SO MATERIAL A CHANGE

AMY D'ORAZIO

This is a work of fiction. Names, characters, businesses, places, events, locales, and incidents are either the products of the author's imagination or used in a fictitious manner. Any resemblance to actual persons, living or dead, or actual events is purely coincidental.

Edited by Gail Warner and Katie Jackson

Cover design by Cloudcat Design

ISBN 978-1-951033-95-8 (ebook) and 978-1-951033-96-5 (paperback)

For all those who, like me, can't seem to get enough Darcy & Elizabeth

TABLE OF CONTENTS

Elizabeth, feeling all the more than common awkwardness and anxiety of his situation, now forced herself to speak; and immediately, though not very fluently, gave him to understand that her sentiments had undergone *so material a change,* since the period to which he alluded, as to make her receive with gratitude and pleasure his present assurances.

— PRIDE & PREJUDICE, CHAPTER 58

CHAPTER ONE

She gently laid one shaking hand on the outside of his door. Her heart pounded so, she wondered that he did not hear it, nor the sound of her panicked breathing.

She had never believed she would grow so desperate as to resort to something like this. In her heart, she thought that he would realise how ideally suited she was to be the mistress of Pemberley and thus would offer for her. However, as each successive year of their acquaintance ticked by, her age advancing accordingly, she had grown increasingly dismayed by his apparent reluctance to propose.

She had come out at eighteen, certain she would receive an offer during that first Season, but it had not been so. A few dances was the most he had afforded her. The second Season proved equally disappointing, and the third, likewise. So now, she was soon to be in her fourth Season, with all of the gentlemen eagerly eyeing those who had just come out, all so fresh-faced and young. She would languish like some bolt of material at the linen draper's that everyone had already seen and passed over.

Nearly all of her friends from school were long since

married—even the ugly ones!—and most of them were mothers as well! Did he not see how beautifully she dressed, how wonderfully she arranged dinners? Her education, her accomplishments, that certain something in her air—did these things mean nothing to him?

She shook her head to clear it of these disturbing thoughts. Now was not the time for doubt and frustration; success was within reach. She simply needed to help things along, particularly in light of the recent events they had attended, which also included the horrid Miss Eliza Bennet.

I have been meditating on the very great pleasure which a pair of fine eyes in the face of a pretty woman can bestow.

She nearly gagged thinking of it. When he said it she could scarcely believe her ears! Nevertheless, it was fortunate she heard it as it served her a warning. Fitzwilliam Darcy—long known for his reserve, his haughtiness, and his general imperviousness to the charms of ladies—was developing some chinks in his armour for a disastrously inappropriate, low-born hoyden.

She shuddered. Who could imagine being so unmannered and uncouth as to think nothing of simply showing up at Netherfield, unbidden and unwanted, her petticoat six inches deep in mud, because her sister had a trifling cold? Such a thing—such a *person*—could not be borne.

Someday Darcy would thank her for rescuing him from this near calamity. Clearly his lusts were overtaking his reason, and now, with Eliza in residence—probably trying to entrap him herself—catastrophe was nigh.

That thought in mind, she removed the housekeeper's keys from the pocket of her dressing gown, inserted the appropriate one into the keyhole and turned it, holding her hand over it to muffle the click. She entered, soundlessly closing the door behind her, then tiptoed across the room to where her soon-to-be intended slumbered.

The fire in the room burnt low, but in the dim light she could see that he had not stirred when she entered and, relieved, approached his bed. Charles often teased Darcy for being such a deep sleeper. He required fewer hours of repose than most did, but when he was fatigued, he could fall asleep in an instant and sleep as if he were dead. What a relief it was to find it was true!

Taking a deep breath to still her nerves, she undid the ties on her dressing gown and dropped it to the floor, revealing a sheer nightgown lent to her by her sister who certainly had no need for it as her husband could rarely remain sober enough to come to her at night. She pulled back the blankets and slid under the counterpane, moving just enough so that her body was close to his.

Her sister suggested that to get things started, she might wish to touch him. Touch *it*, Louisa had said, but now, at the crucial moment, her resolve failed her. But never mind that; she was in his room, in his bed. That was quite enough to suit the purpose.

Of course, she did need to wake him so their tryst could be discovered. To that end, she snuggled closer and wrapped her arm around him, tentatively rubbing his nightshirt-covered chest with her hands. Goodness but he was warm; did he have a fever? She nearly yelped with surprise when he uttered a low moan, turning towards her and encircling her waist with his arm. "Lizz-zz-zy."

It appeared she was intervening just in time. Was he dreaming about Elizabeth Bennet? Ugh. Not a proper dream either, from the sounds of things. Leave it to her to be as ill-behaved in a dream world as she was in reality.

She renewed her efforts to wake him, pressing her body to his. He shifted slightly and pressed his body to hers as well. *What in the world?* Something was poking her in the stomach? *Was that...?* Stifling a giggle, she hesitantly pressed a kiss to his jaw. He turned and captured her lips, running his hand down her back to her leg, which he then pulled up and around his hip. His action brought that which was poking her very close to a certain place—she could not help herself, a small, high-pitched shriek of alarm escaped her, and Darcy startled awake.

"Miss Bingley! What are you doing here?"

DARCY HAD BEEN in the midst of what was becoming a nightly ritual, a highly enjoyable and scandalous dream about Miss Elizabeth Bennet. The first time he dreamt of her was immediately after the assembly. In comparison to what followed, that one had been relatively chaste, involving little more than kissing and caressing her.

His dreams grew more fervid each time he saw her, and he was waking nearly every morning to find himself in an embarrassing physical state. Worse yet, he found himself thinking of his dreams at inopportune moments. Like the other day in the library, when she sat there so innocently reading her book, and he, like a rake, sat recollecting his dream from the night prior and adjusting the book on his lap to cover the evidence of his degeneracy.

He was quite ashamed of himself for his lack of gentlemanly comportment even in his thoughts, yet he felt powerless to stop. There was something about her, something that compelled him and broke apart his control...nay, made him lose his desire to even have control. To have such a woman as one's wife was unimaginable, in more ways than one.

The more he denied what he wanted, however, the more heated and vivid his dreams became, almost as if they were trying to convince his wakeful self of the need to accede to his desires. This particular night had been no different, he and Elizabeth were enjoying his bed at Pemberley—when at once she emitted a high-pitched and un-Elizabeth-like shriek.

It was then that he awoke to his deepest dread.

Struggling to shake off the vestiges of slumber, his heart pounding with fear and distress, he leapt from the bed, frantically reaching for his dressing gown.

"Get out! Get out now! What are you…? Never mind, I do not wish to…but how…? I always make sure the door is locked! How did you…? Get out! Go away now!"

Miss Bingley recovered from her surprise first and cooed, "Darling, you must calm down. This is for the best, you will see—"

"No! You will leave! Immediately!"

As she seemed disinclined to leave his room, he left instead. He went into his dressing room, where he summoned his valet. When the man appeared only minutes later, Darcy asked him to have Mr Bingley woken because his presence in the study was required as soon as possible.

Hastily, Darcy pulled on his clothing and went to await Bingley, using the back servants' stair so he would not have to see Miss Bingley again.

THE SOUND of his door crashing into the wall woke Charles Bingley from a sound sleep. He sat up just as the bed curtain was unceremoniously thrust aside to reveal his hysterical sister.

"Caroline! What in the blazes are you doing here?"

Caroline grabbed his arm, seeming intent on pulling him from his bed. "In Darcy's bed…I thought he wanted to… nightshirt…and I…"

Sitting up, Bingley scrubbed at his face and squinted at the clock on the mantel above the fireplace. It seemed to be about three in the morning. "I cannot understand a word you are saying. Are you ill?"

Caroline shook her head through her sobs, still attempting to pull him from the bed.

"Stop pulling my arm," he snapped. "Is Darcy ill?"

Again she shook her head.

"Then whatever it is can surely wait for morning. Just try to calm down and let us all get some sleep." Bingley settled back into his pillow, closing his eyes.

Just then, a knock came from his dressing room. Bingley sat up, bidding whoever it was to come in. Evidently, he would not sleep in the near future, and he resigned himself to the need to deal with this problem straightaway, whatever it was.

It was his man Perkins, looking sleepy. "Beg your pardon, sir, but you are wanted on an urgent matter by Mr Darcy. He awaits you in your study. May I assist you in readying yourself for the meeting?"

Bingley nodded, again told his sister to go to her room and try to get some sleep, and then rose to dress and meet Darcy.

Darcy's thoughts were a mass of confusion as he paced in Bingley's study. Caroline Bingley! The very notion of having had her in his bed made his blood run cold. What satisfaction might Bingley demand of him for this? Were the servants already gossiping? He cursed himself for being indiscreet in his exclamations—no doubt they were overheard.

At last Bingley entered, his step hurried and his voice breathless. "Darcy, what happened? Caroline could do nothing but sob incoherently at me. Are you ill?"

"No, nothing like that. Bingley, I…we should sit." Darcy forced himself to sit, perching on the edge of one of the chairs across from Bingley's desk.

Bingley did not sit behind his desk, taking instead the seat next to Darcy. "Shall I ring for some coffee?"

"Yes. No! That is to say, no, let us not wake any of the servants." Darcy took a deep breath even as his fingers beat an anxious staccato on the arm of his chair. "It would be best that as few as possible are alerted to the problem."

Bingley nodded just as the door was thrust open and Mrs Hurst marched in, tugging a weeping Miss Bingley behind her. Mrs Hurst had a look of self-righteous indignation about her that did not bode well for the conversation. With utmost disdain she said, "Mr Darcy, our family always believed you were an honourable gentleman."

"And so I am," Darcy retorted fiercely.

"Good." Mrs Hurst was just as fierce. "Then I am sure you will do as you ought and marry Caroline."

"What is this?" Bingley exclaimed. "Darcy? What on earth…?"

Mrs Hurst turned to him. "Mr Darcy invited Caroline into his chambers this evening, and she went! Very unwise, I told her, but she is in love with him and thought he loved her too—and now that he has had his way with her…"

"I beg your pardon," Darcy protested icily. "But such untruth will not be tolerated. I did *not* invite Miss Bingley to my bedchamber, nor would I ever—"

He was interrupted by a mass of incoherent shrieks and sobs from Miss Bingley. Darcy cringed, imagining who must be overhearing them. This story would surely be in every house in Hertfordshire by sunrise.

Bingley was holding his hands over his ears, likely to preserve his hearing from the worst of the shrieks. Speaking over the din, he said, "Can someone please tell me what happened? And do cease with this caterwauling, I beg you."

Darcy spoke quickly. "Your sister admitted herself into my room as I slept and now wishes to persuade you, and apparently Mrs Hurst as well, that it was an assignation between us."

"But it was not?"

"Of course not!"

"She was in his bed," said Mrs Hurst insistently. "Nearly naked, I might add!"

Darcy shot to his feet, feeling desperation grow within him. "I was asleep and hardly able to prohibit her!"

"Regardless, she is ruined!" Mrs Hurst cried out theatrically. "Who else would have her now?"

Bingley looked concerned by this assertion.

"If she is ruined, it was not my doing!" Turning to his weeping tormentor, Darcy ordered, "Tell your brother the truth, Miss Bingley. Surely you would not wish to enter into a loveless marriage with a man whose hand you forced in such a way?"

Miss Bingley looked up at him, teary-eyed. "But I thought you did love me."

Full-fledged panic arose in Darcy's breast as he comprehended that, having come this far, Miss Bingley intended to see her scheme through to the end. Bingley's expression alarmed him still further—he seemed like a man considering what it would be like to have a spinster sister tied about his neck for the rest of his life. Darcy could only imagine what Miss Bingley's Seasons in town cost his friend...no doubt he wished her married with nearly as much desperation as the young lady felt herself.

Sympathy for his friend aside, Darcy would not consign himself to the fate of marriage to Caroline Bingley. She was all that he detested in a lady, and this manoeuvre was clear evidence of the selfish meanness of her character. She would be supercilious and troublesome to his servants, uncaring to his tenants, and a dreadful example to Georgiana. It was a life he dared not even think of, so sure was he of utter misery.

The next moments of conversation became increasingly heated as Miss Bingley insisted that it was a shared assignation and Darcy just as adamantly denied it. Darcy kept one eye on his friend, who looked confused and uncertain, rubbing his hand over his forehead as if he hoped that would make an honourable reply come out.

At length, his gaze fixed on a point beyond Darcy's shoulder, he said, "If there were some other way, Darcy, you know I would agree to it. Alas, I fear gentlemanly honour—"

Pressure rose in Darcy's throat and for a moment he believed he might vomit. What could he do? If he refused, there would be a falling-out between him and a dear friend, talk in London… How would Georgiana be affected by this scandal? It could not be for good, to be sure, not with her health what it was. And what would his uncle say?

"—requires me to insist that you—"

"Bingley…I…I cannot."

"—offer my sister your hand—"

"I am engaged to Elizabeth Bennet." The words shocked Darcy as much as the rest of the room, which immediately fell deathly silent. Everyone stared at him, jaws slack and eyes wide.

At last Bingley said, "What?"

Darcy spoke quickly, ignoring the pang of guilt that smote him as he lied. "I asked Miss Elizabeth Bennet to marry me yesterday, and she accepted me. We are to marry. Miss Elizabeth Bennet and I are getting married."

With a deep breath, he added, "Surely no one thinks I would stoop so low as to invite Miss Bingley into my bed while my…my intended wife slept just down the hall."

There was a short, shocked silence until Miss Bingley renewed her wailing and shrieking while Mrs Hurst began to ring a peal over everyone's heads. At last Bingley mercifully dismissed his sisters, instructing them to return to their beds, then nearly pushing them from the room when they went too slowly.

The two friends were then alone again. Darcy stood, feeling sweat trickle down his back as his friend studied him closely from his chair. "Bingley, you must know that this is… this is all nonsense."

"Which part?" Bingley asked. "An assignation with my sister or an engagement to Miss Elizabeth Bennet?"

Darcy clenched his jaw a moment before replying, "I did

not have any assignation with your sister, nor would I. How long have we known one another? Have you ever known me to behave thus?"

Bingley sighed heavily and scrubbed his face with his hands. "But Miss Elizabeth Bennet? I had not realised that you had developed a regard for her."

"My feelings have surprised me as well."

After several long moments, Bingley added, "You argue quite a lot for people who wish to marry."

"I admire a lady who is unafraid to speak her mind."

Bingley heaved another massive sigh. "Caroline was in your bed, Darcy."

Nausea rose at the recollection. "*Uninvited,* Bingley. I am, as you know, a deep sleeper. She entered as I slept."

"But she is ruined!"

"No, she is not ruined because nothing happened. If this is kept quiet—"

"And now you cannot marry her because you are already engaged?"

"My conduct was unimpeachable save for the fact that I was slumbering when she entered," said Darcy. "In any case, I am engaged. To marry someone else is impossible."

Bingley sighed heavily and began speaking, as much to himself as anyone. "She must marry and soon. Someone, anyone."

He turned his eye to his friend. "The problem is that she refuses to face the facts before her. She has turned away several promising suitors because she had her eye on a bigger prize."

"A bigger prize?"

"You." Bingley regarded him thoughtfully. "She believed you would eventually ask her to marry you."

"I have done nothing to encourage those wishes."

"I know." Bingley rose and went to stare out the window. The sun had just begun to rise over the fields around Netherfield, promising a lovely autumn day ahead of them.

At last, Bingley turned, studying Darcy closely. "May I speak frankly?" On Darcy's nod he continued. "It seems... unlikely...to me that you are engaged to Miss Elizabeth Bennet. I *want* to believe you more than I actually do. But you have long been my friend, and I have no wish to see you bound to a woman you...you..."

He made a helpless little gesture, and Darcy finished his sentence for him, in a manner of understatement. "To a woman I do not wish to marry."

"Yes, exactly."

"Perhaps it will serve us both...my, um, engagement that is," Darcy suggested. "When I am married, your sister will no doubt turn her attention to other prospects."

"Just so!" Bingley exclaimed, as amenable to suggestion as always. "She will realise that unless she acts soon, she will remain unmarried."

"So my marriage will force upon her a bit of urgency. After all, you would not like her always with you."

"No, I would not," said Bingley firmly. "No, indeed. So this matter of you and Miss Elizabeth—as unanticipated as it seems, it will quash any whispers about this business tonight."

"To be sure," said Darcy. "The gossips will presume you found Elizabeth with me, not...not..." He could not even bear to speak it aloud.

"Of course," said Bingley. With uncommon severity, he added, "For what sort of gentleman would I be if I allowed my friend to dishonour my sister under my own roof without demanding justice?"

"Indeed," agreed Darcy flatly.

The two gentlemen left each other then, intending to return to their respective bedchambers for a little while. Darcy knew he would not sleep and therefore did not bother returning to the bed. Instead he took a chair and turned it to face the window.

He had just lied to his dearest friend, and it could not sit well with him. 'Disguise of every sort must be your abhorrence', his father had counselled again and again. No good ever came from deceit. Yet, when it all came down to it, he had lied boldly and completely.

And if I had not, I would be even now bound to Caroline Bingley—through no fault of my own.

He closed his eyes a moment as various scenes ran through his mind. He imagined Miss Bingley triumphantly crowing about 'securing him' to her friends, walking with her during the fashionable hour in Hyde Park, seeing her preen during the theatre as the entirety of the *ton* examined them. Of course, the marriage itself would be even worse—sitting to dinner with her every day, hearing her grating titter and mean-spirited gossip, having to bed her for the creation of his heir! The very notion made him shudder.

It was done and done for the best. The only thing left was to tell Miss Elizabeth Bennet of her role in turning his untruth into truth.

Marriage to a lady like Elizabeth Bennet? Beauty, figure, and wit notwithstanding, she was certainly not the sort of lady he had ever envisioned as his wife. She had an uncle in trade, her mother was crass and vulgar, and he had overheard Miss Bingley once say that her fortune was only one thousand pounds, after her mother's death. London society would eat her alive. For a moment he cursed himself—had it not been for his unconscious imaginings, Elizabeth Bennet would not have been the name to drop from his lips.

But there was no choice here, was there? He had to marry, and it would be either Miss Bingley or Miss Elizabeth Bennet. At least he was not physically sickened by the thought of the latter.

Miss Elizabeth Bennet, your life is about to become something you might never have dreamt possible.

CHAPTER TWO

ELIZABETH WOKE AROUND HER USUAL TIME, HALF-SEVEN. SHE looked out the window to see a lovely autumn day emerging over the countryside.

She dearly hoped that the outlook of the day would be similarly brightened by Jane's improved health. As she retired last night, Jane appeared improved both in looks and disposition. Elizabeth hoped it to be so, firstly because she wished Jane well, and secondly because she anticipated returning to Longbourn to get away from the nasty Miss Bingley, the gossipy Mrs Hurst, the boring and boorish Mr Hurst, and the odious Mr Darcy. Only Mr Bingley was in any manner a pleasant host, but his company could in no way make up for the deficiencies in the other four.

Jane would disagree. Elizabeth smiled as she began to dress and put up her hair. Jane would be inclined to tolerate a great deal to be in company with Mr Bingley.

Her morning rituals complete, she went to Jane, noting with pleasure the return of some colour to her sister's cheeks. "How are you this morning?"

Jane pushed herself into a seated position. "Much better. I believe I owe it all to your good care."

"'Tis always my honour, loath as I am to see you ill." Elizabeth leant in to kiss her sister's cheek, pleased to find it cool.

"I thought I might join the party in the drawing room this evening after dinner."

Elizabeth took a seat next to her on the bed. "I believe they will all be happy to hear that. One gentleman in particular."

"Oh, I am sure you are wrong," Jane demurred, looking shyly at the counterpane.

"I am equally sure I am not wrong! I am confident I am entirely correct! But the others may be equally glad, though for a different reason."

On Jane's enquiring look, she added, "Miss Bingley has made no secret of her wish to see the end of our visit, and after Mama's call yesterday with Lydia and Kitty, I cannot say I blame her."

"Was she very bad, Lizzy?"

Elizabeth pressed her lips together, trying to think of what to say. Finally, having thought of no politic phrasing, she admitted, "She was boastful and excessively familiar. She bragged about your beauty and insulted Charlotte Lucas. She offended Mr Darcy—though I should imagine he takes exception to nearly everything. Nevertheless, he is a guest here. She should not have insulted him."

Jane plucked at the coverlet. "Did Mr and Miss Bingley think ill of her?"

"I believe Mr Bingley is singularly incapable of thinking ill of anyone. He tolerated her with great equanimity. Miss Bingley…yes, she noted our mother's shortcomings."

Seeing Jane's frown Elizabeth added, "But Mr Bingley remained unaffected, and is not his the opinion that truly matters? I think it unlikely our family would have ever earned the good opinion of the likes of Mr Darcy and Miss Bingley, not without a significant change in consequence and fortune."

"I hope it was not so bad as that. I do like Mr Bingley more than any gentleman I have ever known."

Elizabeth patted her sister's hand. "I daresay he likes you just as well. And now, did Mama tell you of the visitor expected at Longbourn today? Evidently, we are to be set upon by none other than the heir of Longbourn, a Mr Collins. He wrote to Papa some weeks past, announcing his intention to visit us. I believe he will arrive today at four o'clock."

Jane's eyes widened. "After all this time?"

"His stated purpose is to 'heal the breach' between our families, but Mama believes he is here to choose a wife from among his cousins."

Jane's eyes widened even further. "Oh, really? Oh, Lizzy, you do not think...would Mama...? If he wishes to marry me, Mama will make me, I know it!"

"My mother is positively certain that you are about to secure Mr Bingley and would not permit Mr Collins anywhere near you, to be sure. No, I fear that if she is correct about Mr Collins and his design in coming here, she will expect me to fulfil that duty."

"Papa would never—"

"I am perfectly able to stand up to Mama. Besides, she might be wrong. He might come for no purpose but to see Longbourn."

"Or maybe," Jane said, an uncharacteristic sly tone in her

voice, "he is just the kind of man a lady would long to marry, and you would thank our mother for forwarding you to him."

With a laugh, Elizabeth said, "I think it unlikely. Rest now, and I shall return later. I must make haste to join them at breakfast."

ELIZABETH DEPARTED Jane's chamber with a glad heart. How good it was to see Jane smile again! Surely they would be able to leave soon; perhaps even tomorrow.

Entering the breakfast room, she noted Mr Bingley, Mr Darcy, and the Hursts already at the table. She forced a smile to her face. "Good morning. I trust you all slept well?"

Not anticipating a response from any of them—even the amiable Mr Bingley appeared uncommonly out of sorts—she turned towards the sideboard, selecting toast for her breakfast. She was considering the eggs when, to her astonishment, she heard Mr Darcy say, "Elizabeth, my dear, yes, I slept, ahh…quite well, and, um…I hope you did too?"

Elizabeth dropped the spoon she had just lifted. *Did he say my name? My dear? I obviously misheard him.* Her shock increased as she realised he had come to stand very close by her side.

He leant over her, murmuring, "Just agree with what I say and do."

He took her plate from her hands and held out his arm. Such was her astonishment, she took it and allowed him to lead her to the place next to his at the table. She sat, noticing that Mr Bingley and the Hursts were staring intently at them. One would have had to be a complete fool to miss the air of tension surrounding the group.

Mr Hurst, having evidently got a satisfactory answer to whatever question had been in his mind, emitted a guttural sound and then lowered his head back to his plate. His mouth full, he asked, "Will there be sport today, men?" Mrs Hurst shot him a disgusted look.

"Miss Elizabeth and I shall walk in the gardens after she eats," Mr Darcy announced.

Elizabeth opened her mouth to protest his presumption in making plans for her when she felt the unmistakable pressure of his hand on hers underneath the table.

Not really sure why she agreed with him, she smiled. "As I am known for being an excellent walker, I must be diligent in practising my craft."

Mr Bingley emitted a bark of laughter, but his levity died as soon as Elizabeth said, "I do hope Miss Bingley is not unwell this morning?"

"Indisposed," Mr Bingley replied, frowning at no one in particular. "She is indisposed. She will keep to her rooms today."

Elizabeth swallowed a bite of toast. "I hope she has not the same fever that afflicted poor Jane."

At the utterance of her sister's name, Mr Bingley brightened. "Ah, yes! How fares Miss Bennet this morning? Dare I hope you found her a bit improved?"

Elizabeth smiled at his kindness. "Indeed I did, sir. In fact, she wishes to join the party downstairs this evening after dinner."

"Excellent!" Mr Bingley looked around the table. "Is that not excellent?"

As Elizabeth required very little time to eat her light repast, it was soon thereafter that she found herself fetching her bonnet and gloves from her room in accordance with Mr Darcy's plan for a walk.

What is he about? He appeared almost friendly, and I daresay I saw a smile from him. Very odd behaviour. What could he mean by it? I must, of course, reprove his familiarity with me. It was highly improper.

Although she had taken no more than a few minutes to retrieve her things, she returned to find Darcy pacing the vestibule at the front of the house. His agitation was clear as he made his way back and forth across the marble floor, his steps sharp and firm.

He said nothing as he held out his arm to her. She took it, allowing him to lead her out of the house and into the gardens. When they had gone a reasonable distance from the house, he spoke.

"Elizabeth, I find myself in a position where it is necessary for us to marry."

Shock caused her to stumble, and she tightened her grip on his arm to steady herself. This made Mr Darcy flash a brief smile at her—did he think she did it purposely?

"I know this might seem surprising to you, and indeed it is to me as well. I could never have supposed that I would offer for a lady of such low origins, humble breeding, and lack of fortune. However, I wish to assure you that although you bring little to the marriage, I have no intention of regarding you as any less because of it. As Mrs Darcy, you will want for nothing, and you will have no cause to repine."

He detailed his concerns over her lack of connexion in

society and the recent behaviour of her family, and how he hoped to enlist the help of his aunt, Lady Matlock, to guide her into acceptance among the *ton*. The only thing he said which was not offensive was that Miss Darcy had wished for a sister for some time. *No wonder! The poor thing is probably desperate for amiable company.*

He concluded by expressing some thoughts on the futures of Kitty and Lydia. "Naturally, with our marriage, I must think of all your sisters as I do my own. It must be said that the behaviour shown by your younger sisters—and yes, sometimes even your mother—would not be acceptable outside of Meryton. For your sisters, I suggest we employ a companion or governess, someone who can truly take them in hand and mould them into proper young ladies. Or perhaps sending them to school would be better? What are your thoughts?"

He turned to look at her, and she realised belatedly that she was regarding him with her mouth hung agape. She closed it immediately. Inasmuch as she had no idea what could have led to the scene in the breakfast room earlier, she certainly had no expectation of anything like this.

"I apologise; I seem to have got ahead of myself."

At long last, Elizabeth found her voice. "Indeed! For a moment, it sounded as though you believed we were engaged."

Mr Darcy began to guide them to a more secluded part of the garden. "Yes. To put it simply, we must marry."

Elizabeth felt her cheeks flush as she struggled to suppress the wild giggles which threatened. Surely the man was not serious? However, when in her limited experience of him had he ever told a joke? Yet the offensiveness of his speech—it was all too absurd to be considered anything but a folly.

"Alas, Mr Darcy, I do not wish to marry you. So any further discussion of wedding plans—or of your very generous concerns for my sisters—is unneeded."

"Not marry me?" He favoured her with a puzzled look. "I can and will give you more than you have ever imagined in terms of wealth and consequence, and I daresay you will be the envy of nearly every woman in England. Do you not realise what a match you will have made in accepting my suit?"

The envy of every woman in England? Good Lord, the pride of this man is beyond the pale.

"Mr Darcy, I cannot decide whether I have gone mad or you have. By the looks of you"—*he truly does look quite fatigued and distressed*—"my inclination is to guess that it is you."

"I do not see how my offer is ridiculous or mad. I wish to marry you. Surely you recognise the compliment I pay you with the declaration of my affections?"

Tugging her hand free from his arm, she turned to depart, her good humour turning to vexation. Nevertheless, she managed to be composed and polite. "Mr Darcy, of course I shall not marry you. You and I do not even like each other. We argue incessantly, and that speech you just gave was so offensive, I would not agree to your offer if you were the Prince Regent himself. Now, if you will excuse me, I must bid you good day." She turned and began to move away from him.

"Wait!" he cried, sounding panicked. "Elizabeth! Stop! You simply must marry me!"

"No, Mr Darcy, I must not, and I shall not. I also must

insist that you cease referring to me in such a familiar manner. I have overlooked it thus far, but will continue to do so no longer."

"Eliz—Miss Elizabeth, please, a moment, I beg of you. Please just listen to me, listen to what I intend for you, and then you will see it is in your best interests to marry me."

Elizabeth pressed her lips together and turned back to face him. She took the smallest of steps in his direction. "You have five minutes, Mr Darcy, and then I shall return to the house."

"Five minutes? Very well." Mr Darcy's countenance took on the appearance of determination. He gestured to a nearby bench where they might sit and even dusted it off with his handkerchief before she sat.

He spoke quickly and confidently once he had seated himself. "You have likely heard the rumours of my income, ten thousand pounds a year. It is a good deal more than that. Pemberley alone brings in more, and I have had considerable success in my investments in the past five years. Thus, your future will be quite secure, as will that of your family."

"I am not overly concerned about my family," she replied airily. "My mother tells me the man who is heir to Longbourn will come soon to visit and intends to select a bride from among my sisters. If that is indeed so, my mother, my sisters, and I shall have no cause for concern for we shall always have our home at Longbourn."

He gave her a sceptical look. "Surely you would not wish to be always at Longbourn?"

"I never said I intended, or even wished, to marry him; however, his marriage to one of us would necessarily secure the rest. However, I also must add that Longbourn and Hertfordshire, in general, are lovely places to live. You might think this neighbourhood beneath your notice, but I assure you, sir, I am quite happy and comfortable. Spending the remainder of my days here would certainly be no hardship to me."

"Of course," he said hastily. "I only meant that with such a lively mind as yours, I believed you would appreciate the opportunity to see more of the country, spend more time in London, perhaps, with its opportunities for experiencing the theatre, the museums, the opera. Derbyshire is also a very agreeable place to live. The Peaks and the Lake District are both an easy distance—we would often go, I am certain."

He gave her a searching look; no doubt he hoped he had tempted her in some way, but she kept her face carefully blank.

"Being the mistress of Pemberley would suit you. 'Tis a large estate; I am not even entirely certain how many servants we employ. We are the first family in the district, and you would be much sought after as my wife."

Elizabeth sniffed and looked at her hands. "Seems like quite a lot of work. I might prefer to marry a gentleman with a small estate, or perhaps even someone in trade. The wives of such men have far fewer demands on their time."

He cast a quick look heavenward before he continued. "You would never need to worry for pin money or anything of that nature. I shall ensure you have more than you could ever spend. You can shop every day and buy thirty, forty, fifty gowns if you wish; I would never speak a word against it. You will have anything your heart should desire."

With a sigh, Elizabeth rose, once again set to leave. "Mr Darcy, it is clear that you know me but little if you believe such things will promote your suit. I do not like shopping and undertake it only by necessity. To have to select so many gowns—to say nothing of all the fittings! It would be nothing short of torturous."

"Think of what marrying me would mean for you and your family. The Darcy name has a long and illustrious history; my grandfather was an earl! Anything you desired would be yours, anything at all."

"If any of that was what I sought in a marriage partner, be assured, I would have accepted you without hesitation. However, I have lived for twenty years now as the daughter of a gentleman of little consequence, and I am exceedingly happy to remain that way."

Elizabeth began to move towards the house but not fast enough to miss hearing Mr Darcy mutter, "The one woman in all of England who would not leap at the chance to be mistress of Pemberley, and I have the luck to need to marry her. Any other lady, I would already be speaking to her father."

She turned back to him, one hand on her hip. "I beg your pardon?"

"You simply *must* marry me."

"No," she replied emphatically. "No, I must not."

Elizabeth began again to walk at a quick pace, and he leapt to his feet, drawing abreast of her just as she said, "If you are suddenly so eager to marry, I wonder that you do not simply propose to Miss Bingley. Certainly each of the things you have mentioned is of great interest to her. I do not believe you would be required to discuss many details before she agreed."

From the corner of her eye, she saw him give a slight shudder which made her smile a little. Although small, it was enough to encourage him.

"If marriage to a wealthy gentleman with a large estate

and fortune, and all the status and fine things that come with that, are not to your liking, tell me what it is you *do* want. I assure you, I shall see to it."

"It is not so easy as that."

"Name it, and it will be yours," he vowed earnestly.

"What I wish for can be neither bought nor sold."

"Ah," said Mr Darcy immediately, "you wish for love."

"Does that seem so terribly absurd to you? It seems very reasonable to me that the person I should choose to spend my life with, to leave my family for, should love me, and I, him. And, by the way, for all the dreadful things you think of them, they do nevertheless love me deeply and have cared for me well these twenty years. So that is six people who love me dearly that you wish me to relinquish in order to become the wife of *one* person to whom I am merely tolerable. That seems a poor trade, does it not?"

"I hold you in great esteem, and what is more, I respect and admire you," Mr Darcy informed her.

Elizabeth raised her brow at him to communicate her doubt. "Come now, Mr Darcy, I am not a fool. There are no two people less suited than you and I, as evidenced by the fact that we have done nothing but argue since the day we met."

"I thought you did so to draw my notice."

A gasp of laughter escaped her. "Surely not."

"You would be astonished at the varied arts ladies employ to court a man's favour. Arguing is not common, but neither is it unheard of."

"I argue with you because I disagree with much of what you say."

At this, the conversation seemed to reach a standstill, and they walked silently for a short while. Elizabeth stole several glances at him as they walked. His face bore an expression she concluded was a mixture of confusion and sorrow.

"Sir, I cannot imagine what has compelled you to offer for me today, but I implore you to consider the very likely possibility that I do you a great favour by refusing you."

"No, I assure you, I want—"

"You made it amply clear on the evening you first saw me that I was not handsome enough to tempt you. Since that time, we have done nothing but draw swords, so evidently our temperaments are ill-suited. And, as has already been stated very clearly, I am nothing but a liability to you so far as fortune and connexions are concerned. There is nothing that speaks in favour of this union."

With quiet stubbornness, Mr Darcy replied, "I think we are quite well suited actually."

Elizabeth heaved a sigh. "Mr Darcy, please—"

He interjected quickly. "As it happens, I think you are among the most handsome women of my acquaintance."

Elizabeth rolled her eyes.

"I only said what I did at the assembly because Bingley was plaguing me and I…but never mind that. It was untrue, and exceedingly rude of me to say it, and I should have apologised to you the minute I suspected that you overheard me. I pray you would accept my humblest apology."

"Thank you. Nevertheless, I…well, we simply could not be happy together."

He stopped walking then and stared at her. His eyes were dark with…pain? Anxiety? "So you are truly refusing me then? You will not, under any circumstances, consider my offer?"

She reached out, laying her hand on his arm. "This is madness! We are not well suited, and although you are confident in your ability to offer me great things, I do not think I can offer you happiness, which appears to me to be exactly what you need most."

His expression changed then from sorrow to frustration and then anger. He turned his head, muttering some soft imprecation. Elizabeth's brows shot upwards in an expression of displeasure, and he apologised immediately.

Elizabeth put her hands on her hips. "There is something you are not telling me here. To have such a sudden and violent desire to marry me—tell me what is behind all of this."

He studied her intently for a moment and then, quite inexplicably, a slow smile spread across his face. "I should have known you would not accept anything less than the truth."

He indicated a path that would deviate from their current route back to the house, wordlessly asking her permission to digress. She nodded her assent.

They walked for a few minutes, the only sound the crunching of the fallen leaves on the path beneath their feet. At length, Mr Darcy said, "You might have noticed that Miss Bingley is in pursuit of me."

Elizabeth laughed, and he looked at her quickly, frowning. She pressed her lips together to stop her mirth, then said soberly, "I had indeed noticed that, sir."

"She has made no disguise of the fact that she wishes to be Mrs Darcy. She cares nothing for me, of course; it is just my fortune and the status afforded by my name that she wants. She has grown increasingly forward over the years, but last night, she did something I could not have imagined any gently bred woman doing."

Mr Darcy was red cheeked, and he would not look at her, his eyes fixed on the ground beneath them. As he seemed disinclined to continue, Elizabeth prompted him. "What did she do?"

"Um, well…it was…she tried…" He shot her an embarrassed look and then returned his eyes to the ground.

Elizabeth bit the inside of her cheek, trying not to laugh. "She made an attempt on your virtue?"

He muttered, "I suppose you could say that."

She swallowed the laugh which wanted to burst forth. "How did she do that exactly?"

Stiffly, he said, "I would not wish to embarrass you with the details."

When she was sure she would not giggle, Elizabeth said, "Oh, that sounds quite scandalous. I am certain that the reality could not be nearly as bad as what I might imagine."

Mr Darcy frowned a moment before shaking his head with a little laugh. "Very well, I shall tell you, but do not say I did not try to spare you. Last night as I slept, she entered my room wearing a revealing nightgown and got into my bed. She woke me by…let your imagination do what it will, but suffice it to say, I awoke quickly and removed myself with as much haste as possible."

"That is indeed"—Elizabeth disguised a laugh as a cough —"quite dreadful and shocking."

"I fled, leaving Miss Bingley in my chamber, and went to Bingley. I explained to him the truth of what had happened. I do not know what he does and does not believe, but the fact of the matter is that his sister was in my bed. How she got there is immaterial."

"Did Mr Bingley demand an offer for his sister's hand? Or shall we have a duel here later?"

"Bingley wanted me to offer for his sister but…I explained I could not, because…"

It took a moment for her to understand his meaning. "Because you are promised to another."

He nodded.

She closed her eyes a moment, her former good humour fleeing at the same rate that, no doubt, Mr Darcy had fled Miss Bingley. "So our supposed engagement prevents you from being engaged to Miss Bingley."

"Yes," Mr Darcy said quietly. "I realise it is a terrible position to put you in."

"Terrible?" she exclaimed. "Terrible does not begin to describe it. Firstly, it is a lie. Secondly, this is your problem, not mine! How could you involve me in such a scheme? And then divulge it to Mr Bingley?"

"And the Hursts."

"That makes it even worse! What did you suppose? That I was simply yours for the asking? Nay, you did not even ask! You…you…"

Beholding his expression, she stopped berating him. She had never seen him in such misery, and it quieted her tongue. Elizabeth took a deep breath to calm herself. She pressed her hand across her eyes and lowered her head, thankful for the soothing chill of the autumn air.

"Would being married to Miss Bingley truly be so dreadful?"

In lieu of an answer, he simply cocked a brow at her, and ruefully she admitted, "Silly question. Forget I asked it."

He leant into her, looking earnest. "I know you have a very low opinion of me right now, but I assure you, we would have a happy life together."

"How could I marry someone on the mere possibility that

one day I might be happy? A lady puts herself wholly in her husband's power, wholly under his control. The risk is even greater for you and me. Even if I were to discount all of our quarrels and my present poor impression of you, what do I know of you, really? I know nothing of your character and little of your disposition."

"You would learn—"

"No." She shook her head. "Forgive me, but I cannot. If there were any other way I could help you, I would do so, but I cannot relinquish all of my own hopes and wishes for your sake. I am sorry."

He sighed heavily and, for a moment, touched two fingers to his forehead. She watched him, feeling a strange tug at the unhappiness on his countenance.

They walked in weighty silence, their steps falling into odd synchronism. Then, just as the shadow of Netherfield reached towards them, she said, quite without thinking about it, "Of course, I need not tell anyone that."

CHAPTER THREE

Mr Darcy stared at her curiously. "Need not tell anyone…what?"

"That I have refused you." Elizabeth shrugged and grinned. "Ignorance is bliss?"

"You mean to deceive them?"

"No, you have already deceived them. I am merely offering to not expose you."

Mr Darcy pondered that as they stood in a patch of autumnal warmth that was too comfortable to be relinquished to go indoors. "I should not have done any of this. I was always taught that disguise of every sort should be an abhorrence to me, yet…"

Against all natural inclination, Elizabeth found herself warm with pity for Mr Darcy. It was not fair that by no fault of his own, he should suffer his whole life. He seemed to feel acutely the misery of the situation although he was not nearly so inclined towards railing at the injustice of it all as she might have done. It almost made her admire him a little.

"How did she manage to gain entry?"

"The housekeeper's keys? Or so I suppose."

"Jane and I shall leave tomorrow. If I were to remain silent on the matter until then..."

He raised his head, seeming to have come to some new resolve. "I could leave for London soon. Bingley wishes to see Miss Bingley settled and believes that with hope of securing me gone, she will decide on a husband rather quickly."

"So you would merely stay out of his way—"

"Until she was engaged to someone." Relief made him look younger and certainly much happier.

"Very well, then," she said with a broad smile and a tiny curtsey-like bob. "You may be assured of my silence."

He grabbed her hand and bent low over it. "I am forever indebted to you. If ever you have need of me, just ask."

Mr Bennet sat in his study, looking upon the sweating, pompous creature before him.

His cousin, the heir to Longbourn, Mr William Collins. A man who would become Elizabeth's husband.

Mr Collins was presently the recipient of the living in the Hunsford parish, granted to him by Lady Catherine de Bourgh of Rosings Park, and it was a distinction he felt keenly. Most of his conversation thus far—and there had indeed been quite a surfeit of it—had been in praise of his benefactress. Although it could not be said that it was an ill-considered strategy to admire the one on whom you were dependent, it was inarguable that Mr Collins was neither sensible nor witty.

When Collins had written, informing Mr Bennet of his intention to visit Longbourn, Mr Bennet had anticipated no more than an agreeable se'nnight spent silently mocking the man. But now? Now he had a far different opinion of the matter.

On the night of Mr Collins's arrival, when he and Mrs Bennet had retired, she had called him excitedly into the sitting room adjoining their chambers. He met her there, wondering at her enthusiasm.

"Oh, Mr Bennet, we are saved, we are saved!" his wife had exclaimed, her voice a loud whisper.

"I did not realise we were in peril, Mrs Bennet, but it is good to know it will come to naught. Good night, then."

His teasing had no effect. She continued to speak effusively, eyes wide and hands waving frantically. "Mr Collins intends to offer for one of our girls! How delightful, is it not?"

As it was, Mr Bennet thought such a notion was quite absurd. Mr Collins lacked any attribute which might render him agreeable to any of the Bennet ladies. He was neither handsome enough for Jane nor witty enough for Lizzy. The absence of a red coat meant the two youngest ladies would not like him. And Mary? Well, Mary would not likely wish to marry anyone.

"Is there a daughter in particular he admires? Or will they draw straws, see who gets him?"

Mrs Bennet tittered, too ebullient to let her husband's teasing distress her. "It should be Lizzy. She is next, you know."

"Has Jane married?" he asked in mock astonishment. "I was not informed!"

"Well, for Jane, as beautiful as she is, only a wealthy man like Mr Bingley will do. No, it must be Elizabeth for Mr Collins." Then, in a stroke of uncommon brilliance, Mrs

Bennet said, "Are you not always going on about how much quicker Lizzy is than the other girls? I daresay Mr Collins will need her help if he is not going to run the place into ruin."

His wife's surprisingly astute insight struck Mr Bennet silent, and he retired that evening with a racing mind and a heavy heart. He had been a disinterested steward of Longbourn and had not done as he ought for either his heritage or his daughters. Now it seemed both of those errors might be remedied by one act, the uniting of Elizabeth to Mr Collins in matrimony.

Could he truly commit his Lizzy to life with such a foolish man?

Then again, if he did not, what would become of them all when he died? What if they did not marry well? What if Longbourn declined? Beauty and wit could not overcome lack of fortune in the case of his death. Were there not many who withered in genteel poverty from just such circumstances?

Surely marriage to Mr Collins would be preferable to poverty or employment. Lizzy was, above all, a reasonable girl. If there were any of his daughters who could make an agreeable husband out of this fool, it would be his Lizzy.

As Mr Collins blathered on about the chimneys at Rosings Park, Mr Bennet allowed his mind to wander. Elizabeth would comprehend her duty as a daughter. She would see the advantage to the family, to Longbourn, that would be realised with her acquiescence. She would understand what must be done and done for the best.

HAVING BEGUN in a most strange manner, Elizabeth's day did not improve.

Miss Bingley remained in her chamber; Elizabeth had overheard the maids discussing the tantrum she had thrown when she learnt of Mr Darcy's betrothal. There were shattered vases, a gauzy nightshift rent into pieces, and a hairbrush thrown at her unsuspecting maid. Fortunately, her maid had ducked; nevertheless the brush had hit the girl with a glancing blow that was of sufficient force to leave a bruise on her face.

Mrs Hurst gave up any pretence of politeness and either ignored Elizabeth or spoke with thinly-veiled spite. Mr Bingley regarded both Elizabeth and Darcy thoughtfully, though he was amiable enough. Mr Hurst behaved as usual, ignoring mostly everyone in favour of drinking and eating to excess.

Mr Darcy at first seemed determined to play some sort of love-struck suitor, giving Elizabeth his arm whenever she wished to walk more than three feet, sitting close by wherever she sat, and even once calling her 'my dearest' right in front of Mrs Hurst. With that she knew she needed to put a stop to it all.

He was escorting her on her return to her chamber to dress for dinner, and in a low voice she said, "Please behave as you usually do. This is too strange to be borne."

"I am simply behaving as a man would who has just become engaged." He sounded affronted.

Elizabeth rolled her eyes. "Let them think we had an argument, something to account for a bit of distance between us, I beg you."

Dinner was a desultory affair as their hostess was still in self-imposed exile in her chambers and Mr Bingley merely wanted to reach the portion of the evening when Miss Bennet would appear. When at last she did, Bingley occupied himself in having the fire stoked and ensuring that Jane's chair was drawn near enough to it. Then he decided it was too warm and insisted her chair be moved away from such a punishing heat. So it went for nearly a half an hour, providing Elizabeth with a good bit of amusement.

She sat off to the side with her needlework, occasionally glancing up at her sister, whose flushed face, she suspected, had little to do with her recent illness or the 'punishing' fire. *Jane is falling in love.* Elizabeth lowered her head to hide her smile.

Was Mr Bingley growing likewise attached? She did not know him well enough to say, but he certainly showed favour to Jane. Although she hated to speak in haste, she could not but reflect on how well settled Jane would be to find herself wife to such an amiable gentleman with a fine income and living so close to her family.

It was for Jane too, she realised, this little farce in which she had engaged herself. Surely Mr Bingley wanted to see his sister settled before he married, so if Miss Bingley were engaged, it was to Jane's benefit.

Mr Darcy was much occupied with his book for the first part of the evening, or at least it seemed so to Elizabeth until she noticed that he never turned any pages. She glanced at him, noticing a rather worried and drawn look on his countenance that made her feel a bit of pity for him. His was a difficult spot through no fault of his own save the fact that he chose to keep society with the Bingleys.

He happened to glance up and see her looking at him, and for a moment their gazes were locked. She offered him a small smile, thinking for some reason that she wished to reassure him.

MR BINGLEY'S carriage bore them back to Longbourn early the next day. Nearly as soon as Elizabeth had settled in to being back at Longbourn, she was set upon by Mr Collins.

He at once began to expound to Elizabeth the many benefits of Rosings Park, Lady Catherine de Bourgh, his position as rector, and the parsonage house at Hunsford. When she was at last able to interject, she attempted to excuse herself, but he would have none of it, remaining at her side wherever she seemed to go. Elizabeth was discomfited when, having looked to her father for one of the secret, mocking glances they liked to share in such situations, Mr Bennet merely looked away.

Dinner was much the same, with the added degradation of Elizabeth, on several instances, catching Mr Collins leering down the bodice of her gown. The gown was modestly cut, yet somehow she suddenly felt naked.

After dinner, Mr Collins offered to read to all of the ladies and selected *Fordyce's Sermons* as his reading material. He began in a slow, ponderous voice, punctuating the important passages with serious looks around the room at each of the ladies in turn. Elizabeth had great difficulty not giving way to laughter at his undue ceremony. However, she did manage to restrain herself, unlike her youngest sisters, who laughed more freely with each passing moment, finally disregarding him altogether and forming their own tête-à-tête. At this, Mr Collins grew offended and closed the book with a resounding thump. All were thus relieved when the time to retire drew close.

Elizabeth woke in the morning feeling an inexplicable nervous dread in her stomach. An early morning walk was her custom, and one she did not intend to alter this morning, particularly as the day had dawned fair and unusually warm for the middle of November. Donning a morning gown and quickly pulling her curls into some semblance of a tidy arrangement, she quickly descended the stairs, only to find Mr Collins already in the breakfast room.

"Good morning, Mr Collins," she greeted him. "I hope your sleep was restful?"

"Oh, indeed, it was; yes, it was, Cousin Elizabeth, and how kind of you to ask." He rose and began to pull out a chair for her.

She forestalled him with a raised hand. "It is my habit to partake of an early morning walk prior to breaking my fast. I believe it will be at least an hour before the rest of the family are down." She smiled politely, and in it, he evidently saw an invitation.

"I shall join you, for I believe the body is as much a temple…" And with that, he was off, expounding upon his theories of walking and exertion and the benefits of both. She had to conclude, however, that these were benefits he likely partook of but little, for he was breathless and perspiring within a few feet of the house despite Elizabeth slowing her customary pace by a substantial measure.

Even through his panting he continued talking, gasping out his opinions on topics ranging from the views of his esteemed patroness on the subject of physical exertion to the places to promenade in Rosings Park, the splendour of Rosings Park, how greatly she would enjoy Rosings Park, how much she would find to admire in Hunsford Village, and finally ending with how she would likely wish to walk to attend the parishioners in Hunsford Village.

Having not fully attended what he said, she startled a bit when she heard the last sentence. "Why would I be attending parishioners in Hunsford Village?"

He smiled at her, and she noticed a large piece of something brownish stuck in one of his teeth. "Why Cousin Elizabeth, naturally it is the duty of the wife of the parson to visit the sick and the needy of the parish."

She looked at him with a flutter of panic in her breast but managed to be calm and sweet as she said, "Of course, sir, but I am not the wife of a parson."

With a patronising smile, he took her hands inside his own, which were curiously feminine and moist, a disgusting sensation. She struggled valiantly to keep the polite smile on her face as she attempted to tug her hands free from his, to no avail.

"Your modesty is to your credit, my dear cousin." He took a deep breath. "It cannot surprise you that I have come to Longbourn to select my bride. Lady Catherine de Bourgh herself thought it an excellent idea to choose from 'those who had called Longbourn their own lo these many years'. She wished that I might choose a gentlewoman, but one not brought up too high, a lady who was both modest and useful. I believe she will be very pleased with you."

He paused significantly and leant into her, requiring her to inhale a deep and searing whiff of his unwashed body. "Although I am loath to excite your anticipation, Lady Catherine has already indicated to me that she will herself visit you and instruct you in your new role."

Elizabeth might have laughed were she not so actively

engaged in attempting to free her hands and breathe clean air into her lungs.

"Of course, a man in my position, having received the living of such a noble personage, must have many choices for the companion of his future life, and I cannot but think that to receive such a distinction might surprise you given your lack of means. I am fully aware, of course, that your portion is merely one thousand pounds, but please be assured, when we are married, you will never hear mention of this from me."

At this, Elizabeth felt she must speak, and indeed wondered that she had not stopped him earlier. "Mr Collins, I thank you for the compliment of your addresses, but I fear I cannot accept."

Mr Collins looked confused for the briefest of moments, then assurance flooded his countenance. "You must be trying to increase my ardour by giving me first a rejection when naturally you mean to accept me. I believe such is the usual practice of elegant females."

"I assure you, sir, I certainly am not trying to do any such thing. That sort of artfulness is not an elegance to which I aspire—if indeed it could be called elegance. I thank you for the compliment of your offer, but I must decline."

"Cousin Elizabeth..." Mr Collins spoke patiently, as one might to a small or misbehaving child. "I hold an exceedingly valuable living and will one day inherit this estate. You surely would not be so foolish as to reject me and the security I offer to you as well as your mother and sisters? You will never receive such an offer again, I assure you."

Elizabeth was also trying to be patient. "Indeed I do reject such an offer, Mr Collins. I could not be a suitable companion for you, nor you for me. Our situation would not be felicitous." Deciding it was likely ideal to return to the house, she turned, wrenching her hands free in the process, and began to walk quickly.

The panting at her side told her that Mr Collins had not given up. "I assure you, madam, when I speak with your mother there will be a different outcome to this conversation."

"If you wish to speak to my mother, I encourage you to do so, but neither she nor you can persuade me to enter into such a union. Please, I beg you to desist. Surely there are other candidates for your affections."

Mr Collins uttered a bitter laugh. "I indeed have many candidates for my affections. However, I must also consider the wishes of Lady Catherine in my decision, and none of those other candidates, I believe, would be so favoured by her as would you."

By then, they had reached the door, and Elizabeth quickly ran inside and up to her chambers, where she intended to wash her hands repeatedly until every bit of Mr Collins's touch was removed. She was in the midst of her third wash when she heard her mother's screech. "Lizzy! Get down here this instant!"

Pausing for a moment, she pressed her fingers on the spot between her eyes. Of course, her mother would wish for this. Who better than her least favourite daughter to sacrifice to such a man for the sake of having the right to remain at Longbourn? Thank heavens she knew she could always depend upon her father to save her.

She walked slowly down the stairs, giving her mother ample time for two more deafening shrieks of "Lizzy!" as well as the audible mutter describing what an ungrateful, selfish creature she was. She first went to the sitting room, assuming she would find Mrs Bennet within, but surprisingly, her mother was in her father's study.

As she walked in, both of her parents looked at her, but it was Mrs Bennet who initiated the tirade.

"You are going to walk right out there this instant and tell Mr Collins that of course you will marry him! Foolish girl! Who else do you imagine would wish to marry such a headstrong girl? You are fortunate he wishes to have you! He is all that stands between us and starving in the hedgerows, and you dare refuse him? I shall not stand for it! Turn yourself right around and get out there before he decides that he will not have you either!" With that, Mrs Bennet began to make shooing motions at Elizabeth with her handkerchief.

Elizabeth wondered why her father did not speak up. Surely he would not wish to see her tied to such a man for all her life? She looked at him standing beside his desk, expecting to see an amused twinkle in his eye. Alarm fluttered within her as she saw the look of resignation on his countenance and the way he turned his head to avoid meeting her gaze.

"Papa? You must know why I cannot marry Mr Collins."

Then her father said words she would never have imagined coming from him, looking at his shoes while he did it. "Mr Collins is a respectable man, Elizabeth. He is not vicious or cruel. The two of you will rub along well together, I believe."

Elizabeth stared at her father with a sinking feeling. He could not mean it. Any moment now, he would surely lift his brow in his typical image of sardonic amusement, or he would tease and vex Mrs Bennet or something! Yet, he did not.

"Sir, I beg your pardon...you do not...will you...are you

in favour of this match?" At last her father looked at her, raising his head with unbearable sympathy on his face. Panic settled into Elizabeth's chest like a large, rapidly moving butterfly trying to escape its confines, and she tightened her shawl around her shoulders, feeling a deep chill.

Mrs Bennet erupted once more in a veritable deluge of nervous effusions, the sum of which was that Elizabeth was a miserable, wretched, uncaring daughter, and she would either marry Collins or be disowned.

Mr Bennet spoke. "Mrs Bennet, perhaps it would be best if I spoke to Elizabeth alone."

At his words, Elizabeth began to shake, for as much as Mrs Bennet's threats and pronouncements troubled her little, Mr Bennet's kindness frightened her to her very soul.

When Mrs Bennet had gone, Mr Bennet took Elizabeth's hand, leading her to a little sofa by the fire. Elizabeth sat, clasping her hands together tightly to control her tremblings.

"A man such as Mr Collins can only improve with marriage to a witty and sensible wife. As for the estate, it will need a mistress who can guide the master and is well regarded in the neighbourhood. Under you, Elizabeth, Longbourn will become more than what it is now, but I fear if Collins has his way with it, it will descend quickly." Mr Bennet sighed heavily. "You must marry. I could be gone tomorrow, and then what would become of you all?"

You must marry. An image of Mr Darcy's face sprang into Elizabeth's mind.

Mr Bennet continued to speak. "The feelings we think are love in our youth are only a sort of infatuation, almost like an inebriation that quickly fades—"

Could I marry Mr Darcy? Does his offer yet stand? How has it come to this? Elizabeth released her hands, and smoothed them over her skirts.

"—and what is left is a union of two people joined for the purpose of procreation and, in the case of the landed gentry, to continue a family estate. For that—"

With a deep breath, Elizabeth interjected, "Mr Darcy proposed to me, and I accepted him."

"Who?" Mr Bennet fell into an abrupt, stunned silence.

"Mr Darcy has made me an offer of marriage, and I have...I accepted him. Mr Darcy has not spoken to you yet to obtain your consent, so naturally I could not tell Mama or Mr Collins."

For several long moments, there was no sound save for the loud tick of the mantel clock. "Mr Darcy?"

Elizabeth nodded, trying to look happy.

"The same Mr Darcy who slighted and insulted you at the recent assembly?"

"He apologised for that," Elizabeth explained hurriedly, looking down at her hands.

Mr Bennet again said nothing, simply looking at her intently and thoughtfully for several long minutes. Finally, tentatively, he asked, "While you and Jane were at Netherfield, did anything...I mean, was there any sort of...sometimes a gentleman will..."

"He did nothing of that nature, I assure you. He was a perfect gentleman." Elizabeth looked at her father in exasperation.

"Of course," her father demurred quickly. "You do realise how wealthy, how great, Mr Darcy is, do you not?"

"I do."

"I would not have you so tempted by such things that you overlook the fact that he is a proud and disagreeable man.

Do you really wish to be bound to such a man? Fortune can only compensate for so much, Lizzy."

The irony of such concern was not lost on her. Her father would object to her marrying Mr Darcy for prudence's sake but would see her bound to Mr Collins for the same? Looking into her father's eyes, so like her own, she had a peculiar sense of never having known him before.

In carefully neutral tones, she said, "Is not prudence the reason you wish me to marry Mr Collins?"

Mr Bennet removed his glasses and rubbed his hands over his eyes tiredly. "Well, yes."

"So, if I am being prudent, will not Mr Darcy do as well as Mr Collins?" Elizabeth tilted her chin defiantly. "Although he does not have Longbourn, it seems Pemberley will do for those of us left behind when you are gone."

"You are determined to have him, then. I daresay there is nothing for me but to await his conference." Mr Bennet rose and went to his study door, opening it. "Mrs Bennet?" he called. She appeared in a moment, looking down her nose at her daughter, prepared to crow her triumph.

"Elizabeth will not marry Mr Collins. She has my full support in this matter."

Elizabeth fled to her chambers, a headache pulsing at her temples, leaving her mother wailing behind her.

CHAPTER FOUR

DESPITE LAYING IN THE DARK FOR HALF AN HOUR, ELIZABETH'S headache remained unabated, the product of anger with her mother and father mixed with fears for her future. Her father would ask her to marry a foolish man like Mr Collins for the sake of saving an estate that *he* had neglected for decades? The injustice of it made her burn with indignation. And now she was left to choose from marriage to the taciturn Mr Darcy or the ridiculous Mr Collins.

A knock at her door prevented her from becoming engrossed in her anguish. "You are wanted in the drawing room, Miss Lizzy," said Mrs Hill when she entered. "Mr Bingley and Mr Darcy have come to call."

Elizabeth scrambled off the bed where she had tossed herself earlier. A few minutes alone with her mother, and Mr Darcy would likely decide to leave her to Mr Collins. She arrived just as a scheme had been proposed whereby Mr Bingley and Jane were to walk out. As soon as Mr Darcy saw her enter, he spoke. "Bingley, perhaps you will permit Miss Elizabeth and I to join you?"

"Oh, that is not necessary," Mrs Bennet cried, no doubt wishing Jane and Mr Bingley to be alone.

Elizabeth spoke over her. "An excellent idea, sir."

As soon as they left the house, Elizabeth began to walk quickly, seeking to put enough distance between them and the house to enable her to speak to Mr Darcy privately. With Mr Darcy's legs so much longer than hers, it was not difficult for him to match her pace, though he no doubt wondered at her haste. Mr Bingley and Jane, strolling slowly, were soon far behind them.

They strode on rapidly in silence for some time, until Mr Darcy enquired, "Miss Elizabeth, are we fleeing someone?"

"No, no…I…" Elizabeth stopped and looked around her in consternation. They had put quite a bit of distance between them and the other couple, and she decided it would have to do. "I…I told my father I was engaged to you."

"You did?"

She nodded, mortified to feel tears well up in her eyes. She struggled for a moment, not wishing to give way to them, but her emotion proved too powerful. She lowered her head and turned her back on him as the first tears rolled down her cheeks.

Her misery was great, yet she could not forget he was there. He moved close behind her, touching her shoulder more gently than she might have imagined and pressing his handkerchief into her hand.

It took her some minutes to be again mistress of herself, but soon she only sniffed and sighed, dabbing at her eyes and feeling strangely comforted by the masculine smell on the fine linen. When at last she was calm, Mr Darcy offered her his arm as they began to stroll slowly through the woods.

"You might recall that I mentioned to you that my cousin would visit, the cousin who stands to inherit Longbourn."

Mr Darcy nodded. "Yes, you believed he intended to make an offer of marriage to one of your sisters, I think?"

Elizabeth nodded. "Before I came home, Mr Collins and my mother decided that *I* should be the ideal wife for him. Thus, when I returned from Netherfield, there he was, ready with a proposal of marriage he felt was sure to be accepted. Ordinarily, refusing him, as well as my mother, would not be a problem because my father would support me in my decision. However, this time…"

She paused, feeling more tears sting her eyes. "This time, my father appears to agree with my mother that becoming wife to Mr Collins should be my lot."

Mr Darcy understood immediately. "Unless of course you had already accepted the offer of another man."

Feeling numb, Elizabeth nodded.

"And you do not wish to marry this man? As your father's heir he would be rather eligible."

"Eligible!" Elizabeth snorted. "The only thing which makes him eligible is being my father's heir. The man is the most stupid, ridiculous, arrogant… Forgive me, I am unkind."

She drew a deep breath. "I fear I would be excessively unhappy to bind myself to a man like Mr Collins, and no doubt it would soon lead to his misery too."

"I see."

Mr Darcy was silent for a moment as they slowly picked their way along the path through the woods. She wondered whether her outburst had scandalised him or he regretted his hasty offer of marriage. Perhaps, given time to think about it, he no longer thought it the answer to his own problem, and was even now preparing to tell her he could not support her claims.

She had to know, even if the news was bad. "But perhaps you…perhaps you have thought of another solution to your own problem? Perhaps your offer does not stand?"

He looked at her, seeming a little offended. "Of course it does. I am a man of my word."

They fell into silence again, and Elizabeth lost herself in thought, imagining what it would be like to be married to such a grave, silent man. Mr Darcy's chuckle broke her from her reverie, and she looked over to see him grinning rather broadly.

"Mr Darcy, if there is humour in any of this, I do wish you would share it with me. From my vantage point, both of us have been forced into a lie based on the betrayals of those around us. To me, it is a bit unsettling if not outright vexing."

"Fitzwilliam," he said.

"What?"

"We should start calling each other by our Christian names. Darcy, if you would prefer it. That is what most of my friends call me."

Elizabeth heaved a great sigh, looking towards the sky for a moment. "Very well. *Fitzwilliam,* will you tell me please what about our situation you find so amusing?"

"I cannot say I find it amusing so much as I find it ironic. Both of us placed into similar situations where we are forced to choose between an unwanted suitor or each other, and only days apart. One could see the hand of Providence or Fate in the matter."

"Hardly," Elizabeth said. "In any case, if the thought of us being destined for one another is what caused you to laugh, I would then have to laugh with you. Ours is more a story of mutual desperation than love."

He gave her an earnest look. "I cannot deny that. Nevertheless, many people marry for lesser reasons."

"I can scarcely credit that such a fate should befall us."

"I daresay it is not so dreadful."

"Come now," she said, "let us be frank. I do not want to marry you, and you do not want to marry me."

"I was at the front of this entire scheme, in case you forgot," he said. "In any case, we are getting married, and there is nothing for either of us to do but reconcile ourselves to it."

She laughed aloud then adopted a teasing simper. "Such pretty, romantic words! Sir, you will cause me to swoon!"

He gave her a faint smile as they continued walking. "I do not think it will suffice to merely say we are engaged. Most people expect that I should make a brilliant match in terms of fortune or connexions so—"

"So since you have made a shabby choice instead..."

He shook his head at her. "I only mean to say people will expect it is a love match."

"A love match? I must pretend to be madly in love with you?"

Darcy replied stiffly, "And I, you, naturally. After all, it is I who proposed, and you who gains the advantage. So I must appear the love-struck suitor most of all."

She perceived she had offended him, and so, in her first act of wifely concern, she reached for his arm and patted it before inserting her hand into the crook of his elbow. "You did a fine job of it at Netherfield. I am most fortunate." She thought a moment, then asked, "How did you ask me to marry you?"

"Does it matter?"

"Of course it matters! People will ask, and I do not think that 'he took me in the garden and told me I must marry him' has much of a romantic shine to it."

"That does bring to mind one more thing," he said. "As we are supposed to be so very much in love, I think a long engagement would seem...peculiar."

His words had the effect of leaping into a cold pond on a hot summer day. She could not breathe for a moment, and the words *'what have I done'* pierced her consciousness. It seemed her breath was caught in her lungs, unable to move and allow her to breathe. "That is...that is probably true."

"I can go back to town and get the licence," he mused, seeming unaware, by this time, of her presence. "Before Christmas would be best, I suppose, but then again, January may do just as well. We should do it here, I suppose. Most go to the bride's county."

"Do I have any say in this?" Elizabeth asked impatiently. "Perhaps you would prefer to speak my vows for me?"

"Forgive me. When do you wish to marry?"

"Next summer?" The words had slipped out before she was able to stop them. From the expression on his countenance, he was much against that idea. "Or in the spring, early spring even."

"We cannot marry during Lent, and we really must have you in town before the Season commences in earnest."

Swallowing against her fear, Elizabeth asked, "Very well then, when do you think we ought to marry?"

He shrugged, a bit dismissively, she thought. "I shall speak to your father about it. January or February would do, I suppose."

Elizabeth could only look off to the side, at once flooded

in indecision and dismay as well as the sure realisation that nothing in her life could ever be the same.

Darcy knocked on Mr Bennet's door and was admitted after only a short, uncomfortable wait. Mr Bennet stood behind his desk. "A good day to you, sir."

The two gentlemen bowed to each other, and Mr Bennet gestured to the younger man to follow him over to chairs by the window. After the appropriate offers of refreshment were made and declined, Darcy realised it was time to speak.

"Thank you for receiving me. I believe Elizabeth has told you that she has accepted my offer of marriage, and as she is not yet one and twenty, I wish to secure your consent."

Mr Bennet stared at him with flat eyes behind his spectacles. His countenance was inscrutable, causing Darcy to feel even more unsettled than he had been previously. After some interminable moments he said, "You are the sort of man to whom I should never dare refuse anything once you condescended to ask for it."

Unsure what was meant by such a reply, Darcy said merely, "Thank you."

An awkward pause ensued, and then Mr Bennet spoke again. "May I ask you a question, sir?"

"I am sure you want to go over the financial details, and I must tell you I plan to visit my solicitor—"

"No, that is not my question."

After a moment of surprise, Darcy apologised and urged him to continue.

"I am sure I shall have no worries regarding your ability to provide for my daughter. No, what concerns me more is that I have not detected any particular favour from you towards Elizabeth. In fact, I might have imagined quite the opposite."

"Although my…this engagement was unanticipated, I assure you in the strongest terms that you need not doubt my attachment to Miss Elizabeth."

"No?"

"No," Darcy replied with more confidence than he felt.

"What is it exactly which draws you to my Lizzy?"

After a moment of shocked silence Darcy asked, "You wish me to account for my attachment?"

"I do indeed."

"Very well." Darcy licked his lips and thought for a moment. "Miss Elizabeth is generous and kind, and I admire her wit."

"Mm." Mr Bennet was not impressed.

"And she…she has a caring nature."

Mr Bennet stared at him.

"She is beautiful too…and I enjoy her teasing. She can make the most serious subject seem rather light and that is something one does not often see. So many ladies mistake spite and sarcasm for wit, but not Miss Elizabeth. Your daughter is able to earn a smile or a laugh in a manner that is sweet. One cannot be offended by her." Darcy suddenly realised he had been carried away a bit and stopped speaking, slightly chagrined.

Mr Bennet nodded slowly. "And what of your estate? Are you not concerned for her management of it?"

"Not in the least. She is capable and intelligent, and I do not doubt that what she does not know she will learn quickly."

Mr Bennet cocked his head and stared at Darcy, though

he seemed to see him not. Darcy half expected some sort of prophecy or judgment to be handed down, but instead Mr Bennet said only, "No doubt you will wish for a short engagement, then."

"I do, yes."

"Before Christmas, perhaps?"

Mr Bennet seemed to be offering a challenge, his gaze steady on Darcy's; looking, it seemed, for any sign of wavering.

"I thought the very same, but Elizabeth wishes to delay until after Christmas—so we will. We shall marry in January."

"Deferring to her already, are you? Best to begin as you mean to go on, sir."

"Happy wife, happy life," Darcy retorted. "Or so my father always said."

Mr Bennet chuckled at that and then rose. With nothing further said, he began to walk out of the room. Darcy followed him into the drawing room where the ladies of the house sat. Elizabeth glanced up at him as soon as he entered, a private smile curving her lips gently, and it warmed him.

He took a step towards her but was immediately stopped. A foul odour accosted him—something like the time he was hunting with a hound who had stolen into the chicken coops and eaten a lot of eggs. Wrinkling his nose, he looked around to see that a clergyman had approached him from behind.

Seeing that his presence had been detected, the man went into a flurry of bowing and scraping. "Sir, I do not believe we have been acquainted. I am Mr William Collins, and if only it had been my honour to be made aware that a distinguished personage such as yourself was residing at the neighbouring estate, I should have called directly. I am fortunate in my patronage, being selected by your very own dear aunt, Lady Catherine de Bourgh, to serve as the rector of the Hunsford parish in Kent, and indeed it is a distinction which, although I do not consider myself worthy, I am determined to do credit to the utmost of my ability."

Darcy could not imagine what he could say in response to such verbosity, and was overcome with astonishment at the boldness of the man to introduce himself in such a manner.

"It brings me a great deal of pleasure, sir, to be able to tell you that when last I saw Lady Catherine and your delightful cousin Miss de Bourgh three days ago, they were both in excellent health. I can only feel the greatest of dismay that I had not the felicity of understanding that I would have the great and undeserved honour of making your acquaintance on this visit to my cousins, else I would have surely brought correspondence from them to you.

"As a clergyman, I feel it is my solemn duty to promote the bonds of devotion within families, and it was for this cause that I have come to Longbourn, that I might heal the breach that has long existed between Mr Bennet and my dear departed sire. You see—"

"Mr Collins, if you please, I have something I would wish to say," Mr Bennet interrupted him.

The ladies, Mr Darcy, Mr Bingley, and Mr Collins looked at Mr Bennet expectantly. Without preamble or ceremony, Mr Bennet said calmly, "Mr Darcy and Elizabeth are engaged to be married."

For a moment, blessed silence entombed the room. Then a maelstrom erupted. Every lady spoke at once, save Elizabeth and Jane.

Mrs Bennet's voice was the most piercing. "Lizzy! Why

you sly thing, you never dropped so much as a word! Oh, I just knew how it would be, just as soon as I knew Netherfield had been let, though of course I would not have expected such a wealthy man to take a liking—"

"Mama!" Kitty wheedled. "I shall need new gowns! We cannot go to Lizzy's wedding wearing our shabby old—"

"You shan't get a new gown for you got two new last month!" Lydia protested.

"It is not my fault that I grew out of the old gowns."

"Yes, you certainly did grow, and not upwards. I think you had best give up on the cakes with your tea."

"Mama! Did you hear what Lydia said to me?"

"Girls, girls!" This was from Mrs Bennet, and Darcy hoped it meant some form of chastisement would come forth. "Oh, we shall all have new gowns! I have no doubt at all that his gentlemen friends who come to the wedding breakfast will take quite a liking to all of you! I should not be the least bit surprised if you would all be married within the year! Oh what a fine thing..."

Mr Bennet, having shot his cannon, gave a wink and a nod and left the room, presumably to return to his study. This was the signal, it seemed, for the squabbling and exclaiming to resume.

Elizabeth rose. "Mr Darcy? You should have no objection to a turn about the gardens, I am sure."

He nearly protested—after all, they had been in the garden not half an hour earlier—but realised she wished to escape, as did he. With a nod, he rose and followed her.

CHAPTER FIVE

ELIZABETH WAS SO EMBARRASSED BY HER FAMILY'S BEHAVIOUR that she could not think what to say, and as Mr Darcy was similarly inclined towards silence, they strolled without speaking for some time. Finally, Elizabeth said, "Mr Darcy, pray excuse the exuberance of my mother and sisters."

"Your apology is unnecessary. In any case, I have never found anything wanting in you or Miss Bennet. You are both, in every way, elegant and well mannered."

"Thank you," Elizabeth said. *I think?* After all, although he had complimented herself and her sister, he simultaneously insulted the others. *Did they not deserve it?* She would think him a simpleton indeed if he approved of their behaviour. Still, it did sting a bit to face obvious contempt and disapproval of her family from the man she intended to marry.

Glancing over at him, she saw on his face an inscrutable blankness. Not for a million pounds could she even begin to imagine what he must be thinking, but that was likely for the better. She struggled with feeling as though she might cry. A silly thing; there was no reason to cry over the antics of her family. She had grown used to them embarrassing her a long time ago and certainly would not allow Mr Darcy to alter her sensitivity to them.

Impulsively she stopped and turned to him. "Are we making an enormous mistake?"

He considered it for a long moment. "Perhaps. But in truth, I simply do not know what else to do. I...to be perfectly frank, the notion of scandal, it...I cannot abide scandal."

"Yes. And even less can I abide the notion of life bound to Mr Collins." Quite unthinkingly, she muttered, "Such a sweaty, stupid man."

She had not intended to say the last aloud and immediately jerked her eyes to Mr Darcy's face. He was not attending, his head turned to stare blankly at the fields in the distance from them. She murmured an apology and began to walk forward. They continued at a slow pace. Elizabeth found herself lost in miserable contemplation of her choices for the future and presumed her companion did likewise.

At length he spoke. "Neither of us wants this, to be sure, but if we must do it—and I daresay we both have reason to suppose we must—then we should make the best of it."

After a brief moment to consider his words she said, "You are correct, of course. There are many ladies in my position who find themselves in marriages not of their choosing."

"Many gentlemen, as well. Hardly anyone can just follow their heart. Some consideration must always be given to the prudence of an alliance."

"Well, in your case, there is nothing prudent about our alliance, I fear." Elizabeth gave him a rueful smile. "Quite the opposite, in fact."

After another few moments, she asked, "Shall I write to your sister? I would like to—"

"No!" It seemed rather harsh, the way he said it, and she drew back, surprised.

"Um…I mean, not yet. I shall tell her first and then…then you can write."

Mystified she said, "As you wish."

They parted when they were back at Longbourn. Mr Darcy, having evidently exhausted his need for the society of Bennets for the day, bent over her hand, then turned towards the stables. He paused for a moment before he left her.

"Elizabeth?"

She turned back towards him.

"I cannot promise you that I shall always be the perfect husband, but I do promise I shall do the best I can to see to your happiness."

"Thank you," she said, feeling touched by his earnestness. "I promise you the same."

He touched the brim of his hat. "And if nothing else, I vow to never be sweaty, not in your presence in any case. Whether or not I am stupid is for you to decide, but my man Fields and I shall make sure to conquer the perspiration."

And so it was that Mr Darcy left his future wife laughing.

THE LEVITY of his last moments with Elizabeth was almost immediately replaced by something far more familiar—guilt. Her words—'*there is nothing prudent about our alliance*'—reverberated in his mind.

Bingley was awaiting him in the stable and began rattling away cheerily as Darcy accepted his animal from the lad and mounted, all the while thinking of the Darcy men who had come before him; all of them married to beautiful, accomplished women from notable families and possessing excellent fortunes.

He had been taught that gentlemanly honour meant reason before emotion and duty before desire. A gentleman did not succumb to lust, but he had done just that. He had not forgotten the dreams he had had of her, and even now, watching her walk away from him, he had felt it burning beneath his skin, his want of her. It embarrassed him deeply. He would face the derision of society because of a most improper dream and a harridan who woke him in the midst of it.

But there was nothing for it, was there? It was done. He was engaged; he had given his word to her father. He would marry Elizabeth Bennet.

He imagined the news spread about town. Caroline Bingley would surely be merciless in her description of Meryton and the Bennet family, most particularly Elizabeth. *His wife.* For a moment he imagined the worst, doors closed to her, ladies tittering at her behind their fans while the men he knew made sly remarks about lust and country manners.

He felt a film of cold sweat break out over him. *Think of the alternative. Imagine taking Miss Bingley as your bride.*

Of two poor choices, he had taken the best one—he hoped. The scene in the drawing room dismayed him, but surely Elizabeth would wish all that put behind her just as much as he wished it for her.

IN THE NEXT DAYS, Darcy and Elizabeth both went about the business of appearing happily betrothed. Darcy called at

Longbourn with Bingley every day and remained for as long as he could withstand the pandemonium.

The first soiree at which their betrothal was known was a party at an estate called Ashworth, the seat of a local baronet, Sir Arnold Goddard. Sir Arnold had two sons and two daughters, and of these, only one daughter, Miss Lillian Goddard, remained unmarried.

Darcy had asked permission to bring Elizabeth to the party in his carriage, with Mary accompanying them as Elizabeth's chaperon. Mr Bennet agreed to it, as well as a scheme to permit Jane to ride in Mr Bingley's carriage with Caroline and the Hursts. Privately, Elizabeth thought she might have preferred to walk the twelve miles, but Jane was happy, so she kept her thoughts to herself.

They began the journey in silence. Mary was quick to remove a book from her bag and make herself invisible, but this did not spur Darcy into conversation, so Elizabeth began. "Have you met Sir Arnold?"

"I do not think I have. I believe he called on Bingley before I arrived."

"I think you will find the family agreeable. They travel a great deal within England and Ireland as well as on the Continent, and always have a number of interesting anecdotes to relate."

"Such extensive travel certainly does alter one's perspective," Darcy noted. "I remember when I returned from my tour, abbreviated though it was, I felt I had learnt more than in all my prior years at university."

"How so?" Elizabeth asked. "I have always longed to travel, but as I have not, I must rely on the accounts of others more fortunate."

Darcy paused for a moment, seeming to contemplate his

reply and then began to speak, more easy and verbose than usual. With great animation he told of people he had met, the places he had gone, sights seen, and music heard. He was an excellent storyteller; she admired his ability to paint a faithful picture of his experiences for her.

He appeared as astonished as she was when Mary looked up from her book and announced, "We have entered the drive."

"Why, we have made excellent time." He pulled his watch from his pocket, seeming a bit distressed by the idea of his own prolixity. "That is to say, we have arrived at the time expected. I…have I really spoken so long? I hope I did not bore you."

Elizabeth smiled at him just as the coachman opened the door. "Not at all. I enjoyed it. I almost felt as though I had visited those places myself."

He smiled at her again, looking more warm and sincere than she had ever seen him. "Thank you," he said quietly before exiting the carriage.

The party had nearly fifty people in attendance. Darcy was surprised, looking around him, that the manor was as well situated as it was. The house was one of the oldest in the county, but the owners had apparently been fastidious in keeping it repaired and refashioned, and the result was charming.

Darcy's custom was to linger on the periphery of most parties, but Elizabeth evidently felt quite the opposite. She immediately entered the fray and appeared determined to hold a conversation of some sort with each and every person in the room. He found himself relaxing, and even enjoying himself, as Elizabeth led the way from person to person. Everyone liked her, and by extension, liked him too, with very little effort on his part. It built hope within him that she would find a welcome in London.

But these are simpler people with simpler manners, he reminded himself. The cats and pigeons of London would hardly be so agreeable to her.

Darcy was given the seat of honour at Lady Goddard's right hand, with her daughter on his other side. "I am acquainted with your cousin, Mr Darcy," the younger lady told him after he helped her sit. "Viscount Saye."

"Indeed?" *These people know Saye? Perhaps they are higher than I had thought.*

"We had a few dances this Season," Miss Goddard said dismissively. "He was horrid to me, scarcely spoke a word."

"Saye?" Darcy asked with surprise. "That is a surprise. He customarily talks the paint off the walls, though very little of it makes any sense."

"Hm," she said with a non-committal sniff. "But do tell me, how did you woo Miss Elizabeth? Do say you proposed at least twice; a lady like Miss Elizabeth deserves it."

"Ah...well, not...not exactly." Darcy was saved from Miss Goddard's romantic inclinations by her mother, who leant over and asked him about Derbyshire as her other daughter was settled near Pemberley. From there it was easy to leave the particulars of his engagement behind.

He glanced down the table towards Elizabeth's chair; she was seated between Bingley and a gentleman he would later learn was a cousin of the Goddards', a Jennings from Oxfordshire. Jennings was about his age and appreciated the appeal of his dining partner far too much for Darcy's liking.

Then again, how could Jennings not like her? She was alternately teasing and sweet, kindness commingled with good humour and wit—intoxicating Jennings just the same as she had Darcy.

Although continuing his conversation with Lady Goddard, Darcy found his eye often drawn to Elizabeth. Jennings flirted with her more boldly with each passing moment, and Darcy swallowed against feelings of jealousy. *Calm yourself man, it will not do to behave possessively.* Elizabeth would hate that, and in any case, he trusted her—even if this Jennings appeared to need a lesson in how to treat an engaged woman.

They were in the middle of the fish course when Elizabeth caught him looking at her. Glancing up at him, she offered a small smile that was as intimate as could be in their current circumstances. She then, barely perceptibly, offered a slight eye roll and an amused grin. The relief which swept through him was absurd, he knew, but much appreciated.

THE CARRIAGE RIDE home was uneventful until, as they travelled the road towards Meryton, they hit a rut and one of the wheels on Darcy's carriage broke. They stopped immediately, and Darcy got out to speak with his men.

Elizabeth looked over at Mary, who had fallen asleep. She had blearily opened one eye when they hit the rut, but then closed it almost immediately. Elizabeth smiled at her fondly—she looked so gentle in repose.

The night had been pleasant, and Elizabeth was encouraged by the time spent with her betrothed. He had shown the ability to be pleasing in society, even among strangers. He had been attentive to her and kind to her sisters. All in all, an unqualified success.

The door to the carriage opened, carrying with it a gust of the cold November wind. Darcy re-entered, telling Elizabeth, "The coachmen will be able to fix it well enough to get us back, but it will require some time. I am sorry for the delay—I do hope your parents will not worry."

Elizabeth smiled. "My parents rarely worry about anything, except in Mama's case, securing husbands. Jane will worry."

Darcy laughed and then beckoned her to the seat beside him. "Come sit here."

"Oh…well, but what if…" She glanced at her sleeping chaperon.

"Yes, what if someone saw us? We might be made to marry," Darcy said wryly. "Come."

Taking her hand, he helped her move. "We will pass the time more easily if we can speak without fear of waking your sister. I must say, of myself and Bingley, I have earned the better part. Your sister is an exceedingly indifferent chaperon."

Elizabeth laughed quietly. "That she is. So long as she is supplied with a book, she will spare us little of her attention."

She settled into the seat next to him as he placed the blanket over her lap. "I am not quite accustomed to the notion that we shall marry. When I recall it, the thought of it surprises me still." She smiled up at him, thinking nervously that she had never been this close to him before.

"I hope it will not be too difficult for you to leave your home," he said. "You seem to have many friends."

Beneath the blanket she felt his hand, large and warm, seek hers. She slid her hand willingly inside his grasp, surprised to realise that his glove was removed. She wondered whether she should remove hers or it would be too bold. *Oh, there are so many rules to courtship, and I feel I know none of them.*

"I hope to make many more friends," she replied lightly. "And most of all, I hope we are friends."

"I have never had a lady friend before."

"I had a male best friend for most of my life." On his surprised look, she said, "My cousin Philips—I called him Phils. We were inseparable from an early age, much to my mother's dismay. She blames him for my tendency to ramble wildly about the countryside."

"Philips? Have I met him?"

She shook her head. "No. He died when I was fifteen and he was sixteen. A shooting accident."

"How dreadful. I am sorry to hear it."

"I do miss him still," she admitted. "And my aunt has really never recovered from the loss. It is why she entertains so often, I think; she keeps moving so her grief cannot find her."

She felt Darcy squeeze her hand lightly, but alas, an unpleasant thought intruded. If Phils was still alive, he would be yet another person she would be forced to give up. Mr Darcy of Pemberley would surely not admit to his circle a Mr Philips, son of a lowly country solicitor, who likely would have become a lowly country solicitor one day himself.

But such thoughts would not do. With a little shake of her head, she forced herself back towards happier thoughts. "So, tell me everything I do not know about you."

Such a directive made him chuckle softly. "Shall I tell you about Pemberley?"

"Sometime, yes, but for now, I believe I might rather hear about you."

Darcy seemed uncertain so she prompted him. "Likes, dislikes, embarrassing stories from your youth, perhaps?"

"Embarrassing stories from my youth? That seems a bit imprudent. Likes and dislikes might be easier."

"Well, then...?"

"I like riding, fencing, and boxing. I do not enjoy shooting so much, and my skill at it is only average, but I am good at fishing. I like reading, as you might have realised already, on nearly any topic, but I particularly enjoy history. Oh, and this might surprise you, I do like dancing. I only avoid it because once you ask a lady to dance, suddenly the entire room thinks you will offer for her."

"I would imagine that does dampen one's enthusiasm."

"And what about you?"

Elizabeth smiled. "I love to dance."

"Good...and what else?"

"Reading as well, including history, although I must own, I do not particularly like the accounts of war that my father enjoys. I do well enough with a needle, though it makes me feel a bit restive if I am at it too long, and I also like to sketch, but with few creditable results.

"I enjoy being outdoors far more than is considered proper for a young lady. Walks, of course, are my favourite, but I have been known to fish with my father," she admitted, wondering what he would think of that.

"I have longed for a fishing partner, so now you will be the one."

"So I shall. We shall scandalise the servants." She had grown accustomed to it, the feeling of her hand within his. It was surprising how quickly it became natural to her.

"You seem to be particular in your choice of foods," he said.

"Yes, my mother has long lamented my fastidiousness at the dinner table."

"It seems you hate potatoes."

"Oh, I do! Detestable things...they always taste like dirt to me."

"And cheese?"

How does he know all of this? "I do not like much of anything made with milk, and much to Mr Hurst's dismay, I prefer plain dishes to ragout. I also hate bacon."

"You hate bacon!" Even in the darkness she could see she had shocked him. "But bacon is...it is—"

"It is a pig," she informed him. "And I have always despised pigs."

"You will need to avoid my cousin Fitzwilliam, then. He eats bacon at nearly every meal. My first memory of him is fighting him for trying to steal my bacon."

She laughed, enjoying the notion of a child Darcy in some hijinks with an unknown cousin. "Your cousin is also named Fitzwilliam?"

"Fitzwilliam is his surname. It was my mother's family name."

"Ah, I see. What about your preferences in dining?"

"I eat anything. You will have no trouble arranging menus on my account; although I must tell you now, I am far too inclined to indulge in sweet things. It will be your job to control me."

"Control you? Surely not!"

When their chuckles had died down, Elizabeth ventured to say, "Miss Lillian Goddard mentioned some slight acquaintance with your family?"

"She knows my cousin Saye—eldest son and heir of my uncle, the Earl of Matlock. Fitzwilliam, who I mentioned earlier, is his younger brother."

"I see."

"It is a position he feels keenly and makes the most of," Darcy said. "Strangely...it seemed he was rather silent to her."

"He is customarily more talkative than his cousin?" Elizabeth teased.

"Infinitely so. He rattles away at anything unless... No. That cannot be."

"What?"

He tilted his head, seeming to consider something. "She said that he had danced with her and hardly spoke to her. I wonder if he likes her."

"She seems very sweet, very pretty."

"She does," Darcy agreed. "But enough to render Saye speechless? That would make her an uncommon lady, and I just cannot imagine... But you will meet him soon enough and see what I mean."

Mary moved in her slumber, startling them both; Elizabeth had forgotten she was there. Her sister's lap blanket had slid down, and Elizabeth leant across the carriage to adjust it, rising up off of the seat, and then re-seating herself, again becoming conscious of just how close she was to Darcy, who reached over to tuck her own lap blanket more securely around her.

"One can really feel winter coming on tonight," she remarked, feeling a sudden rise in tension caused by his nearness.

"In Derbyshire, it snows in November sometimes. Do you like snow?"

"Certainly. I like all the seasons. In winter, the ice on the trees and snowy fields are lovely, but then spring comes with all the new leaves on the trees and the flowers begin to bloom. And then summer arrives, and I am outside enjoying the warmth with every opportunity. Then autumn is upon me, and I have the changing leaves to admire."

"That is quite like you," Darcy remarked, his voice sounding as though he spoke more to himself than to her. "You do not delight in complaining and misfortune, instead finding contentment in whatever situation you are in."

"I do hope so," she answered. "I have always learnt that true happiness is a choice."

He did not reply.

"And yourself, sir? How well do you like the snow?"

"Well, I usually enjoy the colder weather more so than the warm," he admitted.

"Why is that?" She looked at him curiously. "I believe most people would say the opposite."

Speaking with uncommon candour, he said, "It seems that most of the difficult things in my life have occurred in the summertime. My mother and father both died in the summer, and Georgiana…."

He paused a moment and she saw him swallow hard. "Georgiana had some…difficulty…this past summer."

"I see," Elizabeth said. She reached for his hand again, having dropped it when she moved to adjust Mary's blanket. "I am sorry to hear that. She is your younger sister, I believe?"

"She was sixteen in September."

"It can be a difficult age," Elizabeth said gently. "I am sure she will grow out of it, whatever it was."

He did not seem inclined to say more, and Elizabeth

thought it likely that the difficulties of Georgiana were more than he was prepared to discuss with her. For his sake, she changed the subject, "How did you enjoy the evening? Did you find the Goddards agreeable?"

"I did," he replied and turned his head to look at her. She looked up at him, feeling keenly the awareness of their proximity. He lowered his voice, admitting, "As enjoyable as the party was, however, my favourite time has been this, in the carriage."

He moved his thumb in a slow circle on her glove, creating heat that she felt far more than on her hand. She drew a breath, wondering what it meant and thinking how strange it was to be here in a carriage with a man whom she had so recently believed she disliked, but whose caress was now thrilling her. Her voice a whisper, she replied, "I am enjoying this too."

She saw it then, a quick glance at her lips that enflamed her nearly as much as the caress to her hand. What would she do if he kissed her? He was to be her husband, so it was likely to occur sometime in the months leading up to their wedding. Tonight? Would he try tonight? Would she permit it here in front of Mary?

The sharp rapping on the door startled both of them. Darcy hastily rose and stepped out of the carriage.

The cold night air seemed to clear the confusion in Elizabeth's mind. She moved back to sit next to her sister, a feeling of commingled relief and disappointment coursing through her, even as the sensation of his thumb on her hand remained.

"We shall be on our way shortly," Darcy told her as he entered the carriage again.

As reluctant as he was to be parted from Elizabeth that night, the solitude of his carriage after he left the sisters at Longbourn afforded Darcy a time for occupation nearly as agreeable, reflecting upon the moments he had shared with Elizabeth.

Darcy knew his danger very well. He had felt a sudden and almost irrepressible longing to kiss her earlier, right in the presence of Miss Mary Bennet. He had exercised restraint, but he knew quite well that his restraint was worn thin by the end of the night. It was the feel of her hand, so soft and delicate within his. He felt powerful and mighty, protector of something delicate and exceedingly precious, all from the feel of that hand.

He had spent a great portion of the journey considering whether she would permit him to remove her glove. He would nearly persuade himself to do it, and then he would dissuade himself, only to begin again. *I should have just done it. We are engaged and it is only a hand.*

She is so lovely, he thought, recollecting the way she had looked bathed in the silvery moonlight. Raising an eyebrow at him, teasing him, smiling at him… *So very, very lovely.*

Their conversation had been silly and rather inconsequential, but it had made him happy. It was not his way to share information of himself in such a way as he had done tonight. Yet, to do so with Elizabeth was an undeniably happy feeling.

What she had said was endearing—that she would wish to know more of him. Not Pemberley, not Derbyshire, but him. How extraordinarily charming, and so very sincere. How wonderful to know that nothing she did or said was artful or done to entrap him; he had entrapped himself, and he found that daily he was yet more pleased to be there.

My heart has become engaged in this. This is no longer merely an arrangement for me—was it ever? More than once, he had wondered at the ease with which his lie to Bingley had emerged from his mouth. *I asked Miss Elizabeth Bennet to marry me only yesterday, and she has accepted me. We are betrothed.* The words had slid from his mouth quite readily, nary a hesitation or stumble to impede them. Was his mind only just accepting what his heart had known all along?

CHAPTER SIX

It scarcely needed saying that Mrs Bennet was in raptures over Elizabeth's grand match. Her bliss was matched only by her surprise that Elizabeth, long regarded as her least favourite daughter, could have secured the affections of such a wealthy gentleman. She had no qualms in announcing these sentiments to any of their callers. "I should have thought such a man would fall in love with Jane! But Bingley was there first, of course. Beauty is not the only virtue, I daresay, and these great men do need a witty wife to ensure their estates are well run." After the third lady had called, Elizabeth thought she might well expire from her vexation with it.

Her younger sisters, silly as they were, provided a much-needed distraction. They had returned from a trip to Meryton and were filled with stories about the regiment quartered there.

"…and then Denny came and brought with him the handsomest man ever I have seen!"

Kitty interjected excitedly, "He was tall, nearly as tall as Mr Darcy!"

"He is a lieutenant?" Mrs Bennet asked.

"He has only just joined," Lydia proclaimed, "but I daresay when he is in his regimentals, another man so handsome will not be found, not in this regiment nor any other."

Kitty interrupted her. "We invited him to Aunt Philips's party, too!"

"Oh yes!" Mrs Bennet exclaimed. "The most handsome soldier in Meryton—your aunt would not wish to slight him!"

Elizabeth rolled her eyes at the brazenness of her younger sisters as well as the fact that Mrs Bennet did not see fit to censure them. It was far too bold to invite a man of new acquaintance to come to a party, particularly when the party was not their own.

"But Lizzy, what will you wear?" Kitty asked.

"Something that will make Mr Darcy wish to tear it off of you, no doubt," Lydia teased.

"Lydia!" Elizabeth said with genuine shock.

"Oh, come now," Mrs Bennet scolded. "Do not be so missish."

"Good sense and propriety are not missish," Elizabeth protested. "Has my aunt even invited the Netherfield party? Perhaps with so many of the officers—"

"Of course, she has!" Mrs Bennet cried. "She would not wish to slight Mr Darcy, not when he is nearly family!"

Elizabeth winced, imagining how little Darcy wished to call such connexions his own, but fortunately her mother did not see her chagrin.

Mrs Philips came to call later that day and could only increase Elizabeth's consternation. Her aunt was in raptures herself at the notion of such elevated personages coming to her gathering and had ordered expensive teas and coffees brought in, as well as a particular French wine.

"Do not ask me how I got it," she said in an exaggerated whisper. "But I got it. These London gentlemen will not think my party wanting."

DARCY RECEIVED the invitation from Mrs Philips in a packet which also contained letters from his steward, one from his solicitor, and two personal letters, one from Lord Matlock and the other from his cousin Colonel Richard Fitzwilliam. Looking at the latter two, he could not help but feel trepidation. These gentlemen rarely wrote, and receiving missives from both on the same day seemed to foretell disaster.

Darcy's uncle, his mother's elder brother and the Earl of Matlock, was an honourable gentleman who many saw as a bit disagreeable. He did not suffer fools gladly, and for those he disapproved of, he saw no reason to guard his tongue against them. But he was a good person at heart, and he loved his family dearly, including his nephew.

Lord Matlock had been of the opinion, on Darcy's father's death, that Georgiana would be best left to him and his wife to raise properly. A combination of duty and fear of loneliness had caused Darcy to refuse, but subsequent events had taught him that was folly.

Several months past, Georgiana had gone to Ramsgate with her companion, a Mrs Younge. The particulars of what had happened to his sister in Ramsgate were undefined; however, what Darcy did know was that Georgiana had believed she loved George Wickham and had allowed him the liberties of a husband. She was heartbroken to learn it was all a scheme.

But Georgiana did not suffer heartbreak as most ladies might have. She declined rapidly from mere crying into a state of near-madness, and it seemed Darcy's presence made it worse. Lord and Lady Matlock eventually persuaded him to leave her, to allow her the space she needed to recover her spirits, and he, reluctantly, heeded their wisdom. Even this, however, had not helped, though neither had it hurt. According to his lordship's letter, Georgiana's condition was steady.

"Let us hope it remains steady when she learns of my engagement," he muttered to no one.

Then he opened Fitzwilliam's letter, which included much of the same information, as well as the added fact that his cousin had discovered Georgiana had contrived to give Wickham a fairly large sum of money. It had been given in the summer, shortly before the incident in Ramsgate, and Fitzwilliam had just discovered the missing funds in a review of her accounts. Georgiana had grown hysterical when confronted with it, but Fitzwilliam told Darcy not to worry.

"Not to worry?" Darcy sat back, rubbing his head. Life was certainly inconstant, and at times he felt as though he had little control over anything. Georgiana went to Ramsgate and spun things off in a direction that resulted in him coming to Hertfordshire and finding himself an engaged man. How had that happened? He had tried only to do what was best for her and now found himself wholly upended.

Suddenly, he felt like a very, very old man. The weight of the world itself felt as if it were pressing him down and surrounding him. He knew not whether he could bear even one more complication.

Leaning back in his chair, his eyes again fell on the stack of letters, and he noticed Mrs Philips's invitation on top. One thing was certain: he could not go out in society this evening, not even to a humble card party. He was not even sure he could summon the wherewithal required to rise from the chair.

Any humiliation Elizabeth might have felt at the absence of her suitor could only be magnified by the dismay that her aunt Philips, eager to fancy herself in higher circles thanks to her niece, must have asked after the Netherfield party at least one hundred times in the first hour of the party. Then, when a small group rolled up the rugs in another room and began dancing, she lamented loudly how terrible it was that poor, dear Lizzy was missing her preferred dance partner.

Would an hour or so in undistinguished society have been so impossible? She would do her best to make herself agreeable to his friends and relations; was it too much to ask that he would do likewise? Yes, evidently it was. It was the way of the world, and she knew it, but it still rankled. The fact that her aunt was not a countess did not mean she should not be afforded courtesy.

At last resolved to put it aside, Elizabeth rose from her chair. If Darcy chose to leave her unattended, then she would enjoy herself as best she could.

George Wickham had scarcely been a part of Forster's regiment for an hour before he knew all about the current residents of Netherfield Park. It was a stroke of bad luck to find himself in the same county as Darcy, and for the moment, he considered decamping. But Darcy would leave soon, he was sure of it.

Then Denny told him some truly amazing news—Darcy was engaged to marry a daughter of one of the local families. "You are certain?"

"An elder sister of Miss Lydia," Denny informed him, with a quirk of his brow.

Wickham chuckled. "Miss Lydia is charming, and I assume her sister is as well but it did not seem to me that the family was grand enough for Darcy."

"Mr Darcy is rather high in the instep," Denny agreed. "But Miss Elizabeth is a delight. You will see for yourself tonight."

Wickham spent the first hour of the party watching Miss Elizabeth Bennet and awaiting the opportunity to make her acquaintance. As he was at the card table with her two youngest sisters, the differences among the Bennet girls were readily apparent. He understood Darcy's choice as he watched Miss Elizabeth circling the room, talking and laughing with her friends and relations. On first glance, he comprehended why the neighbourhood thought Miss Bennet the beauty, but Miss Elizabeth Bennet had a liveliness about her that could stir a man's blood. *Yes, yes indeed. I daresay I would choose her too.*

Seeing her join her sister, he made haste to approach them. "Miss Kitty Bennet, would you do me the honour of introducing me to your friend?"

"Lizzy, this is Lieutenant George Wickham. Sir, my sister, Miss Elizabeth Bennet."

They enjoyed easy and light-hearted conversation until

Miss Kitty excused herself to join a table for whist. When she was gone, Wickham turned to Miss Elizabeth and smiled in his most guileless manner. "How disappointing that Mr Darcy is not with you this evening!"

He knew he did not imagine a slight tightening of her smile. Ah, but the lovely Miss Elizabeth was not pleased her suitor had not come to the gathering. "Are you acquainted with Mr Darcy, sir?"

"We grew up alongside one another," Wickham replied warmly. "My father was the steward at Pemberley when he and old Mr Darcy were both still alive. I was privileged in that old Mr Darcy saw fit to support my education, so I was sent to Eton and Cambridge along with his son."

"How fortunate that you have both found yourselves in Hertfordshire at the same time. Mr Darcy will be delighted to see you, I am sure."

"I must admit, Darcy and I suffered some disaffection in our later years. Things become so complicated when we grow older, do you not find?"

"They do indeed."

"But never mind painful subjects. What has Darcy told you of Pemberley? I think it the finest place in England." Wickham assumed the very countenance of cheer, seeing he had provoked Miss Elizabeth's curiosity.

She looked away a moment, touching the curls at her neck briefly. "It must have been quite wonderful to grow up in such a beautiful place."

Her discomfort intrigued him, but he could not ask about it. "It is my greatest wish that one day Darcy and I might reconcile, both for our friendship's sake and to once again regard the place I truly view as my home."

Wickham knew he needed her to enquire about his

breach with Darcy—if she were to leave here and ask Darcy, any hope of gaining her sympathy would be destroyed. There was something in her discomfort that suggested to him that he might gain her trust. *She does not love him.*

"Allow me to say that I wish that for you as well, sir." Miss Elizabeth changed the topic only moments later. "Have you been long in the militia?"

"My commission is fairly recent based on my...reduced circumstances."

"My apologies." She looked demurely curious.

"I was destined for a life of service to the church. It was what old Mr Darcy had wanted for me, and it was what I desired for myself as well. Alas, Mr Darcy, when his father died, did not think it should be so. So, I must make my way in some other fashion and have chosen to see whether the military life will suit me. I daresay I shall like it as well as anything I have done."

"You are very good, though it does surprise me to know that Darcy did not honour his father's wishes."

"I was not surprised at all." Wickham lowered his voice to a confiding tone. "His father was exceedingly good to me, and at times, far too hard on his son. He only meant to build his son's character of course, but it must have built resentment in Darcy to see me so favoured. I had the rights and privileges of a son without the responsibility and expectations."

Wickham had to restrain his chuckle of glee at the kindness in Miss Elizabeth's eyes. He gave a deep sigh. "But now I am a poor soldier, and he lives in wealth and privilege." He smiled and added, "With the hand of a beautiful woman no less. Darcy is blessed indeed."

Miss Elizabeth blushed lightly and looked down.

"Indeed, I think it must be I who envies him now!" Wickham chuckled. "But you wished to hear more of Pemberley; forgive me for speaking so much of myself." With that, the conversation turned to a more agreeable topic as Wickham told Miss Elizabeth story after story of that great estate and its inhabitants as he had known them.

CHAPTER SEVEN

The day following Aunt Philips's party saw Darcy and Mr Bingley calling at Longbourn. Bingley brought with him an invitation to a ball he intended to host at Netherfield, and as might have been imagined, its appearance brought great joy to the parlour. When the effusions began to abate, a walk to Oakham Mount was proposed, and soon four of them set off, Darcy with Elizabeth and Bingley with Jane.

As they walked, Elizabeth considered Darcy carefully. She could not deny that she was hurt and angry at his slight of her aunt. Hearing Mr Wickham's story could only increase her consternation. Although she had tried determinedly to put aside all dismay over these things, seeing him renewed her distress. She did not wish to argue about any of it, but neither could she feel as warmly as she had just days before. It was dizzying, these swings in her sentiments, for he charmed her one day and made her furious with him the next.

"I must go to London after Bingley's ball," he announced. "I think I must tell my family of our engagement."

"Shall I give you a letter for Miss Darcy?"

"No, let me speak to her first," he replied immediately. "Should I tell them we will marry in January?"

"I would vastly prefer to marry in February," Elizabeth said, for no more reason than a contrary spirit. Did he intend to let her see his sister before the wedding? Or was she never to know the girl? She forbore to ask.

"February? Why?"

"February is a more romantic month," she replied, as though that made perfect sense.

Darcy paused, clearly considering it, then said, "Lent begins on the twelfth so likely some day in the first week is best."

"What about the tenth?" She said and he, after a curious glance at her, assented.

She said little more than that, walking beside him in the cold November air, but nevertheless he must have perceived she was not happy with him. At length, he turned to her and said, "I should have accompanied you to your aunt's home last evening."

She did not look at him. "It was a very enjoyable evening."

"I do hope Mrs Philips received my regrets."

"No, I do not think she did," Elizabeth replied coolly. "She seemed to have every expectation that you would arrive at any moment."

To this Darcy said nothing. He turned his head forward again as they walked slowly. He appeared lost in thought and decidedly unconcerned for any inconvenience or ill feeling he might have created with Mrs Philips. Elizabeth swallowed hard against her pique. "It was exceedingly unfortunate you did not join us. I met an old acquaintance of yours there."

"Who was that?"

"Mr Wickham."

His response shocked her; he stopped immediately on the path and rounded on her, his face pale with rage and shock. "What?"

"I met a Mr Wickham there last night. He sent you his regards." He had not, not exactly, but Elizabeth said so anyway. "He seemed a kind, gentlemanly sort of man. I was pleased with the acquaintance."

"Sent his regards?" Darcy's eyes burnt with fury, and he leant over her, gripping his walking stick by his side. With his jaw clenched, he ordered her, "Stay away from George Wickham. You will avoid him at all costs."

Elizabeth took a step back from him. "I can hardly escape the—"

"No!" Darcy said, his voice raised enough to make Jane and Mr Bingley, ahead of them on the path, turn around to look. Through gritted teeth, Darcy spat, "You will stay away from him."

Elizabeth quickly turned her head from him to hide her gasp and to disguise the tears of anger and mortification which had risen into her eyes. She managed to choke out some syllables of assent, though it was contrary to every feeling within her.

Jane and Mr Bingley hurried towards them, Mr Bingley's face almost comically concerned. "Darcy? Is everything well?"

"No. No, I…I must return immediately." Darcy turned on his heel and began to stride quickly down the path. "See Elizabeth back, will you?"

Elizabeth lowered her eyes, humiliation setting her face aflame. She could feel, rather than see, Jane and Mr Bingley exchanging glances, no doubt wondering at the scene they had just witnessed. It was too embarrassing, and she could say nothing in her defence. She was angry and had meant to provoke him, and this was the result.

But Mr Bingley was amiable as ever, speaking quickly to dispel the discomfort. "How very fortunate I am! Two beautiful ladies to escort instead of one! Miss Elizabeth, your sister tells me this is the finest prospect in Hertfordshire. Do you agree?"

"Um, yes," Elizabeth managed to say and forced her feet into motion once again.

Mr Bingley offered his arm and, when she took it, kindly patted her hand. Evidently his friend's behaviour did not shock him as much as it did her.

THE RAGE in Darcy's bosom very nearly left him breathless. Wickham! Following him here, always eager to wreak havoc in his life! Fuelled by an anger that rendered him insensible, Darcy returned to Longbourn where he went immediately to Mr Bennet. After a short conference with his future father-in-law, he returned to Netherfield and closeted himself in Bingley's library, careful not to slam doors or kick things as he might have liked to do. Elizabeth's voice within his head repeated, *'He seemed a kind, gentlemanly sort of man...'*

"Arrgh!" This time he did kick something, a pillow that had fallen from a chair onto the ground in front of him. Then he picked it up, threw it down, and kicked it again.

Elizabeth had been 'pleased with the acquaintance' and no great shock that was; Wickham certainly knew how to please when he wanted to. Rage boiled in his gut, imagining Wickham speaking to Elizabeth, leaning into her, breathing the same air as she breathed. To think that he dared speak to her! The thought of Elizabeth's fine eyes shining with pity or amusement as she looked upon Wickham nearly made him gag.

She is mine. Mine and only *mine, and how dare he—*

He paused and, after a moment, slowly went to sit down on a chair.

Was he jealous? Yes, he was, of course he was. And angry and disgusted and most of the usual things that he felt when Wickham was around him. Wickham borrowed on the Darcy name, he had taken Darcy's money, partaken in his education, shared in his home—but Darcy would be damned if he would share Elizabeth with him.

By the time Mr Bingley returned the Bennet ladies to the care of their mother at Longbourn, Darcy had already been to see Mr Bennet. Elizabeth was not given any clues as to the substance of their discussion, but when it had concluded and Darcy departed, Mr Bennet summoned her.

"Lizzy, Mr Darcy instructed me that I must not allow you to walk alone in the fields," he teased. "Husband's orders."

"I am not yet married, sir," Elizabeth protested hotly. "And I do hope you told him that as I am still under your house, I am permitted to do as I have done all my life."

"Well, as it is, I happen to agree with him."

"Agree with him? That is ridiculous! In twenty years, I have not encountered anything more dangerous than a barking dog in these woods, and now you want me to give way to a man who—"

"Elizabeth, you are engaged to a wealthy man. There are people who might wish to harm you, and you should be aware of that. In any case, you will be very soon under his rule—might as well accustom yourself to it now."

With a nod and a smile, her father dismissed her.

The notion had incensed her; her walks were her time of solitude and reflection in a life that was all too often marked by chaos. She did not relish the prospect of a footman tagging along after her everywhere. *My life is no longer my own.*

CHAPTER EIGHT

The Bennets were all surprised that Mr Collins had neither departed Longbourn nor proposed to another of the young ladies of the house. He seemed to have put aside his matrimonial ambitions in favour of lurking about, giving speeches, eating, and making cutting remarks about those who reached beyond their stations. He did appear to hold some agreeable expectations of Mr Bingley's ball, so Elizabeth hoped it meant he intended to partake in an enjoyable evening and then go back to Kent.

As Elizabeth alit from her father's carriage, she stood a moment contemplating Netherfield and the evening ahead of them. She had not spoken to Darcy since the scene on the path to Oakham Mount. The Netherfield party had been absent from church on Sunday, and Monday had been plagued by rain. She hardly knew whether she should be in anticipation or dread of the evening ahead of her.

"He awaits you," Lydia teased, poking her. When Elizabeth looked up, to her surprise Darcy was looking out from the second storey. "He must be violently in love with you."

Hardly. But Elizabeth gave him a little wave and saw him

smile down at her. She hoped it would mean a pleasant evening ahead for them. *I must believe in Darcy's good character. The matter with Mr Wickham must be set aside, for now at least. If nothing else, there is danger in trusting so implicitly in an acquaintance of only a few hours.*

She entered the hall where Mr and Miss Bingley were receiving their guests, and offered her compliments to Miss Bingley. Miss Bingley pressed her lips together a moment, and it seemed as if her reply—a simple thank you—pained her. Elizabeth left Miss Bingley just as Mr Darcy appeared in the doorway. For a moment, her heart jumped a bit, and her breath caught.

Darcy was turned out impeccably, every inch of his attire perfect, from his snowy white cravat to his shining dance pumps. His face, though unreadable, was very handsome, almost artistic in its classic and noble lines. It was, at times, quite astonishing to imagine that he would be her husband, this wealthy, powerful-looking man approaching her.

And then he broke into a smile on seeing her, becoming even more handsome. She felt a strange surge of…something. She knew not what it was, but it made her blush.

"Already blushing?" he asked her as he drew near. "I have not yet even told you how exceedingly beautiful you look tonight."

"It might be best if you do not," she teased, trying to gain her equanimity. "I would not like to enter the ball with my face afire."

"I cannot help myself," he murmured as he drew her hand to his mouth and kissed it lightly. "You are too lovely, and I am reminded of what a very fortunate man I am."

This seemed to be playing it rather bold—had he forgotten that this was good fortune for neither of them? Or was it? She hardly knew anymore. She wanted to change the subject and found herself stammering as she said, "I wanted to say first that I…I regret our argument the other day…on the way to Oakham Mount. I admit, I was upset and should not have—"

"I regret it too," he said quickly. "I hope you will forgive me. Come, let us greet your friends."

Elizabeth paused, not liking to brush it aside so easily. Was she to ignore being left on a path with scarcely a word? And what was the nature of his disagreement with Mr Wickham? It seemed more than what she had been told, but it did not appear Darcy wished to discuss it.

"It seems you and he have had some falling-out?"

"Let us not sour the evening with a discussion of Mr Wickham," Darcy replied disinterestedly, his gaze roaming the room. "Just know that he is not an honourable man."

Darcy was amiable enough as he escorted her about before the start of the dancing, chatting to the rest of Bingley's guests. Elizabeth felt her worries and fears beginning to ease as he walked with her. She was pleased by his agreeability to all who he met. He even complimented Mrs Bennet on her gown, which caused Mrs Bennet to blush and Elizabeth to smile at her mother's pleasure.

HAVING DECIDED to forget his many cares for a night—Georgiana, his family, George Wickham—Darcy found himself in high spirits as he walked about with Elizabeth on his arm. He hoped they could put aside any mention of the likes of George Wickham for the rest of the evening, if not permanently. He had done what he could to get rid of him in an

"Oh? And what might that be?"

The pattern of the dance required them to clasp hands and move together, and he used the opportunity to pull her towards him, the slightest bit closer than was strictly proper.

"Your heart," he whispered, and she was permitted only time sufficient for an uncertain glance into his eyes, before the pattern removed her.

The dance was over disappointingly quickly, and he was forced to relinquish her to Bingley while he partnered with Miss Jane Bennet. Before Elizabeth went to Bingley, he bowed over her gloved hand, kissing it lightly, and then asked, "Will you do me the honour of dancing the supper dance with me?"

She nodded. "I shall, sir, I thank you," and then Bingley hied her off.

ELIZABETH WAS grateful for Mr Bingley's ability to maintain inconsequential chatter throughout their dance for she found herself discomposed by Darcy's flirtation. *Teasing, teasing man! What can he mean by saying such things?* She felt still the heat of the blush he had provoked in her, and still more, the fluttering feeling in her stomach, an oddly pleasant sense of combined excitement and anxiety. The most surprising thing was, of course, how exceedingly disinclined she was to dance with anyone else this evening.

And how easy it was to forgive his less charming behaviour! She frowned, thinking of it, unsure whether it was good or bad for a wife to forgive so readily.

She glanced over to where Darcy danced with Jane. He was looking in the direction opposite her, and so she allowed herself the indulgence of clandestinely admiring his form. At once she heard in her mind his voice saying, back in the garden at Netherfield, that she would be the envy of nearly every woman in England for having accepted his suit. *I daresay that indeed I might well be, to have such a husband.*

Elizabeth found herself extraordinarily sought after as a dance partner the entire evening. After Mr Bingley, she danced with Charlotte's brother John, then Lieutenant Chamberlayne, Captain Carter, and Mr Hurst. She was shocked to learn that the portly Mr Hurst was an able and light dancer, almost expert in his rendering of the figures.

Oddly, Mr Collins had asked her to open the ball with him and seemed offended that she had, as would be expected, arranged to dance the first with her betrothed. Then, rather than ask for another set, he simply abandoned the quest, moving on to ask Mary to dance the first with him, followed by Kitty, Jane, and Lydia. He did not ask Elizabeth to dance at all. She counted herself fortunate, particularly after watching Jane suffer through her time with him.

The most surprising part of the night was when she danced with Lieutenant Denny, who made a special effort to apprise her of Mr Wickham's absence from the ball. "My friend Wickham has asked me to bid you farewell on his behalf. He is presently preparing for departure from Meryton and will not attend tonight."

"I am surprised he should remember me in such a way. Mr Wickham and I were scarcely acquainted."

"Perhaps the connexion had more meaning to him than it did to you?"

This made her frown briefly before asking, "Has Mr Wickham received a transfer to another regiment?"

Mr Denny shook his head. "I beg your pardon, Miss Elizabeth, but to tell you more would be a disrespect to Mr Darcy."

"Mr Darcy? How so?"

Mr Denny would only shake his head, remarking vaguely, "The rich can afford to arrange things to their liking, though what harm it does Mr Darcy to have Wickham in the militia, I shall never comprehend."

Elizabeth looked over where Darcy stood in conversation with Mr Goulding and his son. Could Mr Darcy have had Mr Wickham removed from his position? Because the man had *spoken* to her? She remembered his rage from the day at Oakham Mount, rage she had been determined to forget.

Mr Wickham is no one to you Lizzy, and Mr Darcy will be your husband. She cast another glance towards him and this time he saw her, flashing her a quick smile. She returned it, and almost immediately, he excused himself and began to move towards her, weaving through the crowd purposefully.

Arriving beside her, he murmured, "Oh no, it seems I have shown my hand."

He offered his arm and she slid her hand into it obligingly. "How so?"

He bent his head towards her, his breath warm against the skin of her cheek. "One smile and you command me."

It was an undeniable thrill, though she laughed lightly to cover her consternation as they moved towards the dancers. She glanced up at him, seeing the faint smile he wore and feeling the same on her own countenance. She imagined they must look quite the picture of romance.

He must have had good reason for his interference, she thought. *I must accustom myself to a man who has the power to do as he likes.*

DARCY DERIVED no inconsiderable amount of pleasure from his second dance with Elizabeth. She was somewhat subdued for the first part of it and asked him some odd questions—enquiring whether he thought the militia was a good occupation for a man, and might it not strengthen a wayward character and set it to rights—but was mostly rather quiet. It allowed him to truly study her, to imagine her as she would soon be—his wife, his partner, always by his side. This satisfaction was followed by the further joy of entering the supper room with her on his arm.

It was thence that pleasure was ended. Mr Collins was intent on becoming his most intimate acquaintance, flattering him unendingly on the de Bourgh branch of the family. The man smelt dreadful, was excessively loquacious on disinteresting subjects, and presumed far too much upon his position.

"—and I have often said that dear Miss de Bourgh, with her delicate constitution, would surely bring honour and beauty to even the highest—"

"Sir, your compliments to my family are not unheeded," Darcy replied impatiently. The last thing he wished to hear about was his Rosings relations. "Your father is recently departed, I understand?"

"My dear and wonderful father, himself a parson, left this earth but a year ago, but truly a finer man..."

Mr Collins went on for some time, and Darcy divided his efforts between avoiding his fetid breath—not an easy task, as Mr Collins continued to lean in closely, evidently suspecting Darcy was hard of hearing—and attempting to ignore the exhibition of poor comportment being made by

Elizabeth's family. Miss Catherine and Miss Lydia were behaving like tavern wenches, flirting determinedly and shamelessly with the red coats. Mrs Bennet seemed drunk and was speaking loudly about things she ought not—mostly his and Bingley's fortunes. Miss Bennet was unaffected as always, but her usual smile looked as if it had been painted on.

The scene was noticed by Mr Collins as well. "I have always thought that if I had had any sisters, I should have superintended the development of their characters most strenuously, for a lady's reputation is brittle and—"

"So you do not, then, have any sisters?" *Those who have never had the care of a young lady always tend to presume to imagine it so easy to protect them.*

"I was not so blessed, unfortunately; no sisters, nor any brothers, but if I had..." He continued rattling away while Darcy's attention moved to another Bennet spectacle.

Miss Mary Bennet had risen to play and sing for the gathering. Her performance was overwrought and affected, though her fingering was good. The sorrowful song she played, so ill-chosen for a festive evening, seemed never-ending. At last it was done, but unfortunately, she was too gratified by the smattering of polite applause she received and prepared to begin another. This roused Mr Bennet from his previous indifference. He rose and chastised her publicly, humiliating her and the family in the process.

An appalled silence settled briefly over the room as the guests absorbed the spectacle playing out before them. Darcy glanced over at Elizabeth, who sat with her scarlet face in careful contemplation of her lap.

Rage grew within him on her behalf. How on earth she had managed to come through a childhood with these people and develop such a fine character was beyond him. It was as though she had decided to be the precise opposite, becoming a well-mannered person despite such examples. His admiration for her grew as he considered it; she, who had been given few advantages and had so many impediments to overcome, had succeeded in becoming a lady of true worth.

He had pondered it too long. She glanced up at him and, seeing his stare, abruptly rose, and with quick paces exited the room.

ELIZABETH WALKED OUTSIDE onto the terrace, heedless of the chill of the November air or the gusts of wind that stung her cheeks and arms. She would not cry. She simply refused to cry.

Why, oh why, did her family behave in such a way? It was so humiliating. How could her father just sit there, chatting away to Mr Goulding as if he had not a care in the world? How outlandishly would her mother and sisters need to act before he could bestir himself to intervene?

Of course, she recalled, he did intervene with poor Mary, poor pedantic and arrogant Mary, who had quite lost herself in her brief bit of enjoyment of the ball. What Mr Bennet had done with Mary could only amplify the mortification of the family. He would have done much better to subdue Lydia and Kitty or persuade Mrs Bennet to lower her voice as she boasted of Mr Darcy's income.

Looking back into the room from which she had come, she noticed Mr Darcy had entered, giving the appearance of looking for someone. *No, no,* she told him silently. *Leave me be, I cannot face your satirical eye just now.*

Almost as if he had heard her, he disappeared, and she breathed a sigh of relief. She would not have expected him to follow her into the cold in any case. Likely he just wished to be certain she was not off making a spectacle of herself somewhere as well, in keeping with the rest of the Bennet family.

Heaving a great sigh, she walked farther along the rail, that she might be completely hidden from view of the room. She stood overlooking the parterre, wishing she might somehow relieve herself of the heavy cloak of humiliation which her family never ceased to place upon her shoulders. Jane managed to smile through it, but Elizabeth always found herself burning with frustration and helplessness over it all.

She was so sure of her solitude she nearly shrieked when she felt the warmth of a thick, luxurious coat settle over her. She whirled about, looking up into Darcy's countenance. From the look on Darcy's face, it was impossible to determine what he might be thinking, finding her outside in the frigid November air. He said only, "It is very cold out here, Elizabeth, I would not wish you to become ill."

He held out his handkerchief, and surprised, she realised her cheeks were damp with tears, despite her determination not to cry. She took the handkerchief gratefully.

"I did not know where your pelisse was, else I would have brought it. I hope my coat will suffice."

Looking down at the ground below, she admitted, "My pelisse is of little use but to ornament my gown. Your coat is very warm."

He reached out, adjusting the coat to sit more securely on her shoulders. "I must confess, I find the pelisse a somewhat baffling object. Ladies are much more likely to take a chill, yet men's coats are always much thicker and more serviceable. Should it not be the other way around?"

"I believe it must be reflective of the fact that ladies are not meant to be out of doors." Elizabeth smiled ruefully, giving him a brief glance. She had to admit, it felt quite nice to have his coat upon her arms. It was heavy and quite warm, and smelled of bergamot and spice, among other things. *His scent. This is how he smells. It is pleasant.*

He looked out at the scene she had been shedding tears over, seeing the lawn which rolled away from the house into the wood. The trees looked bare and forlorn from the terrace, the scant moonlight making them appear nearly menacing. Despite the warmth of his coat, she shivered, covering her sudden unease with a quick smile at him. "We should go inside. I would not have you ill either."

"You need not worry for me."

"Is that not the job of wives?" Elizabeth asked, forcing herself to be arch and teasing. "You must allow me to practise my wifely skills."

Her effort earned her a chuckle. "I believe I must then practise the art of permitting someone to care for me. It is not something I am accustomed to, but I do believe I might enjoy it." He took one finger then and traced it down her cheek.

She felt a blush in the wake of his fingertips, even as the air between them seemed to become charged with tension. Before she knew what he, or she, was about, Mr Darcy had taken her chin in his hand, tilted her face towards his own, and gently laid his lips against hers in a soft kiss.

She did not pull away, allowing him to kiss her a second time and then a third. By the fourth time, she stepped closer to him, and he slid his arms beneath the coat, wrapping them around her and pressing her against him. He began tracing his kisses down her neck, and she grew flustered, wondering whether anyone was watching them, or if they were, whether she should care.

She made some awkward little sound, and he understood her immediately, removing his lips from her skin but keeping her in his embrace. She could hear and feel his heart pounding, amazed by how comforting the sound was.

How long they stood thus, she knew not, but at length he murmured, "Shall we go in?" and she agreed with a surprising reluctance.

CAROLINE BINGLEY WAS DISGUSTED by the manner in which the Bennet family comported themselves during supper. When she saw Eliza Bennet run out of the room, barely able to repress the tears in her eyes, she felt strangely satisfied; when Mr Darcy followed her, she nearly crowed her victory. Surely now he would see he simply could not marry into this family! *Whatever scandal might result, what difficulties might arise, he must needs extricate himself from the Bennet family.*

She had gone after them, discreetly lingering in the shadows, hoping to hear the sounds of a quarrel. She did hear Eliza weep—that was most promising—but then, horror of horrors, she saw Darcy go out on the terrace, and before long, he kissed her! She stood, as appalled as she was intrigued, watching Darcy pull Elizabeth into his chest and kiss her with obvious passion.

The worst of it all was that she knew her brother could not long be behind his friend. Charles, seeing Darcy married to one Bennet sister, would quickly settle matters with Jane

Bennet and then she would be connected to these people and this dreadful place. How on earth would she make a splendid marriage with relations such as these? She could not save Darcy, but she knew she needed to somehow turn Charles away from Miss Bennet.

It was then that Mr Collins entered her line of sight, seemingly by Providence. The idea came to her as if by magic, and in a moment she knew just what to do. Affixing a kind and welcoming smile on her face, she approached him. "Mr Collins, I do hope you are enjoying the evening."

Mr Collins startled. "Indeed, I have not had such a happily diverting evening in a very long time. Such elegance, such beauty before me, and the kindness and hospitality of Mr Bingley and yourself. I daresay it is quite a privilege to count you among my acquaintance."

"It is clear you are accustomed to superior society, sir."

"I flatter myself that I am as easy in high society as in low. Why I consider it to my great advantage, as a clergyman, to—"

Caroline interrupted, not wishing to spend the rest of the night accomplishing the small task she had before her. "Yet how very well it will suit you when you take your place at Longbourn. I do believe I understand you to be Mr Bennet's heir?"

"A great honour indeed, as well as my birthright, that I should find myself, once a humble—"

Caroline interjected smoothly, "You will do the neighbourhood great credit, I am sure. Might I imagine that you will choose as your bride one of the Bennet girls? They are lovely ladies, first to last. Any one of them would be a superb helpmeet to you, though I have always felt the eldest should marry first. It is how it was in my family—I could not think of being out until Louisa was settled with Mr Hurst."

Mr Collins looked discomfited. "The matter of a wife remains uncertain. I had felt it my duty—one I felt more than pleased to fulfil—to select my bride from the ladies who would be displaced on my inheritance. I thought it a surety that I would find acceptance of my suit with much to recommend me, beginning with the beneficence of Lady Catherine de Bourgh herself—"

Caroline cleared her throat delicately. "So have you selected a wife?"

It did serve to redirect his verbose speech, and he answered, "I had offered for Miss Elizabeth you see, not realising she had an understanding with Mr Darcy."

"Ah! Now that you have come to know her better you must surely know that was for the best!"

This silenced him for a blessed, albeit far-too-short moment. He had been prepared to relate to her his indignation in full, but her words made him stop, mouth agape, while he considered them.

Caroline continued, speaking assuredly and eagerly. "Miss Eliza, with her tendency towards the impertinent, could not serve your parishioners well. Nor would Lady Catherine suffer her gladly, of that I am sure!"

"You think not?"

"Oh no, sir, I know not. Lady Catherine is no stranger to me"—*although I am a stranger to her!*—"and she would not tolerate such blatant disregard of rank! No, a demure, gentle girl would be much more to her liking."

Mr Collins appeared thoughtful. "I had supposed Miss Elizabeth's vivacity and wit would be tempered when in the presence of one so distinguished as Lady Catherine de Bourgh."

"Perhaps…but perhaps not. I think it not a chance you would wish to take." Caroline nodded sagely. "Of course, Miss Jane Bennet is the eldest sister in any case. She should marry first, or at least be engaged."

"Miss Bennet?" Mr Collins stared at her with an almost comical confused expression on his countenance. "I understood that Miss Bennet had an attachment already."

Caroline widened her eyes and looked as guileless as possible. "Really? I had not heard of any prior attachment, but then, being family yourself, you must know more than I. I hope you will not think me a dreadful gossip if I ask you to indulge my curiosity on the matter?"

Mr Collins looked towards the wall where Jane and Bingley stood in conversation. "I, uh…I had believed her to be on the verge of an agreement with…well, with Mr Bingley."

Caroline stared at him for a moment before chuckling. "You cannot mean my brother?"

Mr Collins nodded solemnly.

"Oh no!" Her feigned amusement turned to feigned concern. "Oh dear! Really? There are rumours spreading about Miss Bennet and my brother?"

Mr Collins lowered his voice, glancing around him. "It would not do for a man of my position to be heard spreading tittle-tattle in this manner. However, as I am not uninvolved in this case, I shall tell you. Mrs Bennet told me an offer is expected."

With a dramatic flourish, Caroline began to fan herself, nurturing a look of deep distress on her face. "You see, this is why… From the very start, I said we must not… Secret engagements are never… If only it could be known…"

"Secret engagement?"

"Ah! You have guessed it. Well, now I must tell you what no one else knows." She paused and then lowered her voice to a mere murmur. "What no one else *can* know because it involves the reputation of another young lady—Lady Catherine's very own niece."

Mr Collins nodded his head and leant forward eagerly.

"There is an understanding of sorts, you see, concerning my brother and Mr Darcy's younger sister." *An understanding by* me. *In that I understand that Charles marrying Miss Darcy will elevate us all.* "Miss Darcy is not yet out, so it cannot be made formal as yet, but of course, you are aware of how things are done in noble families."

Mr Collins looked appropriately sombre to be party to such a confidence.

"So, you see, my brother can have no serious intentions towards Miss Bennet. Oh, my dear, I do so hope she has not harboured wishes and expectations towards him. She will be quite heartbroken."

Caroline abruptly placed her fingers over her lips, shook her head, and gave a little laugh. "Oh, Mr Collins, I beg your pardon. I should not presume to say what I just thought. It is indeed most impertinent of me. I would not dare repeat such an idea as has just occurred to me."

"I would appreciate your condescension in allowing me to learn of your opinion, Miss Bingley, for it has not escaped my notice that you are a refined and elegant lady whose air will always be—"

"If you insist, then I shall tell you what just entered into my mind—quite unbidden, I do assure you! I would not have the effrontery on such a short acquaintance to make any recommendation for a match for you, Mr Collins!"

Mr Collins nodded eagerly.

"Well, you do need a wife, and Miss Bennet is beautiful, yet so modest! Charitable too—I am sure I have not seen her equal. I cannot help but think she would be ideally suited to be the wife of a clergyman. How very well Lady Catherine would approve!"

Mr Collins seemed dumbstruck, visions of his benefactor's approbation dancing in his head.

"Of course, what a fine thing for Miss Bennet and her family to have the comfort of knowing she would one day succeed her dear mother as mistress of Longbourn. Who could be more deserving of such a thing than dear Jane! Surely nothing else could be so pleasing to them!"

Mr Collins remained pensive.

"Pray, forgive me. I have spoken too freely." She offered him a deep and respectful curtsey, then took her leave of him.

She chanced a look back as she came to the doorway of the room, pleased to see his glittering eyes fixed appraisingly on Miss Jane Bennet.

As the Bennets' carriage pulled away from Netherfield Park, Mr Collins permitted himself a satisfied smile. How neatly disaster had been averted! Cousin Eliza was entirely unsuitable, but Cousin Jane was perfect! Now that he knew the truth of her attachment to Mr Bingley, it was plain what he was meant to do.

Still, he would not wish to move in error again. He would

send an express to Lady Catherine, currently visiting at her brother's residence in London, first thing in the morning—not in an outright request for her presence here in Hertfordshire, but perhaps to drop a few hints that might persuade her ladyship to pay a visit? He could only wish for her to meet Miss Bennet and offer her opinions on his selection before anything was done irrevocably.

His gaze travelled about the carriage, landing on Cousin Eliza. A smile stole over his face as he wondered whether his benefactor had been apprised of her nephew's treachery as yet, and if not, what beneficence might await the man who informed her before it was too late.

CHAPTER NINE

THE DAY AFTER THE BALL WAS A DULL ONE FOR ELIZABETH. Most of the inhabitants of Meryton and its environs were sleeping off the effects of dancing the night away and overindulging in food and drink. Elizabeth sat in her mother's drawing room, a book which failed to draw her interest discarded beside her and too many thoughts plaguing her.

The memory of her family's behaviour pained her. Although Mr Darcy had said not so much as a single reproachful syllable to her, she had seen the expression in his eyes in the supper room as he looked upon his future relations. How painful it was that she could not defend them. To do so must defy all reason. They had behaved appallingly, first to last, save for Jane, and he had witnessed it in full, with the sour breath of Mr Collins washing over him to sear the memory into his mind.

How odd it was to love so deeply people who brought you such pain! To know how much good was in them and wonder that they seemed deliberate in their attempts to excite scorn. Were they unaware of the expressions of distaste on the faces of those around them? Or did they simply not care? Surely, they had to realise that no other family created such a scene. They had to know what it meant when people looked awkwardly in some other direction or gave pointed and poorly hidden glances to one another.

What good could it do to think on these things? She would marry soon and then—

A dreadful thought interrupted her musings. Would Darcy feel this way about her? Would he be ever mindful, awaiting the arrival of Mrs Bennet's shrieks from his wife's lips? Would he look for Mr Bennet's sarcasm or Lydia's unbridled animal spirits in *her*?

She imagined Darcy looking at her across the room in the same manner in which he had looked upon her parents and sisters in the supper room at the ball. Her heart began to pound, and her cheeks flushed with just the imagining of it. No. Surely he must understand enough of her character to know she would always behave well in company.

Yet there were things about her to embarrass him, things that were unalterable.

There would be some of his set who would never like her simply because she was the daughter of a gentleman of little importance, no fortune, and no connexions, and she could not change that. Some, like Miss Bingley, would sneer openly. Others might be more subtle but would nevertheless close their doors to her.

She was not what the wife of Mr Darcy was expected to be. Her birth, she could neither disguise nor alter. Her accomplishments were far too few, and her education…she winced thinking of it. She had tried, of course she had, but who could properly educate herself? Access to her father's library was the chief of it, despite the sporadic hiring of masters and the like. She had done all she could, propelled by an inherent desire to learn, but it could not be denied that it was insufficient.

With a shuddering sigh, she rebuked herself. "Well, Lizzy, this is a fine state you have yourself worried into. No one has said a thing to you, and you have already condemned yourself to scorn and universal rejection."

She forced a nervous laugh. She believed herself capable of meeting any situation with self-possession, although she had to admit, when she thought of it, this felt more intimidating than anything she had faced in her life thus far.

Abruptly, she rose from her chair. She needed a walk, a long walk, and she wanted to take it in solitude, Darcy's strictures be hanged.

Minutes later, she set off at a brisk pace, drawing the cold air deep into her lungs, swinging her arms and doing all she could to cleanse herself of the disquieting notions in her head. It worked a little, but she found herself going faster and faster until eventually her walk became a run. It was glorious.

The morning air burnt her lungs as she went faster and faster, her thoughts pounded from her mind by the sound of her boots on the ground. Her bonnet came loose and bounced on her back, followed by curls bouncing along with it, no doubt tangling, but who cared, really? She was one with nature, she was forcibly expelling her troubles in the manner of sweat and breath and—

"Elizabeth! Good lord, what is it? Are you hurt?"

She screamed as Darcy caught her, pulling her close and stopping her dead in her tracks. She could feel his heart pounding as much as her own did as he whirled her about in his arms. His hands, unmindful of propriety, were running over her, brushing her hair away from her face, as all the while he questioned her.

"What happened? Where is he?"

"Where is *who*?"

"Wickham! What did he do to you?"

"Wickham?" She struggled, pulling away from him. "What has he to do with it? I was just running."

He stood staring at her for a moment before asking, "Running from what?"

"From nothing," she replied tartly. Turning on her heel, she began to walk. "Do you not find a good run to be exhilarating at times?"

She heard him begin to walk behind her. He did not reply to her question.

"Because I do. I like to run. Nothing was chasing me, no one had hurt me—I simply wished to run."

He drew abreast of her, matching her stride, still saying nothing. She looked up at him, and he offered a brief, distracted smile and said, "Two months seems a very long time right now."

"Two months until…oh, yes, our wedding. Well, a little more than two months, in truth."

"And then I shall not need to fear your safety so much."

"Mr Darcy, I have walked these paths my entire life. Walked them and run them. I am as safe here as I am in my mother's drawing room."

"If that is true, then I fear for your mother's drawing room."

It was an attempt at a jest—or so she thought—but in her present mood it could elicit nothing but a frown. He tried again.

"If nothing else, I can assure you that scampering pell-mell about London will soon have everyone thinking you very peculiar." In a more serious tone, he added, "But surely this is a habit you reserve for the countryside?"

"You cannot think me so foolish as to imagine I would run around London? Yes, I am aware of the behaviour of a lady. In any case, it is no habit, I merely felt the urge this morning. Forgive me."

They walked, Elizabeth's pleasure in her exertion gone, leaving vexation and embarrassment in its wake. Trying to change the subject, she asked, "When do you go to town?"

"Tomorrow," he said. "Bingley will go with me, but he was not feeling up to the task today."

At this, Elizabeth winced. Mrs Bennet had contrived to be the last to leave the ball, and so thorough were her efforts that the sun was rising and both Mr and Miss Bingley were sagging in chairs when at last the Bennets' carriage arrived.

"I hope to speak to my family and sister and tell them our good news," he said. "I shall likely return in a day or so."

She had wondered often how long he intended to be in the county. They had never spoken of it, and she had no notion what the original plans were or how their engagement had altered those plans. Mrs Bennet was eager to take her and Jane to London, sure she would soon be selecting wedding clothes for them both. To this end, Elizabeth mentioned, "My aunt and uncle Gardiner will visit Longbourn for Christmas, and my mother has hinted that we might return to London with them and—"

"These are your relations in Cheapside?"

His tone was careful, but Elizabeth heard the meaning in it nevertheless. "*Near* Cheapside," she said. "Gracechurch Street. They are very dear to me."

"I am sure they are delightful people." He paused, his

expression pensive as he stared at the denuded trees around them. She too paused her steps and turned towards him, seeing the careful set of his countenance. She had a sinking feeling within her, knowing what he was going to say but accursed if she would make it easy for him.

"Yes, they are wonderful. I can only hope you will like them as much as I do."

"Elizabeth." He stopped and sighed heavily. In measured tones, he began again. "A woman takes on her husband's status when she marries—"

"I know that."

"And for Mrs Darcy to visit some merchant in Cheapside—"

"Near Cheapside!"

He looked heavenward for a moment. "Near Cheapside. In any case, surely you must comprehend that you will not help your own cause if you are constantly reminding the *ton* of your low connexions?"

Tears stung her eyes. "You do not even know them, and for you to speak so—"

"I do not need to know them. They are beneath me and, once you marry me, beneath you too. They are beneath you now!"

"You cannot mean to tell me you wish me to forswear my own aunt and uncle?"

He threw his hands up in the air, and she believed she understood him perfectly. Yes, he would no doubt like it very well if any stain of Bennet or Gardiner could be removed from her.

"You may think," she began, "that with your ring on my finger, I shall be in every way a Darcy, that who I am—Bennet and Gardiner and everything you despise—should be wiped away. But it cannot be so. I shall still be Frances Bennet's daughter, and Lydia Bennet's sister, and Mrs Philips and Mrs Gardiner will still be my aunts. If being a Darcy requires me to behave like you, to scorn anyone who is not the grandson of an earl, then I do not think I shall ever be one, no matter what the vicar says!"

With that, she turned on her heel, saying over her shoulder, "Do not follow me. I have above two months before I am your prisoner, and I intend to enjoy it."

He called later that day but she would not see him. She sent word through Hill that she was indisposed but wished him a good journey back to London. He replied with a note telling her that he would call immediately on his return, and signed it 'FD' with a small heart shape drawn beside it. Somehow that tiny drawing caused a softening within her, and she knew not whether she was charmed by it or vexed.

THE NEXT DAY found Elizabeth alone at home, as her mother and sisters went to Meryton and her father had business out among the tenant farms. The sound of horses and a carriage from outside drew her to the window, wondering whether Darcy had not gone to London after all. *Perhaps he is stopping on his way.*

Her eyes widened seeing the fine equipage entering the drive led by four of the most beautiful horses she had ever seen. *Who might this be?* The only person she knew with the means for such a conveyance was Darcy, but it did not look like the one she knew.

Her confusion increased when Mr Collins alit. As far as she had known, Mr Collins had gone with her father, yet here he was, looking oddly triumphant as he stumbled and almost fell in the drive. Elizabeth shook her head, murmuring, "Mind there, Mr Collins. One must at times lower one's nose enough to see the ground."

At the very last moment—perhaps prompted by whoever was inside the carriage—Mr Collins appeared to recall that he ought to assist that person. He turned, reaching in his hand just as an older woman emerged, scowling fiercely. "Who on earth could that be?" Elizabeth wondered aloud.

The lady was elegantly attired, and the expense of her apparel was advertised in every possible way, from the gold-tipped, ornately carved walking stick to the baubles and bedizenments which liberally adorned her pelisse. Jewels and lace abounded; Mrs Bennet would be well pleased.

The older lady eschewed Mr Collins's arm and entered Longbourn while Elizabeth hastily straightened herself, wishing she had time to change into a nicer gown. The one she currently wore had seen better days but was comfortable, and in any case, she had anticipated a day spent alone, not a call from some noble stranger. She rose to her feet, smoothing her skirts as she heard Mr Collins enter, rattling away in what appeared to be an attempt to enumerate Longbourn's flaws.

"...of course, I shall want to make a number of improvements to the outer yard. I do not think I needlessly vaunt my skills in the area of creating a garden worthy of a gentleman of such station as will be..."

Hill entered the sitting room hurriedly, announcing to Elizabeth, "Lady Catherine de Bourgh, ma'am."

Elizabeth felt a jolt. Mr Darcy's aunt! She curtseyed, and said, "Thank you, Hill. Would you bring us some—"

"That is not necessary." The lady spoke fiercely as if she

expected an insult might have accompanied Elizabeth's request for tea. Not waiting to be invited, she selected a seat nearby. Mr Collins stood behind her chair, smug and oddly triumphant.

I daresay she has not called to welcome me to the family. Elizabeth smiled and sat in a chair close to her. As soon as she did, Lady Catherine looked at Mr Collins and said, "This person, I suppose, is Miss Elizabeth Bennet?"

Mr Collins launched into an introduction. "Your ladyship, allow me the pleasure of presenting—"

"No, no," she chastised him. "This is not a connexion I would wish to either form or maintain. I will have my say and be done with this house with no more thought on the matter." She turned angry eyes on Elizabeth. "You can be at no loss, Miss Bennet, to understand the reason of my journey hither."

"It is an honour to have you call, ma'am," was Elizabeth's careful reply.

"I have no intention of paying you any honour, I assure you," the lady retorted angrily. "A report of a most alarming nature reached me two days ago. I was told that you, Miss Elizabeth Bennet, would be soon united in marriage to my nephew Mr Darcy. Although I know it must be a scandalous falsehood, and I would not injure him so much as to suppose the truth of it possible, I instantly resolved on setting off for this place, that I might have this report contradicted."

"In fact," Elizabeth said calmly and evenly, "it is true. Your nephew has made me an offer of marriage, and I have accepted him."

Lady Catherine, large and fearsome, leant forward. "Hear me now, for I shall not repeat myself, nor shall I be gainsaid. You will not marry my nephew. Ridiculous presumption! A person such as yourself, from such a place as this! It is in every way impossible."

"Yet, so it is. Mr Darcy has made me an offer of marriage, and I have accepted him. We plan to marry in February." Elizabeth kept a smile of determined pleasantness on her face, refusing to allow her ire, or her anxiety, to be seen.

Lady Catherine was glaring so fiercely her eyes were almost closed. At once she surprised Elizabeth by relaxing, sitting back in the chair with a chuckle. "Foolish, foolish girl. My nephew is already engaged to my daughter. Mr Collins has heard me say so many times over."

Elizabeth felt her eyes fly wide at this assertion. Engaged to his cousin? She had never heard mention of Miss de Bourgh nor had she any notion of whether the lady had any claim to him. Mr Collins, naturally, bobbed his head in enthusiastic support of whatever his patroness said—no doubt if she told him she hung the moon, he would agree with equal fervour.

"I have heard nothing of that matter, but Mr Darcy is a man of honour. He would not have made me any offer of marriage were he bound to another, so I must conclude that he is not, therefore, bound by either honour or inclination."

The last was said to satisfy herself and caused another scowl to emerge on the lady's face. "You are determined to have him, I see. Do not expect such a union to be noticed by his family or friends if you wilfully act against our inclinations. You will be censured, slighted, and despised by everyone connected with him. Your alliance will be a disgrace; your name will never even be mentioned by any of us."

Lady Catherine could not know how such words affected her, but Elizabeth was determined to maintain the appearance of sedate confidence even as her cheeks began to burn. "If that is nothing to Mr Darcy, then it can be nothing to me."

"So you refuse to act according to good sense. He will be the laughingstock of London."

Elizabeth pressed her lips together a moment before saying, "I refuse to act on any consideration but that of my own heart and Mr Darcy's."

Lady Catherine shook her head angrily and stared at Elizabeth for several long moments. Finally, she gave a little nod. "Very well, then. I now know how to act. Five thousand."

Confusion silenced Elizabeth for a moment before she said, "What?"

"I know what you want, Miss Bennet, and I shall give it to you for the sake of my family dignity. Five thousand pounds."

"You are offering me money for…for what, exactly?"

"To act as you should, scheming girl. Ten thousand and you never intrude upon his notice again."

"You wish to pay me to jilt your nephew?"

"Ten thousand pounds. Have the articles been signed? I had hoped to find your father about."

"I have made Mr Darcy a promise, and there is no money you will offer me sufficient to break my promise and ruin my reputation."

Lady Catherine rolled her eyes. "Your reputation was in question the moment you declined the offer of your cousin, thus rejecting the chance to make a suitable match and save your family from ruination on your father's death."

"Excuse me." Jane stood in the doorway of the sitting room, a hand-wringing Hill at her side. Jane looked at Lady Catherine. "Madam, I beg your pardon. I am Miss Bennet. I know my mother will be greatly grieved to have missed your call, but may I offer you some refreshment in her stead?"

Lady Catherine looked utterly confounded by Jane's interruption. She was further confused when Mr Collins leant into her and began to whisper, loudly and moistly, into her ear. "Miss Bennet is the loveliest of all of the Bennet girls, and should her arrangement—"

"Obstinate, headstrong girl." Lady Catherine spoke contemptuously and pityingly, turning her attention back to Elizabeth. "You cannot know what your life will be, and what a wretch you will become. You will not be noticed nor acknowledged, and he will soon come to despise you for mortifying his consequence. I appeal to your reason. My final offer is fifteen thousand pounds."

"What makes you think—" Elizabeth began, but she was quickly interrupted.

"It is sense, Miss Elizabeth, sense borne out of a long time on this earth in which I have come to understand the ways of men and the world in which we live. My nephew may have forgotten what is expected of him due to some spell of lust with which you have drawn him in, but it will not last. I should not be surprised that a few days in London completely sets him to rights. He will return, ashamed of his weakness, and end his engagement with you, and then you will be left with nothing. You can anticipate this inevitability now and gain fifteen thousand pounds, or you can wait and have nothing. Surely you must see what is best?"

"I do not wish for your money," Elizabeth said firmly. "And your nephew is not so capricious as you think."

Lady Catherine shook her head, glaring spitefully at Elizabeth as she rose. "I send no compliments to your mother. She has raised an impertinent and wilful girl, who is determined to bring ruin upon herself. Do not think that I shall not carry my point. My daughter's happiness is at stake here, and my wishes will be gratified."

Turning, she swept from the room, Mr Collins scurrying madly in her wake.

Jane was quick to go to her and tried to pull Elizabeth into her embrace, but Elizabeth could not permit it. "Forgive me, Jane; I…I need some air." So saying, she fled the house.

WHERE SHE WENT, she knew not. Rage, dismay, and sorrow jumbled about in her mind, disordering her thoughts, and her feet behaved accordingly, taking her here and there, aimless and purposeless.

'You will be censured, slighted, and despised...'

Such sentiments were too close to her own thoughts to be discounted. How she longed to say Lady Catherine was mad or officious or ridiculous, but she could not. Many of Darcy's circle *would* despise and ignore her; many *would* refuse to receive her. Darcy himself might grow to regret his choice—was it lust? Would she someday be like her mother, her husband's ardour cooled into disdain?

Her fury could only be heightened by remembering the sight of Mr Collins gloating behind her ladyship. She wished she had pointed at him and told Lady Catherine 'You see your little toady behind you? This is his doing. Had he not offered for me…'

Yet, it was not wholly him. Mr Collins's proposal she might have withstood had her father not shown his ill-timed iron will. It was Mr Bennet who held true culpability in the matter.

The rain had begun to fall without her feeling it, but when it soaked through her coat she realised she ought to go home. It was in some ways relieving; the burn of her humiliated fury was diminished into cool despair. What could be done now? She had, as she told his aunt, given her word to him.

The intensity of the rain waxed and waned as she walked, the mud of the roads becoming increasingly difficult to navigate, particularly as she had neglected to change her shoes before she left. Briefly, she considered going to her aunt's house, but a quick survey of her person persuaded her that such a plan might not be sensible. She was muddy and wet, and her hair, having begun to fall from its pins during her run, was in utter disarray. Her mother and her aunt would both be scandalised and horrified to imagine her in town in such a way, never minding the forces of nature which had caused it.

In truth, she did not herself wish to be seen. She had begun to feel the folly in her actions and hoped to return home unseen by anyone.

She had come upon the river that bordered the town, one which also touched the eastern boundary of Longbourn. She had crossed over it using the ancient bridge but did not wish to return that way, as that would put her in good view of anyone passing by on the road. From childhood she had known of a series of rocks spanning the river and had skipped over them numerous times to reach the other side, and it was this route she opted to use now.

She was nearly half of the way across when she realised that she had significantly underestimated how swollen the river was, with several of the rocks already obscured by rapidly moving waters. She paused, feeling all the danger of her situation and uncertain how best to proceed. Deciding to turn back, she slipped and nearly fell into the river. She was forced to reach down to touch the rock beneath her to steady herself, a move that resulted in dipping nearly half of her skirt into the river and soaking it. She looked down in dismay, as the cold, wet fabric clung to her legs.

"Miss Bennet! Do not move, I am coming to assist you!" She looked up in surprise and horror to see Mr Wickham on horseback, preparing to enter the river.

"Sir, no! I…do not…I can manage, I assure you."

Mr Wickham was busily searching his saddlebags, finally finding a rope that he evidently intended to use to secure himself. "You are in danger of falling into the river!"

"I know! Do not concern yourself for me. I intended to cross this way, but now I see that I cannot."

"You must permit me to assist you!"

"It is not necessary!" Seeing that he was undeterred, she realised she would be required to return to the shore. To that end, she hesitantly began to pick her way back in the way from which she had come. She tried to smile at him, to show him that she could manage, even as she made her way right up to the next to last rock. Despite her protestations, he nevertheless had begun to wade in, intent on coming to her aid.

"Really, I am—" She cried out as her foot slipped and twisted painfully on the wet surface of the last rock, and she began again to fall, feeling the water already swirling and pulling at her.

Mr Wickham was quick to lunge forward and grab her, preventing her from toppling into the river. With one forceful tug, he had pulled her across the last rock; Elizabeth tried to leap to the safety of the shore and stumbled awkwardly on her injured ankle.

Her heart pounded from the averted danger, but she was not insensible to the impropriety of the situation. She glanced around nervously, relieved that the rain had kept the town's inhabitants off the streets where they might have seen her with Mr Wickham, soaking wet, muddy, and bedraggled. She quickly stepped back, preparing to run across the bridge, ignoring the pain in her ankle.

"Thank you, sir, but please excuse me. I must be off." She offered him an absurd hint of a curtsey and moved to go, but her ankle had other ideas, and she again stumbled and almost fell. Mr Wickham caught her once more.

"Allow me to escort you home on my horse." Mr Wickham moved to help her onto the animal.

"No, I truly could not."

"I understand your discomfort, but modesty aside, I only want to help you."

"I am very embarrassed," she admitted with a chagrined smile that turned into a grimace of pain as she tried to put her weight on her ankle.

"With your ankle hurt as it is, you will not be able to walk quickly at all. You will likely have caught your death by the time you are able to hobble back to Longbourn."

Elizabeth considered it. Based on the pressure in her boot, it would seem her ankle was swelling even as she stood there, and she was getting colder and wetter by the moment. She would be fortunate at this rate if she did not take ill. If Mr Wickham could just deposit her on the border of Longbourn's property, she still might be able to evade notice.

"May I count on your discretion?"

"Of course. Upon my honour," Mr Wickham assured her.

With another quick glance about her, Elizabeth moved towards his horse, struggling to get herself into position as best as she could with her now throbbing ankle. Mr Wickham placed his hand on her only briefly to help her up, and they were moving towards Longbourn within minutes, Elizabeth sighing in relief. A carriage rolled by at one point, and she closed her eyes, praying it was not Lady Catherine to witness her in such a state.

As the Hursts' carriage rolled through town, Caroline Bingley sat back, hiding a gleeful snicker behind her hand.

Eliza Bennet was being fondled by George Wickham right in the middle of the town, as muddy and unkempt as she could ever be! For a brief moment, Caroline tried to recall what it was precisely that Mr Darcy had against Mr Wickham. An unpaid debt? Some boyhood indiscretions? She hardly knew, and it did not matter. Darcy hated Wickham, and would likely be enraged at the thought of the man having had his hands all over his betrothed as her sodden gown clung to her every curve.

Perhaps Darcy was not out of her reach after all.

CHAPTER TEN

ELIZABETH WAS EXTREMELY THANKFUL, ON RETURNING FROM her walk, to be able to slip up to her bedchamber unseen. The family had returned, and she could hear them talking in the sitting room.

Entering her bedchamber, she caught sight of her reflection in the mirror and groaned. Her face was blotchy and flushed, her wet gown was nearly transparent—in the few areas not covered by mud—and her hair was almost completely loosed from its pins. Rachel, the young upstairs maid who sometimes dressed the younger Bennet ladies, gasped as she entered. "Oh, Miss Elizabeth, what happened?"

Elizabeth smiled at her ruefully. "This rainstorm is what happened. I chose the wrong time to take my walk, that is all, but Mama will not be pleased with me, so I hope you can have me cleaned up quickly. Pray, do not mention it to her."

Rachel had already begun to select clothing, "Of course, miss. Will you want a bath then?"

Elizabeth shook her head. "Mama surely would wonder what I was up to if she heard I was ordering a bath in the middle of the day. I wish I could, as I am quite chilled, but I shall just sit by the fire to warm myself. I need to dry my hair in any case."

As Rachel prepared her things, Elizabeth brushed her hair by the fire and thought over the ride home.

Mr Wickham had comported himself as every bit the gentleman, avoiding all contact with her person other than that which was necessary to assist her onto his horse. He had then escorted her quickly back to Longbourn using a shortcut through the wood that, while it required them to go over the town bridge, minimised the risk of being seen to the greatest extent possible.

They had spoken little; the rain made it easy for them to be silent. Mr Wickham had evidently been to the barracks for whatever personal effects remained and was off to parts unknown; it was plainly not a subject he wished to explain to her, so she asked nothing more of it. When they arrived at Longbourn, he assisted her down and then departed immediately, bidding her farewell with an appropriate bow.

She shook her head, unable to understand what Mr Wickham had ever done to earn Darcy's ire. He had every appearance of goodness, and it made no sense, but so it was. She dreaded Darcy's reaction on telling him of the day's escapade and Wickham's involvement, recalling how he had behaved when Wickham had merely spoken to her.

Unless, perhaps, she did not tell him?

Darcy had been vehement that she should avoid Mr Wickham at any cost, but she had tried, had she not? She had refused Mr Wickham's help even while amidst the peril of the river. Indeed, Darcy ought to be *thanking* Mr Wickham, for Elizabeth might have drowned without him.

In any case, was it not Darcy's own fault that Wickham was out riding at that moment? Had Mr Wickham still had his position, he would have been doing whatever soldiers did during the day instead of leaving his post.

DARCY'S first order of business in town was to inform his family of his betrothal. Being that those in Hertfordshire knew, he thought it best he do so as quickly as he could, and thus the morning after his arrival in town, betook himself to Matlock House.

He wished to see Georgiana but deferred that until after meeting with his uncle. He could not imagine what might be Georgiana's response to the fact that he was engaged. Of course, it was likely she would not even agree to see him.

Lord Matlock was in his study, standing by the window and looking out on the streets below. As soon as Darcy entered, he turned. "Darcy, wonderful to see you. How was Hertfordshire?"

"Hertfordshire was…surprising." Darcy sat down in a chair by the fire and poured himself some coffee. "I am engaged to marry."

Lord Matlock took a seat, looking concerned. "Not to one of Mr Bingley's relations, surely?"

"No, my intended wife's name is Miss Elizabeth Bennet. Her father is a landowner in Hertfordshire near where we stayed."

"Miss Elizabeth Bennet," said Lord Matlock in contemplative tones. "Who does she know?"

"No one," said Darcy. "Or at least no one of importance."

Lord Matlock rubbed his hand across his face. "Nothing scandalous in it, is there?"

"Nothing more than Darcy went to Hertfordshire and lost his head for a penniless country lady."

"Penniless?"

"The Bennets are not in debt, not that I could see, but Bennet has not provided for his daughters. The estate is entailed on a cousin, so when he dies, he can only hope the charity of his heir will sustain them."

Lord Matlock pointed at Darcy. "The charity of his son-in-law is more like it."

Darcy grimaced. "Indeed."

Lord Matlock rose and walked to his fireplace, staring into it, and inhaling deeply. "What about Anne?"

"I have never given Anne cause to think she should have expectations of me," Darcy replied shortly. "And in any case, Anne has Rosings and has told me herself that she cannot think why she would ever want a husband to take it from her."

"It will cause talk," said Lord Matlock, turning to give Darcy a piercing stare.

To this, Darcy could only shrug.

"Well, then." Lord Matlock raised his cup. "To the future Mrs Darcy. May she be long-suffering and kind."

Darcy chuckled. "That she is."

"By the by." Lord Matlock set his drink down on the table. "You have come to me, but I am afraid I need a little something from you as well."

"Anything, of course."

"There has been some talk linking Richard with Lady Susanna, the daughter of Lord Orford."

"Oh no, really?" Darcy winced. Lady Susanna was a lovely young lady, but the sins of the father were many and ranged from abuse of his servants and his wife, to debt, and the alignment with many, many strange and radical political causes. The Matlocks wanted no such connexion as the Orfords, to be sure.

"I know he does not really like her, but his behaviour is such that his honour will be engaged before he knows what he is about. And do not think those people will hesitate to take advantage of matters if they can."

"I shall speak to him straightaway."

As the men sipped their drinks, Darcy sent a note to Georgiana, requesting a moment of her time on a matter of import. Georgiana refused to acknowledge it, so Darcy went and stood outside her door.

"Georgiana? I have news I wish to share with you."

Silence greeted him and he knocked gently. "May I enter?"

He stood, his ear pressed against the heavy oak door, straining to hear any sign of life within.

"You have long wished for a sister…have you not?" He paused and then added, "I am engaged to marry. A Miss Elizabeth Bennet."

After another few moments of silence, he added, "Shall I bring her to meet you? She is eager to know you."

At last he heard some response, given as quiet as a whisper. "No."

He knew better than to press her and instead asked, "Would you like to hear about her?"

But Georgiana had reached the end of her talking for the day. He tried several other questions and inducements, only to hear silence. With a heavy sigh, he said, "Good-bye, Sister, and accept my best wishes for your health."

DARCY WAS EATING breakfast the next morning when Fitzwilliam was announced looking uncharacteristically agitated and harassed. He thudded heavily into the nearest chair, waving off Darcy's footman and offers of coffee. "Darcy, bad news."

Darcy half rose from his chair. "Georgiana?"

"No, no, sit." Fitzwilliam raised his palm. "As you might have known, Lady Catherine is staying with my parents, and went on some undisclosed errand yesterday. She said little about it but that she had received an express Wednesday and had urgent matters out of town. Apparently she has been to Hertfordshire to see your Miss Bennet."

"What!" Darcy exclaimed. His blood ran cold as his mind began to race with the implications of such a thing. "Blast her! What did she do?"

Fitzwilliam was shaking his head, looking grim. "She has been in my father's study all morning, ranting and storming and insisting we act immediately to separate you from this impudent upstart and get you wed to Anne as soon as may be. Naturally, she had much to say of Miss Bennet, and none of it good."

Darcy's hands began to shake and he clenched them into fists to stop them. "How dare she! This is none of her business. How did she even know about it? I certainly have not yet informed her! Thankfully, I told your father of my betrothal yesterday, otherwise he would have been wholly thunderstruck."

"Forget my father's discomfort—what about your intended bride? A poor welcome to the family indeed!" Fitzwilliam shuddered. "Just be glad you had all decamped Bingley's place by then. For she went over there and—"

"Decamped? But Mrs Hurst and Miss Bingley remained, and Bingley had intended to return in a day or so."

"According to her, Netherfield Park was closed up. In any case, she is determined to see you, and I recommend you come to Matlock House—our servants have already been subjected to her rant." Fitzwilliam rose and gestured with his arm towards the door.

While they awaited Darcy's overcoat and hat, Fitzwilliam said, "The news of your betrothal was a surprise to me."

"Your father did not tell you then?"

"No, though he might have informed my mother. She did not seem so surprised when Lady Catherine began to rage."

"I had planned to tell you as soon as we met."

"I was not aware you were even considering offering for anyone."

The coat and hat arrived, and Darcy and Fitzwilliam exited into a biting wind. "It happened suddenly."

"That much is clear to me. Might I have the pleasure of knowing more of the matter? I hear she has no money and no claim to anyone of note…all your repressed lust finally drove you mad?"

Darcy winced; Fitzwilliam had hit uncomfortably close to the truth. "Not so bad as all that, but the tale does not show me in the best light. I am glad to tell you the truth of it —for a price."

"A price, is it?"

"You must stop flirting with Lady Susanna."

"Not you too! Father has set his back up for nothing!"

"Nothing can turn into something in the wink of an eye, we both know that. I can myself illustrate the point very neatly, in fact."

Darcy then proceeded to relate the circumstances that

had led to his engagement, holding none of it back. Fitzwilliam was satisfyingly enraged, aghast, and supportive in turns—but on one matter he could not be satisfied.

"You will be shackled to this woman for life! Surely any claim to Miss Bingley could have been resolved in a manner less irrevocable?"

"How?" Darcy asked impatiently. "It was I who did it—I lied, to be frank. To then come back and say, 'apologies, it was all false,' would not have done. You know I was not raised that way."

"But it was not your fault!"

"It *was* my fault that I said I had a prior understanding. I simply could not...to marry Miss Bingley—"

"You need say no more on that subject. I would have chewed off my own arm if I needed to rescue myself from a similar fate."

"You do not censure me for what I did?"

"Certainly not. But, Darcy, my father could surely help extricate you from this."

I do not wish for that. Darcy had known, of course, that Lord Matlock might have helped him. The night after the incident with Miss Bingley, when Elizabeth had said she would remain silent and not expose his lies, he had wondered what his lordship could do. And the thought that astonished him then, and even a little bit now, was how little he wanted to be freed. He wanted to marry Elizabeth.

He had been silent too many moments, and he saw from the corner of his eye that his silence had roused Fitzwilliam's interest. "What truly amazed me, above all," he said, "was that in all my persuading—I spoke of fortune, position, gowns, travel—nothing would do. She continued to refuse me with witticisms and teasing."

"And what proved to change her mind? Your handsome face?"

Darcy shot his cousin a look. "The idea of helping me. I am sure my misery was plain, and she wished to help me. In any case"—he took a deep breath—"my fate is not wholly bad. She will in time learn to be a suitable wife, and save for her unfortunate family—"

"*Her* unfortunate family?" Fitzwilliam asked, with a friendly scoff. "Let us not forget they have met Lady Catherine."

Darcy frowned. "Yes, well, Lady Catherine notwithstanding, our marriage is a significant elevation for her, and the prospects of her sisters—"

"Unless Georgiana gets worse," Fitzwilliam replied in a matter-of-fact tone. He gave his cousin a clap on the shoulder. "Lady Catherine, Georgiana...and let us hope Saye behaves, else this Miss Bennet might just run screaming."

"See here," Darcy began but stopped. They had arrived at the Matlocks' residence. The front door was flung wide and revealed Saye, his elder cousin, standing in his dressing gown. "Come men, no need to leave all the fun to me!"

"Speak of the devil," Fitzwilliam muttered. "Saye, get inside; you are not dressed. What if people see you?"

"Let them look," he said grandly. "Perhaps it will distract them from all the shouting."

"Richard," Darcy said in a hush; his cousin turned to him. "Everyone else must think Elizabeth and I are in love, including the family."

"You need say no more," replied Fitzwilliam with a nod.

"And you and Lady Susanna?"

Fitzwilliam groaned. "Very well. You need say no more there either."

THE ROOM FELL silent as a footman opened the door to his uncle's study, allowing Darcy and his cousins to enter. Lady Catherine stood by his uncle's usual chair, holding her cane in a manner that suggested she might hit something with it. Lord and Lady Matlock were sitting together on a settee by the fire, but his lordship rose. "Darcy, welcome to Bedlam."

Darcy shot his uncle a frown before greeting his aunts.

Lady Catherine advanced on him immediately with a snarl. "You have disgraced the family name."

"As I am the only Darcy in this room, any problems with my marriage are mine and mine alone. Lady Catherine, I hope you will tell me that the report I have heard of your visit to Miss Bennet was untrue."

She was fairly quivering with rage as she replied, "If I do not oversee your concerns, who will?"

"I shall," Darcy replied firmly. "I neither need nor wish for your interference."

"You are being made a fool."

Ignoring that, Darcy said, "I shall expect your apology not only for myself but for Elizabeth and her family as well."

Lady Catherine looked to her brother. "Do you hear this insolence? This girl has drawn him in so, he even begins to sound like her! A ruder, more impertinent piece of baggage I have yet to be acquainted with and hope I never shall."

"He is right, Catherine" Lord Matlock said. "You had no right to do as you did. I am ashamed of you and agree with Darcy—you must apologise to his lady and her family."

Lady Catherine sputtered, her lips forming soundless syllables, until at last she fell back on her predictable protest. She walked towards Darcy, her cane thumping decisively on the floor beneath her. "You are engaged to Anne, and you will marry Anne. Surely you cannot be so lost to decency as to imagine that you may jilt my daughter for such an insignificant, unexceptional, ill-bred, low-born, nothing of a girl!"

"I shall not permit you to insult my future wife in such a manner. You will cease doing so immediately, or this interview will be ended and our connexion with it. I am not engaged to Anne. Anne and I have spoken on this many times, and we agreed years ago that we would never marry."

Drawing a deep breath against his ire, Darcy spoke evenly, "I shall marry Miss Elizabeth Bennet on the tenth of February. You have two alternatives before you. You may accept my decision and apologise to my betrothed or continue to bluster and fight and find yourself excluded from the Darcy family hereafter. The choice is yours, for mine has already been made."

"And if this is how you will conduct yourself, you may consider yourself removed from your Matlock relations as well," Lord Matlock added.

There was an extended silence during which Darcy went to the fire and his aunt went silent, no doubt considering her next mode of attack, which was an attempt to coddle him into obedience. Walking closer to him, she spoke more gently. "It is not your fault this has happened. This girl has enticed and allured you grievously and wantonly. You have been entrapped by a fortune huntress."

From across the room Saye—who was at grave risk of exposing himself, lolling on a chair with one leg flung across the arm—said, "That cannot be true, can it?"

When he was sure all eyes in the room had turned to him, he said, "Auntie, after all, if money was all she wanted, Miss

Bennet would have taken your fifteen thousand pounds and gone on her way."

Darcy gasped, inadvertently taking a step towards the offender. "You offered her money to break off our engagement?"

Lady Catherine dismissed his protest with a sweep of her hand. "Is that not what all the harlots do—seek payment for their feminine wiles?"

Rage blinded him in a manner it had not often done. He stumbled, even as Lady Matlock rose and came to him, placing one hand on his arm to steady him while Lord Matlock took his sister and began to move her from the room, the colonel hastening to help him.

But Lady Catherine would not go quietly. "She will not be received, I assure you of that. People will see her for the insignificant…" The rest of her words were lost as Lord Matlock pushed her from the room.

Darcy forcibly exhaled as Saye rose and tugged him towards a chair. He sank into it, then dropped his face into his hands.

"First thing," Saye announced, "is to go get your Miss Bennet a present. Jewellery, something costly, obviously."

"She is not entirely wrong," Darcy said tiredly, raising his head. "Some may not receive her…us, that is."

"No." Lady Matlock said firmly. "Not while I live and breathe. If someone takes issue with Elizabeth, then they will be excluded from my circle as well."

Relief swept through Darcy, and he nodded at his aunt. "Thank you. That is generous of you."

"Assuming, of course, that she is not an 'impertinent piece of baggage' as accused," his aunt replied.

"I daresay one might require a certain amount of impertinence to face down that old dragon," Saye remarked. At his mother's gentle frown he added, "She has already earned my approval. What fun that drawing room must have been!"

Fitzwilliam re-entered the room. "Lady Catherine is resting now. Banks brought her a posset for her nerves."

"Let us hope it was a strong one," said Lady Matlock. "Darcy, I shall write to your Miss Bennet. I would like her to come to me before your marriage so that I may introduce her to some of my friends. We must make it known we support her—even you, Saye."

"Even me? What does that mean?"

"It means you are rude," Fitzwilliam told him. "If we were not brothers, I am sure we would never speak."

"That's because you are dull, not because you are poor," Saye replied. "In any case, I just said I already like this Miss Bennet. I think she might be braver than I am. I am sure I should have taken the old bird's money and run for the hills."

"I cannot believe it. I cannot imagine what Elizabeth and her family must have thought, my own aunt offering her a fortune to jilt me."

"What Lady Catherine has hurt, we shall remedy," Lady Matlock promised. "You have my word. Your bride will be the talk of the Season by the time I am done."

CHAPTER ELEVEN

Bingley, having received a summons from Caroline at the rooms he kept, hurried across town to meet his sister at Hurst's town home. He entered the uselessly fine, overheated parlour to find Caroline and Louisa awaiting him.

Although they had not invited him to do so, Bingley took a seat opposite them. "What are you doing here? Why did you not remain at Netherfield? I intend to be back by—"

"We must have misunderstood you," Caroline replied quickly, while Louisa motioned to the housekeeper to bring the tea cart. "We closed the house behind us, I am afraid."

"Misunderstood me? I should have thought it perfectly clear when I said—"

"In any case, Charles," Louisa said firmly, "I think it for the best that we all remain in town. That horrid little village did nothing but cause us trouble."

"A pity you feel so," Bingley replied, warmly, "for it is very likely I shall purchase Netherfield Park for my wife and I to live in."

The two ladies exchanged a look, and Caroline asked, "Your wife? Who might that be?"

"It cannot have escaped the notice of either of you that I was quite taken by Miss Bennet."

"Taken? Or taken in?" Louisa asked and then tittered. Caroline gave her a little poke on the arm, then indulged in her own mean giggle.

"What do you mean?"

"Those Bennets have abused us all abominably," Caroline said. "All of them are quite beneath your notice, that Jane Bennet most of all."

"I thought you liked her?" Bingley exclaimed.

"I did...until I realised she was one of those ladies who aspires to elegance by tormenting a respectable gentleman."

Bingley laughed. "What on earth are you speaking of?"

"I heard it from Mrs Bennet myself that one wedding should beget another—and so it will. The future of Longbourn is secured."

"How so?"

"Because Mr Collins will marry Miss Bennet," said Caroline. "As you surely knew."

"Miss Bennet? Which Miss Bennet?"

Caroline gave him a look that was at once both scornful and pitying.

"But...but I thought she..."

"Her preference for you was rather unseemly, given the arrangement that existed," Louisa opined with a sanctimonious little pout.

"You are both wrong," Bingley said. "I heard nothing of this! And you, Caroline—why should I believe a word you say after your comportment with Darcy?"

She did not like that. Her jaw clenched, and her eyes narrowed as she spat, "I tell you the truth now as much as I did then. I heard it from many people. Surely you noticed he danced with her twice at the ball?"

"So did I!"

"Well, yes, but he is a parson," Louisa said.

Bingley wondered what that should have to do with it. "You must have misunderstood. Mr Collins proposed to Miss Elizabeth, not knowing of her engagement to Darcy. That must surely be what you heard…someone must have mistaken—"

"Mr Collins himself told me of it, Charles," Caroline said. "In any case, as the first daughter, it is Jane's rightful place to be the future mistress of Longbourn. Who would wish to deny her that? Naturally, the Bennets would not consent to Miss Eliza being engaged unless Miss Bennet were also engaged."

Bingley found himself gripping the arms of the chair tightly. "Miss Bennet showed no indication of being attached to Mr Collins—none at all."

"'Tis hardly a love match after all," said Louisa.

Caroline added, "The Bennets were not blessed with a son and now must turn to this alternative to ensure Longbourn remains in the family. Miss Bennet knows her duty."

There was a dreadful pause while Bingley considered that.

Caroline then added, "You know as well as I that in many families the first born cannot marry to suit themselves."

Miss Bennet had not ever really given him leave to believe there was anything more between them—had she? Was this true, that it was all some last bit of fun in society? And who better than the handsome young gentleman who was new to Hertfordshire and did not know of the prior attachment?

An emotion most unusual to Bingley made him flush hot. "I cannot believe it until I know it for myself."

"You will just have to ask her, will you not?" Caroline asked.

"But pray do not make a cake of yourself," Louisa added. "There has been enough of that already."

BINGLEY LEFT Hurst's town house feeling like a caper-witted fool. Surely his sisters were wrong!

But it all made too much sense to allow him to dismiss them. Jane was a dutiful girl and the eldest sister. Of course, the Bennets would wish to secure their home for the next generation, and Jane would be the most likely to do it. Furthermore, why would his sisters want to deceive him? They liked Jane and no doubt would have happily welcomed her as a sister.

Thoughts of his lovely, gentle angel as wife to Collins made him sick to his stomach. He recalled once seeing them walking into Meryton shortly after Miss Bennet had returned home from her illness at Netherfield. It had been Miss Bennet and the three youngest sisters, and now that he thought of it, it seemed as though the younger girls walked apart from Jane and Mr Collins. Was that arrangement deliberate? In hindsight it seemed like it probably had been.

A fervent, lovesick idea at once came into his mind. He imagined himself challenging Collins, snatching up Miss Bennet and riding off, like some hero in a romance novel.

Then he shook his head, feeling foolish. No doubt Miss Bennet wanted to do this. She loved her family. She would wish to do what she could for them. In any case, it was a good match for her, to be the future mistress of Longbourn. He did not even have an actual estate to offer to her, just a leased home and a promise. Collins, as much a fool as he was, at the very least offered her the chance to secure her home for her family and her future children.

I heard nothing of this! Caroline must be in error.

Except that generally, Caroline was correct about such things. She made it her business to know the status of the marriageable young ladies and gentlemen in any society in which she found herself. If there was some understanding in existence, she would have learnt of it.

In any case, Caroline liked Miss Bennet and had even invited her to dine in a party with Louisa. They had said they wished to know her more. She would not put up some impediment to his courtship unless it was completely valid.

Would she?

He sighed. Perhaps Miss Elizabeth's refusal had caused the Bennets to encourage Mr Collins to another daughter. Or possibly Collins had admired Miss Bennet all along and she had only wished for a last bit of fun and flirtation before settling into life as a clergyman's wife and the future mistress of Longbourn.

How can I know for certain? He hardly wished to continue appearing to pay court to a woman who was promised to another. Good lord! He supposed it was fortunate Collins had not challenged him already!

Having left his relations, Darcy went directly to his club with Saye. His aunt had urged him to make known his delight in his betrothal. "You need to get ahead of the gossip,"

she told him. "If it is known that your own aunt tried to interfere and end things, it will look very bad."

So off he went, forcing himself to do that which was least natural to him: talk about himself. There were one or two of his friends present who were glad to hear the news and professed a desire to meet Elizabeth; this he counted as enough and took a seat with the newspaper and the promise of oyster stew from the waiter. Saye kept him company for a time but soon drifted off to the card room.

Minutes later he looked up, seeing Bingley had entered the club. As Bingley glanced around, Darcy motioned to him, beckoning him to come to his table.

He watched as Bingley handed his greatcoat, hat, and gloves to the waiting servant, immediately noticing that something was amiss in his manner. Bingley was decidedly lacking in his characteristic cheer. He walked towards Darcy slowly, without even smiling at the other gentlemen in the room.

The two friends greeted one another, and Bingley sat. "How do, Darcy?"

"I am well," Darcy replied, studying him carefully. "And you?"

"Well enough, I suppose," Bingley replied with a little nod. He was distracted and began to toy with some crumbs that Saye had left on the table linens. "Um, there was some misunderstanding and my family have all left Netherfield."

"All of them?"

Bingley nodded, his gaze drifting aimlessly over the room.

"Will they wish to return to Netherfield with us, or do they intend to remain in town?"

"I beg your pardon, but I do not think I shall return to

Hertfordshire with you. Please do as you will at Netherfield. I shall send word that the house should be closed again after your departure."

Not again. Darcy barely suppressed his groan, understanding very well what happened. It was Bingley's usual way—attend some country house party, fall in love with a local beauty, and then return to town and forget all about her. How many times had he seen it? Too many to count. The true difficulty lay in the fact that Bingley never sought to deceive anyone. When he was there, he genuinely believed himself in love. He was not a rake so much as he was…forgetful.

I should have warned Elizabeth of Bingley's tendency to fall in and out of love easily and rapidly. I can only hope Miss Bennet is not too heartbroken.

"Tell me, have you seen anyone since you returned?" Darcy was posing a specific question, one he knew Bingley would not misunderstand.

"I had some business with Hepplewhite earlier today. His sister was there and sat with us a bit once our business was concluded."

Miss Hepplewhite was a noted beauty with a fine fortune.

"She is a lovely girl," Darcy remarked disinterestedly.

"Very handsome," Bingley agreed without enthusiasm. "I enjoyed the call. Her conversation is delightful. She speaks rather little but listens very well."

After a moment's pause, Bingley spoke up. "Darcy, do you think that…" He stopped himself, shaking his head and looking at the table.

He needs reassurance that this will not come between us, but he cannot continue on, raising expectations as he does. How will he go back to Hertfordshire if he has publicly disgraced Miss Bennet? Heaven only knows what Miss Hepplewhite might now expect.

Darcy cleared his throat and began to speak, a little sternly. "Bingley, you and I both understand the pleasures of a flirtation."

"Was that all it was?" Bingley asked earnestly.

"You tell me," Darcy replied. "Miss Bennet might have been engaged but… That is to say her heart was…" His last words were drowned out by a burst of rowdy laughter from the table of young men next to them.

Bingley's startled gaze came around quickly to his friend. "So you knew? About Miss Bennet that is?"

Of course, anyone could see that her heart was becoming fixed on you, Bingley, Darcy mentally chastised his friend. His voice mildly rebuking, he said, "Yes, I could see it rather clearly."

Bingley groaned, and placed his head in his hand. "How did I not see it?"

"I suppose we all see as we wish. But you must learn to take care. Heartbreak is as real as any illness."

With a sad shake of his head, Bingley agreed. "That it is."

The men stayed together only a brief time, for Bingley, as precipitously as he had come, seemed eager to leave. Darcy confirmed with Bingley that he would go to Netherfield the next day, with plans to remain for a week before returning to London to spend Christmas with his family.

"I believe I had best hasten home." Bingley was given his coat and hat and paused for a moment before informing his friend, "We shall be for Scarborough within the week, so I likely shall not see you again until sometime in January. Do enjoy the Christmastide."

Darcy nodded and Bingley left. Shaking his head, he said,

"I suppose it is to me to break my future sister's heart in your stead? Ah, Bingley."

CHAPTER TWELVE

DARCY LEFT LONDON AT FIRST LIGHT THE NEXT DAY, BEARING a note from Lady Matlock for Elizabeth and a gift from himself. As he travelled, he was forced to consider that which he had not previously—that he had not left her happy. She had been angry with him, referring to herself as his prisoner, and the actions of his aunt had surely done nothing to advance him in her opinion. *At least she did not take the money and leave.*

He could not bear to imagine her unhappy with him, and too much time in the carriage allowed him occasion to do just that. By the time he was at Longbourn he was, if not agitated, nearly so, and thus greeted with dismay Mrs Hill's words. "Miss Elizabeth is unwell in her bedchamber, and the rest of the family are from home."

"She is ill?"

"Was dreadful ill, I am afraid," said Hill. "Had a fever until yesterday but now is a little better. She is asleep in her bedchamber, and I am sure you can see why it is best she not be disturbed."

"Of course. May I leave a note for her?"

Hill procured paper and pen and waited patiently while he wrote a short missive to his ailing lady.

Elizabeth, I am sorry to hear you are unwell. I am longing to see you, and I hope I may have the pleasure soon.

FD

He looked over it when it was complete, feeling it inadequate but also wishing to send it quickly, rather than labour over it, as would be his wont. Folding it neatly, he handed Mrs Hill the note, and she left with it immediately. He heard the sound of her footsteps overhead, first ascending the steps, then moving away from where this particular parlour was situated, evidently going towards the eastern side of the house.

When Hill returned, she brought his coat and hat with her, and he took them. She offered to summon the stable boys for him, but he informed her he would go to the stables instead. She looked at him oddly but said nothing, then curtseyed and left.

Darcy exited the front door. Standing a moment, he looked around, feeling the absence of the house's occupants—save for one. He wondered how long the rest of the family would be gone.

Feeling like an errant schoolboy, he sneaked around to the rear of the house. He entered again quietly through a back door. Taking great pains to be silent, he crept up a back staircase he had seen on a prior visit, thinking of how utterly humiliated he would be if someone caught him. *Yet I do not care enough to stop.*

Pausing as he reached the top stair, he looked down the

hall on the eastern side of the house, seeing four or five closed doors before him. Which one? Still treading lightly, he went to a door he selected at random and knocked softly. There was no response, so he went to another. Knocking again, he heard Elizabeth's voice say, "Come in."

He opened the door and entered, seeing her immediately. Her face was pale, and her eyes looked tired, but she was beautiful. She was not asleep, and the room he entered was not her bedchamber, but rather a small sitting room. She reclined on a fainting couch, a blanket around her.

When she saw him, her eyes flew wide and she gasped, "Mr Darcy!" She hastily pulled the blanket up to her neck. "What are you doing here?"

"I needed to see you," he said quietly. "Pray, do not give me away."

He seated himself on the edge of the couch so that he faced her, unable to resist the lure of caressing her hair, which was unrestrained and fell over her shoulders in waves. "How do you feel? You are ill?"

"A trifling cold. When did you return?"

"Minutes ago." He chuckled. "I was desperate to see you."

"You were? Why?"

"To apologise. I cannot like how we left things."

"I understand that you wish to protect me. I am…unaccustomed to someone having such interest in my actions."

"Is that not the job of husbands?" he teased. "To protect wife and family? You must allow me to practise my husbandly skills if I am going to become proficient."

She looked surprised, but then, to his relief, she laughed. "We both have to accustom ourselves to such things."

He could not miss the shadow that went across her face then. "Your aunt came to visit me here," she told him.

"I know, and please allow me to convey my deepest apologies, as well as that of my aunt and uncle, Lord and Lady Matlock." He removed the note from his pocket that her ladyship had written to Elizabeth. She took it carefully.

"I wish I had been here to help you. My family is embarrassed by what she has done. I told her, as I shall tell anyone who does not treat you respectfully and kindly, that I shall have no part with her until she renders a suitable apology to you."

"Do not say so. I understand the source of her dismay."

"You do?" Darcy could not imagine that Elizabeth would be inclined to take the part of Lady Catherine. "Such as what?"

"She believes you are promised to her daughter."

"I am not," Darcy replied firmly. "I never was. Anne knew that."

After a brief pause, Elizabeth continued. "She was quite certain. I understand Miss de Bourgh is unwell, and likely her ladyship believed she was taken care of, promised to you, such as it was. No doubt it was an unpleasant shock to have that surety taken from her. Mothers feel things deeply."

Darcy studied her, noting the compassion in her dark eyes. He expected outrage, fear, or perhaps sarcasm from her and instead found her reasonable and calm, and exceedingly endearing for it. It stirred within him a powerful desire to vanquish any and every problem she had or would ever have. He moved a wayward curl from her shoulder, enjoying the silky feel of it in his fingers.

He was pleasantly surprised by the feeling of Elizabeth's hand reaching up to the back of his head, her fingers winding gently into his hair. He closed his eyes, hearing her murmur, "I have a great deal of experience with difficult mothers who enjoy exerting their will. I suppose it must come naturally to me by now."

He chuckled, even as one part of his mind considered how near her lips were to his. "So she has not frightened you off?"

"No." He felt the warmth of her breath as the word was released from her lips. "If anything, she made me more determined."

She is perfect. Darcy felt himself falling, tumbling into something he knew not. Words were rising up to his lips, words he was ill prepared to understand, and to stop them, he kissed her.

She received his kiss and returned it first with the hesitation of innocence, then with greater alacrity, pressing close to him. She allowed him to slide her down on the settee and move over her—not completely, just a little—while he deepened the kiss. It seemed to surprise her, but she did not shrink from it.

Gentlemanly restraint soon pulled him back, and they sat upright again. He revelled in the look of her, so well-kissed with prettily tousled hair. Reaching towards her, he tucked one curl behind her ear and then just looked at her until she grew shy under his gaze.

With a self-conscious smirk, she looked down at his aunt's letter still in her hand. "Um, so your aunt—"

"There's the way," he said with a chuckle. "Nothing like the mention of an aunt to dim a man's ardour."

She joined him in a laugh and then opened her note from Lady Matlock. As she perused it, he said, "Lady Matlock feels that spending time in London before we are married might be beneficial to you." He hoped she understood the importance of such a gesture. He remembered then, her mention of the aunt in Cheapside, and the delicacy of that subject—well, surely she knew this was the better choice by far.

With a smile, Elizabeth said, "I shall write to her this afternoon and accept her invitation. She has asked me there until the end of January; I shall see how long my mother will allow me to forestall the wedding duties."

"My aunt would not wish you to neglect bridal obligations to be sure," he said, relieved. "We can settle on a date of return that satisfies Mrs Bennet and my aunt both, I am sure."

"Did Mr Bingley accompany you here this morning?" Elizabeth asked. "He must be wondering where you have gone."

Bingley. Before he could stop himself, he groaned. Elizabeth's eyes flew wide. "Bingley did not return to Hertfordshire with me."

"No?"

He looked into her face, willing her to understand his regret in the matter—though what he might have done about it, he knew not. "I do not think Bingley will return to Hertfordshire."

Elizabeth looked at him but said nothing.

Darcy cleared his throat, feeling as awkward as he ever had in his life and wishing he could pummel Bingley for putting him in this situation. "Bingley is..."

Darcy stopped, drumming his fingers against his leg, and finally decided the only way to go about it was to be frank. "Bingley is easily persuaded in matters of the heart. It pains me to say it, but he falls in and out of love quite readily. I...I hope Miss Bennet will not be too dreadfully disappointed."

"Yes, I fear she will," Elizabeth replied. Her gaze dropped

to the coverlet beneath her hands. "He certainly had me fooled. I thought him violently in love with her."

Darcy resolved that his first order of business, when back in London, was to invite Bingley to Jackson's boxing parlour for the purpose of thrashing him soundly. "Likely he was. His feelings are true; they are just not...constant. I hope that one day he will be different—he is, at heart, a very good man—but he is just full young and has not had the responsibilities of life to help him mature."

"One can only hope." She offered a wry smile through her sadness.

Darcy yearned to make her look happy again and remembered, just in time, the present he had brought. "Um, I...I saw this." He reached into his coat pocket, extracting the gift. "It was pretty, and I thought...I hoped you might like it."

"Oh!" she exclaimed, seeing the beautiful pin he handed her. It was rendered to look like three flowers, bound in a small bouquet. The pin itself was of gold, and the flowers were decorated in tiny gemstones. "This is beautiful! Yes, I like it very well indeed."

She leant over to him and kissed him lightly on his cheek, saying softly, "Thank you."

He felt his colour rise, and before he could dissuade himself, he leant even closer, cupped her face in his hands, and kissed her back.

It was even better than before. This time she slid herself down the back of the chaise, allowing him to lean over her and feel the shape of her body beneath his. Her taste was ten times as sweet as it had been previously, and the feel of her hands against his chest and the back of his neck was so thrilling it was nearly intolerable. He felt lost in her, incapable of doing anything but experiencing the moment. He found himself pushing her blanket aside, leaving nothing but a wonderfully thin layer of muslin between his hand and her skin. He slid a hand around her waist, marvelling at the smallness of it and the delicacy of her.

Then a door slammed somewhere on the lower level of the house, and Elizabeth jumped, quickly pulling away and bringing her blanket back into position. Darcy leapt to his feet, straightening his waistcoat, flushing, his heart pounding with commingled desire and dread at being caught. He caught Elizabeth's eye and they shared a laugh.

"A maid, I am sure," she said.

"This time. But I should leave. I believe Mrs Hill was suspicious of me already."

"She might have been. With five young ladies around the house, she has learnt to keep an eye on things." She paused for a moment, then added quietly. "But I am glad you came."

Darcy inhaled sharply at her simply innocent words. She did not intend to flirt with him, yet she enflamed him more than she knew with her tenderness and warmth. He permitted himself one more kiss, bending over to place it on her cheek. Then he rose, determinedly turning away from her. "I hope you get well quickly." And then he left.

He was nearly down the steps when he remembered that he had, again, not mentioned Georgiana, but it was not a good time. Not when parting had been such sweet sorrow.

Sometime later, her sister's voice came as a gentle whisper into the darkened room. "Lizzy? Are you awake?"

"I am Jane, come in." Elizabeth pulled herself from the

light doze she had fallen into after Darcy left, immediately recalling the disagreeable task she had ahead of her.

Jane smiled as she entered, and Elizabeth, forestalling her sister's pain, asked, "Did you enjoy the day? Who did you call on?"

Jane continued to smile as she recounted the various neighbours they had seen, but Elizabeth noticed that when she got to the Lucases, the pleasure on her face seemed to dim.

"And what happened at Lucas Lodge that was so disagreeable that you nearly did not smile about it?"

Jane heaved a sigh. "They spoke endlessly of Mr Bingley! Mama had to revisit every moment of the ball and relate her disappointment that he had not paid me his addresses that night. She is also displeased he has not written to my father as she expected."

Jane moved to where her sister lay and began tucking the blankets around Elizabeth as she spoke. "Lady Lucas had it from her housekeeper that Mrs Nicholls was keeping the house only for Mr Darcy's return. She said Mr Bingley was not expected."

Elizabeth's heart broke, knowing it was true. She could not tell Jane that, of course, for to do so would be admitting Darcy had been there. Instead she only said, "I am so very sorry, Jane."

Jane looked at Elizabeth, and in her blue eyes was an expression of sadness and despair the likes of which Elizabeth had never seen, and it brought tears into her own eyes. Elizabeth leant forward and pulled her sister into her embrace. Once within the sanctuary of her sister's arms, Jane permitted her tears to come.

Eventually Elizabeth said, "When I am married, you will

come to me in London, and just as Mama has always said, we shall put you in front of Mr Darcy's rich friends—"

"Oh, what use could that be?" Jane cried out in frustration, pushing herself away from her sister's arms. "So more of Mr Darcy's wealthy friends might find me wanting?"

"Mr Bingley is young and easily swayed and—"

"And I am a fool for being unduly flattered by his attentions." Her head turned, and her eyes fell on the table beside the settee where sat the pin Darcy had given Elizabeth. Jane reached for it and examined it. "What is this?"

"It's a pin. Dearest, you must not blame yourself for Mr Bingley's capricious—"

"I can see it is a pin, Lizzy. Where did it come from? It was not purchased on your allowance, to be sure." Jane held up the pin. "Did Mr Darcy bring this to you?"

Heat prickled her skin as Elizabeth admitted, "He did."

"Did he steal up here to see you?" Mr Bingley was for the moment forgotten, as Jane, delightedly scandalised, appeared to wish to tease her sister. "Come now. No man would buy such a pretty thing for a lady only to pass it off to her through the housekeeper or her father."

"Very well," Elizabeth admitted. "Yes, he was here, but pray, do not tell Mama!"

"I shall not! You know I would not—for a price."

Elizabeth groaned.

"It just seems to me that if he took all the trouble to sneak up here, there might have been something more to it than gift-giving." Jane raised one brow questioningly.

"I kissed him, yes, but no more! And it was not the first time."

"The first time while wearing a nightgown," Jane observed wryly. "But Lizzy—I think you are falling in love with him. And certainly it must be seen as a testament to his affection for you that such a proper man would do something so decidedly improper as to sneak into your bedchamber and see you this way!"

"You know as well as I do that love is not a part of this. He is maintaining our charade, that is all."

"How does a secret visit support a charade?" Jane cast a sceptical smirk in her sister's direction. "No matter where it begins, why can it not end in something more true? Is it because you cannot allow yourself to love him?"

"Loving him might be easier were there more days like today and fewer where he seems determined to play my gaoler."

"Your gaoler, Lizzy?" Jane shook her head. "I fear Papa has done you a disservice in granting you the freedoms that he has. It has given you an unrealistic expectation of what marriage will be."

"Perhaps it has." Elizabeth took the pin back from her sister, examining it as it laid in her hand. In her peripheral vision she could see Jane watching her. "I have never aspired to raising myself through marriage, you know that. I could not ever have expected to marry someone of Mr Darcy's status, and now I am. Lady Catherine did do me one favour —his family is now inclined towards helping me, to make amends for their relation's bad behaviour."

"That is very good."

"I hope it will be. I have always made friends easily, but I would be a fool if I did not see reasonably the adversity ahead and did not recognise that those trials were made more difficult by the fact that he does not love me, and in fact, wishes he could erase all remnant of…well, you know. You know what it is about us that is undesirable, and so does he. A Mr Darcy should never marry a Miss Elizabeth Bennet."

She had never before said it so clearly, and it cast a cold shadow in her heart. Her fears, which had haunted her these past weeks, were now made perfectly clear. Could she become Mrs Darcy without completely erasing Elizabeth Bennet, as Mr Darcy seemed to wish her to do? Could she find happiness in her new life?

"If anyone can do it, it is you," Jane said, with her usual sweet encouragement. "You are liked wherever you go, and I do not doubt London will be exactly the same. You have all you need to succeed and to make Mr Darcy love you too."

"I hope you are right." Elizabeth smiled at her sister, and Jane, apparently relieved, smiled back and threw her arms around her in a hug.

CHAPTER THIRTEEN

DARCY CALLED AGAIN THE FOLLOWING MORNING, BUT MRS Bennet deemed Elizabeth still too pale and ill-looking to receive him. He was with Mr Bennet for a time, and when he left, Elizabeth was given a note. After reading it, she went to her father, confused by its contents.

Mr Bennet raised his head from his book. "Come in, Lizzy. You have received your young man's note, I presume?"

"I have. He says he has arranged to send a carriage to bring me to town on the twenty-eighth."

"Mm."

"Does that not seem a bit foolish? After all, the Gardiners will depart Longbourn for London only two days later. It would seem to save some expense if I were to simply travel with them."

Mr Bennet laughed. "I would not worry about the expense. Mr Darcy can well afford to arrange things to his liking."

"Perhaps he did not know about the Gardiners' plans?"

"I informed him of them myself."

So not only am I to refrain from visiting the Gardiners' home, I cannot even ride in their carriage?

To her father, she said, "If he knew they would travel the same way only two days later, why would he not want me to go with them?"

"You will need to ask him that yourself. I know only that he asked permission for you to leave on the twenty-eighth, and I granted it."

Elizabeth frowned at the note in her hand. "Likely he did not wish a tradesman's carriage to draw up outside his aunt's home. Either that or he wished to prove he could arrange things as he wished, with no regard for sense or prudence."

Mr Bennet had opened his book again and leant back in his chair. "You had better get used to it. It was your choice, after all, to marry a man who would wish you to follow where he led."

"Papa..." she protested, but he was not of a mind to hear her.

"Off you go, Lizzy. My mind is more agreeably engaged in non-romantic affairs this morning."

Elizabeth was permitted to receive Darcy the following day. Longbourn was in its usual uproar, as Kitty and Lydia were in one of their arguments, so Elizabeth invited him to walk out with her.

It was a cold day, as days in December tended to be, but at least the wind did not blow, rendering it more agreeable. The chill made Elizabeth take Darcy's arm gratefully, even snuggling into him a bit more than was her custom. They strolled along for a bit, speaking of inconsequential things for a time. Elizabeth was pleased with him; he had arrived prepared to act the lover, and she enjoyed it and allowed her pique over the travel arrangements to be put aside. In any case her father was right. She knew he was high-handed before she agreed to marry him; it would be silly to allow it to eat at her now.

After a short silence, Darcy said, "I am pleased to see you wearing the pin I gave you."

"My sisters are quite envious of it," she said lightly. "It is best to keep it on me, so it does not go wandering onto the fichu of another."

"I knew you must like it when you insisted on kissing me as you did," he said, and cast her a sidelong, teasing glance. "Modern young ladies are so brazen."

She did like it when he teased her and showed his rare, joking side, and she returned it happily. "Forgive me—I must not have heard your protest."

"Oh, there was no protest." He stopped and turned to face her. "I was just hoping to get you to do it again."

"I could not. I do not wish to offend your sensibilities." She took his hand, and made as if to walk on. "In any case, I have never protested against any of your kisses, so I have to presume that if you wanted a kiss, you would ask for it."

"I might," he agreed, strolling slightly behind her and caressing her hand lightly. "Though I like it when *you* kiss *me*."

She looked at him over her shoulder. "I fear we are at an impasse, then, for I, too, like when you kiss me, and in any case, that is more proper for a young lady and her suitor."

"More proper, is it? Nevertheless, I intend to prevail."

She stopped and turned then, one hand on her hip. "As do I."

He studied her, his head tilted, and she had a moment to think that turned out as he was, he looked like a gentleman's fashion plate—tall and lean, expertly tailored, and exquisitely handsome. "Would you have me beg?"

"Beg?" She laughed and drew closer to him. "That would lead to pity kisses, I fear."

"No, I do not want those. What if I became angry, threw a tantrum perhaps?"

"Amusing to see, but coerced kisses are almost as bad as pity kisses."

She found herself stepping very close to him, almost pressed to his chest, and looked up at him. This little game pleased her; seeing this playful side of Darcy reassured her that they were more compatible than she initially believed.

"This is certainly unfair," he said. His eyes had grown soft, and his voice sounded deep and a little husky. "You have unsheathed your weapons."

"I have no weapons."

"Oh, yes, you do." The snow began to fall gently and lightly around them, and Darcy used his thumb to tenderly brush a few flakes from her eyelashes, then allowed his thumb to remain stroking her cheek. "Those eyes," he murmured. "When you look my way with those beautiful, sparkling eyes, I am yours to command."

His words and the caress of his hand on her face did her in, and she raised herself up on her toes, kissing him on the lips. He was quick to deepen the kiss, pulling her closely to him and indulging himself hungrily. She put her arms tightly around his neck and pressed against his body.

She had only just become aware of the difficulties inherent in kissing someone who was so much taller than she was, when Darcy pulled back. He did not let her go, nestling her against his coat while both caught their breath. After a few moments, he murmured, "I win."

Elizabeth burst into laughter, stepping back so she could look at him. "Yes, I suppose you did. It is likely for the best, as I think it might have been too much a shock to you had it gone any other way."

Kissing her hand, he placed it within his arm, and they began again to walk. "Do you think me spoilt?"

Lightly, she replied, "I think you like to have things your way."

"I am too accustomed to it, I am sure. But Elizabeth, surely you must know…"

She turned to look at him.

"I want you to be happy with me. If there is something you want and it is in my power to give it to you, I shall."

Elizabeth blushed at his words and quickly looked away to gather her composure. "Except your kisses, evidently."

"Foolish error. Never again shall I enter into any contest with you in which I must refrain from kissing you. Upon my honour."

"A very good answer, Mr Darcy," she said with a light laugh.

They did not return to the house straightaway, instead following a meandering path. Elizabeth showed Darcy some of the parts of the estate he had not yet seen, such as the small river that bordered it and was graced by willow trees, and the grove of apple trees, some of which resolutely retained a few shivering brown leaves even in December. At last they returned to the house, their ardour finally cooled by the outdoor elements.

Mary sat reading her book in a corner of the drawing room, but paid them little notice. Hill bustled in with tea, and a footman built up the fire. Darcy drew the settee a bit nearer to the fire, and they settled in to regain their warmth.

Almost as if she had been summoned, Mrs Bennet appeared with an invitation for Darcy to join them in a family dinner. A refusal on his behalf was on Elizabeth's lips when she realised the alternative—that he would eat alone at Netherfield. But would he prefer it? She saw him stiffen at her mother's entrance, and his voice took on its usual haughty accents. But he did not decline, and her mother seemed pleased.

Dinner was as dinner often could be at Longbourn, loud and chaotic, but with good food. Elizabeth scarcely ate—too occupied by wincing, cringing, and diverting her mother and sisters from subjects unsuitable for a polite meal—but Darcy appeared to enjoy her mother's table. After dinner, he remained for some time with her father, so long that Elizabeth grew concerned over what they must be discussing. When the two men at last joined the ladies, Darcy seemed thoughtful.

"You and my father were closeted for some time," she said. "Did he compel you to play chess with him?"

"No," Darcy said, still abstracted. "He, uh…he mentioned that Lady Catherine wrote to you. The earl did intend to make her apologise."

"And she did," Elizabeth told him. "Very nicely at that. I shall write back to her straightaway and thank her for her condescension."

"You are kind," he replied, but it was as if by rote.

"Sir?"

After a moment, he said, "I have the faintest black thread of a memory floating about…something your father said pricked at me…but I cannot quite grab onto it."

"Oh, I hate that," Elizabeth said, relieved he was not upset by something. "No doubt you will remember it at three o'clock in the morning. Was it something to do with Lady Catherine?"

Darcy shook his head. "It was when he told me Collins would return in January."

"He will? Why?"

"I do not know, but your father and I spoke then of the breach between your family and the Collinses. The senior Mr Collins was an illiterate and miserly man and had asked your father for money for a business venture. Your father rightly refused him. In any case, as you see, nothing of it is any of my concern, but something niggles at my mind. It will either be forgotten or recalled, I suppose, and it would likely be ideal that I should put it aside."

"I cannot help you. I had never heard of Mr Collins, save as the heir of this house, until November last."

"Being that I must leave you tomorrow, discussing Mr Collins is certainly not my preference." Darcy smiled at her.

"So what shall we talk about?"

"We have never yet been in want of a subject."

"We have not, though there is one subject I have not heard much of."

"Oh?" Darcy asked.

"I would be much obliged if you would tell me more of Miss Darcy." Elizabeth smiled prettily at him. "I only know as much of her as I have heard Mr Bingley's sisters say."

An alarming pale shade went over him, and he became grave. With a severe frown, he said, "I would not hold to any of what those two say on any topic, particularly my sister. They are scarcely acquainted with her."

"I confess, I thought them all the dearest friends. I am

relieved to hear it is otherwise." She waited for him to continue, but he said nothing. "Will you tell me about her?"

"Of course," he said, still appearing uncomfortable. "Georgiana is...she is...she likes music."

"Which composers does she favour?"

"I am sure I could not say."

The pained silence which ensued both surprised and dismayed Elizabeth, but before she could prod him from his silence, Mrs Bennet set upon them. "Mr Darcy, now, you must tell me—for Elizabeth tells me nothing—who will stand up with you at the wedding?"

With that, Mrs Bennet was off, rattling away and seeking his opinion on every inconsequential matter that bounced about in her head. Far from being disgusted by it, Darcy seemed to engage eagerly, plainly delighted to leave behind any mention of his sister.

When the night ended, Elizabeth walked with Darcy to meet his carriage, knowing she must at last broach the topic she had put aside. "I wondered whether you would rather I go to London with my aunt and uncle. It would spare your people the need to travel."

"They will not mind coming for you," he said reassuringly.

"But perhaps your aunt and uncle would mind..."

He watched her, waiting for her to finish her sentence.

She recognised it was likely a sentence best left incomplete. She knew his feelings, and likely his family's as well. What more was there to say?

Yet he appeared to comprehend her. Reaching for her hands, he said, "I am afraid my reason for this haste is entirely selfish."

"Is it?"

He nodded, pulling her hands to his lips, then tugging her close enough to murmur in her ear, "I find being away from you rather insufferable."

Elizabeth closed her eyes, and he lowered his head onto hers. "For a man being forced to marry, you say very pretty things sometimes." She meant it to sound teasing and light, but it emerged plaintive and searching.

"Have I made you uncomfortable?"

"It is not that. Not that at all. Only...I sometimes cannot tell what is real and what is not."

He looked at her intently, his eyes searching and dark, and her heart gave a little flutter. He glanced over his shoulder and in a low voice, asked, "Has your father retired?"

"Likely not. He usually reads in his study before he goes up."

"Come." He beckoned with his finger, and she followed him out into the cold December night. He saw her shiver and motioned her to stay a moment. She watched as he went to his coachmen, who quickly stepped down and walked back towards the stables.

"What they must think!"

"They think a man needs some privacy once in a while with the lady he is going to marry. As enjoyable as Longbourn is, there is not much privacy to be found here."

As he helped her into his carriage, she said, "Now you understand my fondness for long rambles through the countryside. I enjoy both the exercise and the solitude."

They settled into the seat, Darcy beside her. The lanterns sputtered outside but inside was hushed and dark. Darcy reached for her hands, enclosing them within his, and she realised he must have removed his gloves. She had not put on hers, having not planned to be outside. Her heart gave a skipping flutter as his thumb began a slow trace over the back of her hand.

"Please come on the twenty-eighth," he whispered, placing a gentle kiss on her temple. "I have no other reason, no motive, but that I shall miss you."

Elizabeth shivered again, this time from the feel of his closeness and intensity and turned her face towards his. "Very well, then," she responded quietly, "I shall."

"Thank you." He kissed her neck and painfully slowly began to make his way up towards her lips, one hand leaving hers so that his fingers might play lightly with the curls which always fell from her coiffure to lie upon her neck. It was a heady feeling being in the dark carriage entirely alone with him, with a freedom that came from knowing it was unlikely that anyone was concerned for where she was, except possibly Jane.

He kissed her for some time; she knew not how long. Darcy was bolder and more urgent than he had been before. He twisted, bringing her part way across his lap and reclining them ever so slightly. She moved to ease an awkward tilt of her neck, but that left her precariously balanced on the side of his leg. To steady herself, she laid her hand on him.

It was not until he inhaled sharply that she realised her error. Her hand was not on his abdomen as she had intended, but rather on his...she jerked her hand away. "Oh! Forgive me! I did not mean to—"

"No, no. It is not your fault."

"It is very dark—"

"It is, yes."

"I was...you see, I felt as if I might fall so I—"

He quieted her with a kiss, then said reassuringly, "I hardly think you were trying to...you know..."

After a short pause, she said, "Do as Miss Bingley did?"

After a fleeting moment of shocked silence, they began to laugh, discomfort fuelling them until both were sitting up and wiping tears from their eyes. When it had passed, he said, "Elizabeth, I do not think it should surprise you to know that you...affect me."

"Do I?"

"You do. You have for some time now. It is why..."

After a pause, she asked, "Why what?"

"Why I...so easily said your name that night. I had been dreaming of you."

His confession made her blush hotly—he had dreamt of her?—and she was grateful for the dark, which hid her face and expression. She did not dare ask about the nature of his dreams; she was not so much a maiden that she could not guess.

"I confess, I had wondered why it was that you said my name to Bingley that night when surely many other ladies would have done."

"It was you, only you, in my mind."

There was a long silence between them. Elizabeth had no idea what to say to his revelation, or even how she felt about it herself. At length, she said, "Your men must be wondering what became of you."

He sighed heavily, then gently kissed her cheek. "Until the twenty-eighth then."

CHAPTER FOURTEEN

Darcy's carriage was far more luxurious and well-made than any other she had ever ridden in, yet Elizabeth's journey to London was difficult. What should have taken three or four hours took nearly twice as long, as an icy rain had begun to fall, causing their pace to slow to a near crawl. Despite their painstaking approach, the carriage slipped and slid in a number of places, and the coachmen were required to make frequent stops to warm the horses and remove ice from their manes and tails.

Darcy had sent a maid to accompany her, a sweet young lady called Martha, who told her proudly that Darcy had given her one pound complete for her assistance. "How generous," Elizabeth said.

"Indeed, ma'am, but I am sure I do not need to tell you the master's a generous sort. Never a cross word for us either, even if he does like things just so. But you do not know what all goes on in some of these great houses. We are all just glad to be at Darcy House."

"I am glad to know that," Elizabeth agreed with a smile.

The two women talked for a little while, but Elizabeth

could see that Martha wished to sleep and so eventually removed her book from her valise and allowed the girl her rest.

It left her, alas, with far too much time to revisit the disquieting thoughts she had on the nature of Darcy's attachment to her. She had already been possessed of the inklings of it, and Lady Catherine had supposed it as well; then, in his carriage that night, he had confirmed it. He, for lack of more delicate expression, lusted for her.

She had always vowed she would never find herself in a marriage such as that of her mother and father. Mrs Bennet had wished to elevate herself, and Mr Bennet had been captivated by his wife's vivaciousness and beauty. The rewards of the union had disappeared too quickly for them both, and their daughters bore daily witness to the strain.

She could not have imagined someone like herself driving a man like Mr Darcy to surrender to his baser instincts, yet here they were. He had admitted it himself—the reason that he spoke her name that fateful night was because he had been dreaming of her. She had been in his mind, and not because he was captivated by her wit or appreciative of her intelligence.

And had he not, you would be, even now, Mrs Collins. She must continue reminding herself of that.

The trouble was that she, unlike Mrs Bennet, had not aspired to elevate herself. Naturally the Beau Monde interested her—who did not like to read about the doings of the lords and ladies of the first circles?—but she had never imagined nor desired it for herself. Now she would be plunged into it and hoped beyond hope she would be a success.

Lady Catherine's cruel truths echoed in her mind. *'I am certain my nephew is utterly bewildered by the spell of lust with which you have drawn him in—but it will not last.'* Lady Catherine had sent a note of apology, but her apology was for the audacity and effrontery of the visit itself—not for what she had said. Elizabeth had no doubt that the lady stood behind the truth of each and every utterance.

Her aunt had taken her aside and spoken to her when they visited. At first she had not understood what Aunt Gardiner was about, telling her about Pemberley and Lady Anne Darcy, but soon she realised her aunt meant to warn her. "No doubt everyone, him included, expected a match to further elevate the Darcy name. The daughter of an earl, at the very least."

It made Elizabeth laugh when her aunt said that the talk around London had always been that he did not marry his cousin—a young woman of extensive fortune and property —because she was 'merely' the daughter of someone who had been knighted. Her reply to her dear aunt had been somewhat plaintive. "What would you have me do, Aunt Gardiner? It is done; I am engaged, and Papa has signed everything."

Aunt Gardiner had smiled, though her forehead was creased and her mouth pressed in at the corners just a little too much. "Just think of it carefully, Lizzy. London can be a cruel place, and I know you love him, but make certain it will be enough."

'I know you love him.' Elizabeth smiled ruefully even now, remembering how she had not disabused her aunt of that notion. Her aunt, like everyone save for Jane, had been left to believe this was a match made in love. Her aunt could not be allowed to know the truth.

At length she put aside her worries and dozed, only to be woken by the sounds of the city. *We are here.* The thought gave her considerable relief. Across from her Martha stretched. "That was a long ways, miss. It must be near time to eat."

Matlock House was in St James' Square, a part of London Elizabeth had, in truth, never seen before. She felt like quite the country bumpkin, gazing about her at the handsome limestone edifices, well-lit and exceedingly warm looking. The carriage came to a stop in front of what seemed to be one of the largest and prettiest, but before she could spend too much time contemplating it, the door was jerked open and Darcy nearly burst in on them.

"At last!" Pulling Elizabeth from the carriage, he embraced her, exclaiming over the chill of her. "And just when you are so lately recovered from an illness. Where is Mrs Banks?"

Mrs Banks—or so Elizabeth presumed–appeared behind Darcy, and he began ordering her about. "She is chilled through and will require a hot bath and some tea in her bedchamber. Get my aunt's maid to assist her, and I shall—"

"Mr Darcy!" Elizabeth placed a hand on his arm. "I assure you, I am not as bad as that. Really, we were quite comfortable. I was napping until we entered the city, and then I was too busy looking around me to give much care for the chill."

They began to move indoors as she said so, and he lowered his head and murmured, "I was alarmed when you did not appear at the hour I expected. I anticipated all manner of dreadful things, carriages overturned, highwaymen—"

"Plague of locusts?" She laughed, looking into his eyes. "Truly, I am perfectly well, and I think I ought to meet and thank my hosts before I hie off for baths and tea."

"Very well, but I do not want you to take ill." Darcy reluctantly took her into the drawing room to greet his relations. The room was as grand as Elizabeth might have imagined, high ceilings, silk wall hangings, uncomfortable-looking chairs, and thick carpets. A pianoforte sat regally in one corner, causing dread—Elizabeth knew she would be called upon to exhibit, likely often.

Lady Matlock stood with her husband, a vision of aged blonde beauty surrounded by her menfolk. The three men deferred to her for introductions.

Darcy had not told her what to expect of his cousins, but she imagined they might be as haughty as Darcy himself was wont to be, perhaps reserved as well. She found them, however, quite the opposite. Colonel Fitzwilliam was not a handsome man, but he was in person and demeanour every bit the gentleman.

Viscount Saye was exceedingly handsome, and Elizabeth could see that he was well aware of the fact. He greeted Elizabeth by telling her how much he disliked most everyone. "Ladies most of all. I have no use for a woman who mistakes *arts et attraits* for *personnalité*."

"Then we agree," she said amiably. "I do not think coquettishness is any mark of an interesting character."

"Ahhh," said Saye, "and she was not flustered by my French. Well done, Miss Bennet. What else can you do?" He proceeded then to question her mercilessly on her accomplishments which, though scant, appeared to satisfy him.

"Let us permit Miss Bennet a few minutes to change and refresh herself," Lady Matlock decreed at last. "Mrs Banks will help you, Miss Bennet."

Mrs Banks was a kindly woman, though with all the dignity of her position. As she led Elizabeth into a luxuriously fitted guest apartment, Elizabeth considered asking her about the family member who had not received her—Miss Darcy. All attempts to hear of, speak of, or know of the girl who would be her sister had been dismissed or disregarded, and Elizabeth had no little concern regarding the possibility of befriending her.

Mrs Banks was swift and efficient, changing Elizabeth into her best evening gown, which was, she realised, woefully inadequate for her environs. She examined herself in the looking glass. *I am a country maiden, and this does not disguise that.*

Elizabeth's hair was always a struggle, even in the most practised hands, and Mrs Banks appeared startled by how much of it there was once she had released it from its pins. "My mother has always said that my hair belongs to a savage," she said cheerfully.

Mrs Banks smiled. "I was a lady's maid a long time ago, but I must admit, I have not seen its like. Quite beautiful my dear, but I must say, it does not seem to want to obey my orders."

As she began to plait and prod it into order, Elizabeth said casually, "I understood that Miss Darcy was in residence here."

The lady's hands did not still, but they did momentarily slow. "She is."

"Is she...?" Elizabeth paused, unsure how to ask whether Miss Darcy's absence was a protest against her brother's engagement. "I had hoped to meet her," she concluded.

Mrs Banks raised her eyes, and Elizabeth thought she seemed surprised. After a few moments, she lowered her eyes again, and continued her work. "What has Mr Darcy told you, dear?"

"Told me? Um…not…not very much. I know she is much younger than he is."

The lady worked in silence for some minutes, her brow furrowed and her lips pursed, but Elizabeth did not know whether it was the subject or her hair which caused Mrs Banks's consternation. At last, she quietly said, "It is not my place to tell you what ails the young lady—in truth, I hardly know myself—but she is not well."

"Of course," Elizabeth said immediately. "Forgive me for asking. I had no idea of anything…anything amiss."

IT WAS NATURALLY a matter of curiosity for her. What manner of problem ailed Miss Darcy? Sickness? Consumption? Why had Darcy told her nothing of the matter?

She put those thoughts aside as she returned to the drawing room, finding Darcy in close conference with his uncle and the colonel. All rose as she entered the room, and Lady Matlock announced, "Dinner is ready. We shall not stand on ceremony this night; we are family, so let us be at ease."

Darcy led her into the dining room, seating her on Lady Matlock's left. He sat across from her while Viscount Saye sat next to her. "Elizabeth, have you been much in London?" the viscount asked genially as the servants placed the soup on the table.

Elizabeth hesitated for a moment, knowing that they likely knew she had relations who lived in Cheapside and not wanting to introduce that subject just now. "Just a little, and mainly to visit relations. I know the amusements of town very little, as my father preferred to remain in the country."

"Certainly there is no shame in that," Lady Matlock proclaimed. "Until a young lady reaches a certain age, it is best, I think, that she be sheltered from much of what goes on. Too many a young lady has her head turned by some scoundrel simply because he dresses well and possesses a fine carriage."

"Yes, but enough about Saye," Colonel Fitzwilliam quipped from across the table.

"Why is my good name besmirched?" Saye protested, but Lord Matlock intervened.

"Your brother needs nothing more than a good wife to settle him, as do most young gentlemen in his position." His lordship gave serious looks around the table. "Marriage, as you know—"

"This conversation will not end well," Saye announced. "Time for a new subject. Elizabeth, you are the no one from nothing and nowhere who has managed to secure the second most eligible bachelor of the *ton*—the first being me, of course. Tell us how you did that."

The way he said it could only make Elizabeth laugh, even as she privately wondered who among Darcy's relations were privy to the truth of their engagement. Before she could reply, however, Saye continued, "I think I might know a friend of yours, another young lady who comes from Hertfordshire."

"Oh? Who is that?"

"A Miss Lillian Goddard."

The colonel hid a smirk before asking, "Miss Goddard is from Hertfordshire? I do not think I knew that."

She quickly tried to explain, "I cannot claim any great intimacy with her, but in fact, Darcy and I dined at their house, Ashworth, shortly after—"

Saye put down his fork with a loud clatter and glared at Darcy. "You dined with Miss Goddard?"

"It was back in November," Darcy replied.

"That is no excuse."

"In any case, she told me she had danced with you several times and you were as silent as a nun throughout."

"A man who felt less might speak more," the colonel teased.

"I am hardly the sort to go silent in the presence of a lady," Saye replied, sounding haughty. "I must have been ill."

"But you are usually so adept at lovemaking," the colonel replied.

"And do not forget it," Saye replied sternly.

"Yet somehow fumbled about with Miss Goddard? I cannot think why."

"I did not fumble anything," Saye replied, enunciating each word carefully.

"The report cannot be denied," Darcy said. "Or do you call Miss Goddard a liar?"

"I was probably drunk."

"When has that stopped you?" asked his brother.

"Boys..." His lordship was plainly displeased by the discussion, his brow deeply furrowed as he looked sternly about his dinner table. "Is this the best we can do for dinner conversation? If so, I despair of your generation."

Turning to his father, Saye said, "Miss Goddard's father is a baronet, but her uncle is Lord Winchester."

"Now that is a fine connexion," Lord Matlock said,

suddenly looking at Elizabeth with interest. "An intimate of yours?"

"No, not at all," Elizabeth replied honestly. "Ashworth is twelve miles from my father's house."

"We shall fix that straightaway. To Miss Bennet's new best friend," Saye decreed, raising his wine glass. Elizabeth, with a laugh, followed suit.

Her eyes fell upon Darcy. He was across from her, watching as his cousin teased her, and he had a soft, pleased expression on his countenance that gave her a flutter. When he saw her look at him, the corner of his mouth lifted in a half smile and she liked it; it felt sweet, a private moment in a crowd.

It was pleasing to watch Darcy among his relations. He was relaxed and more lively than she had ever seen him. His behaviour towards her was an equal source of pleasure—he was all ease and friendliness, paying her so many compliments that she found herself blushing nearly continually. On the whole, it made for a pleasant dinner, and as she and Lady Matlock withdrew, she felt there really might be some hope for felicity after all.

CHAPTER FIFTEEN

It was an unusual experience to withdraw with only one other lady, and Elizabeth remarked on it to Lady Matlock. "If nothing else, I am nearly always accompanied by at least two sisters, so there is never just myself and my hostess."

Lady Matlock smiled. "Yes, it certainly does me some good to have another lady about."

They entered the drawing room, and Lady Matlock nodded at the large pianoforte on the side of the room. "Do you play?"

"A little, though I would not consider myself proficient."

"Would you play for me now?"

"Of course." Elizabeth went to the instrument, running her hand along the fine polished wood surface. It was certainly an expensive instrument. There was music stacked on a table hidden behind it, and she shuffled through the selections, finding a piece she knew fairly well. "Shall I sing?"

"Please do." When she finished, Lady Matlock had nothing but compliments. "That was well done, my dear. Your voice is lovely, and you played very well."

"Thank you, ma'am." Elizabeth offered a slight curtsey as she left the instrument, joining Lady Matlock on the settee. "I fear I have not practised as I ought."

"There is always time for improvement, though once you are married, fewer will wish to hear you." She patted Elizabeth's hand. "I fear that dinner was not pleasing to you. You ate very little."

Turned as she was towards Lady Matlock, Elizabeth had a view of the door. It was slightly ajar, and she detected movement in the hall. To Lady Matlock, she said, "Not at all; it was delicious. Perhaps you are simply more accustomed to a table of gentlemen's appetites."

"That is quite likely," Lady Matlock agreed.

Again, Elizabeth perceived movement and believed she heard a footstep. Had the door opened a fraction of an inch wider?

"I hope you will consent to making some calls with me soon. I would like to introduce you to some of my friends."

Elizabeth understood that she had passed some sort of test and smiled, relieved. "I would be very pleased. Thank you." She stood then and asked, "Lady Matlock, would you excuse me a moment?"

Lady Matlock understood immediately—or presumed she did—and answered Elizabeth as if a call of nature were her object. "Of course."

Elizabeth thanked her and moved towards the door. Listening carefully, she believed she perceived some footsteps moving quickly as she left the drawing room. She climbed the stairs slowly, taking time to observe the elegance of the Matlock town house, from the wide stair treads beneath her feet to the paper used on the walls. About halfway up, her suspicions were confirmed; she heard a door close exquisitely softly as though the person closing it was taking care to avoid detection.

She went first to her apartment. Having presumed Miss Darcy to be like most young ladies her age, Elizabeth had brought her a present. She hoped she would appreciate the gesture if not the gift itself. "No one will speak of you to me," she murmured, "so it is to me to find out about you."

From the sounds of it, the room whose door had closed so softly was just beyond hers. She went to it, pressing her ear to the heavy oak and saying, "Miss Darcy?"

There was no sound from within.

"If you will forgive my impertinence, I would very much like to meet you. After all, we are to be sisters, are we not? I have brought you something. If you like ribbons, and I hope you do, I have taken what little patience I have for needlework and put your initials on them."

Still nothing.

"Initials were necessary, you see, for in a house with five sisters where ribbons, gowns, shoe roses, and reticules were always floating about, if you did not mind carefully where your things went, they could just as easily be claimed by another sister."

There was no sound, but Elizabeth fancied she could feel a presence from the other side of the door, as though someone was listening.

"I often think of the words of Cibber—you must know it —'*no Fiend in Hell can match the fury of a disappointed woman*'? But I think he was not quite correct, for truly, there can be no rage, no fury that is equal to that of a sister whose bonnet has been torn apart and made up new by another! Even if the bonnet in question was quite ugly and—"

Elizabeth stopped as the door was jerked open, and a girl

stood before her, looking at her with no little astonishment on her face. "I began to think you would never stop talking," she said with ill-disguised vexation.

It was a struggle to hide her own astonishment, for to see Georgiana Darcy was beyond all expectation. She was tall like her brother, and her figure was womanly and well-formed, but from the look of her hair and the condition of her fingernails, it had been some time since she had tended to her toilette. Her hair hung down her back, flat and lifeless, and she was wearing what must have been a servant's dress, old and grey and clumsily mended. The whole effect made Elizabeth feel a deep pity for her.

"It is a fault in my character," said Elizabeth with determined cheer. "Once I begin, I rarely find reason to stop. May I come in?"

"Come in here?"

"If I may," Elizabeth replied with a friendly smile. "I would not wish to intrude upon your privacy, but I have longed to meet you."

Miss Darcy looked at her, considering for a moment, then stepped back, wordlessly acquiescing, and Elizabeth entered.

The room was elegant but had plainly not been done up for a young lady. The furnishings were heavy and ponderous, made of ornately carved dark wood in the style of at least two decades past. The fabrics were dark-hued brocade with tassels and fringe in colours such as puce, olive, and mustard. The only mark of a young lady's presence was a shawl, cream-coloured, tossed over a cordovan chair.

Elizabeth turned her head to find the girl studying her. "You are pretty, Miss Bennet."

"Oh, do call me Elizabeth—we are to be sisters after all.

And thank you. You are quicker to think so than your brother was, but perhaps he has not shared that tale with you."

Miss Darcy shook her head, and Elizabeth told her of their first meeting and Darcy's ill-tempered 'tolerable but not handsome enough to tempt me' remark. She told the tale with great spirit, adding a giggle. "No, I can assure you, if you had told me that night that I had just met my future husband, I should have thought you mad!" She winced, hearing herself say the word 'mad' but it did not appear Miss Darcy noticed.

"So you married him?"

"Not yet. February tenth."

She realised then that she had not actually given the girl her gift and passed over the small parcel. Miss Darcy received it almost absently, staring at Elizabeth as she asked her to call her Georgiana. "Did you see me peeking at you?"

"I saw movement at the door. I thought it might be you."

"I wanted to get a look at you and see what you were like."

"I felt likewise towards you," Elizabeth replied lightly.

"And now that you have seen me…?" Georgiana raised her head quickly, her gaze almost challenging, with her chin thrust forward and an air of defiance about her. "Perhaps you wish you had not. I must not be at all what you expected."

There was hurt in the girl's eyes, and Elizabeth, having been told nothing about her, had no idea why it was there. One thing was certain, Georgiana Darcy, raised with every advantage that the Bennet sisters had not, was miserable. Elizabeth was stirred to befriend her.

"While it is true I knew not what to expect of you, it does

not follow that I am not glad to know you—because I am," she replied gently. "I look forward to knowing you better and hope you will allow me to come back soon. Will you?"

Georgiana seemed to consider it and, with a quick nod, agreed.

As Elizabeth descended the stair returning to the drawing room, she met Darcy, who had a worried frown creasing his countenance. He rushed towards her, taking her hands in his. "You are well? My aunt said you had gone to your bedchamber for some time. We thought perhaps you had taken ill."

"I am well. Forgive me, but I could not deny my curiosity to meet Georgiana. You have told me so little about her, I had begun to fear she already hated me."

Darcy's reaction to this news she could not have anticipated. He dropped her hands and stepped back, a deep shade of hauteur spreading over his face. He hissed, "You did what?"

"I knocked on the door," she replied, crossing her arms over her abdomen. "I…I had brought her some ribbons, which I gave to her and—"

"Ribbons? You brought her ribbons?" Darcy muttered some curse and turned away, raking his hands through his hair. "You have no idea—"

"Of course, I have no idea, because you have refused to utter so much as a syllable about her," Elizabeth replied with hushed ferocity.

"Now is neither the time nor the place to discuss her."

"She seemed to enjoy the visit."

"No!"

"Surely a friend would—"

"See here," he barked, seeming almost menacing. "My sister is not one of your country folk whose characters you can study."

Elizabeth drew in an unsteady breath, blinking back the angry tears stinging her eyes. She had not imagined arguing with Darcy right in the middle of his exalted relations' home on her first evening in residence. "I am not trying to study her character, but I am staying in the bedchamber adjacent to hers. Surely you cannot expect—"

"What I expect," he said, biting off each word, "is that you will do as I bid you."

Darcy's voice was loud, and Saye suddenly appeared from behind him. "His lordship wishes to retire," he said. He cast an eye over Elizabeth then looked at his cousin. "All is well?"

"Yes." Darcy scowled at him.

"Because it all seems rather shouty from where I stand. Really, Darcy, why are you being so missish? What is going on out here?"

Darcy ignored him and continued speaking to Elizabeth. "Georgiana is not well, and you should not trouble her."

Amid such a mixture of anger, embarrassment, and fear, she could do no less than say, tightly, "I had no intention of upsetting her."

"Good. Just leave her alone."

Elizabeth found she could not utter the least syllable, and indeed, could not bear to even look at Darcy. She allowed one stiff nod of her head to acknowledge him.

"Thank you." He relaxed by the slightest degree and held out his arm. "Join me then while I thank my aunt."

She laid her hand on his arm and allowed him to lead her

back into the drawing room. Saye had gone ahead of them; she could not imagine what he might have thought of it all.

WHEN DARCY HAD GONE, taking his black cloud with him, Lord Matlock retired. Elizabeth rose, thinking she ought to do likewise, but Saye forestalled her. "Mother? I learnt tonight that Darcy has kept Elizabeth quite in the dark about our dear Georgiana."

Lady Matlock, who had also risen, froze. Turning to Elizabeth, she said, "Indeed?"

Elizabeth flushed scarlet immediately and stammered, "Ah...no, I did not know...she is ill?"

Across the room, the colonel groaned and said, "Nothing? He told you nothing at all?"

Lady Matlock was studying her intently, and Elizabeth addressed her remarks to her. "Forgive me, but I thought I saw her looking through the door after we withdrew, and I... I went up to see her. I...I am to be her sister, after all, and my intentions were good, I assure you. I was not trying to intrude upon any family concerns."

"Our family concerns shall soon be yours as well." Lady Matlock sat heavily and passed one handsomely bejewelled hand over her forehead with a delicate sigh. "You must have been shocked to see her."

Elizabeth also re-took her seat, but slowly. "A little."

"He ought to have said something," Fitzwilliam opined with a significant look at his brother.

"Tell me something I do not know," Saye replied, then looked at his mother. Looks then continued all around the room while Elizabeth waited, wondering whether she was betraying Darcy by listening to that which he did not wish her to hear.

At length, Lady Matlock said, "She may seem mad, but she is not. At least…I do not think she is."

"Is not the wish to *seem* mad," Saye asked, "evidence enough that one *is* mad?"

The two gentlemen then began to tell Elizabeth the tale. Elizabeth felt anxiety twist in her gut—Darcy clearly did not wish her to know all this, yet his Fitzwilliam relations gave her no choice.

"It all started when Darcy and I hired a companion, a woman highly recommended but in whose character we were frankly deceived," said the colonel. He continued, explaining that Miss Darcy had been the mark of a seducer while on holiday at Ramsgate. She had been stopped within hours of leaving for Scotland, where the man would have married her over the anvil. "Had it happened, I have no doubt that she would have been even now abandoned by the man, her fortune of thirty thousand pounds in his grasping hand."

"How terrible," Elizabeth breathed. "Poor dear."

"That is, alas, not the end of it," Fitzwilliam continued. "Georgiana now does not see anyone, especially men, likely because…because…"

Uncertain, the colonel looked around and Elizabeth, imagining she understood him, said delicately, "She was most particularly injured?"

"As a man can injure a lady," Lady Matlock concluded. "Yes, dear, how good you are to understand us. She has been unwell—"

"Mad," Saye said flatly.

"Not mad," Fitzwilliam countered. "But not…not wholly

sane. Clearly we did fear for some time that she might be… increasing, which might have accounted for her behaviour."

"Her behaviour?" Elizabeth asked.

"For four months now, she does not leave her bedchamber, she sees no one, she scarcely eats," Saye told her. "As you likely saw, she does not tend to her appearance."

"She has not responded to cajoling, threats, punishments, or inducements of any sort," Fitzwilliam added.

"If it is discovered how she is, it will…it will be a blight on the family," Saye said. "We have considered sending her away for a bit, to rest and, we hope, improve."

Lady Matlock was shaking her head and frowning severely. "You mean *you* have considered it."

"And our father," the colonel told her. "It is not what any of us want, clearly, but she is not improving."

"No one is ever helped in those places," his mother argued. "And if the *ton* finds out, she will never be able to hold her head high in this town again."

"If she is prancing about dressed in Darcy's old breeches, I daresay she will not hold her head high regardless," Saye said.

"I am not surprised he was reluctant to speak of the matter," Elizabeth interjected.

"It was particularly painful for Darcy," Lady Matlock told her. "The poor boy always does feel guilty over everything, even that which is not his responsibility, and in this…well, his guilt was keen."

"Darcy brought her to Pemberley after it happened," Saye continued. "It was disastrous. Georgiana disappeared for three days altogether, no one knew where until someone in one of the villages found her. Then she locked herself in her room and would not leave, save at night."

"She refused to eat," Fitzwilliam added. "Made strange cuts on her arms with Darcy's letter opener, threatened to take poison..."

"My mother offered to take her in because Darcy tends to hover, and Georgiana needed, more than anything, some time to herself," Saye explained. "We hoped it would be of benefit to them both."

Elizabeth considered that, thinking of the man she had met back at the Meryton Assembly in October. How differently she should have judged him then, had she known the burdens that weighed upon those broad shoulders, the worries that were hidden behind his handsome brow!

"She was always the most pleasing child," Lady Matlock interjected. "She had the sweetest temper one could imagine."

"She was very kind to me," Elizabeth assured her.

"We do not know what will come of her. She is simply not recovering her spirits."

"I confess, I had no idea." Elizabeth looked around the room, seeing each of those remaining studying her carefully. Hesitantly, she added, "It seems Darcy wishes me to stay away from her so...I daresay I must."

"Of course," Lady Matlock said, sounding soothing. "While I cannot agree with him—"

"Nor I," the colonel interjected. "It seems...counter to the purpose. But allow me to speak to him on the matter. Darcy is a reasonable man above all and likely only reacted from surprise."

CHAPTER SIXTEEN

Her argument with Darcy, paired with the revelations of his aunt and cousins, made for a poor sleep, and Elizabeth thought she showed it plainly when Darcy called the next day. Saye immediately joined them in the sunny morning parlour, taking a seat very close to them and smiling in the manner of someone who expects a good show.

"I need a few moments with Elizabeth," Darcy told him, gesturing to other chairs at a greater distance.

"As you like," Saye mimicked Darcy's gesture but towards Elizabeth.

"I do not need a chaperon."

"My father thinks otherwise." With great ceremony, Saye opened the book he had brought in tucked beneath his arm. After a few long moments, he looked up and said, "Do go on. I presume you have not come here merely to stare at her?"

"Saye, I am hardly some green lad unable to control himself with a woman."

Saye licked his finger and turned a page with an elaborate sweep. "I am honour bound, Cousin."

Darcy rose and bent over the chair to murmur into his

cousin's ear. After a few indiscernible phrases, Saye protested, "Well, I attended the argument, ought not I be privy to the making up?"

Darcy straightened and sighed. "I thought you were going to Yorkshire today. Some house party or another?"

"I sent my regrets."

"Why?"

"Because I would rather be here."

Darcy towered above his cousin, clearly vexed, while Saye, unperturbed, feigned reading. At length, he closed the book and said, in much aggrieved accents, "If you must know, I got into a fight with Moore."

"About what?"

"A horse."

"A horse?"

"He wanted it, and I decided I did too. So I bought it."

"You bought your friend's horse out from under his nose? How could you do that to your friend?"

"It was prime horseflesh, and Moore is a flapdoodle," Saye retorted with a roll of his eyes that would have put Lydia to shame. "Are we here to discuss my horse or are you going to make amends with your lady? What matters is that I am going nowhere, and I have nothing else to do but read my book right here." Locking his eyes on Darcy's, Saye opened the book, again licked a finger, and turned a page.

Elizabeth bit her lip to hide her grin; for all their gentlemanly airs and titles and fortunes, at times they really were just overgrown boys.

"That is my book," Darcy said, his jaw clenched. "You are doing all that finger licking in my book."

"How else am I meant to turn a page?" Saye, wholly unrepentant, did it again.

Darcy studied him for a moment, towering over him with a glare that did not seem to bother his cousin in the least. Then, without warning, Darcy swiftly leant over, thrust his hands into his cousin's hair and mussed it about wildly. Saye cried out as if he had been burnt, rearing away from the assault and sending the book flying across the room. He leapt to his feet to get away from Darcy's hands. "What in the blazes is wrong with you?"

"I want you to leave!"

"Anyone might call, and here I am with lunatic hair!" Saye glared at his cousin. "And you might have caused material damage to my hair follicles!"

"True," Darcy agreed. "You ought to let your man see to you as soon as may be."

Saye pointed at him, scowling fiercely. "This is not over. You had better hope I do not lose any of them or there will be hell to pay."

Elizabeth giggled as Saye stalked from the room with one last resentful frown at his cousin. Darcy rescued his book and moved towards Elizabeth's sofa, sitting down beside her. "He cannot abide the notion of losing his hair. He will have his man massaging his head and applying tonics for the next half an hour at least."

Elizabeth laughed lightly, but her eyes were trained on Darcy. He was the first to speak and did not—unsurprisingly —offer a direct apology. "Elizabeth, Georgiana...um, I intended to speak to you of Georgiana many times since we became engaged."

Elizabeth laid her hand on top of his, sliding her fingers between his. "It must have been difficult to speak of, particularly when we were often with so many others."

"Yes, that is true. She is ill, as you might have seen. That is to say, of course you saw, I would think you a simpleton indeed if you had not noticed—but of course you did—and I am well aware you are not a simpleton. She is not well…not since last summer when…"

After he trailed off, Elizabeth said, "Your cousins spoke to me about what happened."

"Do not blame her," he said immediately. "The fault is mine and mine alone."

"I should think the fault belongs to her seducer."

"She is severely melancholic and at times has no wish even to live. Fitzwilliam and I had hoped that staying here with Lady Matlock would help her, but so far it has not."

Elizabeth nodded. "And the physicians? What have they said of her condition?"

"There is nothing wrong with her that can be fixed by medicines or even with bleedings. She bears no fevers, no rashes, no broken bones, and no ill humours." He paused and then said, "They believe it is likely an affliction of her mind, and that at this point, it is…unlikely to improve without…"

"Without what?"

"A stay at some place like Ticehurst." He paused, misery etching sorrowful lines on his countenance.

"What is Ticehurst?" Elizabeth asked gently.

Darcy did not look at her but frowned at the carpet by his feet. "A place where a young woman of means who has…run into difficulty…might go for some rest."

"You do not mean…?"

"Not that sort of difficulty," he said hastily. "Happily, we have been spared that much at least. Nervous complaints—that sort of thing is what I mean."

For a moment Elizabeth did not understand, but then she suddenly did. "An asylum?"

Darcy did not reply for a moment, then nodded. "It is nothing at all like Bedlam. I have been categorically opposed to the very notion of it, but Fitzwilliam thinks it might be needful." He raised his head then to look at her and said, "And perhaps it is. Perhaps my wife might not like this potential scandal in her house."

Elizabeth opened her mouth to demur, but Darcy stopped her. "Please consider—there are implications that far outreach one pleasant little chat in a bedchamber. You and I have difficulties enough already, and we shall have, one day, our own children to consider."

Although she could not argue his point, it did seem rather drastic. From what she had seen, Darcy's sister was no raving madwoman. She was suffering from heartbreak—suffering it more theatrically than most, but still, it was heartbreak. His inability to allow her opinion in the matter was frustrating. After all, she did have four sisters. She knew something of young ladies, certainly more than this band of young men did.

"I think she needs a friend," Elizabeth offered. "I cannot think it good for her to be locked away in that dark room, fine as it is, all alone all the time."

"Elizabeth. I do comprehend that you wish to help." He sounded as if he were speaking to a small child who wanted to stir Cook's bowl of muffin batter. "But right now, what I need you to do is devote yourself to the tasks ahead of you here that will help you forward yourself in London. That will be of use to us all, more than you can possibly know. Do not worry yourself for Georgiana."

"Do you mean to forbid me to see her?" she asked carefully.

"I would rather you did not, but I shall not forbid it."

It made no sense to her. Why would he wish her to ignore a lonely young woman living mere steps down the hall from her, a young woman who clearly needed a friend? It made her wonder whether *he* was the one who was mad, but she could not say that.

"It seems strange to me. I know you thought your aunt might help, but I am nearer in age to Georgiana and well accustomed to ladies of her years, and having young sisters and—"

"And I am embarrassed." Having said so, Darcy was immediately on his feet and across the room by the fire, stiff and enraged. Elizabeth bit back a sigh. *Well, it has been nearly twelve hours since our last quarrel.*

She rose and followed him. As soon as she drew near to him, he began to speak, "Do not think me insensible of the irony. I was hard in my judgment of your younger sisters and their behaviour in Meryton, yet my own sister is guilty of worse. Perhaps that is why I was critical, for I have seen what may come from even a moment of negligence."

"But this is nothing to do with them. It has only to do with Georgiana."

"Yes." He turned to look at her. "And what has happened to her is entirely my mistake. *Mine*. And I shall be the one to help her get well again. I did not wish for Lord and Lady Matlock to shoulder the burden of her care, but Fitzwilliam is also her guardian, and he insisted. But the notion of sending my...my...you in there to fix what I have broken is positively insupportable."

It was the '*my...my...you*' which truly set her hackles up. Could he not refer to her as his betrothed? His future wife? His intended? But she did no more than press her lips together in a thin line before saying mildly, "Well, that is certainly a prideful view of the matter. I should think you would want her well no matter who helps her accomplish it."

He opened his mouth to reply but was prevented from so doing by Colonel Fitzwilliam, who very nearly burst into the room. "What on earth did you do to Saye, Darcy? I have never even heard of half the curse words he is using to describe you, and that includes those used by both the French and Spanish armies."

LADY MATLOCK'S object in bringing Elizabeth to London had been to introduce her to the ladies of her circle, and thus did the two ladies begin almost immediately to make rounds of calls. They were more arduous than pleasant, and it did not take Elizabeth long to realise that most of the ladies she met had less a desire to meet her than to examine her.

The first call was to a Lady Wellburton and her daughter, Lady Grace, a languid blonde of fine fortune. Lady Wellburton was evidently an intimate of Lady Matlock's, and the two of them were soon giggling like schoolgirls over some *ton* gossip while Lady Grace sipped tea next to Elizabeth. Elizabeth made many attempts at conversation with Lady Grace, with little success; the lady answered as briefly as possible, asked nothing of Elizabeth herself, and in all manner of doing, made it nearly impossible to hold a conversation.

A Mrs and Miss Davies were next. They were both quite nice, talking animatedly and asking questions and the time flew by. When they moved to depart, however, Elizabeth was obliged to return to the drawing room unexpectedly, for Lady Matlock believed she had dropped her handkerchief. As Elizabeth approached the door, she heard Miss Davies speaking to someone else—other ladies had called while they were there—saying, "...certainly not a beauty, no great wit, even her figure was very nearly boyish! I cannot think what Mr Darcy sees in her! She yammered on endlessly about Hertfordshire as if anyone should care—what must he be thinking to offer for such a lady?"

Her head high, Elizabeth re-entered the room. Miss Davies startled, her mouth agape—she did at least have the graciousness to blush—and then said, "Oh, Miss Bennet. I thought you and Lady—"

"Lady Matlock seems to have misplaced her handkerchief. Ah, I see it over there." With quick steps, Elizabeth retrieved the lost article, then thanked her two hosts again and left.

Similar scenes were repeated over the next days in one luxurious drawing room after another. Elizabeth thought it a shame how her mother might have gossiped for days at even a glimpse of the silk wall hangings and carved wood furnishings in the rooms she entered, but such views could not compensate for the chilly receptions. A Miss Rhodes and a Miss Owens spoke the slightest number of syllables to Elizabeth that civility required while their mothers conversed with Lady Matlock. The home of a Mrs Archer was next—she was sitting with her mother, Mrs Featherstone, and younger sister, Miss Featherstone. The two younger ladies were falsely kind with a patronising air. "You have never been to town for the Season? Never?"

Elizabeth contrived to keep her voice even, though the other ladies' voices had risen in dramatic disbelief. "I have not."

"Why, I do not think I have ever heard of such a thing! Alice, could you imagine it?"

"I assure you, it was not such a hardship."

"Oh, but it is! It surely is! Why, I think I might have simply died! Would you not have died, Agnes?"

"Oh, yes. I would certainly have died," Miss Featherstone agreed. "Or at the very least, wished for death."

To this, Elizabeth could only offer a small, disingenuous smile.

It was not all horrible. There was one lady, Miss Jane St Claire, who seemed to be truly amiable and kind. The two ladies spoke easily on music and poetry, as well as Miss St Claire's plans to marry in March. She was disarmingly honest about her betrothal. "My dowry is generous, and his family, while ancient and titled, is in dire need of funds. It is not any great romance between us, but he is a good man, and I enjoy his company. And..."—she shrugged—"he is the tallest man who asked me. I have no wish to tower fearsomely over my husband." It was then Elizabeth noticed that she *was* a rather tall lady.

Alas, by the end of Elizabeth's first week in London, Miss St Claire was the only lady who had shown promise as a friend. It came as something of a shock to her, she who had always been well-liked among her peers. She stood thinking of it late one afternoon, watching the carriages pass on the street below.

There was a sinking feeling in her chest and gut that did not respond to reason or reassurance. She began to find meaning in everything and anything. Darcy had not yet taken her to the opera or the theatre. Was it a sign he was ashamed of her? Did he regret her already? Had she disappointed him?

She had considered it often of late, what Darcy's opinion meant to her. It was not easy to own to it, but somewhere along the way she had formed a desire to make him proud. *Of course, I want to be a good wife to whomever I should marry.* But she knew, in more honest hours, that was not the whole of it.

In any case, it did not seem she would make him proud. She seemed to be failing miserably, in fact.

Darcy himself seemed quite different to her as well. They had argued in Hertfordshire, it was true, but there were other times, happy times, and those times had been increasing in both frequency and duration. Now they were never alone; they never had time to really talk or laugh or... or kiss. Much as she hated to admit it, she missed that. What did it all mean? *You are being silly,* she scolded herself, but she did not think she was. It was difficult enough to marry a man one scarcely knew without being thrust into a strange society as well.

All she could think of was her happy life in Hertfordshire and what she would leave behind, and panic began to beat at her ribs like a trapped bird, furiously seeking relief. She was not given to self-doubt and ill-humour, but neither was she accustomed to scenes where she felt such inadequacy.

Alas, these scenes, these people, she could not escape. It reminded her of Netherfield Park. She had known immediately that she was unwanted when she arrived to care for Jane and so had remained upstairs as much as she could without being rude—not because she feared them, but because she had no wish to be where her company was so clearly unwanted.

And now she had the duty of not only remaining where she was unwanted, but in making herself desirable to them, to Darcy himself first and foremost. She could only hope it would not prove a Sisyphean effort. A woman took on her husband's status; the material change would be hers. Elizabeth Bennet would become Mrs Darcy, but Mr Darcy stayed Mr Darcy. It was the way of the world after all. For the first time she wondered what becoming mistress of Longbourn might have been like. At least she would have had her friends.

Before she knew what she was about, she was in the hall, tapping gently at the door of her soon-to-be sister. "Georgiana? May I come in?"

At length, the door was opened, and Georgiana stood before her. Today she wore breeches—Darcy's? They fell to her ankles, so likely so—and a child's gown over them which was only as long as her knees. Her hair hung unbound but at least it appeared to be clean, which Elizabeth thought was a good sign.

"What is it?"

"I…uh…" Elizabeth stammered, having not considered what she would say to the girl. "H-how are you today?"

"The same as I usually am," the girl said, though her words were not bitter but emotionless, merely reporting a fact.

Elizabeth cast about desperately for something to say to the girl, but it was Georgiana who broke the silence. "Has my brother forbidden you to see me?"

"Not exactly. I believe he thinks that…" Elizabeth had no idea how to finish her sentence and so gave a little shrug.

"He thinks lunacy is catching," Georgiana said and made a little snorting sound that Elizabeth realised belatedly was laughter.

"It is not that," Elizabeth told her. "He…he wants to be the one to help you through your troubles and likely worries that I shall impede your progress. I just do not know… A gentleman might not understand how much a lady sometimes needs her sisters."

Her words made Georgiana's countenance harden. "Do not think you need to come in here and heal me. I do not need anything."

With a rueful smile, Elizabeth said, "No, I meant *me.* I need a sister. I, um…I am accustomed to always having someone about who I can talk to about the troubles of the day, both large and small. I…I guess it seemed natural to me to seek out…seek out my sister here in London. I mean we are not yet sisters, of course, but…I am engaged to your brother so…"

It sounded selfish and almost ridiculous to her ear even as she said it. The poor dear was struggling under the weight of her own misfortunes; surely she had not the energy required to listen to Elizabeth rattle away about some silly women who did not like her.

"You want to speak to me about the troubles of the day?" Georgiana asked, clearly shocked.

"Forgive me," Elizabeth said, turning. "I should not have disturbed you. I shall leave you to your rest now."

Before she could take a step, Georgiana cried out, "Wait!"

Elizabeth turned back. The alteration in Georgiana's air was striking. From contrary and tired, she seemed to have become almost eager. Colour had appeared in her cheeks and even her eyes seemed brighter.

"I have never had a sister," she said. "I am afraid I do not know much of anything to help you."

"A willing ear will do," Elizabeth told her with a gentle smile. "Just listen to me whinge, and then assure me that anyone who dared to cross me is vile and due a vicious case of spots all over her face."

To this Georgiana laughed outright, and the sound was pleasant. "Or that she will be cursed to trip and make a fool of herself when she dances at Almack's." She stepped out of the room and closed the door behind her. "Shall we go to your bedchamber?"

Elizabeth followed Georgiana into her own guest bedchamber; light and airy, it was one in which a young lady should reside. In marked contrast, Georgiana's bedchamber seemed like it should contain a dyspeptic old man who read religious treatises and thought music was evil. She wondered why they had chosen to install Georgiana in that particular room.

Georgiana, looking around her, asked, "Do you like it here?"

Elizabeth thought about that simple question framed in the context of her panic only minutes before and hedged her response. "Lord and Lady Matlock have been very kind to me."

Georgiana walked across the room and took a seat at Elizabeth's dressing table, facing away from the looking glass and into the room. "I can hear most everything that is said on the first floor from my room, you know—some trick of the chimneys, I think, and the way things echo through the antechamber. I have heard almost all."

So that is why she chooses that room. Elizabeth sat on the bed and said with a nervous chuckle, "I am sure I probably do not want to know half of it."

"Saye likes you, which is something. Richard does as well, but he is more inclined to approve of people than the rest of them. My aunt does too, and the earl…well, he is starting to like you. Lady Catherine, as you might have guessed, despises you."

"Yes, that is no surprise."

"She has long wanted my brother to marry Cousin Anne, but that was never going to happen, no matter how much Lady Catherine fussed about it."

"I understand Miss de Bourgh has a sickly constitution?"

"She makes much of small problems. A headache sends her to bed for a week, and she is so often abed for her monthlies that she ought to just call them her weeklies."

Elizabeth laughed, and Georgiana looked startled; evidently she had not meant to be funny.

"Do you love my brother?" she asked. She had a piercing way of studying a person—she pinned them in her gaze, seeming to expect dishonesty. Under such scrutiny, it was impossible to lie.

"What have you heard of our engagement?" Elizabeth asked, watching as Georgiana arose and perambulated about the room, examining the book on Elizabeth's night table and her handkerchief, and even uncapping the little bottle of scent on her dressing table.

"Nothing, really. I heard when my brother called on Uncle to tell him, but I noticed that he did not say he loved you. In such cases as these, however, love is assumed."

"He does not love me," Elizabeth admitted. "Our engagement came about in a rather unusual way."

It was likely very wrong of her—indeed, she was quite certain Darcy would be displeased—but she found herself confessing the truth to Georgiana. Georgiana was in turns shocked, amazed, and appalled. "Miss Bingley did that?" She looked wide-eyed and as though she was suppressing a laugh. "I should never have imagined her to be so…or to do anything like... And so you chose my brother over your cousin?"

"It was an easy choice. My cousin has little to recommend him save being presumed heir to my father's estate. I knew I could never respect him. I can respect your brother, but um..."

Unexpectedly, a sob rose up in her throat, and she coughed around it. Her failures among Lady Matlock's set were evidently weighing on her more than she had realised. She dropped her face into one hand and sighed. "I fear that neither of us considered...or at least *I* did not consider that..."

"What?"

"I do not really belong here," Elizabeth said quickly. "Not with a man like your brother, not in drawing rooms such as these. I have nothing of my own and...and I fear marrying into it does not bring acceptance in this circle."

She would not cry—in this she was determined—but she did need a moment to compose herself. A hand, thin, bony, and cold, touched her, and Elizabeth nearly shrieked but stopped herself at the very last moment. Instead, she raised her head to see Georgiana looking at her with a worried frown. "But you have only been here a week, have you not?"

Elizabeth swallowed and forced herself to look more cheerful. "A bit early to declare failure, I know. I assure you, I am not always such a ninny."

"I think it might be daunting for any lady, no matter how brave, to spend endless hours simply meeting new people," Georgiana said, sounding very loyal, much to Elizabeth's surprise. "But you must be doing other things too. Do you like shopping? I am sure that must be occupying much of your time as well."

"Shopping? Oh, well..." Elizabeth made a face that was half smile and half frown. "I am afraid I do not much like shopping."

"But you are a bride!" Georgiana looked shocked. "And you know, a new-married lady does require many new clothes, and you, well, might...that is to say..." She trailed off, blushing deeply, then dipped her head awkwardly.

After a pained moment—pained for Georgiana but not Elizabeth—Elizabeth reached out and touched her arm. "Please dear, you can speak plainly to me."

"Town and country are not the same," she said, looking terribly uncomfortable. "You do not want to appear as though you do not know the difference. Everyone here has an entirely different wardrobe for London than for their country homes, and Mrs Darcy will be expected to have the same."

"A whole different wardrobe? Good heavens!"

Georgiana nodded. "My aunt is forever shopping. Every day, almost. And my friends from school...well, they spend years poring over the plates, getting ready for their first Seasons, and then after that, getting their trousseaux... Forgive me, are you well?"

Elizabeth laughed. "Yes. Only slightly faint, that is all. Would that I might have a second Elizabeth to buy all those gowns for me! But no, I know you are entirely correct. I think my mother will have expected me to shop, in fact, and will likely box my ears to find I have not."

"My aunt will love to help you, I am sure."

"And I shall be most grateful for it." On an impulse Elizabeth leant over, kissing the girl on the cheek. "Of course you are right. Thank you."

CHAPTER SEVENTEEN

As was his custom on Twelfth Night, Sir William Lucas hosted a gathering for nearly all the younger people and families within the district. Lucas Lodge was already humming with revelry when the Bennet carriage arrived. The men of the militia, bored and a bit discontented after all the Christmas festivities, had arrived *en masse* and were prepared to dance, which delighted Sir William to no end. Jane smiled seeing Charlotte Lucas in a corner, speaking once again with Lieutenant Denny, who had always been attentive to her.

There were several local gentlemen in attendance. Mr Howe was a pleasant though plain gentleman of six-and-twenty, who was heir to an estate approximately ten miles from Longbourn; Mr Willmer was the friend of Mr Howe, reported to be the second son of a baronet from somewhere in Essex; Mr Abell, at four-and-thirty, was likely the eldest of the unwed gentlemen and the current master of an estate about the size of Longbourn called Aylesbury; and finally, Mr Scott, who was the handsomest of the gentlemen, and was heir to an estate worth nearly as much as Netherfield.

His father was a squire, and alas, it seemed the distinction was felt keenly by his son, who was largely regarded as haughty. *Perhaps he is not, not truly,* Jane thought hopefully, thinking of Mr Darcy. *Perhaps he is only misunderstood.*

During the course of the evening, she learnt that Mr Willmer was recently engaged. Her mother had it from Mr Howe's mother, who it would seem had harboured hopes for her own daughter and was grieved by the announcement. The dancing began, and Jane noticed the approach of Mr Howe. She gave her mother a look, and Mrs Bennet gave a proud nod in return, both of them anticipating Jane accepting his offer to dance.

"Miss Bennet, you are looking very well this evening," he said.

"I thank you, sir."

"I wonder, Miss Bennet, whether you would be so inclined—?"

"It would be my pleasure."

He drew back. "I beg your pardon."

"Forgive me," Jane said, feeling all the discomfort of presumption.

"Think nothing of it," he said with an easy smile. "My sister, you see, is exceedingly shy, and since her come out, she has not had much success in recommending herself to the other young ladies. I wonder whether I might introduce her to you."

"Of course," Jane agreed through gritted teeth, and thus it was that she spent the first two dances with Miss Howe, an awkward girl of seventeen, who had little to say on any topic and seemed vexed by her brother's interference.

Silence having fallen between the two ladies, Jane finally excused herself, walking towards her mother. As she passed the pianoforte, she was approached by Mr Scott, who looked bored.

After exchanging the required pleasantries, Mr Scott gestured towards the instrument. Her sister Mary was seated there with Maria Lucas, playing for the dancers, and they moved to the side so as not to disturb their playing.

"Miss Bennet, I do not believe I have ever heard you play."

"I am afraid I am not gifted musically," Jane admitted.

He shrugged. "Perhaps you simply did not take the time to practise."

Jane did not know what to say to that. She merely smiled and replied, "Likely, you are correct."

"You do not sing, then?"

"No. I do like to draw, however." Mr Scott did not seem to hear her, so Jane, summoning her courage, said, "Perhaps, if you would like to call sometime, I may show you my sketches. I have several of the landscapes around the neighbourhood, which I think turned out well."

Mr Scott offered her a disinterested smile. "Thank you. Alas, I am to leave Hertfordshire next week, off to visit some friends in Derbyshire. I believe your sister will soon be a resident of that county, is that not so?"

Next week? Jane blushed at his gentle rebuff. After all, if he had wished to call, surely he would have found time in the course of a week to do so. He simply did not wish it. "Um, yes, my next younger sister, Elizabeth, will marry Mr Darcy of Pemberley in Derbyshire."

"Very well for her." Mr Scott grinned in a way that was half wry and half roguish. "You know, I always had a bit of a *tendré* for your sister, but...well, I am nothing to Mr Darcy, to be sure! I hope she is very happy with him."

Mr Scott liked Lizzy? I never would have guessed it. She said, "I believe she will be."

She danced with Lieutenant Chamberlayne after that and then went to her mother, who scolded her violently for not having danced enough. Jane smiled demurely through the tirade, hoping no one noticed.

The rest of the night passed in much the same way. She danced with several soldiers, which prompted another lecture from her mother on how she was far too beautiful to be a soldier's wife. She watched Denny continue to flirt with Charlotte, and she spent some time sitting beside her mother listening to the town matrons' gossip, the bulk of which centred on Lizzy—Lizzy's great match to Mr Darcy and the beautiful gowns she would need to purchase for her new life as Mrs Darcy.

These were the things they used to say of her: the great match she would make, the many gowns she would have, the house, the carriages. It had always been Lizzy they fretted over, fearing she would never attract a wealthy husband. Oh, she begrudged her sister none of it, to be sure! The shoe had been shoved onto the other foot quite unexpectedly, however, and Jane could not deny that it pinched.

SEVERAL DAYS LATER, Jane Bennet sat quietly pretending to crochet some lace, but in truth, she was so upset, she could do little more than make knots and snarls. Her younger sisters had gone to call at Lucas Lodge, and she had been left alone with her mother when Mrs Philips called.

Mrs Bennet and her sister were discussing yet again Jane's failure to secure Mr Bingley.

"Perhaps it is her age," Mrs Philips suggested. "Once Elizabeth marries, it may be prudent to suggest that she is the eldest sister. Otherwise the men might think Jane has been passed over and is on the shelf!"

"Three and twenty is certainly not on the shelf, not by any means!"

"But in London, these great men meet ladies coming out at only eighteen or nineteen years old. Compared to them, twenty-three likely seems very old indeed! Best if they think her only twenty or twenty-one, like Elizabeth."

Mrs Bennet clucked nervously, "I am just worried that if she does not marry soon, her beauty will begin to fade, and then who knows what might happen!"

Were they right? Was she old? It was as good a reason as any, for try as she might, she could think of no reasonable explanation for Mr Bingley to have abandoned her. He had seemed so sincere, and she had been certain he felt for her just as she had for him. Could his affection have waned so quickly? Jane blinked rapidly, seeking to dispel the tears which had sprung into her eyes.

Mrs Bennet lowered her voice, though Jane was still able to hear her quite clearly. "Now that other gentlemen see how Bingley has put her aside, they will do likewise. No man wants what another has discarded."

"But surely Lizzy will help her."

"I count on very little where that girl is concerned," Mrs Bennet announced, giving Mrs Philips a significant look. "And in any case, Mr Bingley is Mr Darcy's closest friend. I am sure whatever it was that put him off will be spread abroad to the rest of their friends."

Was that true? She had never considered that before, and the thought appalled her. She knew why Mr Darcy was marrying Lizzy, even if her mother did not, and it was not romantic. Furthermore, she was well aware of how much their family dismayed the gentleman and how little he would likely want them around him in the future—even his wife's dearest sister. No doubt he would wish to forget the Bennets ever existed. She swallowed against the hurt of that thought.

Jane looked at her mother and aunt gossiping carelessly over Jane's lost love, and for a brief moment she felt a pulse of anger the likes of which she could not remember ever feeling before. If she had grown old, it was because she had wasted too many years being particular—and all because her mother had taught she could ignore prudence. It required Mr Bingley's defection to teach her to be sensible about how far her beauty would get her with a wealthy bachelor. A lady like herself—pretty but with no fortune or name to offer—was good for some diversion in the country, but nothing more.

"What time will Mr Collins arrive tomorrow?" She heard Mrs Philips ask her mother, and Jane sat up a bit straighter.

She excused herself from her mother's parlour and went to her bedchamber, where she sat staring at herself in the looking glass, her heart pounding in her chest while she tested her own resolve.

What if I were to marry Mr Collins? I would have a home, and I would be married. His living is good, and one day I would be mistress of Longbourn. Mama would never need to worry on that account, ever again.

As for Mr Collins himself…his person was not so very pleasing, but as his wife, she might encourage him to indulge a little less and bathe a little more. Perhaps a different style for his hair might suit him better.

As for his character, he was neither mean nor vicious. He

was not the most intelligent of men, but he was educated, was he not? He could not be entirely stupid, and he had made a fortunate alliance with the noble house of de Bourgh. Surely a woman such as Lady Catherine would not select a parson for her parish who was entirely without merit.

I could do it. I could be wife to Mr Collins and find contentment in my situation.

"Mrs Collins," Jane whispered into the mirror. "Mrs Jane Collins."

CHAPTER EIGHTEEN

INTENDING TO ACT ON GEORGIANA'S GOOD COUNSEL, THE next morning Elizabeth went to Lady Matlock's dressing room. She resisted the impulse to shift on her feet as she stood there watching the great lady in her corset and petticoats—but somehow still resplendent—sitting at her dressing table having her hair arranged. It had not escaped her notice that whether at the breakfast table or in her formal portraiture, Lady Matlock always looked impeccable and beautiful. Did Darcy expect that of her? No doubt his mother had been much the same, and she thought, not for the first time, of how incongruous it was that a lady like she should end up married to a man like Mr Darcy.

"What is it, dear?" Lady Matlock asked over her shoulder, looking around her maid who was putting the finishing touches on her hair for the morning.

"I wondered whether I might ask something of you."

"Of course."

"As has been said, I have not been much in town, and in not so many days here I can see that my gowns are"—she glanced down at her simple muslin frock—"not as they should be."

"Your gowns are very pretty, dear, and quite becoming, but I believe I understand you. The town bronze they call it." Lady Matlock smiled. "In any case, any woman about to be married needs new clothes, not just you."

Not just a lady undertaking such a substantial elevation in station, you mean. Elizabeth smiled wryly but did not voice those thoughts. "Just so. I understand the Season will require quite a lot, but in truth, Mr Darcy has not even told me how much he intends to be here or whether he wishes to remain at Pemberley."

Lady Matlock laughed lightly. "If I know my nephew, he might like to run off to Pemberley and never again be forced to make idle chit-chat in a ballroom, but we shall shop regardless."

Lady Matlock's maid finished with her hair, and her ladyship nodded at her, then rose from the little seat to don her morning gown. "Let us begin today."

DARCY HAD BEEN WELL pleased to hear that Elizabeth and Lady Matlock intended to shop. In fact, so pleased was he, and so eager to undertake the bills, that it shamed her—was her mode of dress really so bad? She had not thought it as dreadful as that.

But everything had been arranged, and Darcy kissed her hand and would not hear of Mr Bennet awaiting any bills. It was a good thing too, for the first bolts of fabric Elizabeth laid her hands on were already far in excess of anything she or her father had ever seen before. Evidently, Mrs Darcy would require a full wardrobe—shoes, pelisses, day gowns, night gowns, evening gowns, walking gowns—and she should have been at it from nearly the second she set foot in London.

It was a piece of good fortune for Elizabeth that at one of Lady Matlock's favourite dressmaker's, they came across an order that had been cancelled only hours previously, which meant she could have something for immediate use. The gown was a silver gauze muslin over white satin with sizeable puffed sleeves and a little train. It was nothing Elizabeth Bennet would have chosen, but perhaps Elizabeth soon-to-be Darcy should.

The gown fit nearly perfectly save for the bodice. Elizabeth was light and athletic, and whomever this gown had been measured for was evidently far more endowed. "No matter," said the dressmaker. "I have made less fit more. I have a secret weapon, you see."

She disappeared a moment then came back bearing what looked like two small, kidney bean pillows, and before Elizabeth could speak a word, she had thrust them into the bodice of Elizabeth's gown, poking and tugging and arranging the busks such that the illusion of an ample breast was created. So long as she did not dare breathe, she did credit to it. "You do not think it too flashy?" she asked Lady Matlock quietly while the dressmaker pinned her hem.

"Flashy?" Lady Matlock asked. "Oh, no, of course not. It is very elegant, particularly for evening."

And as she looked on, somewhat amazed by seeing herself—this town version of herself—emerge, the dressmaker made further suggestions. "You will want your hair a bit more this way." She pushed Elizabeth's hair higher, arranging some of the curls here and there, leaving some down. "And let these tumble like so. Tell your maid; she will know what I mean."

"Oh yes," Lady Matlock agreed, a beaming smile on her lovely face as she stood behind Elizabeth. "Just like that." And Elizabeth thought she could perhaps seem like she belonged in this woman's sphere, that no one would look askance when she was introduced as the future niece of this elegant countess. She did not look like herself at all, but then again, was that not the object of all this?

"I think," said Lady Matlock, coming closer to her, "this will do very well for my friend's ball two nights from now. Do you know all the dances?"

"As long as there is not a waltz," Elizabeth said with a smile.

The dressmaker chuckled. "You had better not waltz in this dress, not unless you batten down the hatches first, if you take my meaning."

London had been full of arguments and distance, conversations held in the presence of inquisitive cousins, and little else, and Elizabeth was determined that tonight, at least, they would have something more. Something more akin to the tender moments, the private times in her sitting room or his carriage, something which could reassure her that the more ardent Darcy she knew in Hertfordshire was still within him.

She continued to feel all the dismay of believing that her engagement—unorthodox as it was—had come about largely as a result of his…well, his lust for her. But now she worried that even that had cooled. What would they have if he lost his attraction to her even before they married? She had reconciled herself to it, or so she believed, and hoped they might build upon it. But what if all chance of that was gone before they began?

Each successive day in London produced a greater distance between them—more politeness, more discomfort, and less ease. Darcy was not unkind to her, but she wondered whether she had disappointed him, whether he had begun to regret their engagement or his hasty words that night at Netherfield Park. She could only hope that seeing her in an elegant, expensive gown purchased at a London dress shop and worn at a London ball would relieve him. And even as she hoped it, she wondered when what he thought and felt had grown so important to her.

The preparations for a ball at Longbourn were noisy, chaotic, even violent at times, as shoe roses were hunted for, gowns were exchanged, hastily mended, or altered, and necklaces exchanged or lost or found. Fights broke out over the least thing, anticipation made them all mad—it was in all ways terrible and wonderful. Elizabeth found that she missed it rather awfully as she was trussed into her gown within the relative peace of the Matlock town house before the Barrington ball.

Lady Matlock's maid had studied the latest hair arrangements from France, and between her own ideas and the directions of the modiste, an elaborate contrivance of curls was situated atop Elizabeth's head. Nothing about any of it bespoke comfort—and at a certain angle she feared she looked like Miss Bingley—but there was no doubt she looked like she belonged in town.

Lady Matlock entered just as the maid finished. "Elizabeth, are you ready? Well! I see you are! Let me have a look. Very, very nice my dear. Only one thing missing." Elizabeth opened the case she was handed to reveal a three-strand silver and seed pearl necklace with matching ear bobs. Lady Matlock added, "Darcy might have another idea, but being that he has not seen the dress, perhaps not."

The maid was already fastening it—apparently, a demurral was quite out of the question—so Elizabeth uttered her thanks. "I cannot tell you how much I appreciate it. It is beautiful, Lady Matlock, and suits perfectly."

Elizabeth descended the stair of Matlock House cautiously. The town bronze required a certain rigidity, it seemed, or things might fall out of place. She wondered whether this was the 'certain something in her air' that Miss Bingley had said was the mark of an accomplished lady and had to stifle a giggle.

The colonel and Saye were at the bottom of the stair and gave their unstinting approval to Elizabeth and Lady Matlock. Lord Matlock descended only a few moments later, to the surprise of all. "Why do you all look at me so? Was I not included in the invitation?"

"Of course, you were," said her ladyship. "But I had no notion that you intended to join us."

"I do still like to surprise you, my dear," he said with an almost roguish grin. "Miss Bennet, I shall open the ball with my wife, but if you will permit me a space on your card as well, I should be most obliged."

Such a distinction, Elizabeth knew, would raise her credit substantially. It would be recognised among those in attendance that she had his lordship's favour. "I thank you, sir. It would be an honour."

She had donned her pelisse by the time Darcy arrived, bringing a cold draught and the faint air of impatience with him, and by that time Lady Matlock was keen to get to the ball, so he would see her new gown at the ball. She did see his eyes move quickly over her hair but knew not whether it meant he liked or disliked it; it may have been mere absence of thought.

It seemed to Elizabeth a great waste to use carriages to go to a ball that was only half a mile from the Matlock House, but she knew enough of the manners and airs of town to understand the requirement for it. Still, her agitation nearly overcame her as they all inched along, and from the look of her betrothed, he scarcely fared much better.

"I could do without this, I assure you," he muttered. "Roll up the rug and let me hum you a tune, and we can dance all night long." She burst out laughing at that, likely more heartily than was warranted by such a little jest, but she was gratified to see the return of his good humour.

Yet, while some part of her agreed, another part was eager to be there. It would be the first party she attended that would make the society pages, the kind that Elizabeth and her sisters used to gasp over in their little drab parlour at Longbourn. Never in her girlhood days had Elizabeth dared imagine she would be sitting in a carriage, with an earl, on her way to attend such an event.

When at last they reached their destination, Darcy handed her out with a gentle squeeze of her fingers, then offered his arm as they walked towards the door. He leant in, murmuring, "I hear my uncle is dancing with you. I do hope he has not stolen your first set from me, as I think it would be bad form to have to duel my own uncle."

She giggled lightly. "Fear not, the first is all yours. He will open with Lady Matlock."

There were liveried footmen then, who set upon them to take their wraps, offer a room to refresh themselves, and direct them towards their hostess. When her time came, she gladly surrendered her pelisse to the waiting footman, then turned to Darcy, as shocked to see the surprise on his face as he evidently was by her. Was it her gown? Was there something amiss? He had taken a step back to look at her, and his face was entirely devoid of expression.

"Is something wrong?" She looked down at herself, expecting to see some large crimson blotch or other blemish upon her, but there was nothing. "Are you well, sir?"

"Perfectly so," he said. "You are lovely." He seemed as if he wished to say more then, but did not, merely falling silent beside her as they moved to greet their hostess.

Viscountess Barrington was something of a grand dame, a large woman with noble bearing who had arrayed herself in enough jewellry that she nearly outshone her chandeliers. She was older than Lady Matlock, but one could see the shadows of the beauty she must have once had.

"Bennet," she said, peering closely at Elizabeth with eyes that were beady but bright. "Who is your father?"

"Mr Thomas Bennet of Hertfordshire," Elizabeth answered. "His estate is called Longbourn, near Meryton." So saying, she prepared herself for the inevitable questions or statements doubting her right to be in so exalted a gathering.

Lady Barrington did not smile so much as bare her teeth. "It might surprise you to know that I was acquainted with your grandmother, Miss Elizabeth Rose Morgan. She was quite dear to me. Are you her namesake?"

"I am," Elizabeth replied with a smile. "But alas, I did not know her. She died before I was born."

"Has it been so long? Yes, I daresay it has. The years go quickly at my age. You look just like her. Save for the difference in the fashions, I should have almost believed it was her ghost coming to me."

Elizabeth thanked her after which Lady Matlock asked after the lady's health. Then their party pressed into the throng.

"You have made an excellent friend, Elizabeth," Lady Matlock murmured as they moved.

"Have I?" Elizabeth could not deny that the idea pleased her. Some approbation, for any cause, was sorely appreciated.

"Oh, yes. Her friends and relations run deep. Is that not so, Darcy?"

Darcy had not seemed to acknowledge Lady Barrington's notice of Elizabeth. He stared straight ahead and replied only with a curt, "Yes," in reply to his aunt's query. Elizabeth knew not what to make of him but resolved to put it out of her mind, at least for now. It was important that she acquit herself tonight and fretting about her displeased suitor—who in truth was never particularly happy at balls—would not allow her to do that.

This gown will surely be torn and stained by the end of the night. Elizabeth looked ruefully at her hem, which already bore the marks of dirty shoes and chalky floors. The colonel had appeared, and by virtue of some shift of the crowd was the closest in step behind her. "Lady Barrington prides herself on bringing together couples who eventually make a match," he informed her.

"There can be no wonder to that," Elizabeth replied over her shoulder. "There must be five hundred people here, and I would wager that a good portion of them are unwed. The odds do favour some of them marrying at some point."

The colonel chuckled at that. "Well, she cannot take

credit for you and Darcy, for that was done before you arrived. But where has he got to?"

Surprised she turned, looking around her. "He was right here... I do not know where he went."

She was spared further speculation as Lady Matlock demanded her attention for introductions. As had been seen on their morning calls, some of the ladies were less than welcoming, which Lady Matlock saw as a triumph in itself. "To meet with uniform delight would be a disaster," she said to Elizabeth from behind her fan. "That would mean they thought you too plain to be seen as competition. Their spitefulness is a compliment to you."

Elizabeth quickly discerned her ladyship's method of showing her approval of people—she would touch Elizabeth's person in some way when making the introduction to convey significance. If she was not particularly enthused about the person, she remained aloof, showing no trace of warmth to either party.

After an excessively long time that was likely no more than half an hour, the beginning strains of the first set began to sound, and Elizabeth glanced around, looking for Darcy. It was not difficult to find him—not only was he taller than most, but he moved with a command that made groups part naturally to allow him through.

For Elizabeth it was a heady moment; she would have to be better than any woman could be to not triumph a little in knowing he was coming to her. Their eyes met and her heart gave a flutter, and disconcerted, she looked away, a sudden, frightening understanding coming upon her. She wanted to please him. Even when they quarrelled, she liked being with him more than anyone else. She forgave him easily when he was ill-humoured, and above all, she wanted him to be happy.

I have fallen in love with him.

The thought was not a happy one; indeed, it rather alarmed her. Love had never been any part of this arrangement, and she would have done much better to keep some bit of herself apart. Greater attachment could only strengthen the power he had to hurt her. *Stupid, stupid girl.*

But she would not castigate herself, not here, not now. He was to be her husband, and if he would not love her, she should at least do all she could to keep his favour.

She gathered up her wits enough to tease and flirt with him a little when they danced, but he was strangely grave, his disposition better suited for a funeral than a ball. Finally, she ceased teasing and spoke to him more gently. "I fear you are not enjoying all these people around you."

"Are you? My aunt seems determined that you should know them all before the night ends."

She laughed. "Your aunt is very good to me, but I must admit, I am heartily sick of new acquaintances by now."

But alas, the introductions did not cease. If she was not dancing, she was becoming acquainted with someone. Elizabeth reflected that her mother's comment at Netherfield Park about how the Bennets dined with four-and-twenty families seemed sillier than ever. Here she met that many in the room set aside for the ladies to refresh themselves, and her head nearly swam with all the names and estates and relations. How did anyone ever know everyone? London was no place for the forgetful, to be sure.

Her greatest pleasure of the night came when she overheard Lord Matlock remark to his wife that her conversation was very good—she was as able to speak with ease to any person as anyone he had ever heard—and he was glad for it. Lord Matlock believed that under Lady Matlock's tutelage, she might even be able to become, in time, a noted London hostess. *Heaven forfend,* Elizabeth thought. But the sentiment behind it was pleasing.

Between all of the introductions, she danced with Lord Matlock, the colonel, and Saye, who wondered that no one of any importance was at the ball—by this, she gathered he meant the elusive Miss Goddard—as well as a Sir Jonathan Broxton, who she learnt was Mr Bingley's friend and much like Bingley in both appearance and demeanour. Following Sir Jonathan, she was asked to dance by Mr Stubbs, a man who was in school with the colonel and perfectly awful.

He was about thirty and appeared nearly as wide as he was tall. Mr Stubbs had an enormous fortune which yielded him fifteen thousand pounds a year. Fifteen thousand *clear,* he emphasised to Elizabeth. He had a way of leering down her bodice that made her deeply regret every effort made to raise her breasts to their current impressive, albeit deceptive, appearance.

It was another exceedingly long half an hour, but it did pass, however slowly, and eventually she was led back to her betrothed. Darcy soberly handed her a glass of wine and thanked Mr Stubbs for bringing her to him, and Stubbs, recognising his part in the evening was over, had the graciousness to be off. He trundled off to seek his next victim while Elizabeth breathed a deep sigh of relief.

"I have never wanted for a fichu so much in my life," Elizabeth admitted, smiling up at Darcy. "Hang what these dressmakers say is fashionable; they are not the ones in the ballroom, are they?"

With a faint smile, Darcy said, "Allow your own sense to

direct you, Elizabeth, not what they tell you to wear."

There was something in the way he said it, and the sudden comprehension that he had not actually complimented her appearance or gown, that made her say, "You do not like it, do you?"

"Like what?" He stopped, looked outward towards the crowd, and turned to her. "You look very well. I believe I did say so."

"Actually, you did not," she said with an arch smile that belied her words. It would not do to have anyone think they were having any argument. "But so long as I am elevated beyond the tolerable, then I am improving, am I not?"

He gave her a look, then said, "It is a fine gown. Seems well made."

"Well made?" she sputtered with laughter. "Ah, the sweet words of courtship."

"Forgive me. You know I have not the talent for saying the right things in these circumstances."

The right things? She cast him a sidelong look. What right things did he think needed saying? Surely, he had to see that for once she looked as if she belonged here—did she not? It certainly was not a gown any dressmaker in Meryton could have made, and her hair was not arranged as dear old Sarah at Longbourn would have done it, to be sure. Could he not see the difference?

"You need say nothing at all," she said lightly, and so ushered in a tense silence.

After some moments of that, he said, "It does not much seem like...like you."

"No," she agreed. "It does not, nor does having my hair in this way seem like me, but then, is that not the purpose of all of this? I can hardly be Lizzy Bennet of Longbourn here in

London, can I? I must change, materially change, into something else entirely, and I am trying to do so."

This assertion was greeted with a stare—tinged with the faintest hue of malcontent—directed towards the dancers. "I cannot like you resembling Caroline Bingley and her ilk."

"Miss Bingley, no matter what we think of her, is fashionable and pretty. I think—"

"I think she would put lace on a saddle." He pulled his handkerchief from his pocket and ran it across his face, muttering, "And I fell in love with Elizabeth Bennet, whose petticoats were six inches deep in mud."

Fell in love? She dismissed his words as mere hyperbole and instead set her mind on the last part. *Six inches deep in mud.* It was that phrase which made her chin lift and her back straighten with remembered embarrassment, as she remembered all too well the petticoats and the incident to which he referred.

It was the day she went to Netherfield for Jane and had been nowise left to wonder whether she was an intruder. The first evening's dinner she remembered particularly, as it had mortified her painfully. She had quit the dining room but heard them begin shredding her as the door swung closed; to her discredit, she had stopped to listen.

> *Miss Bingley began abusing her as soon as she was out of the room. Her manners were pronounced to be very bad indeed, a mixture of pride and impertinence; she had no conversation, no stile, no taste, no beauty. Mrs Hurst thought the same, and added, "She has nothing, in short, to recommend her, but being an excellent walker. I shall never forget her appearance this morning. She really looked almost wild."*

"She did indeed, Louisa. I could hardly keep my countenance. Very nonsensical to come at all! Why must she be scampering about the country, because her sister had a cold? Her hair so untidy, so blowsy!"

"Yes, and her petticoat; I hope you saw her petticoat, six inches deep in mud, I am absolutely certain; and the gown which had been let down to hide it not doing its office."

"Your picture may be very exact, Louisa," said Bingley; "but this was all lost upon me. I thought Miss Elizabeth Bennet looked remarkably well, when she came into the room this morning. Her dirty petticoat quite escaped my notice."

"You observed it, Mr Darcy, I am sure," said Miss Bingley, "and I am inclined to think that you would not wish to see your sister make such an exhibition."

"Certainly not."

Was this how it had been happening all over London too? She felt her insides begin to quake. Were they all laughing behind her back?

"Elizabeth?"

"Six inches deep in mud." She forced a dry, high laugh. "That phrase is not one I have heard of late, but I did hear it rather clearly that day at Netherfield after the door to the dining room closed behind me. I forgot you were in there too."

Of all, it was the accusation of having 'no conversation' which wounded her. Perhaps she had no style, and yes, her hair did sometimes look wild, but she could converse with ease to nearly anyone—anyone save these London ladies with too little in their brain boxes, it seemed. *Lord Matlock thinks so too!*

Apparently knowing he had upset and unsettled her, Darcy put his hand on her arm where the room could not see it. "Bingley remarked that evening on how pretty you looked, but it was my plainly spoken admiration of you that sealed your fate. I am sorry, Elizabeth, but I am afraid I made them dislike you right then and there, by not only refusing to join their abuse of your petticoats, but also daring to admire your complexion and your eyes."

He brushed lightly the back of her arm with his fingertips and let them travel into her sleeve while he smiled down at her. He was flirting with her, and she drew a shaking breath, feeling like an utter idiot but not willing to make a spectacle over it.

Was this to be her lot? Secretly mocked when she quit a room? Always in the wrong frock? Always doing the wrong thing at the wrong time in the wrong way? Suddenly, all that Lady Catherine had said about quitting her sphere seemed sage advisement.

With great relief, she noticed Lord and Lady Matlock coming towards them. She hoped that it meant that, unlike Mrs Bennet, they did not follow the practice of being the last to leave a place, for she was quite ready to bring the night to a close. The notion of having her hair in a simple plait and being clad in a plain flannel night shift was suddenly vastly appealing.

And as she lifted her eyes to his, she wondered what fresh miseries lay ahead—for surely to allow him into her heart, to give over this last little bit of herself, could lead to nothing else.

CHAPTER NINETEEN

THE REFLECTIONS WHICH TROUBLED HER AT THE BALL continued the night long. She was grateful that Georgiana did not come to her to ask how she had been received because she did not wish to disappoint her. She knew that the girl's advice had been well-intentioned, and in truth, it was good advice. It was only Elizabeth's execution of it which had missed the mark.

She took up a post on the window seat, watching the square below and its associated bustle, which gradually lessened as the night wore on. She saw Saye and the colonel leave again—it was not uncommon for the two brothers to be out all night—and wondered at the habits of men. Were Darcy's the same? Would they continue? Such notions had to be less imperative to her at present than her own, more immediate concerns. Anxiety for her future threatened, and while her courage always rose when others intimidated her, when it was her own mind's torment at play, it was less easily conquered.

She could not come to any resolution save the same one she always had, that she was a person of sense and agreeability who would do her best. She was engaged to him. What was there to do but make the most of things? How much time would they spend in London in any case? Surely, she would meet someone, somewhere who truly liked her?

A painful crick in her neck woke her where she had fallen asleep, her head resting against the cold glass of the window. It was morning, but barely, only the servants and coal boys hurrying along the streets.

"I understand," Saye drawled from behind his newspaper as Elizabeth entered the breakfast parlour later that morning, "that you had a dance with Old Stubbsy last night at the ball. Do say it is true."

The colonel grinned. "Stubbs is a grand fellow, is he not?"

Elizabeth pursed her lips to repress her smile as she took her seat at the table. "He did not step on my feet, and for that I was grateful."

Saye lowered the broadsheet. "My only quarrel with the man is his strange propensity for being observed in the nude. Always wandered about in a scandalous state at school, and now!—one dares not call on him for fear of being urged into his dressing room."

He raised the paper again and remarked, almost idly, "Tell me, Elizabeth—are you fond of shrimp?"

"Shrimp?" asked Elizabeth, somewhat confused by the sudden choke of laughter which burst from Colonel Fitzwilliam.

"Shrimp." Saye said from behind his newspaper. "I have always found them to be rather grotesque, so small and greyish-pale and curled...pink when cooked, of course, which in my estimation renders them even less desirable."

Colonel Fitzwilliam was near apoplexy but controlled

himself enough to give his brother a light punch on the arm. "Stop that."

"Stop what?" Saye lowered the newspaper and shot his brother a look. "I am merely enquiring as to Elizabeth's preferences. Elizabeth, I ask you again, do you or do you not enjoy shrimp? And how much shrimp have you enjoyed?"

"I…I do not…" Elizabeth looked back and forth between the brothers. "I do not think I understand."

But she was destined to be left bemused for Lady Matlock entered then and both men straightened while she greeted them all and asked Elizabeth, "My dear, are you going somewhere?"

"It is a lovely morning," Elizabeth said. "I thought I might have a walk."

She thought perhaps a walk, preferably alone, would help her disordered spirits, but walking alone was not done in London. Lady Matlock seemed hesitant, though might have agreed to it, but Lord Matlock arrived in the breakfast parlour at the last moment and insisted the colonel attend her. Knowing he must surely long for his bed after the undoubtedly long night, she sent the colonel an apologetic look and began to demur, but the colonel was gallant. "The exercise will do me good, I am sure. Let me get my hat."

The mail arrived while Mrs Banks sent a girl for the colonel's hat, but Elizabeth was required to put her letter from Jane aside, for the requested article arrived moments later, and then they were off.

THE COLONEL WAS as agreeable as ever, rattling away on things of little consequence as they went along, telling her tales of him and Darcy as boys. Elizabeth knew he was aware of the truth of their beginning and no doubt wished to demonstrate Darcy's finer qualities to her, hoping to show her what an excellent husband she had caught. Little did he know she was already much too aware of the fact. Nevertheless, she attended him with half an ear, and laughed and gasped in all the right spots.

"...Darcy was very good to me, accepting the punishment right alongside me, although I assure you, when we were alone, he exacted his own penance!" The colonel laughed heartily.

"He is good to his friends," Elizabeth responded with a little smile.

"That he is. In fact, I only recently learnt of a situation where he saved a friend from certain danger in matrimony."

"Is matrimony so very dangerous?"

"At times," said the colonel with a little chuckle. "Our friend was in danger of having his honour engaged due to his attentions towards a woman who was lovely but had a dreadful family. The family was quite ready to pounce on him."

"Were they?" Elizabeth swallowed, her attention suddenly fixed and whole as she comprehended him.

"There was a great deal of advantage to the alliance for them, though for him it could be nothing but a degradation. But he did not see that because"—here the colonel gave her a sheepish grin—"the girl was quite pretty. Fortunately, the gentleman in question had Darcy's aid in keeping a clear head."

Elizabeth flushed, and turned her head quickly to disguise her expression. "There must not have been much affection, in any case, if the gentleman was so easily discouraged."

"I think he did like her, but he is not a foolish man and could see the certain evils in his choice once they were shown to him."

"Would you mind if we return?" Elizabeth said abruptly. "I think I am getting a headache from all the wind."

"Oh, I am sorry to hear it." The colonel peered at her a moment and then turned, directing her back towards the house.

IT WAS NOT A TERRIBLY long distance to the Matlock residence, but by the time they got there, Elizabeth was burning with determination. She would go to Darcy at once and insist on understanding the meaning of his interference in Bingley's attachment to Jane. How could he object to Bingley connecting himself to a family that Darcy himself would belong to?

Unless it was a consequence of Darcy's own revulsion for the Bennets? Darcy would save his friend because he could not save himself.

Either that or, having undertaken the lengths that he had to avoid marriage to Caroline Bingley, the last thing he wanted was to be any sort of relation, even distantly, to her. Was that it? No matter how one looked at it, it was another example of Darcy arranging things with only himself at the centre. No thought for Jane's, Bingley's, or her own feelings —only what suited Darcy.

She went to Lady Matlock, who often spent the time after breakfast writing letters in the small, cream-coloured parlour off her bedchamber. She could not imagine her ladyship undertaking any calls this morning, not after the late night before, and she was correct. From her simple—for her—day gown and satin slippers, Elizabeth could see that Lady Matlock intended to remain in. "I find myself needing to speak with Darcy," she told her ladyship. "Things pertaining to...our marriage."

She had no idea what Lady Matlock might have imagined she meant, but it did the trick. Lady Matlock smiled and nodded and offered to send Mrs Banks with her. "You will be married in a month," she declared. "Who will have anything to say about it?"

ELIZABETH HAD FORGOTTEN about Jane's letter until she returned to her bedchamber to retrieve her pelisse and gloves and saw it there on the table. Jane was a faithful correspondent; it did not occur to her that this particular letter would have any news that might preclude the reading of it in Lord Matlock's carriage, and so it was therein that she received the dreadful news.

My Dearest Lizzy,
Warmest greetings from Hertfordshire. I pray your stay in London is agreeable and that Mr Darcy and his relations continue in good health. We are all very well at Longbourn. It has snowed a little, and the village looks pretty with its covering of white. Some of the village elders have said we shall have much snow this year, more than we have yet seen in our lives, but only time will tell whether they are correct.

I do not have the words to tell you what I must without

shocking you, so I shall say it directly. To wit, I am engaged to Mr Collins.

Please wish me well, dear sister, and do not censure me. Mr Collins was not fortunate enough to secure your regard, but for me, the notion of being his wife is not intolerable. I shall not pretend to some great romance on either my part or his, but he is in need of a wife, and I am grown weary of feeling uneasy for my future. I resolved that if I obtained an offer from a respectable man, I would take it. In Mr Collins I have the promise of remaining at Longbourn all my days. It is enough for me.

Mr Collins arrived to us only yesterday, but I was quick to let him know of my hopes where he was concerned. You are no doubt surprised by my boldness and so, too, was he. But afterwards he spoke prettily and assured me of his ardent belief in our future happiness, and before long, it was done. Our mother and father are both pleased, and Mama is at last able to relieve her nerves of the fear of ending up in the hedgerows.

Lady Catherine feels that I would serve the parish well. From all Mr Collins has assured me, if I perform well in my duty to the parish, I should have every hope of gaining her esteem. I shall admit, I do look forward to days of occupation and service.

Please write back to me soon, dear Lizzy, and reassure me that you do not despise me for what I have done.

Ever your devoted sister,
Jane

Oh Jane, Jane! How could you do such a thing?

Elizabeth read and re-read the letter, finally acknowledging that her eyes did not deceive her. *I have saved myself and, in so doing, sacrificed my most beloved sister.* All this mincing and prancing about London, pretending at being some lady of the *ton,* and for what? So dear Jane would be made to suffer in her stead?

The boil of hot guilt burnt her throat and made her want to cry out. Across from her, Mrs Banks asked, "Miss Bennet? You are well?"

"Yes," Elizabeth said, with almost maniac denial, for she was very, very far from well. Indeed, she felt a mad panic and an impulse to escape, to run to Jane and have her declare this letter a joke—except Jane rarely told jokes and certainly not about such a dreadful thing as this.

"You have not had bad news, I hope?"

She could not answer that directly. Most people would view an engagement as good news, but this, *this* was nothing short of tragic. "My elder sister has accepted an offer of marriage," she said at last.

Mrs Banks, wise woman that she was, comprehended Elizabeth's agitation. "Something tells me you are not pleased."

Elizabeth shook her head and blinked back her tears, but no more could be done for they had then arrived—but she did appreciate the way that Mrs Banks offered a consoling pat on her back.

Of Darcy's house, she observed little save that it was, as she would have expected, sizeable and elegant, its stone face still wider than many of those around it. The housekeeper,

Mrs Hobbs, greeted them eagerly; Elizabeth had not realised Mrs Banks and Mrs Hobbs were sisters, and her visit would give them some pleasure as well. *Someone ought to be enjoying themselves in all this.*

Darcy seemed to immediately understand that something was amiss when Elizabeth was shown into the drawing room. He closed the door behind her, heedless of propriety, and asked, "What is it?"

From those three words, her tears began to flow, a relentless trickle down her cheek. Her voice caught when she said, "It is Jane."

"Jane? Has she taken ill again?" Darcy pressed his handkerchief into her hand and led her to a nearby sofa. She sank into the soft aubergine velvet, dabbing at her eyes as Darcy sat next to her. Then she turned, pressing her face to his shoulder and allowing her tears to flow unchecked. At last she managed to say, "Jane has accepted an offer of marriage from Mr Collins."

"Mr Collins?"

"Indeed," she sobbed. "Oh, poor, poor Jane!"

"Your parents? Did they require it of her?"

Elizabeth pulled back from him, trying as best she could to restore herself to dignity. There was a sinking ache within her borne by guilt and misery that could not abate. "She did not say so, though she did say they were very pleased with her."

Opening her reticule, she removed the letter from it while Darcy rose and went to a sideboard, pouring a glass of sherry for her. Returning, he handed her the wine and sat again. He took the pages from her hand, scanning them quickly, then sighed heavily.

"Has your father signed the articles?"

"I would assume he has. My mother would have been insistent until all was settled."

"I hope there is a chance for her happiness in the union. I myself have had counsel from your father on the beneficial effect of a good wife. Mr Collins surely must improve with Jane by his side."

"Yes, but what of Jane? What good can come of it for her?"

"Jane will gain the respectability of a married woman and, of course, Longbourn, eventually."

Hearing him saying so, in accents so unfeeling and reasonable, could only make it worse. Although she had never been to Hunsford, a perfectly clear image of Jane in a lace cap standing meekly beside her ridiculous husband outside Hunsford parsonage sprang to Elizabeth's mind. It nearly made her sob aloud.

"If that is all that matters, then I might as well have done it myself," she cried. "I saved myself only to toss my most beloved sister into the jaws of the wolf instead. And *you* have all the satisfaction of having spared your friend the undignified connexions you could not escape yourself."

"What are you saying?"

A sob tore itself free from her chest, and Elizabeth bent her head to avoid the look on Darcy's countenance, a look her words had placed there. She needed no more guilt.

It was in this terrible moment that the butler entered, looking flustered and apologetic when he found Darcy with her. "Oh, sir, um…Mr and Miss Bingley to see you."

"Right." Looking at Elizabeth, Darcy said, "Yesterday, I told Bingley to call at this time, but I shall put him off."

"Pray do not. I would not interrupt your plans." Elizabeth was on her feet in an instant. There could be no two people she wished to meet less, but between the crying and the raised voices there was already enough to raise curiosity.

"Of course you do not interrupt. Please wait—you have only just arrived."

Elizabeth lowered her voice. "Miss Bingley would not scruple to gossip if she found me here alone with you. She cannot know Mrs Banks is just below stairs."

"I shall summon Mrs Banks," Darcy replied firmly. "Stay."

Leaving did not seem to be her choice, and so she did not.

Of her appearance, Elizabeth dared not think. She smoothed her hair, and hoped the fact that she had wept was not too obvious, as they awaited the arrival of the Bingleys in the drawing room. When she entered, Miss Bingley had a decided air of triumph about her, and Elizabeth could not think why. Could she know about Jane? Already?

Mr Bingley appeared notably downcast but searched her face as they all sat, looking for what, she could not imagine. "Miss Elizabeth Bennet, how good it is to see you. Are your family all well?"

"They are, sir, thank you."

"And all are in good health? I do hope Miss Bennet continues to do well after her illness of the autumn."

"Jane, and all of my sisters, are in excellent health."

Miss Bingley interjected, "How is your dear cousin Mr Collins? Such a treasure he is! I do hope one of your sisters has been fortunate enough to secure his regard?"

Ah, so she knows. Careful to remain calm, Elizabeth said, "Mr Collins is well. He has recently proposed to my eldest sister, Jane, and she has accepted him. I learnt the news myself just this morning."

Mr Bingley went white, and Elizabeth saw him draw a deep breath as his hands clutched the arms of his chair.

"What a great comfort for your family, Eliza! To one day be mistress of Longbourn. No one could deserve it more than dear Jane. You must be so very thrilled."

"It was a shock, to be sure—" Elizabeth began but was interrupted by Mr Bingley whose voice sounded high and thin. "A shock? How could it be a shock?"

Astonishment made her silent for a moment so Darcy spoke in her stead. "Much as it is desirable to have a daughter as future mistress of Longbourn, as of last autumn Mrs Bennet had told Mr Collins he should not entertain any notions of matrimony with Miss Bennet because—"

"But that cannot be!" Mr Bingley looked around him wildly. "I was told that—"

Miss Bingley spoke over her brother, her voice loud and falsely sweet. "I must say, Miss Eliza, it is a relief to my mind to see you so well in looks! I have been nearly consumed with worry for you!"

Her scheme worked. All eyes turned to her.

Elizabeth instinctively felt she would do best not to ask, yet found herself saying, "Why were you worried about me, Miss Bingley?"

Mr Bingley was not ready to leave the subject of Jane's betrothal behind. "Miss Elizabeth, forgive me but I understood your family had an expectation—"

"The last that I saw you, you were nearly drowned!" Miss Bingley exclaimed, her smile a rictus of insincerity. "Such a hearty constitution you must boast, for I cannot imagine many gently bred ladies who could be soaked to their skin and not fall deathly ill."

Elizabeth understood her immediately and cursed the misfortune that had brought Miss Bingley to the swollen creek the day after the Netherfield ball when Mr Wickham had come to her aid.

"I had a cold," Elizabeth said, tossing an unconcerned, airy smile at Darcy. "It was nothing, I assure you."

"Is that how you became ill?" Darcy asked, his eyes dark, his too-interested gaze upon her. "Because you nearly drowned?"

"I was not nearly drowned," Elizabeth told him while across from her, Miss Bingley smiled with scarcely restrained glee. "I have crossed that way my entire life. I stumbled a little on the rocks."

"Such a rainy day it was—not many would have dared stir out of doors in such a cold, pelting rain," Miss Bingley offered. "But no one can accuse you of lacking an adventurous spirit."

With a serenity she did not feel, Elizabeth said, "It was not raining when I set out, and in my haste to return home, I unwisely decided to cross the river on the stones rather than go around by the bridge. They were more slippery than I realised."

Miss Bingley was not finished, and she lifted her chin, looking like a cat who was savouring an entrapped mouse. "How very fortunate it was that Mr Wickham was there to assist you. It was Mr Wickham, was it not? How gallant of him to take you home on his horse."

Elizabeth turned hotly, ashamedly red. She dared not look at Darcy as she said, "Mr Wickham was quite insistent in his efforts to rescue me from the river, and indeed, I might have been in trouble had he not. I went directly home, and all was well. I had a trifling cold afterwards, as I said."

Miss Bingley's satisfaction in the distress she had caused Elizabeth was plain, though her brother appeared baffled. A furtive glance at Darcy revealed that he had gone pale with rage; it made her insides flutter with anxiety.

The dreadful silence which ensued made everyone uncomfortable, and it was Darcy who relieved it by asking after Bingley's relations in Scarborough. No one cared about the conversation that followed; everyone in the room was in some degree of distress, anger, or, in Miss Bingley's case, triumph.

Darcy was angry, but Elizabeth had not done anything wrong. She had tried as best as she could to decline Mr Wickham's assistance. Then, when he would not be refused, she had acquiesced and spent as little time in his presence as possible. What could she have done differently save remain at home that day? Would he have been happier had she drowned unassisted?

You should have told him. Her conscience would not absolve her.

A small flame of unwise indignation flickered in her bosom, for was it not hypocritical of Darcy to become angered with her for withholding information? She could fill a book with all that he had not told her since becoming engaged to him only six weeks ago.

Finally, the Bingleys took their leave, and Elizabeth did not mistake the look of satisfaction on Miss Bingley's countenance. Elizabeth could not be concerned for her, though, thinking she was on the verge of a significant argument with her betrothed, and feeling all of the taut anticipation of a row.

CHAPTER TWENTY

WHEN THE DRAWING ROOM DOOR CLOSED BEHIND THE TWO Bingleys, Darcy went to the window, and Elizabeth followed behind him, wishing to touch him but daring not. "Fitzwilliam, I…it was after your aunt's visit, quite unwisely I-I went for a walk, the rain began and, um, and I fell into—"

Darcy turned, his face frozen into a mask of contemptuous rage. "Into the arms of George Wickham?"

His tone made her pause for a moment to gather her composure. "It was fortunate for me that Mr Wickham was nearby for I nearly fell into the river and drowned."

"Nearly fell? Or did fall? Because the account I just heard had you quite soaked."

"Uh, yes, well I daresay I was, but not because I fell… It was raining rather hard," Elizabeth admitted. "It…it was not as Miss Bingley made it sound…"

"She said you were soaked to the skin."

"Well…yes. I…I had left the house…unwisely, I do admit, in only a…a walking gown…"

Darcy uttered some oath beneath his breath. His jaw clenched, he asked, "And what did Wickham do? Did he hold you in his arms? Share with you his coat? How long did this liaison last?"

Under his glare, she found herself folding her arms across her middle. "I…my ankle was twisted a little because I slipped on the rocks."

Darcy waited, his stare unrelenting and hard.

"So…so he…he helped me from the river and…I was limping. He insisted on carrying me home—it was a mile—on his horse."

"On his horse." Darcy shook his head, his lip curled with disgust.

"What could I have done? It was not as though I planned it or wished it, but I was injured." Elizabeth protested, her natural defences rising. "Would you have preferred he left me to the river? Should it have pleased you better if he saw me in distress and kept riding? I know you do not like the man, though for my life I cannot comprehend your treatment of him—"

"My treatment of him?"

"You have reduced him to poverty, you blacken his character, but in this instance his actions were nothing short of heroic!"

"Are you mad?" Darcy's fists were clenched. "George Wickham, a hero? He was a far greater danger to you than any river could be."

"I have seen nothing nor heard anything of that. I needed assistance, and he provided it. Surely you can laud him for as much."

"How silly of me to think Bennet could watch over her the few weeks until we married," he muttered, clearly not intending her to hear it. She gasped, unable to help herself.

"Forgive me, but I specifically asked your father to

prevent you rambling about the countryside unescorted," he said. "Had you not been so doing, you would not have been in George Wickham's arms, soaking wet."

"My father knew nothing of it," Elizabeth retorted, realising even as she said so that she was proving rather than disputing his point. It could only serve to vex her further. "I have learnt enough of you to comprehend how you would prize such a quality as blind obedience, but it is a quality I do not have. I shall not deny that my father has done me a disservice allowing me the liberties he has, but it is how I have been reared."

She paused and then added, "This is why I shall never be able to make you happy."

"What are you saying?"

She pressed her lips together but no such effort could restrain the words that needed to come forth. "You believe you know what is best for everyone, for Bingley, for me, for your sister—"

"In this case, I do!"

"Well forgive me, but I cannot abide such…such selfish high-handedness. You snatched me up because I suited your purpose in avoiding Miss Bingley with no thought for who or what I really was, and what I *am* is entirely wrong for you."

"Selfish high-handedness?"

"You arrange people like chess pieces, pushing them here and there as they suit your purpose—but I cannot censure you for it as I have done the same. I thought only of my own purposes in agreeing to this marriage. You want something I cannot give you, and I want something you cannot give me. So it was said in the beginning and so it remains now."

He exhaled forcibly and at great volume. It seemed to

leave him weak, and he sank into a nearby chair, turning his head away from her.

"I cannot live my life as a wealthy man's ornament, no thoughts or feelings of my own, my life reduced to sitting in drawing rooms in silks and jewels, eating cakes, gossiping about nothing of consequence–"

"I have never wished for any such thing."

"You dislike everything that is low and countrified in me, yet when I tried to be different you despised that too."

"Because I could not like seeing you dressed like Caroline Bingley? You are too beautiful to—"

"If we were in love, if we did it because of some great romance, it would be entirely different, but we both know that is not the case," Elizabeth said. "Lady Matlock takes me around, introducing me to ladies who have nothing in their heads but marriage and balls and parties… We both knew we were not in love but now…now I realise you do not even like me."

She gestured towards him, feeling like she was losing the thread of her reason. "You will be Mr Darcy, much as you ever were, but I shall…I am expected to be something materially different, something that I simply do not think I can be."

He cast her a strange, baffled look. "How can you say I do not like you? I proposed to you, offered my hand, my life, everything I am and have, and in return—"

"You told me why you said my name that night," she said, cutting into any protestations he might utter. "Because of…" She shook her head, unable to say it outright. "I have seen what it is, witnessed first-hand when two people who are so dissimilar form a union based on…on…a man's…interests and…and those interests change. They grow dim and eventually turn to resentment as the object of his interest grows old."

Darcy's look changed from confusion to horror as he comprehended her, but she ploughed on, heedless and reckless. "I do not wish to be someone's shame, particularly for reasons I can neither help nor alter." She swallowed hard and added, "I cannot change sufficiently to please you, or anyone else in this town, nor do I want to try."

Evidently he did not plan to speak, so Elizabeth walked over and stood in front of him, clasping her hands in hopes they would stop shaking. "It was an error for me to have agreed to this arrangement, and I think it would be best if I released you."

One fist clenched and unclenched by his side, and his face was nearly frightening with pale rage; but when he spoke, it was with calm superiority. "Your anger has made you a fool, Elizabeth."

Elizabeth drew in a deep, shuddering breath, doing nothing more but looking at him for a moment. "I do not think it foolish. In fact, I think it the first wise thing I have done since this began."

Darcy turned his face away from her. "As you would like, then. I am certainly not planning to beg you."

"I would not have you do so."

They remained in silence for several long minutes until at length Elizabeth said, "I should go." Her voice squeaked and broke on the word 'go'.

He rose and went to the bell, rang it, and then informed the footman summoned that Miss Bennet needed the carriage.

The carriage took an eternity to be brought around. Darcy and Elizabeth were silent throughout the long wait until the carriage drew up. He handed her in, but at the last, he squeezed her hand tightly, stopping her just as she entered. She turned back to look at him. He stared at her intently for a long moment, and then pulled her hand to his lips for a kiss before releasing her and telling the coachman to move on.

Elizabeth nearly fell into the plush navy squabs of the Matlock carriage, her emotions boiling beneath a tightly held mask of serenity. She was resolved to retain her equanimity in front of Mrs Banks. One word, she felt, would be the end of her. She could not bear to think of the consequences of what she had done. Clearly, she would need to go home, but how to explain that to Lord and Lady Matlock? Perhaps Darcy would want to inform them? Or perhaps he thought it her duty. She could not guess which was right in this circumstance. Should she begin packing? Should she write to her mother and father?

They entered Matlock House, and Mrs Banks turned to take her coat and bonnet. Feeling the prickle of ready tears accompanied by a rising need to escape to something familiar, Elizabeth said, "Excuse me, I…I forgot…there is something I must do."

She turned then, nearly running out the front doors as Mrs Banks called behind her, "Should you wish for the carriage?"

Elizabeth replied with only a raise of her hand and then was gone.

DARCY STALKED into his house after seeing Elizabeth off, strode into his study, and closed the door. The shock of all she had said, of what she felt and believed, took his breath away. He had been such a fool, imagining her content, thinking she was of like mind with him—hoping she was falling in love with him as he was with her. Instead, she was admiring George Wickham, her hero!—and thinking him arrogant and selfish and ruled by lust. Fury burnt a hole in his gut and made him rise from his chair to glare out his window at the street below.

So much of what she said could not be denied. They were not well suited to one another, and they did quarrel more than most engaged people would. She challenged him, though with a sweetness and archness that made it all palatable. Nevertheless, he had been the master of his house and his affairs for some time now. He had expected to marry a woman who would fall into her place in his world and be delighted for it.

But that was not the sort of lady Elizabeth Bennet was, was it?

She was beautiful last night. She was always beautiful. But she was not beautiful in an Elizabeth Bennet way. She was beautiful like any ordinary lady of the *ton*, any diamond of the first water who arrived at her matchmaking mama's side, fresh out of the right schools with the right connexions and boasting all the right accomplishments. The very sight of it made his stomach turn, and he despised himself for any part he might have played in making her believe he demanded it of her.

Ladies of the *ton* were like the grounds of Rosings Park—raised to be cultured and fashionable and strictly adherent to certain lines. The main gardens around his aunt's home had been designed by a man who studied under Le Nôtre, and this man evidently thought Rosings Park should be no less grand than Versailles. Roses grew to precise heights at Rosings Park, shrubs were tortured into complex and unnatural shapes, and weeds dared not encroach. There were times to bloom and wither, and paths went in Euclidian formations.

Not so at Pemberley. Pemberley claimed an unrefined, uncultivated loveliness, where trees and shrubs were oft left to grow unbound, and roses tumbled about in colourful, heady-scented disarray. Certainly there were more orderly gardens too, but it was in the wild places where he had dreamt of seeing her, her own wildness showing, her beauty unbound as well. Elizabeth was perfect as its mistress just as she was. Elizabeth was no drawing room ornament nor did he wish that of her, though it seemed she thought he did.

If we were in love…

She could not know how her words wounded him. Yes, she had told him over and over again how this match was not founded on affection. But in his case, it was, and had been for some time now. That first night at the assembly he had been offended by her; the manner in which she dismissed him after his insult was unprecedented. He would have dealt with tears or anger, but she gave him a look that made him feel ridiculous—him! Ridiculous! No one had ever made him feel that way, and his pride had demanded he be offended by her.

But she would not leave his mind. He had thought of her almost incessantly until their next meeting when the Bennet ladies called at Netherfield. He doubted she would remember their conversation—something about books—and indeed, he hardly remembered it himself. He only recalled that it enchanted him because it was so honest. She did not play the coquette but spoke with genuine intellect and feeling, and he could not get enough of her.

His danger had become truly apparent the day he came upon her muddy from the fields, having walked from Longbourn to nurse her sister. She cared not what Miss Bingley and Mrs Hurst—even he—might think. She was there for her sister. Who would not want to be loved by someone like that? And he remembered thinking 'I could spend the rest of my life with a woman like this'. It was that, not lust, that drove his thoughts and dreams on the fateful night Miss Bingley entered his room. Yes, he found her desirable—he was a young man of seven-and-twenty, and there would be something amiss with him if he did not—and his body wanted her as much as his heart did. He would not apologise for that.

And then he was engaged to her, and whether he admitted it or not, he was falling in love with her. By now, he simply could not imagine living his life without her. Unfortunately, that was precisely what she wanted—to live her life without him.

If we were in love... Had she not heard him say it? It had not been said purposefully to be sure, but he had admitted it, apparently to no effect at all. Though perhaps she had not heard him, as the ball was noisy, and he had said it quickly.

But how could she imagine Wickham a hero? He exhaled, forcibly, disgustedly. When she knew what he had done to Georgiana?

It could not be denied, he ought to have told her the truth about Wickham. He should have informed her of Georgiana's condition, as well as the reason for it, but selfishly, he had wished to leave such unpleasantness behind. The time he spent talking to her, walking with her, and kissing her was too precious, too sweet to introduce such disagreeable subjects. He had always believed he would tell her the 'next' time he saw her…except the 'next' time had never come.

The fire, recently stoked, had grown too warm, and Darcy tugged at his cravat, feeling the heat of the room as well as of his own frustration. He opened the window an inch or so to allow in some fresh, wintry air, but it proved too much; the frigid January wind burst inside with great zeal, catching his pile of papers and blowing them wildly off of his desk and towards the fire.

Darcy cursed, watching the papers tumble about. He slammed closed the window, then hastened to gather up the papers. A whirling dervish could not have disarrayed them more, he mused, as he knelt down to gather them.

It was a fresh source of sorrow that the pages were the marriage articles that Mr Bennet had signed. He sighed as he began to smooth, sort, and reorder them. It was in the process of so doing that his eye fell upon a page bearing an odd date, that date being June 29, 1806. It was a date significant to him, being the day that his father had died. It was evidently a date significant to Mr William Collins as well, being the date of his christening.

His brow wrinkled, Darcy looked more closely at the page. It was something not meant for him; evidently it had been mixed in with his pages, likely from others on Mr Bennet's desk. From the state of that gentleman's desk, he could not be wholly surprised.

The document pertained to Longbourn's entail, naming Mr Collins as presumptive heir. It also indicated he had been christened less than six years previous. Darcy was not sure how old Collins was—a heavy young man, he was the type who would look the same at twenty-five and forty—but he knew he was not a child. Why would he have been christened in 1806?

His ire was, for a moment, set aside as newer feelings of suspicion replaced it. Something was amiss here, though he could not imagine what. He could still recall Mr Collins proclaiming proudly, *'My dear and wonderful father, himself a parson, left this earth but a year ago.'* Darcy could not imagine any circumstance in which the child of a parson would not have been christened until adulthood.

He rose, moving back to his desk, where another memory hit him. It was during the time Elizabeth was ill and Mrs Bennet would not allow him to see her. He had spent time with Mr Bennet, and Mr Bennet had told him of the quarrel with his cousin, Collins's father. *'My cousin Collins was an illiterate and miserly man.'* Furthermore, Bennet had indicated that their quarrel was about money, funds that the elder Collins thought Bennet ought to lend him to start some business or another.

Nowise could a parson be illiterate; and what sort of parson would engage in a decades-long quarrel over funds for a business venture? It was exceedingly odd.

From nowhere, another comment Mr Bennet made came to mind. He had remarked on the oddity that Collins, like himself, had many daughters, though had obviously, at some point, managed to sire a son as well. Yet, had not Collins stated he was an only child? Darcy cast his mind back. He could not recall it with complete certainty, but he was quite sure the man said he had no sisters.

Oddities first to last, but Darcy had to own that Collins spoke so often and so much that it was easy to ignore him. He might well have clarified or explained these evident inconsistencies in his, versus Mr Bennet's, accounts of things.

But this page was another matter. How could a man of five-and-twenty be christened in 1806?

A simple mistake. Someone erred in their recording of the date of Collins's christening on these documents. What could it signify?

He folded the document carefully. He would go to Matlock House and give it to her to return to her father.

A thin excuse to see her, his heart whispered, but his mind shushed it.

CHAPTER TWENTY ONE

I SUPPOSE THE FIRST LESSON TO BE LEARNT IS THAT I NEED TO stop running off every time I am upset, at least until the weather turns.

Elizabeth's desperation to see her beloved aunt and uncle Gardiner had outweighed the fact that it was far too cold and windy to walk a distance of above three miles to Gracechurch Street. She trembled violently, though how much of it was from emotion and how much from the cold, she could not say. Further, it could only be seen as the hand of God that kept her from getting lost or accosted as she went, although she did need to stop once in a shop to ask for guidance on her way.

At long last she found herself at their home, nearly sobbing with relief at the blessed sight of her uncle's door. The door was opened quickly by Richards, her uncle's man, and moments later she heard Mrs Gardiner's light and graceful steps hurrying towards her. "Elizabeth! What on earth! Never mind, let us begin by getting you warm."

In very short time, Elizabeth found herself ensconced by the hearth, warmed as much by her aunt's kind solicitude as she was by the fire and the blankets heaped upon her. Mrs Gardiner was astonished and concerned by her sudden, unannounced call—that much was evident—but genteel as she was, she held her curiosity until Elizabeth herself spoke up. "You must be shocked to see me."

"I am always glad to see you, but I can see you are upset." She leant over to smooth her niece's hair. "What is it?"

Elizabeth stared into the fire, oddly reluctant to tell her aunt what she had done. "I have released Mr Darcy."

The only sign of Mrs Gardiner's surprise was a momentary pause. "Why did you do that?"

Elizabeth found it curious that although her tears were lodged in her throat like a large, hard ball, they would not begin to fall. She curled into the blanket around her shoulders.

"I…we quarrelled…and I realised that this engagement was…failing us both. We argue so much, Aunt! So I told him I thought we should end our betrothal."

"It is not uncommon when you argue to feel as though all is lost or you could never love one another again, but it does not mean—"

"Except that we were never in love," Elizabeth replied tonelessly. "I was not honest with you, or anyone else save for Jane, about this betrothal—it was never about love. It was about escaping Mr Collins. I saved myself, but now poor Jane will be the sacrifice."

She told her aunt the truth of her engagement to Mr Darcy, starting with the fateful night at Netherfield and continuing right until that very morning. As Elizabeth related the extraordinary tale, she could see her aunt was surprised but contained it; she did as she always did best and listened. When all was said, she asked, calmly, "Do you truly wish to break this engagement? From the sounds of things, it appears you acted on an impulse, and unwisely at that."

"I am not formed for the life of Mrs Darcy. I believed I could become what he needed, and that perhaps he might be what I needed, but I was wrong, dreadfully so. We can only make one another unhappy. Oh, that none of this had ever happened!"

"Yes, but it *has* happened. You accepted him and have been engaged for nearly two months. I think you know the consequences of breaking your engagement to a man such as Mr Darcy. You would likely never recover your character."

With a weak smile, Elizabeth said, "So it will be doom and despair either way, but if I release him, then at least he shall have some hope of happiness."

"Oh, Lizzy, do not joke, not now."

"I must! In any case, it does not matter! The words have been uttered, and what's done is done. Aunt, you know how proud he is; you know his family. I have injured that pride, gravely. Were I to beg on my knees for another chance, it would not be granted, and I cannot do that. I have my own pride, I suppose, and wisdom too."

"Wisdom? Where is the wisdom in any of this?"

"Whether I live the role of a shamed woman who broke her engagement and is despised by society or a married woman living in subjection and dissension, also despised by society, I shall be miserable. However, in the first case, I suffer alone, whereas in the second, Mr Darcy suffers with me.

"I could not bind myself to a man who scorned me, as my father does my mother. She is insensible, I think, to most of his slights, whereas I understand each and every one of Mr Darcy's remarks."

"Mr Darcy surely does not—"

"Can you imagine the fate that awaits me at the hand of my mother? At least she has Jane's match to console her—another charge which must be laid at my door. Now Jane must suffer such a man her whole life long, all because I would not do as my mother wished. Oddly enough, it would seem this might have been the one case in which Mama was correct."

It was the thoughts of her sister which at last broke her. Elizabeth bent over, tears suddenly pouring down her cheeks. Her aunt touched her hand, and she grasped onto it, holding it tightly to her chest. "Oh, what shall I do? What can I do? I have made such a jumble of it all!"

Mrs Gardiner pulled Elizabeth into an embrace, patting her back and smoothing her hair until she was calm again, then asked, "Elizabeth, how do you feel? Do you like him? Do you love him?"

"No."

"Are you sure?"

Elizabeth drew a deep, shuddering breath. "I do not think he even likes me. He acted like he hated me when I was in his house earlier."

"I did not ask what you think *he* feels. What do *you* feel?"

"This life is not for me." Elizabeth sighed heavily, twisting the sodden handkerchief in her lap. "I do not fit into his life, and I cannot become what he wishes me to be."

She could feel the weight of her aunt's stare upon her for several long minutes. Finally, Mrs Gardiner said, "It is easier —is it not?—when we feel someone might reject us, to first reject them. For a man like Mr Darcy, who seemed so very unattainable—"

"It seemed quite the spur to my genius to despise him

when everyone else wanted to flatter him. But I had secured him. He was mine, and now he is not."

It gave her an odd feeling to speak those words. He had been hers once, but she had lost him; the sharp pain associated with that nearly overwhelmed her.

"Perhaps you felt his love was unattainable, even when the marriage was certain," Mrs Gardiner suggested.

"It hardly matters now. It is done, and there is no hope."

"Perhaps if you went to him—"

"No, no." Elizabeth rose, squaring her shoulders and replacing her sadness with determination. "He is a proud man, and he has boasted that his good opinion, once lost, is lost forever. There is no second chance here."

And then she was crying again and wondering at exactly how many tears she had left within her.

THERE WAS no one at Matlock House but Fitzwilliam when Darcy arrived. His curiosity had briefly quelled his anger, but it was back now in full measure and caused him to immediately demand of his cousin, "Where is she?"

"Elizabeth? No idea," Fitzwilliam replied. "Something wrong?"

Darcy did not reply, going to the window to look out below, as though he expected to see Elizabeth on the street. He drummed his fingers against the sill before raising one hand to rub the back of his neck. "I...I need to speak to her. Where is she?"

"As mentioned two seconds ago, I have no idea. Shall we ask Mrs Banks?"

Mrs Banks was sent for and could add nothing to the

mystery save to say that Miss Bennet had gone out, and she had no idea when she would return. Darcy tried not to growl with frustration and was helped by Fitzwilliam, who clapped his back and said, "Join me at the billiards table, then? I am sure Elizabeth will be back soon."

The gentlemen were silent as they walked to the billiards room, set up the balls, and selected their sticks. Fitzwilliam got them both drinks as Darcy broke, and they began their game.

Three full games were played with no sound but the resounding crack of ball against ball and the minimal conversation required to conduct the game. Darcy took great satisfaction in making shots with fierce and forceful precision. As they began a fourth match, Fitzwilliam said, "Do you want to talk about anything?"

"No."

After a few shots more for each, Fitzwilliam enquired carefully, "A disagreement, was it?"

Darcy took great care in lining up his next shot. As he bent to strike, his eye fixed on his target, he said, "She thinks Wickham some sort of hero, and yes, I disagree wholeheartedly." The violent thwack of his shot was a satisfying punctuation to such ridiculous notions.

"A hero? Wickham?" Fitzwilliam laughed. "You mentioned he was in Hertfordshire, but I assumed you got rid of him before he could meet her."

"She almost fell into a river she was attempting to walk across, and it was high because of recent rain, and he jumped in to help her out. I guess it was somewhat heroic. One lurks near a lady long enough and eventually one will have a chance to be of some assistance. In any case, she did not see fit to inform me of the incident, and I had to learn of it today from Miss Bingley, who witnessed the whole scene."

Fitzwilliam grimaced. "That is unfortunate. Still, if she was in trouble, it was good someone was there to help, even if that someone was George Wickham. Does she realise it was he who—"

"Did you not tell her about that?"

"Saye and I told her the story but never the name—we did not think it signified."

"I see." Darcy took a deep swig of his drink. "Well…even though the situation was unavoidable, she should have informed me of it."

"Indeed she should have," Fitzwilliam said with satiric warmth. "After all, look how honest you were with her about Georgie."

"What do you mean?"

"Meaning the woman who marries you will be responsible for your ill sister, and Elizabeth agreed to marry you knowing nothing of it. Georgiana's situation could still come out and bring scandal onto everyone, including the Bennets."

"The Bennets are—" Darcy began to protest but then stopped. True, the Bennets were not of the first circles, but they were respectable people. They had nothing to besmirch their names, no whiff of scandal about them. He frowned.

"The Bennets?" Fitzwilliam prompted.

"You are right," Darcy acknowledged grudgingly. "She should have known. I daresay I should have told her, and her father as well. I suppose I thought that the elevation in their connexions would make up for any potential for disrepute."

"I do not know her family, but such an elevation surely does not impress Elizabeth overmuch. She seems as likely to strike up a conversation with the dustman as a duchess."

He was right, and not only that, Darcy knew it too. The things she valued were not of town and *ton*. She valued honesty, loyalty, laughter, and love. He cursed, the hopelessness of the situation coming over him. She was everything he had ever wanted in a woman, yet he was nothing she wanted in a man.

He suddenly desired nothing more than to escape. Reaching into his pocket, he withdrew the paper about Collins, intending to give it to his cousin to pass on to Elizabeth, but seeing it arrested him.

"What is that?" Fitzwilliam craned his neck to look, but Darcy did not immediately answer. His mind began to turn, considering the information contained on the page he held. It was such a substantial and unusual error that it was hard to dismiss as mere nothing. But what could it mean?

It was Jane Bennet's engagement that had precipitated this most dreadful of quarrels. Was there some way that this error might affect the entail? Because if it did, and if Jane might somehow be released from her engagement to Collins…

I am trying to brew a tempest in my tea cup. In all probability it meant nothing and would have no consequence for anyone.

"Darcy, what is on that paper?"

But if it somehow brokered Jane's freedom...then I would be the hero. And Darcy wanted badly to be Elizabeth's hero. It was galling that only Wickham had had the opportunity to come to her aid. *Was that why I was so enraged at such an obviously inconsequential encounter and—to be truthful—fortunate rescue? Because I was* never *her hero?*

"What are you doing tomorrow?" Darcy asked his cousin.

Fitzwilliam shrugged. "Nothing that could not be changed. Why?"

"I need you to come with me to Bourne."

"Bourne? Why?"

Darcy did not reply, having heard the sounds of his uncle in the hall. Had Elizabeth returned? His lordship was speaking to someone. "Excuse me," he said, laying his stick aside.

As he exited the room, Fitzwilliam strolling after him, Lord Matlock was coming down the hall, chuckling heartily as he walked with a gentleman unknown to Darcy. The unknown gentleman was smiling amiably as well.

"Ah, there you are!" Lord Matlock exclaimed, seeing the two before him. "Darcy, you must already know Mr Gardiner. Gardiner, this is my youngest son, Colonel Richard Fitzwilliam."

The men all bowed to one another as Darcy searched his mind for the reason why his uncle supposed him to know Mr Gardiner. The name did sound familiar, but he could not place it.

That Mr Gardiner was a person of fashion was immediately plain. He had a clear, intelligent gaze and treated Lord Matlock in a manner that was respectful but not servile. A brief conversation showed him to be erudite as well as amusing, making more than one wry observation that made the gentlemen laugh.

When the carriage was brought up, Lord Matlock insisted on going out to see it, telling the other men, "Mr Gardiner has an interest with Hatchett and Barker, and they have employed all the modern methods in his carriage. Riding in this carriage must be as comfortable as being in one's own bed!"

"You will come for a ride in it some day and see for yourself, though I warn you that the day I did so was the day I went off and spent quite a lot of money. But my wife was increasing at the time, so I told myself it was for her." Lord Matlock clapped him on the back, laughing heartily, as Mr Gardiner departed.

"A good man, that," said his lordship. "Come boys, let us go have a drink in my study."

"Who is he?" Fitzwilliam asked. "I have not heard you mention the connexion before."

"With good cause. It is nearly impossible to get an audience with him, much less partner with him—and now he is family!" Lord Matlock could not contain his glee. The men had entered the study by this point, and settled into chairs, Lord Matlock pouring Cognac for them all. "A gift from the man himself. He wished to thank me on behalf of Elizabeth."

"Elizabeth?" Darcy asked, but Lord Matlock only nodded, watching Fitzwilliam savour the Cognac.

"Wonderful," Fitzwilliam said with an appreciative sigh. "But why is it you have not met him before? I know few who can ignore your summons, Father."

"Gardiner is a man of business," Lord Matlock replied, shocking both his son and his nephew. His lordship was not known for his liberality where the classes were concerned. "Very successful and thus has more penniless earls and baronets coming after him than he cares to deal with. He is highly selective with new acquaintances—I have no doubt I could gain an audience with King George sooner than Edward Gardiner—at least until today."

"What does he do that is so unique?" Fitzwilliam asked curiously.

"He is, simply put, brilliant," said his lordship. "In the

manner of Midas, the things he touches turn to gold. I cannot explain it—if I could, I would do it myself—but he has a nose for investments and is careful who he allows to partner with him. Ratcliff was the first to approach him."

"Lord Ratcliff?" Darcy questioned. "He does not even speak to the untitled!"

"Snobbery is an expensive habit," Lord Matlock agreed. "And one Ratcliff can no longer afford. His estate was hit hard when an epidemic of typhus swept through his tenants, and suddenly his farms were more empty than full. Then his house very nearly burnt to the ground. It was desperate times. So off he went to Gardiner, right as he was on the verge of mortgaging his lands, and Gardiner was able to help him make enough money to keep himself afloat and, eventually, to refill his coffers.

"After that, Gardiner had nearly everyone of consequence coming after him, but he is exceedingly selective about who gets in. He tells you straight off he will not take your money unless you can afford to lose it, and he will not entertain the notion of family heirlooms or mortgaged estates as security. 'Tis an unusual position he has, but the luxury of being a man in trade is that he scarcely cares two straws for status or family name. It is all what you bring to the table, no more than that, and whether you despise him for it, who cares? Most of the *ton* disdain the tradesmen regardless."

Lord Matlock took a long drink. "The world is changing, boys, and do not let it be said that the house of Matlock lags behind. Richard, you have the inheritance left to you by your mother's father—you might want to consider doing more with it than collecting interest. Mr Gardiner might be able to increase it quite handsomely for you, and he would, being that we are all family now."

"How is it that he is now family?" Fitzwilliam asked.

"Elizabeth's uncle," Lord Matlock said. "I met him when he brought Elizabeth back today."

So shocked was he that Darcy exclaimed, loudly and incongruously, "That is Mrs Bennet's brother?"

Lord Matlock, clearly taken aback by the vehemence of Darcy's outburst, said mildly, "Being that his name is not Bennet, then yes, he must come from her mother's side. Really Darcy, you might have told me it was Gardiner. You said he was in trade, like he was some shopkeeper or something."

"I hardly knew myself," Darcy said slowly, thinking how genteel and mannerly the man had been. "I had not met him before." Darcy hoped he had not offended the man by not requesting an introduction. Lord Matlock had not suggested it, assuming they were acquainted, and Mr Gardiner had been gentlemanly enough to overlook the slight.

Lord Matlock rose. "I believe it is well past time that I dress for dinner, and Richard, I suggest the same for you. Darcy, will you dine with us?"

His immediate instinct was to demur, feeling unequal to facing Elizabeth over the dinner table in the presence of his relations. He wondered what else Mr Gardiner had known behind those kindly eyes. His own uncle, he concluded, knew nothing, based on his cheerfulness.

What now? Did she intend to go through with it? Did he? Or would they make peace with one another? He had to find out, uncomfortable though it might be, and resolved to get her alone for a time.

"I shall. Thank you."

CHAPTER TWENTY TWO

Elizabeth remained above stairs until the last possible moment, then descended, pale and withdrawn, having obviously been crying. Watching her produced a contrariety of emotion. His last pulse of anger ebbed into sorrow, and the small bit of lover's elation he had always known, could now be named for what it was. *Yet another way her eyes command me,* he thought, feeling every bit of his powerlessness.

She did not speak and neither did he; he offered her his arm and led her into the dining room. Saye pushed past him. "Take your place over there, Darcy. I sit next to Miss Bennet."

Darcy gave his eldest cousin a look. "It is a family dinner, is it really necessary to—"

"If we do not observe order, then we are no better than savages." Saye gave Darcy a shove and a smirk, taking his seat next to Elizabeth with an overdone flip of his tails. Elizabeth's attention was being commanded by his aunt, so Darcy suppressed a sigh, then walked around the table to take the seat across from her.

Elizabeth kept her eyes fixed carefully on soup she

scarcely touched, and he ached watching her, knowing how she felt. How had it come to pass that the woman he loved did not even think he liked her?

Likely because you did not hide how you wished to take her and mould her into a Mrs Darcy that had no remnant of Bennet left within her—at least until the ball showed you how dreadful that would be.

He had been, he felt suddenly, remarkably unfeeling, staggeringly selfish to her; all he had ever felt since this began was what *he* needed and what *he* wanted. Words from the autumn echoed in his mind, and they were not to his credit. *'I find myself in a position where it is necessary for us to marry.'*

He had not hidden his disgust of her family and friends. Hertfordshire society was not what he was accustomed to, yet who was he to judge? As his cousin had observed earlier, he was kin to some rather questionable characters himself. What difference was there between Mrs Bennet and Lady Catherine, in truth, save for the fact that Lady Catherine's title and fortune meant that people were required to tolerate her better? He had openly censured the brazen behaviour of Elizabeth's sisters, but none of them had attempted an elopement, nor had they been holed up in a room for nearly half a year refusing to bathe. As for his own faults, well…one had only to refer back to the product of his guardianship to see the multitude of his failures. Mr Bennet, a lax guardian? His daughters were healthy, hale, and happy. It was enough.

Lady Matlock's voice intruded upon his reverie. "I saw Mrs Davies and her daughter today, Elizabeth. They wished me to pass on their regards."

Across the table, Saye snorted. "Oh, I bet they did."

"They did," Lady Matlock insisted.

"Well then they were surely more generous than has been historically shown," Saye said with a sniff.

"What do you mean, Saye?"

"Mother, come now. Miss Davies has dangled after Darcy since she came out. No doubt she wishes Elizabeth would come down with a sudden and rapid-moving case of the plague." Darcy quickly darted a glance at Elizabeth, worried she would be offended, but although she did not smile, her eyes betrayed some amusement.

"Not only me," Darcy protested. "You too."

"Yes," Saye replied, "but I was ruder to her, let her know she had no hope straightaway."

"What a thing to say!" Lady Matlock shook her head at her son. "Mrs Davies is—"

"Another desperate mama angry that some unknown country girl reeled in the big fish. Elizabeth, was she overtly rude? Or did she whisper about you behind her fan?"

"Oh, um..." Elizabeth stammered, blushing, but fortunately Saye did not require an answer. "If that ball was any indication," he accused with a wave of his fork, "you seem to have focused your efforts on showing her to the Darcy cast-offs."

Sounding insulted, Lady Matlock said, "Son, you do say the most absurd things at times."

"What is a Darcy cast-off?" Lord Matlock asked. "Sounds like a military term."

"You are thinking of castaway," Fitzwilliam replied helpfully. "Naval term."

"You can hardly say Lady and Miss Hepplewhite, Lady Wellburton and her daughter, Mrs Archer and Mrs Featherstone, and Lady—"

Saye nodded. "Just as I suspected. First to last, Darcy cast-offs. Darcy, be a good man and back me on this."

And then, at once, everyone, including Elizabeth, suddenly looked at Darcy, and Darcy, awkwardly, said, "Not one of them had any reason to believe I had intentions towards them."

"You danced with them," Saye told him.

"Never more than once, if even that!"

"Once is too often for some of them," Saye replied with a pointed glance. Then he whispered something to Elizabeth that Darcy could not hear but which made her smile, faintly, but still... Darcy was sure the joke was at his expense, but he forgave Saye if it brought Elizabeth some small pleasure.

"Many of them had set their caps on Darcy for no other reason than their mother's friendship with my mother," Fitzwilliam added. "It was you or Saye—"

"And I am as barbarous as I am alluring," Saye said. "They want me, they fear me, but most of all, they fear how much they want me."

This pronouncement was greeted with a brief period of silence which Saye himself ended by saying, "In any case, I could have taken Elizabeth to a cockfight in Clerkenwell, and she would have met with better people than this."

"I shall not permit you to take Elizabeth to a cockfight," Lord Matlock said sternly. He cast Elizabeth a warning glance, as if he thought she might insist on attending one.

"My mother has done all she can, but now I shall introduce you to my friends and we shall see how they do for you."

For a brief moment, Elizabeth met Darcy's eye but just as quickly looked away. From his chair, Lord Matlock said,

"But no cockfights. Reputable gatherings, Saye, of wholesome people."

"Obviously." Saye rolled his eyes. "And pray do not forget—we still have not called on your dear friend Miss Goddard."

"I am afraid I do not know her direction."

With a flourish, Saye removed a slip of paper from his pocket, showing it to her. "Almost neighbours, there. We shall call tomorrow. Also the opera. Darcy, why have you not taken her yet? Do you speak Italian, Elizabeth?"

She looked as though Saye's plans were overwhelming her. "I...I am not sure."

"You are not sure whether you speak Italian?" Saye asked dubiously.

"N-no. I mean, yes, I do speak Italian, but..."

"You will explain it to me, then. I have never had much of an ear for languages myself." Saye grinned, moving easily past Elizabeth's moment of discomfort. "I believe we shall enjoy ourselves together exceedingly well."

As he saw Elizabeth's relieved smile, Darcy wondered how it was that Saye—self-centred, arrogant Saye—saw so clearly and quickly what Darcy had not. Darcy had taken her from her family and given her everything she told him she did not want and nothing of what she did—dignity, respect, love. *Because you have only been thinking of what you wanted and what you were feeling and having and wishing her to become. Not her. Never of her.*

His hand began to shake; he had not realised that he was painfully clenching his fork to the point of exhausting the muscles of his hand. He set his utensil down carefully, but it clattered against his aunt's fine bone china nevertheless. He rose, a bit unsteady on his feet. "Ex-excuse me," he said, turning to leave the table.

"Darcy, are you well?" his aunt asked after him.

"Yes," he said. "Just...I just need a minute."

ELIZABETH WATCHED DARCY WALK OUT, half wanting to follow him and half relieved he was gone. She could not think what had induced him to remain that night, but then again, perhaps he thought the same of her. Perhaps he thought she should have been on her way back to Longbourn even now. She had no idea what she was supposed to have done and certainly no idea what to do next. What she did know was that it had utterly discomposed her to be made to sit across from him and pretend to be indifferent to his presence at the table.

In her head, her aunt's voice again asked the question, *'do you love him?'*

She recalled seeing him the first time, standing so haughtily by the door as Sir William Lucas greeted Mr Bingley's party. Darcy, Miss Bingley, the Hursts—they had not been pleased with what they saw, and Darcy's particular disgust had led him to insult her later that evening.

But before that, before any slights had occurred, before she even knew his name, she felt something, a sharp thrill of excitement, the quickening of her heart, and a desire to know more of him. Darcy was a handsome man, there was no question of it, but there was more to it than that. After all, Mr Bingley was handsome as well, and she had not felt that pull towards him, nor had she felt it for other handsome men of her acquaintance. For Darcy, she had experienced an immediate and intense attraction wholly unlike anything she had ever known before.

Of course, her fleeting attraction to him had rendered his insult more potent, enabling him to hurt her in a way that few other gentlemen had ever had the power to do. It was something he had evidently been paying for since, and by her own hand, even though she had not exacted her penance purposefully.

And what of the time since?

A rush of memories came to her: their inconsequential banter the night the carriage wheel broke on the return from the party at Ashworth; his touch when he found her weeping outside of Netherfield the night of the ball; the way he stole into her sitting room when she was ill; her compassion for him when she saw him upset.

His humour she had not expected, but she liked it very well indeed. Laughing with him, talking to him, kissing him —precious moments. A tenderness began to grow in her as the memories of all that was good in him ran through her mind unimpeded, and a lump formed in her throat. *This will not do!* she scolded, reminding herself that she was at a dinner table with his relations.

It is done now. It matters not that you love him. It is unlikely he will even return to the table. He had been gone some time now while she had been lost in her thoughts, mechanically eating and smiling, and making stilted replies to the conversation.

At dinner she learnt he and Colonel Fitzwilliam were going to some place called Bourne the following morning. It was two days there and two back; and thus they would be gone five or six days complete for business known to no one but Darcy.

She was pulled from her musings by Lady Matlock, who had risen from the table. It was time for the drawing room, where she would spend as few minutes as required and then retire.

The two ladies entered the drawing room, and Darcy entered through a different door only a moment later. "Darcy, I hope you are well?" Lady Matlock smiled at her nephew. "They are having their port—"

"Excuse me, but I need to speak to Elizabeth alone for a moment," Darcy said to her in hurried accents. "And then I shall be for home to prepare for my trip tomorrow."

Lady Matlock was taken aback, but a glance at Darcy's face seemed to persuade her to ignore the fact that she had just been dismissed from her own drawing room. "Very well then," she said. "A few minutes cannot hurt. I shall leave the door open."

She quit the room with only a brief backward glance. Elizabeth felt her stomach twist painfully when her ladyship, despite her warning, did close the door behind her.

Darcy's countenance revealed nothing of his thoughts, but given his violent anger of the afternoon, she could only suppose he continued in it. Trying not to show her dismay, she turned partially away from him. "You might have forgotten, but I am meant to depart on Tuesday next."

He walked towards her slowly and deliberately until he stood before her. "Indeed, I had forgotten."

She did not look up. "Perhaps I should go earlier…now?"

He did not reply. She could hear him breathing, deep and somewhat ragged, and then he raised his hands, almost touching her, seeming as though he intended to embrace her —but he did not. A moment later his hands fell again to his sides. "Will you look at me?"

She did, raising her eyes and fixing them on his.

"Do not say there is not love. For whatever you have felt,

for me there is love, ardent love, since the first time you appeared in that breakfast parlour with muddy petticoats and brilliant eyes and a heart so full of kindness it was impossible *not* to love you. You will decide whether it is enough. Our quarrels, my high-handedness, your tendency to run amok, and this nonsense of the Bingleys—it can be fixed, and we can be happy. But I cannot allow you to think there is not love, for there is. I love you, all of you, everything about you, and I pray you will offer me—offer us—a second chance.

"When I return, if you still wish to release me, then one word will silence me on the matter forever. I have not considered any wishes but my own thus far, but such selfishness will not do. The choice is yours, dearest, loveliest Elizabeth, and I am at your command."

He bowed, then paused, then bowed again but more shallowly. Seeming to reach some gentlemanly decision, he moved towards the door, apparently having determined to leave her.

Then, in a rush, he returned and grabbed her hands, pulling them to his chest. In a voice made rough with emotion, he whispered, "I said I would not beg, but I will, of course I will. Anything for you, anything you want...but please do not leave me."

And she, having no notion what to think or feel or do, bent her head, lightly kissing his knuckles. He replied with a light kiss to her head and then dropped her hands and left her.

CHAPTER TWENTY THREE

After such a day that ran from despair to elation and confusion and everything in between, Elizabeth thought she should have fallen to the floor in a heap of exhaustion the moment she retired. But she did not. She sat at the dressing table, failing even to ring for the maid to help her undress, her mind revisiting the scene in the drawing room.

"Lizzy?"

Elizabeth shook her head, rousing herself from her recollections to smile at the girl who appeared over her shoulder. Her smile turned to concern almost immediately; Georgiana looked even more distressed than was her custom. "What is wrong?" She turned and rose from the table.

"I have been on pins and needles all night waiting for you. You quarrelled with Fitzwilliam, did you not? About Mr Wickham?"

"You must not worry about that—everyone quarrels sometimes. How did you know?"

"Before you returned from visiting your aunt, he was playing billiards and talking to Richard. I could hear them."

"Do you remember Mr Wickham?"

Georgiana went still as a deep red flush crept up her neck. "Remember him? I…I…indeed, I do." Hesitantly, she sat on the edge of Elizabeth's bed and said, "Mr Wickham is the man from…from last summer. The man who…"

"Who what?" Elizabeth asked, then inhaled sharply as horror struck her. "Not the man who–"

"The very one," Georgiana replied quickly.

With a gasp of breath, Elizabeth said, "No wonder Darcy despises him so!" She shook her head, astonished. "Pray, forgive me, I had no idea. I never would have spoken of him so, had I known that it brings you pain."

"You did not know?"

"Your cousins told me about what happened last summer, but they never disclosed his name." Elizabeth uttered a small groan of dismay at the remembrance of what she had said to Darcy in defence of the scoundrel earlier that day. How her words must have pained him, particularly if he believed she knew the truth!

"How do you know him, Elizabeth?"

Elizabeth joined Georgiana on her bed. "I knew him only a little in Hertfordshire. He was with a militia there and arrived after I was already engaged to your brother. He came to a party at my aunt's house and told some…some tales to me."

"Tales of *me*?"

"No…really hardly anything at all, something about a living your father left to him but which your brother denied him. But forgive me, I do not mean to pain you more than I already have." Elizabeth shook her head ruefully. "How thoughtlessly cruel I have been, to your brother and to you!"

"How could you have known, if no one told you, of the long history of the Wickhams and my family?"

"Will you explain it to me? If you are able?"

"I am able. Perfectly so." Georgiana then related to her the truth behind Darcy's hatred of Wickham, beginning with their boyhood friendship, which led to pains and hurts, Wickham's various cruelties and libertine behaviour, the friendships he had tried to take away from Darcy. It was shocking, and far beyond anything that Elizabeth could have imagined based on her scant acquaintance with the man who had appeared so charming and agreeable.

"Anything my brother had, Mr Wickham wanted, even if just to *ruin* it—the latest of which was me, my life and my person, though he cannot be wholly accountable for what I allowed. I thought his charm was something to do with me, that he truly had some feeling for me, but it was mere puffery. In any case, although regrets may be had, what was lost can never again be found."

Elizabeth reached for her, squeezing her hand.

"I do not know how I shall ever look at my brother again," Georgiana confessed. Her hands began to twist and chafe in front of her. "He is too good, too upright and honourable, and to think that I have done this, have willingly brought this shame upon us… I cannot bear to know his disappointment in me."

"He wants only for you to be well again, I assure you. He does not censure you."

"Oh, but I wish he would. I wish he would just sit me down and ring a peal over me!"

"If you wish that," Elizabeth teased gently, "you will need to first leave your bedchamber. He can hardly ring a peal over you when you refuse to see him."

"It is too hard. Every time I think of it, I find myself stuck at the door. You have no idea how often I imagine myself among them again." A wistful smile came over her face.

"Then why not try?" The words popped out of Elizabeth's mouth before she could stop them.

"Try…going out there?"

"Why not?" Elizabeth asked. "You come in here readily enough. How much worse could it be to go down there?"

"But you are different," Georgiana said. "You had no hand in raising me. You bear no burden of my shame. I am not your failure."

"You are not any person's failure," Elizabeth insisted. "My dear, you are but sixteen. Scarcely grown! Yes, your life has taken a little turn, but you remain Georgiana Darcy of Pemberley, a beautiful young woman of fine fortune with family who loves her dearly. You are by no means friendless in this world."

Georgiana considered this while Elizabeth considered her, thinking of the strangeness of seeing a girl like her, hair down, so peculiarly dressed in rags, yet with perfect posture, her bearing ramrod straight, and that certain something in her air that Miss Bingley would extol. Georgiana Darcy was of noble birth, even in her present disguise.

"But who would ever marry me?" she asked.

Elizabeth would not lie to her for she knew the truth. Some men *would* turn away from her—but not Darcy. Of this she was certain. To those he loved, he was true. "That I cannot say, but I promise you this, Georgiana, you will always have a place with me. With us."

"Truly?" The look of relief which swept across the girl's countenance was astounding.

"Did you think your brother would not have you?" Elizabeth asked. "He loves you very much, you know. Even when I scarcely knew him, I knew how he doted on you."

"N-no, but...well, I knew he would one day marry, and when that happened she...you...his wife might not...but you would? You would let me remain with you?"

"Consider it a promise. I used to tease my sister that I would never marry, and I would live with her and her husband and teach her ten children to play their instruments very ill."

"Instead, I shall be that sister," Georgiana said happily.

"Save that I have heard that you play very well, so I daresay my children would become as accomplished as you are. But let us hope there are not ten of them!"

But the jest, no matter how it began, had brought Jane and her dilemma to mind; all else was forgot as Elizabeth curled her legs beneath her and began to avail herself of her young friend's willing ear to speak of her elder sister's trouble.

When the night began at length to turn to day and Elizabeth's yawns could be disguised no more, Georgiana rose to leave. But Elizabeth forestalled her. "Georgiana, what we spoke of before? That you might try to come downstairs?"

"Oh." Georgiana laughed nervously. "You do not forget, do you?"

"Your brother and Colonel Fitzwilliam are away. Perhaps it will be easier to face them in stages?" With an encouraging smile, Elizabeth added, "If you come down for dinner, everyone must eat, and that will turn their attention away from you at least part of the time."

The pause between them went on for what seemed an excessively long time until, at last, Georgiana nodded.

In the early hours of the next morning, Fitzwilliam settled into Darcy's carriage with a thud and muttered, "Wake me when we change horses—I still do not know why I am going to Bourne." He pulled his hat over his face, and moments later, he snored.

And I still am not certain why I *am going to Bourne. Perhaps for no reason at all.* With a slight shake of his head, Darcy leant back, resolved to his course of action, and believing, even if not knowing, it would work for good.

Some hours later, when the horses and men were both refreshed, Fitzwilliam gave him an expectant look. "Well then? I believe I am owed some explanation."

"And you will have one, inasmuch as I have it." Darcy removed the now-familiar, creased and re-creased page from his breast pocket and handed it to his cousin

Fitzwilliam skimmed it quickly, no sign of comprehension on his face. When he looked up, he gave Darcy a quizzical look. "What is this?"

"*That* was mistakenly in among the marriage articles that Mr Bennet signed. I was warm yesterday and so opened a window, and the wind blew the contents of my desk all about the room. When I picked it all up and re-ordered it, I found this page."

"A page telling of a William Collins christened on June 29, 1806 in Bourne, and who is the heir to Longbourn. Longbourn is Elizabeth's family estate?"

Darcy nodded.

"Very well. So?"

"While I was in Hertfordshire, Mr Collins presented himself at Longbourn—the families were estranged and did not know him, only his father. Mr Collins is five-and-twenty and holds the living of our own dear aunt at Hunsford parsonage."

"There are likely a multitude of William Collinses. Hardly an unusual name." Fitzwilliam reached across, handing Darcy the page. "A William Collins christened in '06 would still be scratching out sums on a slate, not writing sermons."

"Except he purports to be one and the same William Collins."

Fitzwilliam wrinkled his brow, and removed his hat, scratching his head. "Some parish clerk made a mistake in recording the date—more than likely it means nothing."

"Perhaps, save for the fact that there are other inconsistencies in his life story, things he said which did not match other things said of him." Darcy met his cousin's eyes. No matter how disinterested Fitzwilliam's words, he could see that the puzzle provoked his interest.

"This is not your estate, and therefore not your business."

"It *became* my business when Elizabeth cried in my arms over it."

Fitzwilliam could not argue with such logic as that. "Why did she do that? This is the cousin they tried to make her marry, yes?"

"And who is now engaged to her beloved sister, as of only yesterday," Darcy informed Fitzwilliam, gratified to see comprehension dawning. "I do not think any Bennet, including Miss Bennet, would contradict the statement that the only attraction Mr Collins holds is his standing as the heir presumptive of Longbourn. Which brings me to my concern in this matter—what if he is not?"

"But surely before seeing one of his daughters tied to the man, Mr Bennet looked into this?" Fitzwilliam asked. "You did say these papers must have originally come from his desk."

Darcy shook his head. "Mr Bennet has not exerted himself in the care of his estate. I doubt he has ever really examined the documents pertaining to the entail. He had always planned to have a son and break it."

Fitzwilliam stared up at the ceiling of the carriage considering the angles of it all. It was why he was such a good ally, never one to dismiss an argument without careful deliberation of all sides. "What if," he began slowly, "in the absence of her sister, Miss Bennet has fallen in love with this Collins?"

"Miss Bennet is in love with Bingley," Darcy said. "Has been since last autumn."

Fitzwilliam rolled his eyes. "Poor girl. I might have told her how that would turn out."

"He was different this time," Darcy said with a shake of his head. "He appeared genuinely attached to her. It is why I never did speak to him of Georgiana."

After Ramsgate—when they knew not what would ever come of her—their immediate inclination was to arrange a hasty marriage for Georgiana. When Darcy considered which of his friends might be willing and who would be good to her, Bingley was first on the list. Thus had Darcy decided to go to Netherfield with the primary object of assessing the possibility of seeing his friend married to his sister.

Fitzwilliam said, "I was not sure it was a good scheme to begin with."

Darcy shrugged. "At the time I feared, if she were with child...but no, we have at least that comfort. He might have considered it for the advantage of our connexions. A tradesman's son becoming nephew to the Earl of Matlock would be a substantial elevation."

"Nephew to the Earl of Matlock...and raising Wickham's bastard," Fitzwilliam concluded with a quirked brow. "Is it really worth it? Being a son to said earl, I cannot say myself."

Impatiently, Darcy continued, "In any case, Georgiana is not increasing, and Miss Bennet was left heartbroken by Bingley who went to town on business and suddenly announced he would not return to the country. I was preoccupied with my own matters and assumed he had merely lost interest in her."

"As is his custom."

"Yet..." Darcy drummed his fingers against his leg. "He has been rather downcast ever since. Oddly, he is behaving as if it were he who was abandoned." He thought then of Bingley's repeated questions about Jane's engagement; something was strange there too, but he knew not what. He would need to ask Bingley when he returned. "In any case, Elizabeth's sister accepted an offer of marriage from Mr Collins, heir presumptive to her father's estate, who was inexplicably christened only five or six years ago."

"And thus it is that our hero and his trusted companion are off to Bourne to have a poke about the parish records and see what is what." Fitzwilliam grinned. "Of course, I must maintain it is most likely no more than some little error in the record. You have forgotten philosophy. *Pluralitas non est ponenda sine necessitate.*"

"The simplest explanation is usually correct. No, I do not forget that. But if there is something that could be done, some way my future wife's happiness might be increased, then I shall do all I can for it."

WHEN GEORGIANA KNOCKED on Elizabeth's door, she was sure the girl had come to tell her she could not join them for dinner. But when Georgiana entered, although she was pale and looked even more fragile than usual, she did not demur. "I wonder whether I might ask you for some help?"

"Of course." Elizabeth set down the book she had been reading and stood. "What do you need?"

"I thought I should wear, you know…one of my old gowns?" She held out her hand from which the ribbons Elizabeth had given her dangled. "Maybe put up my hair, if you could help me?"

Elizabeth hid the giddy joy such a simple request gave her. "I do not like to boast, but when you have one maid and four sisters, you do learn to dress hair fairly well."

It was quick work to find in Georgiana's bedchamber the necessary petticoats and corset. She did not have stockings—leading to a rather grim joke about everyone thinking she would hang herself with them—but Elizabeth quickly retrieved a pair of her own. Georgiana had no evening gowns at Matlock House, but Elizabeth assured her that her family would not mind and helped her into a pretty day gown that might have done with some pressing but was otherwise suitable.

Georgiana kept a tight hold on Elizabeth's arm as they descended towards the drawing room. Elizabeth heard his lordship holding forth about something to do with Swedish Pomerania as the footman opened the door for them. The two ladies entered side by side.

Lord Matlock's words died, and he rose, looking grave and solemn. Saye also rose and was uncommonly speechless.

Lady Matlock remained in her seat, a hand clutching her handkerchief held to her lips. She was the first to recover from her surprise, however, and began to speak, her voice too high and too cheerful, and her words far too fast.

"Why…why Georgiana. You look lovely. It is so good you are out of your room. How very well you appear! Just lovely! You are feeling better, I think? You look just wonderful. Will you dine with us tonight? Do dine with us tonight. Will you eat something?"

"May I please?" Georgiana asked, and Elizabeth patted her arm reassuringly.

"Of course! Of course you may! We are thrilled! James… are we not thrilled? Saye? Someone do tell our dear girl how glad we are she will join us this evening."

"We are thrilled," Lord Matlock confirmed gravely. "Quite beyond measure."

They went into dinner, and Elizabeth wished, dearly, she could do something to ease the tension. Lord and Lady Matlock both watched Georgiana as if she were a keg of powder which might explode at any moment, and even Saye was uncharacteristically sombre and watchful. The soup was served, and Lady Matlock seemed to hold her breath in anticipation as Georgiana placed her spoon into her soup and took the tiniest of sips.

Lady Matlock leant forward eagerly. "Do you like the soup, Georgiana? Perhaps I ought to have had the cook make something heartier for you? Your colour is very good. I daresay that this soup will do for you as well. Do you like the taste? Perhaps you need salt?"

Georgiana had startled when her name was spoken and listened to Lady Matlock with eyes wide. Elizabeth decided she must intervene and take the attention away from Georgiana. "I think the soup is delicious," she exclaimed cheerfully. She then looked at Saye and enquired energetically about a book she had seen him reading. From there, she guided the discussion to books in general, including scandalising Lord Matlock with the admission that she had read some of Fourier's works.

"Your father allows you to read Fourier?"

With an arch smile, she replied, "Only in the sense that he did not know of it, sir."

This then led to a spirited discussion of some of Fourier's tenets for utopian society, and the truly surprising admission by Lady Matlock that she, too, had read Fourier and particularly enjoyed those ideas pertaining to women. Georgiana was forgot, for the moment, while she argued her case to her husband.

"Go to any of the great houses and see who truly has the run of the place—the housekeeper, a woman. Mrs Reynolds, for example, has been running Pemberley in the absence of a mistress for fifteen years now—budgets, servants, calendars—I daresay it is well above and beyond any of this nonsense you chew over in the House of Lords."

Lord Matlock had forgotten to eat and stared at his wife with horror. "Eleanor, I assure you, I am as liberal a man as any—having been blessed with a wife who has equal parts wit and beauty—but let us not forget the single greatest contribution any woman makes to society."

Lady Matlock regarded her husband with an air of hauteur. "And what, dear husband, is that?"

Lord Matlock spread his hands wide and said, "Bearing children of course."

"Am I then useless? I shall not be bearing any more children, you may have noticed."

"Of course you are not useless. I only mean that perhaps your most important role is finished."

Lady Matlock dabbed at her lips with her napkin. Then, with a cool glance at her husband, she asked, "Will that corner do?"

His lordship followed the direction of her finely boned finger towards the corner of the room. "For what, dear?"

"For the spot where I shall lie down and die."

Lord Matlock looked about the table, and Elizabeth dropped her eyes to her plate to avoid laughing at his expression of panic. Saye afforded him no such respect and guffawed openly, and even Georgiana hid a small smile behind her napkin.

Elizabeth decided to rescue his lordship. "I have often heard it said that the family is the building block of any great society, and being that a woman—be she wife, mother, grandmother—oft ensures the strength of the home, why I daresay the Empire depends upon her."

"You are very wise, Elizabeth," said Lady Matlock with a toss of her head that looked almost as if it could have belonged to Elizabeth's younger sisters. "Wiser, it seems, than some of these men at the table who are many years your senior."

"I am wise enough to know this much, my darling, that I shall always need you just as much as I love you." And with that, his lordship rose and offered his lady a deep bow over her hand while Lady Matlock blushed like a schoolgirl, and Saye leant back in his chair laughing at them.

It was a sweet moment, but more than that, it was a family moment, unguarded and utterly lacking in the barriers of propriety one had to afford strangers, or even a more distant relation. *I am part of the family circle enough for moments such as these.* It was a warm feeling.

"Aunt, may I be excused?" Georgiana asked as the three ladies entered the drawing room some minutes later. "I…I have a headache."

Lady Matlock's face fell, but Georgiana then asked, "Perhaps I might dine with you tomorrow too? Or do you have plans?"

Lady Matlock recovered immediately. Beaming with pleasure, she went to her niece, kissing her on her cheek and whispering something Elizabeth could not make out but that made Georgiana smile.

When Georgiana left, and the door closed behind her, Lady Matlock heaved a massive sigh. Then, to Elizabeth's great shock, she came to her, leaning in and kissing her cheek too. "Dear girl, what you have done for us!"

"Me?" Elizabeth laughed. "I did nothing more than help her dress."

"You helped with far more than that. I cannot imagine what it was, for I believed that we had tried everything we could with her—but no matter. I am mightily grateful to you."

Elizabeth found herself blushing. "I suppose that sometimes a lady nearer her own age has an advantage."

"You know, I have thought about what Saye said the other night at dinner. About the cast-offs?"

"Oh!" Elizabeth laughed awkwardly. "No, pray do not think I have not been enjoying myself. As you said at the ball, there is a certain ambition among women, and I would be silly to imagine that others do not feel it."

"Be that as it may, I must assure you, you have done very well," Lady Matlock said with an earnest gaze. "I want you to know that his lordship and I shall be glad to call you our niece. Very glad indeed, and I hope you do not doubt it."

And despite the fact that Elizabeth had at times doubted all of it, she could only smile and nod and thank the countess, and be grateful for all the kindness bestowed upon her.

CHAPTER TWENTY FOUR

ELIZABETH'S SPIRITS CONTINUED TO IMPROVE OVER THE NEXT days as she was taken about by Saye. Their first call together was to Miss Lillian Goddard who, she gleaned, Saye had admired for some time. Although Miss Goddard was from Hertfordshire, Elizabeth did not know her well as their homes were enough removed to preclude many meetings, and Miss Goddard had been kept out of society until her older sister married.

"Just act natural with her," Saye instructed, as he sat in his carriage torturing his hair into elaborately careless arrangements. "No good can come from trying too hard."

"I shall be on my guard," she replied drily, watching as he carefully situated his hat on his coiffure, then frowned, removed it and began again to torment his curls.

When at last they entered the drawing room nearly a quarter of an hour later, Miss Goddard was pleasant and pleased to meet them. Indeed, if Elizabeth herself had not known better, she would have thought they were as friendly as Saye had imagined them to be. But whatever amiability existed between the ladies, it was set aside, as Saye was immediately into the fray. Having been accused of prior taciturn behaviour, he appeared determined to make up lost time.

He began by asking after the health of her mother and sisters, and from there rattled away about nearly anything that struck him—his relations, the deplorable state of the roads when visiting his relations, his belief that there ought to be different roads for different sorts of carriages. "After all," he said, "how many of these roads are nearly destroyed by some farmer and his cart heaving about in the middle of it."

"If you had a separate road for more elegant conveyances," Elizabeth asked at this juncture, "would it not be an invitation for highwaymen to accost you? After all, why waste time on the farmer when they could nab a viscount's purse?"

Here Saye paused—it was evidently an angle he had not before considered—and Elizabeth took the opportunity to ask Miss Goddard about her plans for the Season.

"We are quite fixed," she said, sneaking a glance at Saye. "I daresay my mother is determined to see me settled this year, so we shall not stir for anything."

"You have met my mother," Elizabeth replied, "so you must know how well I understand that the plans of mothers cannot be gainsaid."

"No, they certainly cannot." But although Miss Goddard's words referenced Elizabeth's conversation, her eyes followed Saye, who had risen and was perambulating aimlessly about the room, taking up this and that, looking at things and putting them down again, and behaving in all ways exceedingly disinterested.

Evidently noticing that Elizabeth had seen her watching

Saye, Miss Goddard blushed deeply, then dropped her eyes. *These games we must play are confusing for us all.*

When the time for a polite call was finished, Elizabeth rose and was surprised when Miss Goddard offered some information about an exhibition she planned to attend with her friends on the morrow. "Will you join us, Miss Bennet?"

Elizabeth tried to control her smile, to accept with demure pleasure. After all, it would not do to behave as though she had no friends, even if it were true. "I would like that very well. Perhaps, Lord Saye, you will escort me?"

"Who else will be there?" he asked, and Elizabeth struggled not to roll her eyes. Goodness but men were fools at times!

Miss Goddard named a few people that Elizabeth did not know—a Miss Georgette Hawkridge, Miss Sarah Bentley, and a Lady Phee—which caused Saye to sigh. "Oh, Georgette. She is my cousin, you know."

"Yes, I think I did know that."

"I suppose I ought to come, then. No use offending the family, and in any case, my father does not countenance ladies roaming about unattended."

Miss Goddard smiled at him, and he nodded in receipt of it, and then Elizabeth rose and was escorted out, all the while considering how terribly silly were the ways of men, particularly the wealthy ones who had most things in life handed to them.

When they arrived back at the Matlock town house she was surprised to find Mr Bingley awaiting her in the drawing room. He was alone, she was relieved to find, but such relief was only temporary for he was in such a state as could only immediately rouse her anxiety.

He stood by the window, gazing out on the streets below. When he turned to look at her, he appeared as she had never before seen him, with tired, haunted eyes and dolorous lines marring his countenance. His hair was in disarray, hinting at long hours of raking his hands through it. Against her will, she was sorry for him.

"I am for Hertfordshire tomorrow, Miss Bennet. I wonder whether you have any letters you wish me to take to your family."

"Hertfordshire? Is it the sport which draws you?" she asked lightly. "An anxiety of Netherfield being overrun by pheasant or partridge, perhaps?"

"I have an imprudent plan of seeing your sister," he admitted.

"My sister is engaged to be married, sir."

"You do not understand." He stepped towards her. "Caroline told me Miss Bennet had an understanding with Mr Collins—she said their engagement was arranged, that Jane, as first daughter, should rightfully be mistress of Longbourn. It was not until we saw you at Darcy's house, and you said that you were shocked by the news of your sister's engagement that I began to suspect the truth."

"How could you think Jane had an understanding with Mr Collins?" Elizabeth cried. "What, then, did you make of her interest and attention to you? And her clear disinterest in him?"

"I…I thought it was some last time to…to sow her wild oats."

"Sow her wild oats? Good heavens! Jane is a lady!"

"I know, I know!" He hung his head.

"No matter—it is done and she is to be married. You cannot entirely blame Miss Bingley."

He jerked his head upwards and stared at her, wild-eyed. "Caroline lied, she said—"

Elizabeth interrupted, saying firmly, "But you should have learnt the truth of it yourself. Let this be your lesson—you should not allow your sister to lead you about."

Her frankness caused his eyes to fly wide for a moment, and he paused. "I intend to go to your sister—"

"Pray do not."

"—and propose!"

"No!"

"No?"

"I know my sister. If you think for a moment she would end her engagement in favour of you, I must disabuse you of that notion. She will not do it, and in any case, why should she? You might change your mind again tomorrow."

"Change my mind?" Mr Bingley exclaimed. "Not once did I change my mind! Not one day, since the very first that I met her, have I ceased to love her!"

With an angry groan, Elizabeth went to the window. She ran her hand over her head to ward off an incipient headache. "Sir, I am sorry to hear your sister deceived you, but nothing stopped you from returning in November. You believed more in your sister than in your own heart and mind. You might have gone back with Mr Darcy and discovered how things were on your own. Jane was heartbroken when Mr Darcy informed us you would not return."

Behind her, Mr Bingley said, softly and regretfully, "I would do anything, anything at all, to fix this. Truly I would."

Elizabeth turned to him. "Alas, there is nothing to be done. I cannot imagine any circumstance in which Jane will not end as Mrs Collins. You should just go home, Mr Bingley, and forget all about her. I do wish you well."

SAYE ENTERED the room a few minutes later bearing a glass of some drink that he pressed into her hand. She took it from him without much thought for she was still emotional, incredulous, and sad, knowing what Jane had lost. Perhaps it was for the best. Perhaps it was a love that was too changeable and young to have endured. But perhaps, like Darcy had said, it would have grown and matured and been wonderful for a lifetime.

For not the first time, she recognised how she had grown to admire and rely upon Darcy's opinion. She liked his observations and realised that she counted on his sense and his reason.

But now was not the time for such reflections. Absently, she raised the glass to her lips, took a sip and nearly spat the contents back at Saye who was watching her closely. "What is this dreadful potion?"

"Cognac," Saye replied. "Your uncle brought it to us. Only a little, now, it is not meant for ladies. I thought a strong drink was in order after dealing with the likes of Bingley."

Elizabeth wondered how and why her uncle went about procuring such dreadful stuff. Putting that thought aside she asked Saye, "How much did you hear?"

"All of it. Had that very glass pressed to the door." Saye took an enormous swallow of the vile liquid. "It is his own fault, you know. He should not allow that sister of his her own way as much as he does."

"Miss Bingley surely does despise Bennets. She has done

all she can to make us suffer." Elizabeth told Saye how Miss Bingley had reported her to be nearly in Wickham's arms in a river in Hertfordshire, leading to the dreadful row between her and Darcy. From the lack of shock on his countenance, she recognised he had already heard the whole of it.

"Of course, it was all my fault," she finished. "For if I had told Darcy from the start, he would not have been caught unaware."

"Eh, well. Darcy loves you, he will overcome it," Saye remarked casually, and Elizabeth, unaccustomed to hearing such sentiments spoken of freely, blushed and turned towards the window. "Oh, now, none of that missishness here. I heard all about Miss Bingley and the bed and you and the fat cousin they wanted you to marry. But no matter how it started, what I know is that, now, in January '12, my cousin is quite in love with you. But you, Miss Bennet, are something of a mystery. You do tend to keep your own counsel, which I think is why I have not grown bored with you yet."

He finished his drink, then asked, "So how shall we get vengeance on Miss Bingley?"

"Vengeance on Miss Bingley?" Elizabeth laughed, then traded glasses with Saye, as she had not touched it save that first sip. "Hardly necessary. What could be worse for her than seeing me married to Darcy?"

"Oh, I have a few things in mind," he drawled. "Come now, let us think of some ghastly trickery."

Elizabeth looked out on the square. Snow was falling, light icy flakes that would amount to nothing but swirled about rather prettily. "Never mind Miss Bingley; I would rather think happier thoughts. I have come to realise there might be a lesson to learn from this sad business with Mr Bingley and my sister."

"I doubt that."

"Miss Goddard reminds me a great deal of my sister, perhaps a bit timid and guarded with her heart. I think a little encouragement in love would do well for her."

"Well I have surely encouraged her plenty."

Saye must have felt the weight of Elizabeth's incredulous stare for he turned from the window within moments. "What? Do you think I most particularly call on ladies all over the town? She ought to have felt her distinction the moment I walked in her parlour."

"How would she know that?" Elizabeth asked quietly. "She might have thought you called for my purposes or that we were off to call on ten other ladies besides."

"You should know by now that I am not going to be the sort to dance attendance on a woman," he scolded. "Desperation is not a good look for me. Insouciance, wit, and fashion are my marks."

"But a lady likes to feel her power a little." She held up two fingers in a pinching motion, just to show him how little might be required of him. "No more than that."

He rolled his eyes. "I can hardly have the whole *ton* saying I have made a cake of myself!"

"Would you rather have the whole *ton* saying you lost her to another?" Elizabeth gave him a pointed look.

"Another?" Saye scoffed. "Show me someone else who is better than I am—"

"Darcy." Elizabeth made a little face at him. "After all—here I am."

"Aha!" Saye crowed. "So you do love him!"

Elizabeth blushed hotly and turned away. Teasing him had redounded smartly, but nevertheless she would not deny him. It was the truth, was it not, even if she could only admit it to herself?

"Say it to me, and I shall flirt the very stockings off my lady tomorrow. Tell me you love Darcy."

"I think," said Elizabeth, smiling out the window at a Darcy only her mind's eye could see, "that *he* ought to be first to hear it."

She saw, reflected in the glass, as Saye, beaming, quaffed the remains of his Cognac. "That will do well enough. Well then, Miss Goddard, prepare to be made love to as never before, courtesy of your dear friend Elizabeth. And Miss Bingley, prepare to be humiliated, also thanks to your Bennet friends."

"What?" Elizabeth turned about. "No, I said nothing...do not do anything to Miss Bingley. Truly, I...I cannot like the woman, it is so, but I would not like any harm—"

But her words were cut off as Saye, his steps quickened by glee, had quit the room.

THE EXHIBITION WAS, in Elizabeth's mind, a success, or at least she considered it so. She truly liked Miss Goddard's friends, and believed there was a possibility for a real friendship between them. She liked Miss Hawkridge and Lady Phee as well; Lady Phee was recently married and Miss Hawkridge, a Fitzwilliam cousin, was soon to marry, and jokes abounded about how soon they would be strolling in the park complaining of their nurses and nannies and comparing notes on the hiring of governesses. "Let us make a promise," cried Miss Hawkridge, "that whatever mix of girls and boys we have among us, we shall not start with any matchmaking for them!"

Miss Bentley was something of an eccentric, having an enthusiasm for the *phylum arthropoda,* but Elizabeth found her endearing and sweet. In any case, she was evidently quite wealthy, and a wealthy girl could afford to be eccentric. She wondered whether Colonel Fitzwilliam had ever considered her.

Of Miss Goddard herself, she could say rather little, because Saye, a man of his word, nearly monopolised her. Credit was due him, however; it seemed he was better able to play the ardent suitor than he had previously indicated. Miss Goddard was at first disconcerted to find herself so singled out; but, within the first hour of the excursion, she had pink cheeks and dreamy eyes, and her friends were walking behind them and whispering plans for her trousseaux.

"Very well, Elizabeth," Saye announced later that afternoon, as they warmed themselves over tea with Lady Matlock. Georgiana had also consented to sit with them, and although she said rather little and sat a bit apart, Elizabeth saw she had keen interest in all that was said. "You might have had something worth saying there. I daresay Miss Goddard is quite besotted with me now, even more so than before."

CHAPTER TWENTY FIVE

In Bourne, Darcy and Fitzwilliam presented themselves to the curate in the parish house nearby. Darcy had already developed his explanation for his interest in the records of this tiny parish. "It pertains to a matter of an inheritance. We are just ensuring all the proper steps have been taken."

The curate, Mr Mallory, was a sprightly man of seventy who looked no more than sixty. His keen blue eyes bore signs of intelligence beyond his station. He led them to where the parish records were kept, and departed, allowing them privacy.

The books were in a dreadful state, weddings, burials and christenings all mixed together. Things appeared to be in the order in which the clerk decided to record them, not by date, so locating the date for the christening of William Henry Bender Collins was no small task. At last, however, it was found and confirmed to be June 29, 1806.

Fitzwilliam read it aloud. "Son of Reginald Henry Collins and Mrs Sarah Bender Collins."

Darcy shook his head in frustration. "Why on earth would Collins have been christened in 1806?"

"It appears that Mr Reginald Collins was not able to attend." He pointed to a record farther up the page, showing that Mr Collins senior was buried in March of the same year. "The christening would have occurred three months after his father's death."

Once again Mr Collins's words from the Netherfield ball struck Darcy with brilliant clarity. *'My dear and wonderful father, himself a parson, left this earth but a year ago.'*

"Another inconsistency," Darcy said, shaking his head as if willing the pieces to fall into order. "I clearly recall Collins telling me that his father had died one year previous—in 1810 that would be."

"Let us look for that, then." The two men then spent a good bit of time searching for burials in 1810, as well as late 1809 and early 1811, but to no avail. No additional Collins was found.

"Perhaps Mallory will be able to tell us something," Fitzwilliam suggested, having become interested in spite of himself.

Darcy considered it. "I am loath to arouse his interest. I would not wish for it to return to Collins that I was poking about in his affairs."

"Who else could know?"

Darcy nodded, putting aside his uneasiness with the remembrance of Elizabeth's tears for her sister's fate. "Very well. Let us find Mallory."

THEY FOUND Mr Mallory minutes later in the parish house, sitting down to what appeared to be a modest repast.

Darcy apologised immediately. "Do not allow us to interrupt you. Where might we await you?"

"No, no." Mallory stood, wiping his mouth and preparing to attend them. "Pray, join me. It is humble fare, but quite good. The ladies of the parish take care of me in that regard."

Darcy could not think which would be worse, to refuse and risk offending the man or to accept and deplete what looked to be humble resources. Fitzwilliam evidently understood his hesitation and was able to gracefully manoeuvre them out of accepting the man's hospitality. "We ate before we arrived, but if there is coffee, perhaps we may sit with you?"

Approximately ten minutes later, the coffee had been procured, the men were seated at the table, and the mystery of Mr Collins began to unfold.

"We had a question about a christening conducted in 1806. A babe called William Collins."

Mr Mallory nodded vigorously, almost visibly swelling with an uncommon sense of importance; no doubt it was a novelty for him to be the bearer of information of interest to someone other than himself.

"Ah, yes, young William. How pleased his father would have been to know him, but alas, he passed before his son was born. A great tragedy, you see, for the man never to have known his wife bore him an heir when he wished for it so dearly."

Darcy tried not to appear so evidently surprised. "William Collins was born in 1806 then?"

Mr Mallory nodded. "Of course—just around the date of his christening. In June, I believe, though I would need to examine the books to be certain. Mr Reginald Collins, his father, worked here often, so we were intimates."

"Reginald Collins was the parson?" Darcy asked.

"Oh no," Mallory replied with a chuckle. "But we all called him Reverend Reginald in these parts because he did like to sermonise. Carried on something dreadful, mostly about the evils of money and spending money and debt. Good man, but he did like the sound of his own voice."

"He had never taken orders?" Fitzwilliam asked.

"No, no, he was illiterate," Mallory replied. "Could not read a word, I am afraid, much less go to school. But did as much as he could for the church without it, tended the grounds and such."

"And the boy born in 1806—was that his only child?" Darcy asked.

"Had three daughters," Mallory said, confirming what Mr Bennet had told Darcy awhile back. "Then Mrs Collins passed away after near twenty years of marriage! Consumption—I believe it was '95 or '96." Mallory nodded. "He mourned her a long time. Loved her quite dearly you see, and could not even think of marrying again...until he had to."

"Why did he have to?" Fitzwilliam asked.

"He needed an heir. Reginald was set to inherit some property—in Herefordshire, or maybe Hertfordshire, I believe—and if he did not have someone to inherit, it would go to his brother, and that he could not abide. So he married Miss Sarah Bender in 1805. She was a young thing, some distant cousin or the like? Sixteen when she married him and seventeen when she buried him."

Darcy could do nothing but nod, his mind a frenzy of possibilities. Was the man who was Lady Catherine's parson a fraud? Posing as Mr Collins in an attempt to steal Longbourn? Surely he would realise such a scheme would never work; it was too easily discovered.

Mr Mallory continued to speak. "Mrs Collins was with child when Reginald died. I do think she married again, back in her home county. I did not meet the fellow but have heard that he takes good care of her and young William."

Mr Mallory then rose and excused himself for a moment. Darcy and Fitzwilliam leapt on the opportunity to confer about all they had learnt. "So our Mr Collins is not who he says he is. He could not think he would be successful in the scheme."

"No," Fitzwilliam agreed. "The boy is young now, but Reginald Collins would have left information for him on the estate for when he came of age."

"Unless someone were to purposely conceal it from him." Darcy shook his head, still lost in his thoughts. "The Mr Collins I know would have been too young to be executor at that time. Who would have done it? Reginald's brother?"

Mr Mallory re-entered the room, chuckling as he came. "Oh, this conversation does bring back some good memories. I teased Reginald quite a bit about his forthcoming nuptials, you see. He was scarcely a year younger than I, and I reminded him of it as often as I could."

He laughed, while Darcy and Fitzwilliam stared a moment. Darcy asked, "So when Mr Collins wed Miss Bender he was…?"

"He was three and sixty, God bless him, but he did what he aimed to do. He made himself an heir to make sure that brother of his, Mr Thomas Collins, did not get that estate he was always after."

"Does Thomas Collins live around here?" Fitzwilliam asked.

"No, he's dead. He died not too long ago—was it '09 or '10?—in gaol."

Darcy winced. "Gaol?"

"The only real surprise is that it took them so long to put him up there. He was far too fond of the bottle. Why, they even had a drink named just for him over at the local public house—just ask for the Tom Collins, they will know what you are after. And debts… None of the local people would give him credit, but he did manage to run up debt everywhere else."

"Did he have children as well?" Fitzwilliam pressed.

"Just one child, a boy, also called Thomas Collins. He would be, oh, somewhere in the middle of his twenties now, I should imagine." Mallory shook his head, looking down into his cup. "I do not like to speak ill of the dead, but of Thomas Collins senior there was little good to say. Illiterate, like his brother, but Reginald earned an honest shilling. Thomas was a drunkard and a wastrel. Give him two shillings, and he spent four. That was what got him initially; he went to debtors' prison. Then while he was there, he got into an argument with another man and nigh on killed him."

Darcy and Fitzwilliam both gasped.

"The man was as dangerous with two fists as most are with a blade or a pistol. Unfortunately, it was a skill he honed most frequently on his wife. That poor dear would come to church with her boy, scarcely a meal in either one of them, both with his marks all over their bodies, and tell incredible stories of falls and mischiefs. No one ever believed her—we all knew the truth of how things stood, but what could be done? Reginald did what he could for them, but he had his own mouths to feed."

Darcy asked, "Is she still alive?"

"Mrs Thomas died when her boy was only nine years old, a great misfortune indeed, but it made her husband go from hateful and angry to cold and indifferent, so I guess it was a sort of blessing. I daresay the boy was better off ignored than beaten."

Darcy glanced at Fitzwilliam as he asked, for the purpose of clarity, "So, you say Mr Thomas Collins died a little over a year ago, and his son—also Thomas—is about five and twenty?"

"Aye," Mallory agreed. "I do not rightly know what came of him. Some say he took orders. Perhaps he liked sermonising like his uncle but decided to make it official."

"And young Master William Collins and his mother are in…?"

"Bedford, I believe," said Mallory. "Or thereabouts. Cannot say I know her new name, but the Benders were her people. They will surely know her over there."

Fitzwilliam, having no doubt seen the gleam of anticipation in Darcy's eyes, rose. "Mr Mallory, I thank you for your kindness and hospitality, as well as your assistance."

Darcy reached into his pocket, and drew out some pound notes that he laid in front of the man, whose eyes gleamed as he said, "Oh no, I cannot take money just for sitting down to talk."

"You cannot know how helpful you have been," Darcy told him, as he noticed Fitzwilliam, from the corner of his eye, tucking another pouch of coins where it would be found later, once the two gentlemen were long gone.

The man bowed respectfully. "I am in no position to refuse the kindness of a stranger, sir. We are a humble parish with many needs. Bless you both."

THEY MADE one more brief stop by the church before they left, Darcy wishing to confirm Mr Collins's dates once more. As expected, they found a Thomas William Collins, christened in 1786. "He gave his name as William Collins," Darcy told Fitzwilliam.

"I wonder how much of that was to further his deceit versus simply to distinguish himself from his father."

"In any case, the Collins of my acquaintance grew up hearing from his dreadful father about the estate he, or rather, they, were to inherit."

"Uncle Reginald was getting old and had only daughters, so naturally they thought it a sure thing that it would pass to them," Fitzwilliam agreed with a nod.

"So as a young man, with every expectation of becoming a landed gentleman one day, he sees his elderly uncle remarry and then watches as his uncle's young wife is increasing. He fears his dream is about to be taken from him —and it was, with the birth of young William Collins in '06."

"And the exceedingly young widow likely did not know anything about Longbourn or the entailment—or if she did, her knowledge was scanty."

"A solicitor must have been involved," Darcy mused. "Particularly as Reginald and Thomas senior were both illiterate; but Thomas William Collins is not and may have been privy to the wills and so forth."

"In any case, it would appear that they successfully concealed the inheritance."

"Except for this damning page that made its way into Mr Bennet's hand. They could not have known about that, to be sure. But the success of the scheme remained to be determined. Mr Bennet is not dead, no wills have been executed, no inheritance has taken place. The whole thing might have fallen apart, but by then, Jane Bennet would have been Mrs Jane Collins and likely with a brood of children around her feet. I believe, for Miss Bennet, the only thing worse than being married to such a man would be to be evicted from the home that she made such a sacrifice to save."

"The next step must be to determine that William Collins —the true William, that is—remains alive. If he does not, then our Collins is indeed the heir," Fitzwilliam observed cautiously.

"Quite right. Do you mind taking a little turn into Bedford, then?"

ELIZABETH HAD ONLY a few days remaining in London before she was to return to Hertfordshire, and she was determined to do as much as she could with them. Shopping took some part, though she purchased less and looked more, determined to seek her own style within the multitude of patterns and muslins and fashion plates. She spent many hours with Georgiana as well, who began the gradual change towards sleeping less during the day and more at night and spending more time with her family. She eventually prevailed upon Elizabeth to join her in an excursion to her brother's house to find some things she wished to have with her at Matlock House.

It was odd to be at his house without him in it, and still more so once she realised that Georgiana had been absent from it for nearly six months. Mrs Hobbs and the rest of the household were overjoyed to see her, but soon understood it was best to be understated in their effusions.

Georgiana, learning Elizabeth had been there only once

before, was determined to show her everything and to say as much good of her brother as could be said—which was quite a lot. Mrs Hobbs, once she caught on to it, became equally determined to have her say as well. Everything more she learnt, every memory, seemed to clarify some misunderstanding she had of him. Her recollections of the sweet moments between them, the tender kisses they had shared… it was all too much, too dear. There were times she could hardly wait to see him again, and other times when she thought he must surely despise her for all the silly things she had said and the ridiculous things she had foolishly done. It was as if she had been determined to see him in the worst light; only now, in his absence, could she truly comprehend how in disposition and talents he was the one man who suited her above any other.

Several evenings before Darcy's planned return, they all attended the opera. It was one Elizabeth had hoped to see with Darcy, but Lady Matlock would not be put off.

Elizabeth and Saye entered the opera house behind Lord and Lady Matlock, and almost immediately, Elizabeth spied Miss Davies with her mother and, she presumed, her father. Saye poked her arm. "There is your dear friend Miss Davies. I suppose she will try to flirt with me." He sighed heavily. "With Darcy spoken for, her efforts in my direction can only increase. I tell you, people do not know what I suffer."

"Poor man." Elizabeth gave his arm a squeeze. "How positively dreadful to be so desirable. How do you endure it? The orphans who beg for food on the streets are nothing to you."

"The orphans are not forced to dance with simpering chits," Saye replied blithely. He then brightened. "What do you say to giving her the cut direct?"

"You may ignore her if you would like," said Elizabeth,

"but I shall greet her." And Saye did just that, looking down his nose and uttering not a syllable while she observed the required civilities.

They then encountered several of Saye's intimate circle. Elizabeth met a Miss Jackley, who was quite pleasant, and Sir John and Lady Haberton, who invited Elizabeth to tea with great enthusiasm. "We are just a few doors down from Darcy's house, you see, and I daresay we shall become intimates! Just wait and see! I am certain of it! Haberton and Darcy were at school together, and they are quite good friends already. What a merry party it will be when we are all together!"

"And now Miss Bingley." Saye brightened. "Very well, Elizabeth, be ready."

"Ready for what?" Elizabeth asked, but Saye made no reply, dragging her through the crowd at a breakneck pace.

"Miss Bingley," he cooed when they arrived at said lady. "How do you do?"

Surprised and flattered by the viscount's particular notice, Miss Bingley began immediately to preen, only half paying attention as Saye begged to be permitted to introduce her to his particular friend Mr Yates, worth eight or nine thousand a year, who 'favoured the taller, blonde ladies'. Saye's words spewed quick and relentless as he urged Miss Bingley towards the man. "I think you will particularly like that Yates does not require children."

"No children?"

"Come now, Miss Bingley." Saye gave her a significant look. "One can hardly accuse you of being excessively maternal. If I had to guess, I would imagine you do not even like children."

"I do not dislike them," Miss Bingley replied pensively,

but after a silent moment, confessed, "There is just so much noise and filth associated with children! Even in the best families, you see them run amok with dirt on their dresses, shrieking and cackling madly. And so capricious in their behaviour! Such unseemly displays of rage, sorrow, and cheerfulness, all within a moment! It is enough to drive a refined person to distraction. If only they were quieter and more calm, less inclined to displays of unseemly emotion, more reasonable—"

"Then they would not be children; they would be miniaturised adults," Saye replied, giving Elizabeth a look. "In any case, I think you ought to meet Yates. He seems an ideal sort for you!"

Before Elizabeth knew what was what, a time was set for a meeting of Miss Bingley and Yates, and Saye was tugging her away again. It was, bar none, one of the most peculiar things she had seen Saye do, and she thought he did a great many peculiar things. He was a man dedicated to his own diversions to be sure.

"What was that about?" Elizabeth asked as they walked off.

"Nothing to concern yourself over. You came to me for help, and I shall help you."

"But I did not ask for your help," Elizabeth protested. "To be clear, I said you should do nothing."

"That is not how I recall it."

"You should not do anything that—"

"We shall have to agree to disagree then." Saye beamed at her. "Now stop quarrelling with me like a fishwife, and let us go enjoy the opera."

CHAPTER TWENTY SIX

As the carriage entered the drive at Longbourn, Darcy told his cousin, "You should know that Elizabeth's younger sisters have a, um...a fondness for a man in regimentals."

"Do they?" Fitzwilliam cursed. "And here am I, done up like some country squire. You might have said something earlier."

"I meant it as a warning," Darcy replied drily.

Darcy thought he must give Mrs Bennet her due; despite being caught unawares by her visitors, they were received with graciousness and offered a generous collation within a short time. Mr Bennet, it turned out, was away from the house—with Mr Collins—but expected to return within half an hour. As such, the two men sat with Mrs Bennet and her daughters in what was not an entirely disagreeable time. One of Fitzwilliam's finest qualities was the ease with which he entered any society, and the society of Longbourn was no exception. He charmed Mrs Bennet quickly, flirted with her daughters readily, and in all ways proved an excellent guest.

Miss Jane Bennet, he observed, was quiet in the corner, bent over some needlework and offering little in the way of conversation. Darcy moved her way, observing as he did that she was embroidering some fine muslin handkerchiefs with the letter 'C'. When she saw him, she looked up and blushed. "A gift for Mr Collins," she explained. "You have no doubt heard…"

"I have," he said, and after a moment of consideration, added, "My best wishes for your happiness." What he could not say, yet, was how dearly he hoped that her happiness would be without the wretched Collins.

"Thank you." She smiled again. After an uncomfortable pause, she added, "Will you be staying with your friend? You are most welcome here of course."

"My friend?"

She seemed perfectly sedate save for the hand that held the handkerchief. It trembled, though he might not have seen it save for the material, which fluttered lightly. "With Mr Bingley, at Netherfield."

"Bingley is at Netherfield?" he asked. "I confess, I had no idea of that."

"I do not know what has drawn him here," she said with another gentle smile.

He had to admire her; inasmuch as he believed she smiled too much before, now he saw she was merely in command of her sensibilities, offering up smiles when she might rather scowl.

"He has not called?"

"My father has received him." That told Darcy enough. The lady chose not to receive his friend, and he could not blame her.

"We intend to return to town yet this evening," he told her. "Unless my business with your father requires more time than anticipated."

It was not so much later that the door opened and Mr Collins entered, reporting to the lady of the house that Mr Bennet had retired immediately to his book room. As Collins had done in November on meeting Darcy, he freely introduced himself to Fitzwilliam, taking the liberty of shaking his hand but doing so while he was also bowing, so for one terrible, hilarious moment it seemed as if he were about to kiss Fitzwilliam's hand. Fitzwilliam seemed both fascinated and repulsed by him, but Mr Collins had no such uncertainty and set about making a new 'dearest friend'. Darcy abandoned his cousin—reasoning that if he could defend England against Napoleon, he could withstand time with Mr Collins—and sought out Mr Bennet.

He found Elizabeth's father just as he was settling himself in front of a fire with a mug of something hot and a thick book. "Mr Darcy, this is a surprise. I had not expected to see you here until you came to take my daughter from me." Mr Bennet smiled genially. "I hope there is no alteration to the scheme?"

Darcy, unsure how to answer, ignored the question. "I came most particularly to see you, sir. I am afraid I must speak to you on matters of some delicacy."

"Oh? About Lizzy?"

Darcy shook his head. "I hope you will forgive me for looking into the matter I am about to lay out before you. It was not my business, and perhaps I have been officious, but pray, do know my intentions were good."

Mr Bennet's face had changed; no longer genial, he seemed wary, if not outright suspicious. "What is it?"

Darcy began by laying the sheet regarding the christening of Longbourn's heir on the small table beside Mr Bennet's chair. Mr Bennet put his book down and took up the page, skimming it as Darcy began to first tell him how he came to have the page in his possession and then continuing with his tale in a dispassionate manner.

Mr Bennet showed no acknowledgement to the news save one brief, tight frown as he returned the page to the exact spot where Darcy had laid it. Then he merely sat in an attitude of solemn repose and waited for the conclusion.

"And you think this Mallory knew what he was about?"

"We confirmed his story with the parish records," Darcy said carefully. "And to be certain, we stopped in Bedford to see young William and verify that he yet lives. He is indeed alive and well with his mother's people."

With a sigh, Mr Bennet rose and went to his window. "No doubt you think me negligent to have overlooked this. I confess, I have paid remarkably little attention to the entail, determined as I always was to cut it off. But here we are, me with five daughters and a charlatan poised to take one of them."

Although he agreed, Darcy did not reply to such charges, only offering a weak demurral. "There is of course some possibility that a misunderstanding has arisen."

"You do not believe that."

After a short pause, Darcy admitted, "No, I do not. But you should, of course, speak to Mr Collins and allow him the opportunity to explain himself. Perhaps there is some irregularity of which I am unaware." Darcy rose. "I shall take my cousin and return to London, but if there is anything I might do to be of service to you in this matter, please ask it."

Mr Bennet opened his mouth then, but before he could say anything, there was a knock on the door and the man himself entered. The barest civilities were exchanged on Darcy's side, though they were more numerous on Collins's, and once they were exhausted, Darcy departed, closing the door behind him.

Only when he had re-entered the drawing room to collect Fitzwilliam did he think of the page on Mr Bennet's table. He wondered whether Mr Bennet would have thought to put it aside until he was ready to speak to Mr Collins. Some minutes later, he had his answer as Mr Collins's loud voice came from the study.

Turning to Mrs Bennet, Darcy said quickly, "Madam, you may wish to send your younger daughters upstairs to avoid hearing some unpleasantness." Shockingly, she, and they, obeyed him quickly—Mary, Lydia, and Kitty hurriedly gathered up whatever ribbons and books and trinkets were around them and scurried up the stairs. Jane moved to follow, but Darcy forestalled her, saying, "No doubt your father will wish to speak to you shortly."

Jane sat down, her eyes wide, as they all heard, "...a most grievous outrage...wish to know of what I am accused!"

That was followed with still more outrage. "How dare you, sir! I ask, how dare you! A man of the cloth...you dare suggest...Lady Catherine de Bourgh...family for generations..." Mr Collins was scarcely coherent and rapidly becoming less so, but nevertheless, all was said in the strongest possible terms and in as many ways as possible.

At one point, Fitzwilliam said, "Perhaps we ought not be a party to this family matter?"

To which Darcy, loath as he was to overhear what he should not, nodded towards Jane and her mother and murmured, "Yes, but I do not like the idea of leaving them alone." A particularly violent outburst followed to underscore his concern.

Jane had made every attempt to stay calm in her chair,

but the argument was growing in volume and ferocity. "Please, sir," Jane begged, "pray tell me what is happening?"

Darcy began, quickly, to recount the now well-worn tale. He had not got far into it, however, when the voices from Mr Bennet's study ceased. The door was flung wide with enough force to hit the wall, and Mr Collins bellowed out his intentions to remove from Longbourn and never darken its door again. He decried anyone foolish enough to connect themselves with such people as the Bennets and then stormed out, instructing Hill to send his things to the inn at Meryton.

WITHIN AN HOUR, Mr Collins was quite drunk at the local tavern and telling nonsensical tales to all who would hear them. An hour after that, he was removed from the place by some of the militia who overheard him and could not abide such slander against a family who, by and large, had been welcoming to them. He was soon put onto a stage back to Kent, still quite drunk, but having been effective in making it known that he had no intention of honouring his promise to Jane Bennet.

Darcy learnt that part of it back at Netherfield, where he and Fitzwilliam had been persuaded to put up for the night. Bingley had been mightily glad to see them, having been left with too much time and too little society to enliven him.

"You must have had a hand in this, Darcy," Bingley said as the men stood over a game of billiards. He had just heard it from one of the footmen, who had learnt it from the coachmen, who had been in the tavern watching the spectacle unfold.

"Likely more than I should have done," Darcy agreed.

"But it was for Elizabeth. She could not bear to see her sister unhappy."

"Nor can I," Bingley declared. "I intend to propose to her tomorrow."

There was a loud clatter as Fitzwilliam dropped his billiards stick. "Tomorrow, eh? Well, why not rush over tonight? There is a full moon, you know."

Bingley looked as though he might consider it, so Darcy hastened to say, "A joke, Bingley. Miss Bennet has had a shock and—"

"But you think it sound?"

"Do I think *what* is sound?" Darcy would not look at Bingley, instead staring at the table as if absorbed by it.

"Surely for me to go to her and tell her I love her now, when she must be down-spirited…? It is an excellent notion, is it not?"

Darcy cast an eye at his cousin, who was studiously examining the wall panelling. "I cannot say."

"Cannot say?" Bingley sounded amazed, and across the room, the sound of a stifled chuckle came from Fitzwilliam.

"You must decide on your own. I can hardly tell you when to propose to a woman."

"Not just any woman! One who is to be your sister!"

"I have determined of late to reform my character and be less officious," Darcy informed him soberly. "We are all grown men here and should heed our own inclinations." With that, he bent, taking a shot and sinking a ball.

"It was not your turn, Darcy," said Bingley reproachfully.

"No, Bingley," Darcy said with a sigh. "It is yours."

CHAPTER TWENTY SEVEN

THE TRAVELLERS HAD SUFFERED SOME DELAY—ELIZABETH knew not why for the weather had been no impediment, at least not if London was any indication—but finally came the morning when the carriage was expected. Alas, it was only the day before she was due to leave, but she hoped she would have time enough to speak to him and settle things between them.

And tell him I have fallen in love with him? She knew not whether it would do. Their last meeting had been alternately quarrelsome and cold, though markedly better at the end of it. Thinking of his words and the feelings which he had displayed made her weak, but she still knew not how it would go. What if his declarations had been the work of the moment and further reflection had caused him to realise that the obstacles between them really were too great? That thought was too painful to be considered.

She was in fidgets all morning, and at length decided on a walk to calm herself. To her surprise, Georgiana consented to join her, though at such a time in the morning that the chance of seeing people she knew was heightened. But Elizabeth would not be the one to offer discouragement, and so, after pressing a footman into service as their escort, the ladies were off for a perambulation in the park at as leisurely a pace as the brisk air would afford.

They were, evidently, too leisurely, for they returned to see his carriage in the square, just then drawing up in front of Matlock House. Elizabeth felt her heart leap, even as she pressed her lips together to bring them colour and raised her hand to see whether the curls at her temple were tidy. A glance at Georgiana showed her doing likewise.

Georgiana laughed, sounding anxious and somewhat fearful. "I know… How silly to worry about where my curls are when I have been going about so dreadfully of late."

And with that, Elizabeth recognised how much more the young girl's nerves must be affected than even her own. Squaring her shoulders and curving her lips into a smile that belied her trepidation, she led Georgiana forward.

Colonel Fitzwilliam disembarked first, stretching quickly even as he moved towards the door. He did not see them, as they were just then coming up around the carriage, but Darcy, once he had similarly exited, did.

His obvious astonishment at seeing the ladies was considerable; for a moment he stood as still and grave as a statue. Then he took a small, cautious step towards them, his eyes moving from Elizabeth to Georgiana and back again. He bowed, somehow managing to not take his eyes from them as he did so.

This view into his character interested Elizabeth. Knowing him as she did now, and imagining how much feeling must be ranting and storming within him, he nevertheless greeted them in terms of perfect composure—perhaps even more than he might have summoned if he had felt less. It was another way she had misunderstood him in the beginning, thinking him unfeeling, when in truth, he was instead a master at concealing great emotion.

He enquired after Georgiana's health as if she had been laid up with a trifling cold, and he offered his arms to the ladies to walk in. Georgiana, too, became more formal, Elizabeth noticed, but not uncomfortably so. It was clear she esteemed and respected her brother and could not behave as easily with him as she did with Elizabeth.

Colonel Fitzwilliam awaited them in the entry, along with Lady Matlock, who smiled and kissed her nephew on the cheek. "Well? What do you think of our dear girl making such a recovery of her spirits?"

Her words made Georgiana blush and lower her eyes. She mumbled something that Elizabeth could not fully hear.

"I am very pleased to see her so," Darcy said gravely.

"I-if it would please you both," Georgiana stammered, "y-you and Richard, I mean, perhaps we could talk in private? In a little while? I...I would like to refresh myself after our walk, if I might be excused."

The colonel mentioned that he, too, needed to get the dirt of travel off himself and Darcy echoed his thoughts. "But before I do, I need to speak to Elizabeth."

There was something in the way he said it—so serious, and not able to look at her—that made Elizabeth take a step back even as she felt the smile fade from her lips. Their most recent argument and all that was associated with it came rushing back to her, and she felt with great certainty that he had changed his mind.

They were directed to the antechamber where they might be separate without being secluded. The rest of the family went their various ways while Elizabeth walked into the area with Darcy behind her, his measured steps echoing on the marble floor. When she reached the far side of the chamber, she turned and cast one quick glance to his impassive countenance, before beginning to speak.

"I…I am very sorry again for…for the situation with George Wickham. It was not until Georgiana told me herself of the connexion between her and him and you…I should never have defended such a man had I any idea—"

"We need say no more of that matter. I realised once I was no longer angry that you could not have known, and in truth"—he extended his arm, and she, after a moment, realised he was offering his hand and so reached forward, allowing him to envelop her hand in his clasp—"I ought to have told you myself."

Elizabeth released a breath she did not realise she had been holding and offered him a small smile, which he did not return. "There has been a change in the circumstances of our engagement," he said. "You agreed to marry me under conditions that are no longer applicable. Neither you nor your sister will marry Collins henceforth; so if you will marry me, let it be because you wish it, not for fear of another outcome. If you want to be free, I cannot say it will be easy for you, but know that I would do everything I could to help you."

"What do you mean? Jane will not marry Mr Collins?"

He shook his head and told her an incredible tale that began with one of her father's mislaid papers—"My father's papers always look as if they were organised by having the wind blow them about"—and continued with the history of the Collins family, then his own belief that Mr Collins must have been raised believing he would one day inherit Longbourn only to be supplanted by his uncle's posthumously born heir. "Being that the boy and his mother were so young and likely knew little of the inheritance, it would seem Collins intended to take advantage of the situation and claim Longbourn for himself. Likely he felt it rightly his own."

It was news that could only delight and amaze, yet Elizabeth, hearing it, could think of only one thing—that he had undertaken this effort for *her*. He had gone to these lengths, inserted himself in a business of no concern to anyone but the Bennets, and it had been for her. Could there be any greater demonstration of what it was to be loved by him? Yes, he might always be high-handed and arranging things as he thought was best, but he loved her and would endeavour to make her happy, to relieve her worries, and to solve her problems.

She had always thought it merely a poetic device to describe the swelling of one's heart, but now she felt it, like a tide of tenderness within her. She hardly knew how to contain it as she watched him so seriously relating how neatly Collins had been vanquished. He was in the middle of describing his talk with Mr Bennet when she pulled her hands from his grasp and flung them around his neck; rising on her toes, she kissed him as ardently and deeply as she ever had. He was surprised, but only for a moment, and then his hands went to her back, and he pressed her close, returning every bit of her fervour.

"Thank you," she breathed between kisses. "A million times, thank you."

She could not have said anything worse it seemed, for he froze. Pulling away, he said, a bit snappishly, "I did nothing from a desire for gratitude. Elizabeth, pray do anything except marry me because you feel grateful."

But she would not allow his pique. "Are we forever to misunderstand each other? I did not say I would marry you for gratitude, even if I do feel it. Have I not cared for your sister as well? And it was not to earn your gratitude, it was because I have grown to love her as my own." She reached for his hands, entwining her fingers into his even as she saw anxiety still writ upon his countenance.

"Forgive me. It is…I would hate knowing you married me because you felt obligated to me in some way." Slowly, he admitted, "I have also feared that, with your sister in some scandal, you might marry me to avoid more indignity to your father's name. If it is so, I shall accept it, but pray tell me the truth; let me know where I stand."

"I promise it is neither for gratitude nor fear of shame that I wish to marry you," she said and watched as apprehension ebbed from the lines of his countenance. "And I do want to marry you more than anything, I do. Indeed, my greatest fear entering this room was that you had decided against me."

"Never." He slowly shook his head. "I only wish to give you whatever you desire and to make you happy."

"We have something in common, then, for it is my greatest wish to make *you* happy."

"You do," he said in a low voice. "More than you can imagine, I am sure, particularly as you might have seen in me no more than a wish to change you. I have seen the error of my ways, I assure you. Nothing could have been made more clear than that night at the ball when you looked like…well, like everyone else did."

"I can hardly go to a London ball in one of Jane's old muslins," she teased.

"You are more beautiful in one of Jane's old muslins than any of those women could ever hope to be in the finest silks and jewels," he asserted. Then, after a moment spent in contemplation of her face, he added, "But I am eager to see you in the Darcy jewels. Some of them are perfectly terrible, but others..."

He took one finger and began at the side of her face brushing the curls at her temple and then tracing down her neck to her shoulder. "Others will suit you very well, I think."

"Things *will* change," she said. "I know they must. I do not wish to embarrass you or—"

He chuckled, sounding bitter. "Embarrass me?"

"I do understand how I might—"

He stopped her with a kiss that was as surprising as it was thrilling. When he released her, he said, "I am proud of you, especially since I looked past my own nose to really see you. In a very short time you have earned the regard of my relations—"

"Save those in Kent," she reminded him with a smile.

"She likes no one, I assure you. But his lordship and my aunt are not generally those who love unreservedly, and they do love you. I can see it. Saye and Richard as well...and well, Georgiana. I can still hardly comprehend it, the change has been so remarkable."

"I cannot take credit for that," Elizabeth insisted. "She was ready to emerge from her melancholy and knew not how. I opened the door, that was all."

"But by far the greatest change has been in me. I could not imagine being so impatient to marry and so sure of my own felicity, and certainly not after what happened last summer. The man who went to Netherfield Park was wretched and despairing, to say nothing of how angry I was at myself, at George Wickham, and yes, even at Georgiana. I scarcely had capacity in me to be civil, yet into this thunderstorm came a ray of sunshine. Undeserved, but here it is, and I have captured it for my own."

There could be no other reply for such sentiments but to kiss him, and so she did.

"Do not think you have done less for me," she said softly. "I knew the future that lay ahead of me and my sisters, and there were days I could not bear it. I managed it by not thinking of it, but we knew how limited our lives were. But I do not marry you for any of that."

"I know," he said. "I remember still, very well, the day in the garden when I disclosed all before you and you wanted none of it."

She laughed, too loudly perhaps. "I did take some delight in vexing you that morning, but you must know it was rather shocking to be told over breakfast that you were being conscripted into a marriage."

"But you are not now," he insisted, looking at her intently. "Nothing and no one will force you to marry except—"

"Except my heart," she said, looking at him with as much earnest devotion as she could communicate. And then, with her heart threatening to burst from her chest, she added, "Because I have fallen in love with you."

For a moment she thought he must not have heard her, for he stared, not a muscle moving, not even a blink of his eyes. "Tell me again, I beg you."

There was something in the way he said it which made her laugh, though she could not quite look at him again as she repeated, "I love you with my whole heart."

And then she did not need to look at him for he crushed her into him, his lips on hers and his heart pounding in fierce union with her own.

"I shall do my best not to exert undue influence over you," he promised.

"And I shall do my best not to run amok and entangle myself in worrisome situations."

"I shall enjoy the liveliness and ease of your temperament."

"And I shall appreciate your judgment, information, and knowledge of the world that must be superior to my own."

He was shaking his head even before the words left her mouth. "I have tried to change you, and it will not do. You must be, always, my Elizabeth, not some lady of the *ton*."

"I shall be your Elizabeth," she promised, "only a bit less countrified perhaps."

His eyes were soft as he bent to resume his kisses, and she tilted her head, eager to receive them. Before she could, however, a loud crash made them both jump apart.

Saye leant against the doorway, a book that he had evidently just purposely dropped at his feet. "Really Darcy? Right here in full view of the street and the whole drawing room? His lordship is about to have a freak."

Darcy wondered whether he looked as stupidly gleeful as he felt, sitting among his relations in the drawing room that night, side by side on a small couch with Elizabeth. They were in love, and they would be married. Suddenly the weeks until the blessed day seemed long indeed.

To see Georgiana so well quite beggared belief. She was quiet—she always had been—but she was there and she did speak, albeit softly, on several occasions, and he saw her hide a giggle behind her hands when Saye was telling them all about attending the opera.

Lady Matlock began the subject saying, "We saw *The Marriage of Figaro* a few nights past, and it was truly splendid. Elizabeth, I think you liked it very well, did you not?"

Elizabeth opened her mouth to answer, but before she could, Saye interjected, "Elizabeth loved every minute of it until she met Stubbs again. From the stench of things, I do not think he has bathed since Lady Barrington's ball."

"It was not that bad," Elizabeth admonished.

"Stubbs has always believed in bathing weekly, but I daresay he misses quite a few of those weeks. Elizabeth turned a shade of green I have never seen before," said Saye with a chuckle.

"Fortunately, I did not depend upon your assistance! You did little more than stand behind him and laugh at me."

"I was much occupied with Moore at the time, as you might remember. We had important business which had to be discussed that very moment."

"And your business required the pair of you to make waving motions at your noses and mouth the words 'do you smell something?' at me?" Georgiana was giggling freely by now, and even Lady Matlock had her hand covering her face.

"This is all a bit coarse, is it not?" Lord Matlock asked sternly.

Saye shrugged. "We are discussing the opera. My mother introduced the topic, if you will recall."

Fitzwilliam was laughing freely, but asked, "Seems you have mended your fences with Moore?"

With a dramatic sigh, Saye nodded. "Elizabeth made me do it. Moore has offered for Miss Julia Grenville, you know, and I think Elizabeth likes her."

"The infamous horse was an *engagement* present for Miss Grenville," Elizabeth said, shooting Saye a little frown, which elicited groans of dismay from both Fitzwilliam and Darcy.

"Yes, yes," Saye snapped. "I have heard it all in spades, I tell you. Darcy, you will need to endeavour to check that little something bordering on conceit and impertinence which your lady possesses."

"I could not dare," Darcy replied solemnly. "For those happen to be two of the things I love most about her."

This prompted a prolonged moment of silence as Elizabeth's cheeks flamed scarlet and the rest of the room considered, likely with some wonder, the import of his declaration. When Elizabeth had recovered, she gave him a bashful glance, looking somewhat chagrined but nevertheless pleased with him.

Saye was the first to recover from the pronouncement, informing them all, "Well, I sold it to him for a loss, so he must be happy, as is his lady."

When the conversation had turned, Darcy felt the coolness of a small hand sliding into his. Elizabeth turned her head, murmuring, "How did I ever think that Mr Darcy was so taciturn?"

"I was taciturn," he told her. "You have made me into a flirt."

"Just so long as it is reserved for me alone," she teased.

He chuckled. "You may depend upon that."

"Miss Grenville has a lovely woman who was her companion," Elizabeth said to him. "A Mrs Annesley. She was a gentleman's daughter and widow of a clergyman."

"Oh?" He did not immediately understand what she was saying, caught as he was in the more pleasant aspects of flirting and teasing with her.

"Perhaps…later, she might be of use? Miss Grenville will marry and no longer need her." Elizabeth gave a slight nod across the room towards Georgiana. "But forgive me; it is an impertinence that I would suggest—"

"Impertinence? Of course not." He smiled at her. "Are you not the lady of the house?"

"Not quite yet," Elizabeth said, but her smile told him that he had again pleased her.

"Perhaps we can meet her together soon," he suggested, and Elizabeth agreed.

After some time, Elizabeth was prevailed upon to exhibit. For a moment, Darcy thought he might turn pages for her, but Elizabeth sent Georgiana a look and Georgiana was quick to join her, which was likely the best arrangement anyway. They made a happy picture sitting together so prettily, and Darcy even permitted himself to imagine times, perhaps not so far distant, when similar scenes might arise at Pemberley.

When Elizabeth had finished her song, she whispered something into Georgiana's ear. Trembling, and somehow both pale and flushed simultaneously, Georgiana spoke across the room to him. "If it would p-please you, Brother, Richard, I have a song for you, for, um, to welcome you home again."

Darcy was thunderstruck a moment, having not imagined any such thing—even on her best days, Georgiana did not like to exhibit—but Fitzwilliam answered heartily for them both. "Of course!"

She took her seat and began a song she used to play often in her younger years. Darcy could not remember the name of it or the composer, and it could not be denied that she played dreadfully ill, her hands shaking and unaccustomed to the movements that had once been almost instinctive. Nevertheless, it was the most beautiful song he had ever heard, and he released a soft breath, again daring to hope that somehow Georgiana's dark days might come to an end. His eyes slid to the slim figure next to his sister, the dark-eyed beauty whose small, pale hand even now rested on Georgiana's back to provide reassurance. He wondered how much more a man could love a woman without expiring under the weight of it.

About halfway through, the earl came and sat down next to him. "I daresay Lizzy has done her a lot of good," he said with his customary gruffness. "Darcy, have I not told you that you ought to marry? I always said another young woman would do Georgiana good, and it seems I was right. You and Richard had hardly exited the toll gate when she began to come around."

Lord Matlock paused for a drink of his coffee. "She came down to dinner one evening, somehow Lizzy had even managed to persuade her to dress as she should. Now they go out of the house, little walks even in the most abominable weather! I cannot say I think it a good idea to have delicate young ladies outdoors in such weather as we have had, but I have to say, it does not seem to have done any harm."

Darcy wanted to chuckle at his uncle and his ever-present 'I-told-you-so's', but he did not, instead nodding and saying, "I am just happy to see her and happy she will see me."

"Now, once you and Lizzy are married—"

"Is it not rather familiar of you to call her Lizzy?" Darcy asked.

"Familiar?" The earl scoffed. "She *is* my niece…or very close to it, rather. Would you have me call Georgiana Miss

Darcy?" The earl laughed heartily, then continued, telling Darcy all the other advice that he had for his marriage, most of which consisted of always endeavouring to keep the ladies happy. "Strength of the Empire, son," Lord Matlock said. "Happy wife, happy life."

"I do not disagree," Darcy said with a smile.

CHAPTER TWENTY EIGHT

Elizabeth returned to Longbourn in the same manner in which she had departed—in Darcy's carriage but in the absence of Darcy. *It is my last time travelling thus,* she told herself, enjoying the peculiar thrill that gave her even as part of her knew that it was not wholly true. Even married ladies travelled without their husbands sometimes.

They had not had sufficient time the evening prior to talk over all the little differences and discords that had plagued them throughout their courtship. Some of them were likely best forgotten, though others she hoped to discuss more fully. What was important to her—the most important thing of all—was that she knew he wished to make her happy, and that she could make him happy too. Theirs would be a home of love and joy in abundance. The rest could be worked on.

He would arrive in Hertfordshire on the first of February. For some brief, heart-stopping moments, Lord and Lady Matlock had wondered whether they ought to come with him to attend the wedding. Elizabeth tried to imagine, in the best possible light, how it would be to see Darcy's exalted relations seated among her mother and sisters, but no matter what rosy hues she cast upon it, it made her shudder.

Georgiana came to her rescue, telling Darcy apologetically that she did not think herself up to the task of going to Hertfordshire. "Not yet, in any case," she said with sweetly regretful looks at Elizabeth. "Oh, Lizzy, do say you know it is nothing to do with my affection for you!"

"Surely I do. Think nothing of it." And Elizabeth sighed with relief and silent gratitude when the earl and countess said they should remain in London with her if Saye and Fitzwilliam were determined to go. Saye, she knew, would be too busy contemplating his ennui-laden attempts at flirtation to concern himself with her relations, and Fitzwilliam had already been there and no doubt witnessed the worst of it.

The populace of Meryton was horror-struck at the dastardly actions of Mr Collins, and almost all were in agreement that Miss Jane Bennet had suffered a near miss. But it did nothing to lessen Jane's humiliation, for to her there could be nothing worse than being talked of and stared at, and the gossips of Meryton were hardly able to restrain their whispers and nudges. Elizabeth had scarcely been home half an hour before she saw the signs of Jane's melancholy; always quiet, she was now a silent shadow of her former self. Elizabeth's heart ached every time she beheld her.

Mrs Bennet set upon Elizabeth almost immediately, alit with the plans and preparations which had taken place in her absence. Although she had written of each and all of them in exhaustive detail, she seemed to think it still necessary to discuss them as though no one had ever heard it before.

Seeing the pain on her elder sister's countenance, Elizabeth asked, "Mama, do you think we ought to delay—"

"Delay? Indeed we shall not," Mrs Bennet said sternly. "This nonsense about Mr Collins...why I have never understood it myself, how you could take an estate that was not legally your own, and it seems I was right after all! Your father does not listen to me..."

And with that she was off on a litany of grievances against Mr Bennet and his careless ways, as well as the perversions of entails. Elizabeth nodded and made sounds as though she was listening, all the while forbearing to remind her that it was Mrs Bennet most of all who had been so determined to see one of her daughters married to the man.

DARCY ARRIVED in Hertfordshire ten days before his wedding to the plainly evident relief of his friend Bingley. Bingley had been holed up at Netherfield trying—and failing—daily to see Jane Bennet.

"Speak to her," Bingley urged. "You were at the front of this, after all. Tell her I have cut Caroline off—"

"You have?" Darcy asked, surprised.

"Indeed, I have," Bingley said vigorously. "And with no regrets. She cannot simply cut up my peace and throw me around as a party to her schemes. The Hursts have her, she wants for nothing, and even she cannot spend twenty thousand pounds effortlessly."

"I am for Longbourn immediately," Darcy informed him. "If the subject arises naturally while I am there—"

"Darcy!" Bingley exclaimed, and it seemed the very curls

on his head quivered with his urgency. "You cannot be so disinterested!"

"I am not disinterested. But the primary object of my interests is my own beloved lady."

"But tell her this. Tell her I have loved her since the first time I danced with her. I have not told you that, but it is true. I do realise I have fallen in and out of what I thought was love before, but I know now that I never before felt anything like what I feel for her. I must have your word that you will tell her that in my stead."

"I cannot give you my word on it." Darcy accepted his newly brushed overcoat from the butler, shrugging into it. "I shall see how things are. Elizabeth's latest letter to me indicated that Jane does suffer rather grievously from this blow to her reputation, unjust as that may be."

"Hang reputation!" Bingley cried out. "Hang the *ton*. Hang you, if you wish to cut the association because I choose to marry a woman with a damaged reputation, then fie on the lot of you!"

Darcy laughed at him. "Being that the woman in question is to be my sister, I should think my association with Jane and her future husband—whosoever that gentleman is —secure."

Bingley groaned loudly at Darcy's intractability, but another thought had struck him. "Speaking of sisters, I understand your cousin wishes to forward a match between Caroline and a Yates? I had not thought Saye involved in those sorts of schemes."

Darcy shrugged. "You never know what cause will strike Saye's interests. Yates, is it? Well, he has a fine fortune and is reputedly very kind."

"That is recommendation enough for me." And on this,

Bingley was done speaking of his sister, turning his interests back to his ineffectual efforts to woo Jane Bennet. Darcy thought he had never been so glad to mount a horse and ride away in all his life.

When Darcy rode into the yard at Longbourn he received a surprise; Elizabeth awaited him in the yard, her eyes bright with anticipation and her lips curved into a gentle smile that turned beaming when she saw him. It gave him a jolt, that he could not deny, but a pleasurable one.

He dismounted quickly, then offered her a courtly bow. "Miss Elizabeth Bennet."

She curtseyed and then, eyes twinkling, said, "That will do for now, I suppose, though I have hopes for different ere long."

"As do I." He glanced towards the house. "Have we any spies to concern ourselves with?"

She shook her head. "I chose my spot wisely."

He needed nothing further and drew her into his arms for a proper greeting that any young man in love would bestow upon his lady. "How good it is to kiss you without fear of Saye lurking about," he murmured.

"He did take to his role of protector rather eagerly."

"Likely as much to torment me as to protect you."

"He does like to tease you, does he not?"

She was still held within his arms, and he thought how well she fit there. She had not brought her bonnet outside with her, and he allowed his fingers to caress the ringlets at her neck. "He does, though I must say, it is only my recent association with a spirited young lady that has allowed me to tease him back. I used to get angry with him, but now I find turning the tables to be ever more enjoyable." He permitted himself another small kiss. "One of the ways you have changed me."

"I have changed you?" She laughed. "Say it is not so."

"But you have," he replied, taking care to speak lightly. "And I am glad for it because I know that once—even when you agreed to marry me—there was much about me that you disliked. And with good reason! I cannot bear to think of all the foolishly proud things I said and the arrogant, disdainful things I have done."

"You must not think of that, for since then..." She looked down, fixing her eyes on his greatcoat. "Since then, my feelings have undergone so material a change as to render those first impressions wholly inconsequential. I am determined that all else will be forgotten."

"Perhaps you will, but I shall not, for I am determined to be a perfect husband."

"Perfect?" She shook her head. "Do not think of it, for it is our imperfections, I think, that make us so perfect for one another."

"Elizabeth." He whispered her name before lowering his lips to hers, kissing her soundly. "I know it is said so often as to make it almost meaningless, but I shall tell you that you have truly made me the happiest of men."

"Then it is settled between us," she said with a smile that he felt, rather than saw. "We are going to be the happiest couple in the world."

Darcy had resolved, firmly, that he would embrace the society of Hertfordshire as he had not previously. He went to Mrs Philips's house to play cards, he sat with Sir William and heard him wax eloquent on his presentation at St James's, and he even, one painful afternoon, endured a prolonged conversation with Mrs Bennet about muslins and lace. She did not feel Elizabeth's wedding gown had enough lace on it, and she had much to say on the subject. Following that, Elizabeth took pity on him and, with a reassuring kiss and a whispered thanks for his patience, sent him off to spend time in his own pursuits.

It was during one long, tiring ride—from which Bingley was thankfully absent—that he found Jane Bennet walking one of the paths along Longbourn's outer edge. Dismounting, he called out to her. "I had not known you were of the same inclination for walking as your sister."

"Usually, I am not," she replied with a wan smile. "But I find myself more inclined towards it these days."

Darcy chuckled, though in truth, he doubted she meant it to amuse. He asked then whether he could join her; a resolution had formed in his mind, and while part of him wondered whether he ought to speak to Elizabeth first, another believed she would surely wish him to act on the opportunity presented to him.

After a few minutes spent in idle pleasantries, he said, "I am glad you will not marry Mr Collins. He was unworthy of you even when we believed him your father's heir."

"I am not sure you are right, but I…I do admit I am relieved that I need not carry through with the sacrifice I was prepared to make. I am indebted to you, Mr Darcy."

"You do not need to thank me. I am only sorry for the pain all of this has caused you." He paused, then asked, "Has

Elizabeth mentioned anything to you of my sister's troubles?"

Jane flashed another smile, this one kindly and understanding. "She has indeed and was encouraged by how much better Miss Darcy was feeling when Lizzy left her."

"She has improved more than I dreamt possible, and I must think it can only continue through the spring." He looked around him, taking in the silent, dead fields full of mud and last year's faded grass. Before long, this same view would be green and teeming with life awakening, astonishing anyone who cared to look with the rapidity of its resurrection. "She has had a wish to remove to Pemberley for some time."

"I have heard Pemberley is unequalled in all of England," Jane replied. "I am sure I would go, had I the chance."

"That is what I hoped to speak to you about. Elizabeth and I shall be often in town this spring, and I would not like Georgiana to be off in Derbyshire alone. I think she would do better with—"

Jane's face lit with genuine pleasure. "A companion! I would be most grateful if you would consider me for such a position, for I would be most grateful for—"

"No, no," he said gently. "Elizabeth will hire a companion for her. You are our sister, and by extension, Georgiana's as well. I think you would do very well for one another."

Jane had gone red, embarrassed by her misunderstanding, but a faint look of pleasure came over her. "Time in another county would be much appreciated, sir. An alteration of scene and society sounds just the thing."

"Count it settled, then. And I hope you will consider it your home for as long as you wish it."

"You must take care with your words, sir, because you

might find it difficult to get rid of me," said Jane with a little laugh. "A spinster sister who lingers about Pemberley forever."

Quite coincidentally they had come up a rise, a place from which Netherfield stood at some remove. They both looked towards it, while Darcy thought of his friend and his attachment to this young lady. At length he said, "I know of one man who hopes, fervently, that will not be the case."

"Fervour comes easily to Mr Bingley," Jane replied, still with a faint smile. "It is his steadiness that must be proved."

How neatly she had come to the heart of the matter! Darcy tipped his hat towards her then asked whether he could escort her back to Longbourn.

TWO DAYS before the wedding saw the arrival of Darcy's cousins at Netherfield. Saye, having not been there previously, cast a disinterested eye over the vestibule and said to Bingley, "Not too shabby for a tradesman," and then punched him lightly on the shoulder.

"Saye, Bingley is not, nor has he ever—"

"Yes, yes," Saye said impatiently. "But on to more important matters. Darcy, the ancient Greeks had a tradition—"

"Oh, no," Darcy said immediately. "No Greek traditions, Saye, not here where they do not know us."

Saye ignored him. "Before a man can be leg-shackled, he must be permitted to sow some wild oats. So we shall throw you a party here tonight—"

"Yes!" Bingley said eagerly.

"Who is the local madam? I need at least twelve women of ill-repute and... Ho! You there!" He signalled to one of the footmen who had come to attend them. Removing a piece of paper from his jacket, he said, "Take these to the cook. Now, where was I? Ah, yes…women of ill-repute, strong booze, and I think it would do wonderfully if we set Darcy off on a naked run through the lawn of his lady's estate later."

"Not one bit of that is happening," said Darcy with a gimlet-eyed scowl. "I do not see getting married as an excuse to lose all respectability, nor do I wish to see my relations shaming me or the Bennets."

"When have I ever made you ashamed?" Saye rolled his eyes. "We must fete you properly, Darcy!"

"Just say yes," Fitzwilliam murmured, having drawn close to Darcy's other side. "Excessive brandy, cards, and cigars is all that it will be, you have my word."

THE MYSTERY of the paper that Saye gave to Bingley's cook was solved later that evening as the gentlemen gathered at the card table. Saye had decreed that they should play high, and so they were, but the highest stakes of all remained for the one who would run naked through Longbourn's lawn.

"I do not care if it is above ten miles away," Darcy told them all. "If Saye loses, we are for the lawn at Ashworth."

"Indeed we shall," Saye agreed cheerily. "It could only forward my suit for Lilly to see me as God made me. I might do it even if I win."

"Lilly, hmm?" Darcy laid down two cards.

"Things have proceeded apace, then?" Fitzwilliam enquired. "I had wondered whose drawing room you were spending your days in."

"Worry less about the drawing rooms," Saye told him,

"and more about the bedchambers. Ah! But here are the drinks!"

Saye had been to a private soiree at Carlton House the week prior and brought with him to Netherfield the receipt for punch that he swore would be the only thing anyone of fashion drank henceforth. "Prinny's Punch Pare," he told them all as Bingley's first footman served them generous portions. "It has rum, brandy, arrack, but green tea as well, so healthful for the digestion."

Darcy took a cautious sip. It was delicious, he had to admit, and very sweet, having various fruits and fruit juices along with the more potent ingredients. The other men seemed to appreciate it equally well, enough to overlook Saye's peculiar reticence to speak of Miss Goddard.

"I have had a letter from Caroline," Bingley announced as Fitzwilliam began to deal them all a new hand. "She has come to an understanding with Saye's friend Yates."

"Yates? Fine man." Fitzwilliam said, suddenly intent on his cards.

Saye replied, smoothly, "Generous fellow, that Yates. She will not want for any comfort, to be sure."

Bingley was looking at his cards. "She is of age now, so she hardly needs my approval—not that I should withhold it."

Darcy could not say why—for he scarcely knew of Yates—but there was something odd in Saye's countenance as he looked around the table with satisfaction. Not that Darcy was worried overmuch for Miss Bingley's felicity, but Saye was not given to matchmaking and did not like Miss Bingley. It was a strange piece that he had involved himself in seeing her settled, and even more so that he wore an air of glee for having done so. "Has Yates a good fortune?" Darcy asked.

"Four or five thousand a year?" Fitzwilliam offered.

"Indeed?" Saye asked. "I thought it was a bit more. But a wonderful house in Surrey—"

"Surrey?" Fitzwilliam asked. "I thought it was Swansea."

Saye shrugged. "Each would do as well as the other, would they not? Ravenshaw is the house, quite modern."

"No debts?"

"What is it to you, Darcy?" Saye asked. "I did a good turn and formed a love match."

"In any case, she wants to marry him, and I have no objection to it," Bingley said hurriedly while laying two cards down. It seemed that if there was ill to be known, he did not wish to hear it, so Darcy reminded himself again that it was none of his concern.

"And seeing her settled could only help your suit with Miss Bennet," Fitzwilliam added helpfully.

At this, Bingley brightened. "Just so. Well, then—to Yates and his bride!" He held up his glass and all joined him in a salute, though it had to be acknowledged that for Darcy, he drank more to congratulate Bingley than Miss Bingley.

Saye and Fitzwilliam had brought gifts with them as well, and these were presented in due course. Darcy was not sure which horrified him more, Saye's gift of Caracci's *The Sixteen Pleasures*, a book filled with copies of ancient erotic engravings, or Fitzwilliam's gift of champagne and condoms. "Perhaps that," Fitzwilliam said with a sly grin and a wink, "is more a gift for the soon-to-be Mrs Darcy!"

CHAPTER TWENTY NINE

Fitzwilliam Darcy of Kympton Parish and Elizabeth Bennet of this Parish were Married in this Church by licence this tenth Day of February in the Year One Thousand Eight Hundred and Twelve by me, Frederick Chapman, Vicar.

Elizabeth straightened after signing her name to the register and turned to look at her husband with satisfaction. "The last I shall ever sign that way."

It had been a lovely morning, and Elizabeth was grateful to her mother for all she had done to organise things while she was in London. The gown was a triumph of good taste—Mrs Bennet had wanted more lace but had ceded to Elizabeth's preference over her own. As for her new husband, he was in spirits such as she had not before seen. He smiled at everyone he saw, not a scowl or clenched jaw in sight. One could not doubt his felicity, and she hoped everyone thought likewise of her, for it was true.

Jane stood up with her and seemed as content as one might imagine. Elizabeth was delighted with the news that her dearest sister would go to Pemberley to regain her spirits and touched by how Darcy paid her such consideration.

"Mrs Darcy." Saye came up to them, offering her a kiss on the cheek. "Did you perchance have a view of the lawn last night just after the clock struck midnight?"

Elizabeth looked at Jane, who shook her head, mystified. "The lawn at Longbourn?" On Saye's nod, she said, "I fear I did not. All the family was asleep by then."

"Except our mother," Jane recalled. "Her nerves would not permit her to sleep. She said she scarcely closed her eyes for two minutes last night."

"Mrs Bennet, hmm? And is your mother the sort to look out a window?"

Darcy was suddenly all attentiveness to the conversation. "Saye, what is this about? Were you playing cards last night after I retired?"

"I was *winning* at cards last night, which is better than I can say for our poor friend Bingley. He, alas, was not aware of how I enjoy playing a long game and fell quite miserably into my trap." Saye shook his head. "February is a dreadfully cold month, but I daresay the boy acquitted himself nicely."

And with that he strolled away, fluttering his fingers behind him as he exited the vestry.

Elizabeth looked up at her husband. "How did Mr Bingley acquit himself?"

And Darcy leant in, stealing a kiss on her cheek before whispering, "I shall explain it later, but do know you should never drink one of Saye's punches, no matter how delicious they are."

A DAUGHTER MARRIED! And to such a man as Mr Darcy!

To be sure, Mrs Bennet could not have imagined that, of all her daughters, it would be Elizabeth who had earned such a distinction, particularly when Jane stood off to the side, melancholy but still much to be admired. But it would change, and dear Darcy—surely, she could call him that now? He was her son, after all—would see that she was put in front of many wealthy young gentlemen.

Her eyes narrowed seeing Mr Bingley walk across the room to speak to her. He had the wan face of a young man who had indulged too much in drink the night prior, but it was not that which drew her attention. It was the particular bounce in his step, and the overall jauntiness of his air which made her wonder whether…

"Frances, you have outdone yourself with this breakfast."

Mrs Bennet turned to her sister. "Mr Darcy must have two or three French cooks, at least. I could not let it be said that my table was wanting."

"Naturally! But you look very tired. I do hope after all this fuss you will sit in your chair with your feet up." Her elder sister was ever mindful of Mrs Bennet's health, knowing how her nerves suffered, and Mrs Bennet could see the worried lines between Mrs Philips's eyes. She sought immediately to reassure.

"It is not the wedding which has tired me," she said, remembering at the last minute to lower her voice. "We had something of a furor here last night. On the *lawn*."

"On the lawn? What happened on the lawn?"

"Had I not seen it with my own eyes I should never have believed it, but…we had a young man run across the lawn after midnight…*unclothed*."

"No!" Mrs Philips pressed one hand to her mouth. "Surely not naked?"

"Completely." Mrs Bennet nodded gravely. "Trust me, Alice, I am not so old that I cannot recall what a naked young man looks like in the moonlight."

Mrs Philips glanced out the window as if she thought the man might still be there. "But who was it?"

"Of course, my first thought was that it must have been one of the officers. You know, they do so admire dear Lydia! But now..." She nodded across the room to where Mr Bingley stood speaking earnestly to her eldest daughter. "I daresay some recognition has been provoked."

Simultaneously scandalised and delighted, Mrs Philips cast an eye at the young man, allowing her gaze to travel over his form. Turning to her sister, she said, "The moon was quite bright last night."

Pressing her lips together to suppress a giggle, Mrs Bennet said, "It was indeed, and the objects thus illuminated were...not insubstantial." The giggle could not be restrained after that, with both sisters indulging themselves as they had in their youth.

"He is fortunate Bennet did not see him," Mrs Philips exclaimed when she was calm.

"Oh, fie on Mr Bennet! What might he have done? Unless the young man ran directly across the pages of the book, he would scarcely notice!"

"Do you think he hoped *she* would see him?" Mrs Philips gestured delicately at her eldest niece.

Mrs Bennet gave a little shrug. "All I shall say is that if he so chooses to pay his attentions to her again—well, you will not see me objecting to it."

And on that, the ladies were off to giggle more.

JANE BENNET WATCHED PATIENTLY as Mr Bingley crossed the room towards her. She had considered going directly to her bedchamber following the wedding—even if Lizzy *had* noticed (which she would not, because Lizzy's eyes were only for her bridegroom) she would not have been angry with her—but eventually, Jane decided to remain at the breakfast for at least a little while. She would be soon gone to Derbyshire, and in the meantime, she was determined to ignore the stares and the whispers of her neighbours. But with such resolution came the sure knowledge that she would need to speak to Mr Bingley; and it seemed the moment was upon her.

He was full of compliments for Elizabeth, the breakfast, the day, and anything else associated with the wedding, but at length, he turned to the true purpose of his conversation which was to tell her the news of his sister.

"Caroline is engaged. She will marry a Mr Yates just after Easter."

"How nice for her."

"He offered a longer engagement, but she is eager to see things settled. Wants to spend the Season as Mrs Yates."

"He is good to oblige her." In truth, Jane thought it a crime that Caroline Bingley should gain the respectability of a married woman when what she deserved was... Oh! This was not like her at all. She would wish ill on no one, not even Miss Bingley. "I wish them all happiness," she offered hastily.

"I confess, I am less of a mind for her happiness than my

own," Mr Bingley said half-humorously. "Although I would not have her treat him poorly either. She is choosing to marry him, and I told her in no uncertain terms that she should not do it if she intended to make him unhappy. I believe she understood me. I have done my duty as her brother and have tolerated far more than I ought from her. Yates will have a firmer hand, I daresay."

Jane doubted whether any man had a firm enough hand to control Miss Bingley's meanness, but she smiled and nodded so as not to spur an argument.

"With my sister settled, I hope that I might turn my attentions to my own romantic inclinations," he said tentatively.

Discomfort prickled through her, making her long to leap up and run away, but she schooled herself into complaisance. "Sir, I—"

"Do not say anything!" he cried out immediately, far too loud and emotionally. Jane looked around the room, terrified someone might have noticed his outburst. There were a few curious looks their way, and Elizabeth, from across the room, seemed to be looking over with a gimlet eye. It would not do.

"If you will excuse me, sir," she said, rising to her feet. "My mother needs me." But Mrs Bennet was giggling over cake with Aunt Philips and paying no mind to Jane and Mr Bingley at all.

"Pray, do not go." Mr Bingley had also leapt to his feet. "I have not even said what I came here to say!"

"What do you wish to say?"

"I want to marry you."

Jane closed her eyes a moment, hearing words that would have thrilled her to her soul three months earlier. "Forgive me, but I must refuse you."

His arms akimbo, he asked, "Why?"

"Why?" Jane sighed. "Sir, you have heard the rumours—"

"Fie on rumours," Mr Bingley said warmly, but thankfully much more quietly.

"It is all well and good for you to say so," Jane replied with as much severity as she could allow. "But I cannot be so unconcerned. It is my reputation that suffers after all."

"I only mean to say that it cannot matter to me, not when I lo—" He stopped himself, then concluded, "...when I hold you in such esteem. Miss Bennet, you must know that I would do anything at all to go back to that night at my ball and do as I wished to then."

Her heart ached as she beheld him. He was handsome as ever, entreating and amiable and sweet, and she longed to simply acquiesce to whatever designs he had for them. But it could not be—it was leaping into things that had made a confusion of her life, and she would not repeat her errors. Hasty engagements would not do.

"Please, Miss Bennet...Jane. I want to marry you."

"Mr Bingley," she said, watching his face fall at her formal use of his name, "pray comprehend, sir, I have just made a jumble of my life because of heartbreak and hasty decisions. I must have some time to myself to sort through—"

"I can give you time," he said earnestly. "Perhaps...a month? How much time will you need?"

Jane laughed weakly. "Sir, I do not know, but all of this has been just so difficult, and I want only to feel my heart whole again before I offer it to another."

"And will that 'another' be me?" he asked, his eyes searching hers.

She sighed, heavily. How to kindly tell him that part of her dismay had to do with *him*? He was playing the ardent lover now, as he had last autumn, but would he be put off again? Would obstacles arise that would make him go cold? More than anything, she wished for a husband she might depend upon no matter what. Bingley had not as yet shown her he could be that man.

She could not speak so; it simply was not her way. And so she offered him a smile and rose to excuse herself.

"But when will I see you again?" He reached for her, possessing himself of her hand as if he had that right. She allowed it. Why not? With a reputation in shreds, what was one more morsel for the busybodies?

"I cannot say," she told him. "I am for Pemberley, where I intend to remain until...well, I cannot say. For some time."

"May I come see you there?"

"You will need to apply to Darcy for an invitation. It cannot be my place to invite guests to his home."

And with that, she left him.

SAYE LOOKED AROUND THE BENNETS' parlour, amazed to find himself in such unremarkable environs. *These people all need a good study of some fashion plates.* Some round old gent had cornered him for an age, blathering about a presentation at St James's—a ceremonial knighthood, who cared? But he was saved from what would have become peevishness by two things: he truly liked his new cousin, and Miss Goddard was present. She shone like a diamond among these lumps of coal.

Now if he could only rid himself of the happily married couple and get some time alone with her. Lilly sat with Elizabeth on a little couch while he and Darcy stood close enough to them to join the conversation but far enough for some clandestine admonishment of his cousin. "Do you not need to go consummate a marriage or something?" he hissed. "Surely there is an accommodating hay bale nearby."

"We are not animals, Saye," Darcy replied. "It is called a wedding *night* for a reason."

Saye rolled his eyes, but then softened seeing Lilly make a particularly pretty smile in response to whatever nonsense Elizabeth was spouting. "I need to speak to her *alone*."

"Who, Elizabeth?"

Saye frowned at him. He was not certain he found this new droll Darcy much to his liking. "Get your woman, and get *out* of here."

Further discord was obviated however, as the bride herself rose from her seat and slid her hand into Darcy's arm. Darcy looked down at her with such an expression as Saye had not seen, and strangely, he found himself rather wistful. Darcy was as besotted as any man could be, and he looked as though he was rather enjoying it. "Do not hurry your return," Saye said to their departing backs, but they were too busy looking at one another to hear him. He turned to Miss Goddard, who had remained on the sofa. "May I?"

She smiled and agreed, and he sat next to her. Damnation, but this woman made all cleverness flee from him! He found himself in the hideous state of having nothing at all to say and so offered, "Can I get you anything? More wine perhaps?"

"No, thank you." She showed him her full glass. "Mr Darcy kindly brought me one."

"Darcy is all politeness."

"I have never been much acquainted with him," she replied, as they both looked over to where Darcy and Elizabeth had stopped to speak to more of their guests. "But I confess, he seems rather more easy and friendly than has been reported."

"Well, he's in love," Saye replied offhandedly. "Men in love are a strange lot—the unfriendly become friendly and the amiable grow uncivil. There is no accounting for any of it."

"You must be madly in love with me, then," she teased, rather boldly. "For in nowise do you act as I have heard—a rattle, a rake, an inveterate flirt..."

Her teasing produced an alarming effect on him—like vomiting, except words came out. "Perhaps I *am* in love with you."

Miss Goddard's cheeks, so delicate and pale, turned a most becoming shade of pink. "Oh, um, forgive me," she said hastily.

"Why? Do you intend to break my heart?" He turned towards her on the couch. It did not quite bring her into his arms, but it was as close as one could manage among company. "I am rather enchanted by you."

She released a little breath that might have been a laugh and looked away from him. Now it was she who could not speak, so he said, "If I have given up rakishness and flirting, you can hardly blame me. When one finds the love of his life, the rest of the ladies all look like the wilted flowers the morning after the ball. And rattling is hard when one is seeking the words to impress.

"What I am, dear girl, is a *voluptuaire*—dedicated to my worldly pleasures, not the least of which is you. And I would like to see to your enjoyment and pleasure as well." He leant into her whispering, "Darcy might bring you a glass of wine, but I shall see to it that you get the bottle. Nay, I shall buy you your own vineyard if you wish."

She giggled, lightly, and he thought it the loveliest sound he had ever heard.

"So, what say you? How about it?"

Her giggles died into a puzzled look, and she asked, "What say I to what?"

"Marriage."

"To you?"

He wondered whether she had recently sustained a blow to her head. "Yes, my darling, to me. I am violently in love with you and want to marry you."

She looked at him while she considered his words, her slender neck charmingly tilted as she absently twirled one flaxen curl around her finger. Finally, she said, "Maybe."

"Maybe?" He chuckled, delighted with her, although it was, of course, not the answer he wished for. "Why only a maybe?"

"For a man who says he is violently in love, you have not courted me nearly enough. Indeed, you have scarcely paid any attention to me at all. I rather thought you disdained me."

"Nothing could be further from the truth," he assured. "But surely you know enough of me to comprehend I am not the sort to dance attendance on any woman."

"If you want me, you will have to," she said, her blue eyes sparkling. But no, they were not really blue, were they? Nothing so common for his Lilly! They had the colour of aquamarines, and he resolved at once that he would buy her a necklace of aquamarines to match.

He sighed heavily. "You are going to try and bring me to heel, eh?"

She had risen to her feet and turned away from him. Half-turning she looked over her shoulder at him and he thought no woman had ever looked so alluring before. "Something tells me that if I did," she said, "you might like it."

And with that, she left him, half-frustrated and half-admiring, but wholly in love.

THIRTY

June 1812

In her bed in London, Elizabeth Darcy stretched, gently displacing the strong arms that held her tight. Not gently enough, it seemed, for Darcy was awake almost instantly.

"Shoving me aside already, Mrs Darcy?"

"You are very warm when you sleep."

"You sang a different tune in February," he grumbled good-naturedly.

"Four months! How shocking to imagine that such time has passed already!"

For the first weeks of their marriage, the Darcys restricted themselves to the society of each other. Having come late to the understanding of their true affection, they wished to waste no time learning all they could of one another.

Mrs Annesley proved an excellent choice for companion to their sisters. Colonel Fitzwilliam had escorted Georgiana, Mrs Annesley, and Jane to Pemberley, where the three ladies spent contented days in their own pursuits, such as music and needlework and, in Jane's case, a great deal of drawing. In a letter to her sister, Jane said,

Mrs Annesley is fond of sketching and has provided me instruction—such as she could—in the art. Even though I am not very good at it, I find I rather like to draw, and spend many happy hours engaged in the activity.

Jane had included a little sketch of Pemberley at the bottom of her letter. Having not been there, Elizabeth could not say whether it was a faithful reproduction, but Darcy thought it very fine. It was wonderful to see their dear sisters at peace, and Elizabeth believed that all signs showed a full recovery of the spirits of both.

After Easter, Lady Matlock hosted a ball in town to celebrate the newly married couple. It was an unqualified success, and Elizabeth thought she could not have even begun to count how many people were in attendance. She could not say she was universally liked, but she did find herself forming a circle of friends. If there were those who wished her ill for marrying Darcy, she was too happy with him to concern herself about it.

After the ball, the demands on their time increased, and almost every night there were dinners and private soirees, excursions to the theatre or opera, and all manner of diversion. Lord and Lady Matlock, many times with Saye, joined them for dinner on evenings in. Elizabeth was truly fond of her Fitzwilliam relations, and in any case, it was highly diverting to watch as Saye courted Miss Goddard.

On one such evening in the beginning of May, Lady Matlock commented, "Darcy, your friend Mr Bingley has become quite the dull fellow. He refuses more invitations than he accepts, and when he does attend, he seems rather unwilling to dance!"

To Elizabeth, Darcy said, "Finally, Bingley does as I tell him."

"Some have said he seeks a wife. You may tell him from me that skulking about being curmudgeonly is no way to win anyone's hand."

"It certainly worked for me," Darcy murmured, again for only his wife's benefit.

Elizabeth did have some sympathy for Mr Bingley. She knew that his only wish was to win Jane's hand and Jane was at Pemberley. She privately thought it a compliment to her sister, and proof of his constancy, that Bingley appeared to have no interest in the amusements of town and society. Indeed, his only purpose appeared to be to seek the Darcys and procure an invitation to come to Derbyshire from them.

At a party they all attended, he spoke to Elizabeth of his fond reminiscences about Darcy's estate, nearly waxing poetic about it. He concluded by asking, "When do you intend to leave town?"

"Our plans are not yet fixed."

"I would leave tomorrow," said Darcy as he joined them bearing a glass of punch for his wife. "However, Lady Matlock insists on our attendance at some forthcoming parties. But perhaps by the middle of June, we shall go."

Bingley said hopefully, "So, if you are at Pemberley in the middle of June, you might be prepared to receive visitors—"

"Bingley you astonish me," Darcy said sternly. "Mrs Darcy has not yet so much as seen her new home, and you importune her for an invitation?"

"I am hardly the usual visitor! Have I not come to Pemberley in July for many years now?"

"You have, but not with my wife in residence."

Bingley closed his eyes for a moment, seemingly to temper his impatience. "Mrs Darcy, I do hope I count you among my friends?"

"Naturally, sir."

"You must know that I hardly expect you to amuse me or feed me lavish meals. A bed to sleep in is all I require; you will hardly know I am there."

Darcy glanced down at her, giving her a look she had come to enjoy almost above any other. He had come late to teasing but was an enthusiast of the practice now.

Repressing her grin, Elizabeth said, "I could not have any guest in my home but that I could delight him with all the best Pemberley has to offer. Only the finest meals, the most successful sport, and the happiest parties should be experienced at Pemberley. That is why I must not even consider guests until I have fully accustomed myself to Pemberley and its workings."

In a sober voice, Darcy added, "Many of the bedchambers are quite outmoded. Mrs Darcy will likely wish to turn her immediate attention to redecorating and restoring."

"Redecorating?" Bingley asked incredulously, vexation turning his neck blotchy. "Do you think I care about outmoded bedchambers?"

"But we care," Darcy insisted. "The lady of the house wishes to put her best foot forward."

With a sound of pure exasperation, Bingley excused himself and stalked off.

Mrs Caroline Yates arrived in town in early June, triumphantly wed in spirit...if not body.

Alas, Yates proved much less wealthy than she had believed. He was Lord Saye's friend, and she thought all the gentlemen in his circle had heavy purses. But Yates was not even as rich as her brother. *But it is better than living on my fortune,* she reminded herself. As if anyone could even *exist* on a thousand pounds per annum!

In any case, she had other concerns, for having been married for several weeks now, Mrs Yates remained untouched.

The wedding night had been somewhat humiliating. He had entered her room, kissing and caressing...until he suddenly leapt up, very nearly throwing himself out of her bed. "I cannot," he gasped. "Forgive me, but...no. It is not possible."

And with that, he left her.

Perhaps she should have been glad—stories of pain and humiliation in the marital bed ran rampant among ladies of her acquaintance—but she was not. What most confused her was her remembrance of that night in Mr Darcy's bed. Thoughts of it made her wish to die of embarrassment, but there was one thing that raised her curiosity, now that she was married. As Darcy pulled her to him before he awoke, she had felt...*it,* and the feeling of...*it*...was unmistakable. Yates did not feel the same, ever, no matter how much kissing and touching there was.

Was there something she ought to be doing about it? Had she neglected some important duty? She had asked Louisa, but Louisa had merely laughed and told her she was fortunate not to have to endure all the fumbling and grunting that ensued.

Her confusion could only turn to anger when she overheard her brother speaking of the Darcys to Hurst when he thought she was not about. He had said Darcy—long known for his habit of rising early—had not been available to receive him until well after noon on not one, but several occasions! That, and he went about his home whistling like some sort of half-sprung fool, whispering all sorts of little asides to Mrs Darcy, who blushed nearly incessantly.

So she has all the money and prestige associated with being Mrs Darcy, and she has that *too!*

At last, she decided she must speak with her husband about it, no matter how embarrassing it would be. She could not remain a married maiden! If nothing else, she wished to know what it was the other ladies tittered over!

"You did not know?" Yates sighed heavily. "Forgive me, my darling, but I suffered an injury in my youth and now... well, I simply cannot. I thought perhaps if we...if I...but no. Nothing has been sufficiently...rousing."

She stared at him, disbelieving, until finally asking him, "Ever?"

He gave her a little shrug. "Perhaps not."

She was so mortified and dismayed by the report that she spun on her heel and ran to her bedchamber, tossing herself wildly on her bed to recover from the shock.

But such a shock required more than an hour or two to recover from. It was in her mind still when she and Yates went to a play later that week. It was *As You Like It,* and she had seen it many times, enough times to follow it without paying heed.

Lost in her own thoughts, it required a good bit of time before she felt the weight of someone's gaze upon her. A glance to her left showed it was Lord Saye, who met her look with a nod and a smirk, the meaning of which she would not know until much later that evening.

They were both at a post-theatre soiree at Lady St Alban's house, and strangely Lord Saye seemed determined to speak to her. His insistence made her wary. *Lord Saye disdains me on his best days and hates me on the others.*

But there was nothing for it. He had crossed the room to greet her. She curtseyed. "My lord."

His returned bow was of the most perfunctory sort. "Enjoy the play?"

"It was diverting enough."

Saye examined his fingernails. "I might have thought it *plus approprié* to meet you at Hamlet."

"Why Hamlet?" she asked, feeling it would be best not to ask but unable to resist.

"Hamlet is just so full of exquisite verse. Do you know what my *favourite* line from Hamlet is?"

"I am sure I cannot imagine."

"Be thou as chaste as ice, as pure as snow, thou shalt not escape calumny. Get thee to a nunnery, go." Saye grinned broadly. "Marvellous turn of phrase, is it not?"

He knew! Caroline's blood ran cold as she looked at Darcy's cousin, handsome, arrogant, and not above kicking those who crossed him right in the teeth. "I am sure I do not know what you mean."

"Oh, I think you do." He quirked one perfectly formed brow at her, a smile still playing about his lips. "Hoisted by your own petard—another fine turn of phrase."

"Pray, speak plainly. All this Shakespeare goes right over me, I am afraid."

Saye lost his smile at once. "Then I shall hope this is plain enough for you. You tried to trap Darcy into marriage. You failed. You tried to ruin his engagement to my dear cousin Elizabeth. You *failed.* And you tried to ruin the lives of both Jane Bennet and your own brother. The outcome of that remains uncertain, but I daresay you will have failed in that as well. You toss petards about at will, and this time, I threw one back."

He shrugged. "In truth, I was too kind. Yates is a good man, with a good fortune, and if it so happens that he has a perpetual lobcock—"

"What do you know about it?" she hissed, feeling her face contort with anger.

"No more than what *everyone* knows. Poor Yates, so dreadfully afflicted. 'Tis a good thing Ravenshaw is not entailed; he can leave it to his horse if he likes. But you surely do not care, not when you were so clear on your dislike of children."

"I can get an annulment, you know," Caroline retorted, shocking herself with the notion. She could, could she not? An inability to lay with one's wife was grounds for it, she knew that much. Not that she wished for it, but neither did she want Saye to think he had prevailed.

Saye nodded and said brightly, "Just so! But before you speak to a solicitor, you should know how they go about it...'tis rather an embarrassing affair, if Yates would even submit to it."

The humiliation... Indeed, she knew she would never endure anything like it, but for Saye to know—for him to have set her up for this! She seethed and did her best to shoot darts from her eyes to let him know it.

"The worst is, you cannot even take a lover. Heaven forbid you should fall with child—even if Yates forgave you, the rest of society would not. *Everyone* would know."

He went to move away from her then, pausing to murmur in her ear, "You are going to die a virgin," as he brushed by her.

It was a moment that made her burn with rage every time she considered it over the next weeks. She would not seek an annulment, she decided. She and her husband enjoyed many loving moments together, and it would be enough. She would be satisfied with what was, and not worry for what might have been, and when she saw that wanton trollop Mrs Darcy with her whistling fool of a husband, she would just smile to herself, secure in the knowledge that her waist would be forever trim and small, while that diminutive thing would likely swell up like a balloon. See how she liked all of those late mornings when she could scarcely birth one child before he laid her down with another!

DARCY WAS TRULY surprised to receive, in the beginning of June, a request to meet with George Wickham. He had not seen hide nor hair of the man since autumn in Hertfordshire and he was immediately alarmed to hear from him now. Georgiana and Jane were safe at Pemberley—but what of Elizabeth's younger sisters? He went to his wife immediately.

"Elizabeth, has anyone in your family mentioned Wickham coming to Hertfordshire?"

She moved over a little so he could join her on her settee, where she had been reading a book. "No, they have not, and I just had a letter from Lydia today telling me in great depth about every bachelor in the county, so I think we may be reasonably certain he is not there. Why do you ask?"

He handed her the note and watched as she read it. "It

says he has something of yours." Elizabeth looked up. "What could that be?"

"I wanted to be sure it was not one of my female relations," Darcy replied wryly.

"So will you meet him?"

Darcy had already ignited a taper that he tossed into the fireplace with Wickham's note. "The only thing that might induce me to meet George Wickham would be the promise of running him through, and as the note does not seem to be a challenge, I intend to ignore him."

But Wickham would not be ignored. He intruded upon Darcy's notice one afternoon when Darcy was returning from his club, coming behind him and laying a hand on his arm. Darcy rounded on him immediately, grabbing him by his neckcloth and very nearly spitting in his face. "Get out of here and do not come back if you place any value on your life, but I can assure you, I do not."

"I-I have something—"

"You have nothing I want save a thick hide I should like to put my sword through." Darcy released him with a shove. "Now get out of here."

"I have news of Collins!"

"Why should I care about Collins?" Darcy scoffed. "The man is nothing to me."

Darcy moved to go into his house, and somewhat frantically, Wickham reached into his pocket, extracting a ring which he thrust towards Darcy. "The Matlock crest."

Darcy sighed and took the ring. It did appear to be the Matlock crest, and against all better judgment, Darcy thought he ought to learn more. "Very well. Come in."

Wickham followed Darcy into the house. They went quickly to Darcy's study, happily avoiding much notice.

Wickham sat in a chair when he arrived, but Darcy's immediate scowl made him stand again. "This is not a social call. Now, when did you steal his lordship's ring?"

"I did *not* steal it. Collins did."

Darcy examined it again. "I suppose it should be to the magistrate to decide."

Wickham threw his hands up, disgusted. "I am trying to do a good turn here, Darcy, and return your family ring to you. In any case, I won it and many men who were with me at the table will vouchsafe for me."

"You won it? From whom?"

"Well, that is the part of the story which is interesting. I encountered your almost-brother Collins at a gaming hell."

"Indeed?" Darcy sank into a chair, leaving Wickham standing, and examined the jewellery. A surprise indeed. Although Mr Collins had been bound for Kent when last seen, it was not certain he had returned until it was noted that his personal effects were removed from the parsonage house. Lady Catherine had also reported that there were a number of items of no small value which had gone missing from Rosings. Darcy thought little of it in the moment; Lady Catherine accused most people she knew of stealing from her at one time or another. In this case, however, it seemed she was correct.

"Mr Collins at a gaming hell with the old earl's ring," he mused aloud.

Wickham nodded. "He was down quite a lot, though I have heard his debts were nearly all settled in the end. In any case, I had rather hoped you might want to buy it from me."

"How much do you want for it?"

"A thousand pounds."

Darcy laughed loudly and extended the ring towards

Wickham. "You forget—the earldom is nothing to do with me. I could not care less about this trinket."

"It was your own grandfather's ring!" Wickham pretended not to see Darcy's attempt at returning it.

"Go ask Saye whether he wants to buy it."

Wickham rolled his eyes. "If I were on fire, I doubt Saye would lift a leg to put me out."

"Nor would I. Very well, I shall give you ten pounds for it."

"Ten pounds? It is a family heirloom!"

"Not a *Darcy* family heirloom. Actually, make it five pounds."

"One hundred pounds, Darcy, I beg you."

"Have you forgotten what you did to Georgiana? What I ought to be doing is shooting you at ten paces." Darcy levelled a stern gaze at Wickham, and Wickham, surprisingly, quailed a bit.

"Very well, ten pounds. More than generous, I thank you."

Darcy went to the bell and summoned his man to fetch ten pounds from his purse. While they awaited the arrival of the funds, he asked, idly, "And have you seen Collins since?"

"I have not, but the ladies down in one of the Fleet Street brothels found his body stark naked in a bathtub."

"His body?"

"Quite dead," Wickham reported disinterestedly. "Man cannot hold his liquor, there can be no two opinions on that account. All that talking was bound to anger someone, and it did."

Then the money arrived and Wickham, having completed his business, was off. Darcy went to tell his wife that she had one less cousin to concern herself with.

DARCY COUNTED it an extraordinary relief when at last Ascot was upon them. He was eager to take his bride to Pemberley. It felt odd that she had not yet seen the house of which she was mistress, and further, all of those at Pemberley were quite eager to meet her. He had had several letters from Mrs Reynolds on the subject, and no matter how many times he had replied with 'immediately after Ascot' the good lady continued to send letters entreating him to return earlier.

"Lady Matlock cannot dislike our effort," he told Elizabeth. "Many have already left town, yet here we are dutifully going about the business of turning you into the ideal society lady."

She laughed. "Heaven forbid! But no doubt it is the heat that has driven them out early."

London had suffered an early period of hot weather; the heat hung over town like a suffocating blanket, wilting the ladies and making the gentlemen grow short-tempered and quarrelsome. Darcy had suffered his own moments of acute vexation but was always cajoled back into good cheer by the reminder of how good his life really was, courtesy of a pair of fine eyes and his own pretty woman.

Despite the thinning of the crowds in London, Ascot managed to conjure up cheek-to-jowl crowds. Darcy stood on Lady's Day in close confederation with his cousins and Elizabeth, enjoying himself, though not nearly as much as his wife was. Elizabeth, despite her indifference to the equine in general, was invigorated by the races and had developed a fondness for betting.

"I am not sure this is in her best interests," Darcy

remarked to Saye, as Elizabeth exclaimed about another victory.

"Definitely not in yours," Saye replied. "No one fancies having to retrieve his wife from the gaming hells."

He turned then to Elizabeth, accusing, "You, madam, are a sorceress. The odds on Lady Olivia were dreadful, and no one in her bloodline has ever managed a triple win!"

Elizabeth merely shrugged and said, "Sometimes it's the one who knows least who can make the best guess."

And although Saye commented in jest, Darcy began to wonder whether Elizabeth had some knowledge she had not previously disclosed—for although she feigned ignorance, her bets were laid with almost frightening accuracy. Saye lost more than he ought, and Fitzwilliam lost more than he had, yet Elizabeth continued to win and win, her purse growing fatter with each passing race. Darcy shook his head, hoping she had not been set off on a bad path.

Then, in a remarkable and sudden downturn, she lost it all on a side wager with Fitzwilliam. Having mastered the art of the official pools, she had turned her talents to betting on the bettors. Darcy watched with some suspicion as her fortune was rapidly given over to his cousin, who crowed and shrieked triumphantly in a manner most ungentlemanly.

"Really, Richard," Saye scolded. "That behaviour is most unseemly."

Fitzwilliam hardly cared a jot, not when Elizabeth was handing him a roll of pound notes such as would keep in him good stead for some time. "Take it as a lesson," he counselled the group at large. "A thoughtful wager is not merely chance! There is an art to it, art combined with sure knowledge of odds and statistics."

Elizabeth nodded, seeming to appreciate this sage bit of advice, and then they all parted.

He knew what she had done, and it warmed his heart; dear to him as his cousin was, this evidence of her goodness could only delight him. Was this not one of the finest things about her? Her kindness, her arch sweetness—it had drawn him from the start, from the very beginning when he had made his dreadful non-proposal and she had so impishly agreed to not expose his disguise.

When she snuggled in under his arm that night, sliding her feet—really, how did she have ice cold feet in June?—beneath his legs, he said, "You know, you might have fooled Fitzwilliam today, but I was not so misled."

"What do you mean?" she asked with an air of innocence.

"I mean that it was rather a shocking downturn for a lady who was so exceedingly successful with her wagers."

She turned her head, looking up at him. "It is really all math, is it not? Yet some luck must be involved; any horse could throw a shoe or stumble or take a fright."

"Yes, a horse might stumble. And so might a cousin with his finances and find himself in arrears."

She was quiet a moment, then said, "I happened to overhear something of that when I returned with her ladyship one afternoon. He was with your uncle, and Lord Matlock was not inclined towards generosity that day. I pitied him."

"I wonder whether I should be jealous of him as the recipient of your beneficence?" Darcy mused, mostly teasing.

She turned, raising herself up on one elbow to examine him. "Surely not. Although he might have benefited from my largesse, it is only you who has everything else of me. In truth, it has surprised me."

"How so?"

"Well." She pondered a moment, tracing one finger across his chest. "First you had my hand—not the usual course, but it was how we did it. Then my heart—though I cannot say when and how you received that; I was in the middle before I knew I had begun."

"I feel it the same."

"But since we have married…there is more. You have my hand, my heart…but also my mind and my soul. We are inextricably bound." Her eyes shone when she looked at him. "I sometimes find that nothing seems to have happened until I have discussed it with you. You have become my best friend, even above Jane, and that I never expected. I did not even know it was possible for husband and wife to be thus."

It still thrilled him when she was so filled with affection for him—thrilled and frightened him, for he could not imagine how it would be if ever he disappointed her or failed her. "You are my everything," he said simply. "And I feel it more each passing day."

She felt his words; he could see that in her eyes. He reached up, rubbing her back as their gazes met in a few silent moments of tender communion. At length he kissed her and said, "We should go to sleep. It has been a very long day."

Twisting to the side, she managed to douse the lamp while still keeping one hand on his chest. When the light went out, she turned back to him, leaning in and kissing his cheek in a lingering, promising way. "You had better stay awake, Mr Darcy," she whispered. "For I have big plans for you."

EPILOGUE

"SHALL WE REACH THE HOUSE BEFORE NIGHTFALL, MR Darcy?" Elizabeth teased. She had immensely enjoyed their travels over the three days past, but they had seemed long, mostly because she was impatient to see the home of which she had heard so much.

"In just a moment we shall come over a rise and see my favourite view in the world. Then you will at last behold the home of which you are mistress."

When they reached Darcy's preferred spot, the carriage stopped and they disembarked. Elizabeth was filled with awe and delight, seeing both the grandness of the home and, even more impressive to her, the natural beauty of the place. It could not fail to enchant her immediately, and she told her husband so in the most expressive of terms. He was gratified and kissed her soundly, paying no mind to the coachmen, who smiled among themselves and quickly looked away, by now accustomed to Mr Darcy's recent tendency to lose his reserve when in the company of his beloved.

The days after their arrival passed in a flurry of happy activity. The servants had been all anticipation of meeting their new mistress, and were uniformly charmed by her ease and graciousness. Having believed that once in the country, their activity would lessen, Elizabeth was surprised by how busy they were. Mrs Reynolds was eager to acquaint her new mistress with all of the workings of the house, and callers from the neighbourhood set upon them almost immediately.

In August they gratified Bingley's wishes for an invitation to Pemberley. There was to be a small party including Saye and Colonel Fitzwilliam, and Miss Goddard and her friend Miss Bentley. Mr Bingley did not delay in either his acceptance of the invitation or in bringing himself thither, and arrived a week later.

ON THE MORNING of Mr Bingley's first full day in residence, Jane found herself alone with him in the breakfast room. The others were not yet down, including her sister and brother-in-law, and Mr Bingley remarked on it at once. "Mr and Mrs Darcy certainly do not rise early. I am surprised—Darcy has always kept a habit of a morning ride when in the country."

"Mr Bingley, you must know that some of the habits of a bachelor do change for a man happily wed."

Bingley smiled. "I do not know it from my own experience, so I shall bow to your superior knowledge. I am glad to find them so happy. But what of Miss Darcy?"

"Miss Darcy takes a tray in her room in the mornings."

"It seems we are quite alone, then."

"Would you like me to send for Mrs Reynolds?"

"Heaven forbid!" Bingley exclaimed. "No, let us leave the lady to her work. I can be trusted, I assure you."

"I know," Jane said, then added, "I do trust you."

It had more meaning than was immediately apparent, and Mr Bingley knew it, acknowledging it with a grin. "Derbyshire agrees with you, Miss Bennet," he said. "I think you are even more beautiful than when I last beheld you. Do you intend to return to Hertfordshire?"

Jane shook her head. "I would miss Lizzy too much, and I am happy in Derbyshire."

"Then that settles it." Mr Bingley punctuated his words by laying down his fork. "I shall write Mr Morris directly and tell him I am giving up Netherfield."

"Surely not because of anything I said?"

"Exactly because of what you said. On what greater authority should such a plan be laid than that of my future wife?"

Jane smiled, her cheeks growing warm as she looked down at her plate, which still contained nearly everything she had put on it. "I have refused your proposal, sir, lest you have forgotten."

"My first one, yes, but I have many others planned."

"How many?"

"As many as will be required." Mr Bingley's hand crossed the short expanse of table between them in fits and starts. When he finally covered hers, she turned her palm so he could hold it. Part of her worried someone might enter, but she pushed the fear aside.

"Do you know who the last lady was that I danced with?"

"I am sure I cannot imagine."

"You. I could not imagine dancing with any other, certain that if I somehow waited, you would be not only my last dance but my next dance as well, and then my partner, not only in a dance but for life.

"So I shall find you a home of your own in Derbyshire. I

have, in fact, an excellent prospect already in mind. I need only your agreement, my dearest, and I shall have our happily ever after well in hand."

Tears stung in her eyes as she considered the man beside her. She could not deny that she loved him just as much as ever she had. When he had come to Pemberley, she had hoped it was for her and prayed for this very moment. He loved her and she loved him, and she believed in them, that they would make a wonderful marriage and family together.

There might be some who would whisper about them, or about her, and some might disapprove of his choice…but she had already tried to please everyone, and to act in a manner which would secure everyone else's approval. It had not been a success.

"If you have no objection," she said, "I would like to be married at Pemberley."

BINGLEY HAD LOCATED an ideal situation in close proximity to Pemberley and arranged with a land agent to view the place about a week into his visit. It was a lovely estate, vastly smaller than Pemberley, but quite ideal for Bingley. It was settled that Jane and Bingley, in the company of the rest of them, would go to see it. Darcy could not attend, his assistance having been requested by his steward on that particular day, but the others were eager to go. Darcy woke at dawn and was away from the house early, as the day promised to be stiflingly hot, and he hoped to be off of his horse before the sun was too high in the sky.

While the household assembled for breakfast, Elizabeth remained in her chamber, a cool cloth on her head, and a hand across her churning stomach. Although nothing was certain, by this time, the Darcys had been wed for nearly six months, and Elizabeth's courses had been absent for two. Her mornings were plagued by nausea, which seemed to be increasing in intensity with each passing day.

After lying about in her bedchamber for some time, she determined that the idea of being in a hot, bouncing carriage was insupportable, and thus, she sent word to Jane telling her that the rest of the group should go on without her. All were concerned save for Mrs Reynolds, who shooed everyone off as quickly as she could.

Elizabeth rested until nearly noon, when, as if by sorcery, her stomach settled itself. She then became not only hungry but ravenous, and soon found herself before a large, albeit late, breakfast, with Mrs Reynolds happily at her side observing every bite she took. Elizabeth had not told her housekeeper anything for certain as yet, but it had not stopped that good lady from making little forays to the nursery, making little lists of what would need done to make it habitable for the next generation of Darcys.

When Elizabeth was done with her meal, she was at loose ends. A book and the shady spot by the pond, she decided, for what else would do for a hot afternoon and a stomach that might flip at any moment?

A delightful surprise greeted her there. Darcy had evidently finished whatever business had engaged him and had decided to swim. He was just emerged from the pond when she arrived and was standing by the water's edge, his sodden breeches clinging to his thighs, as he removed his shirt and wrung it out. She watched him for several shocked but thrilled seconds, unwitting as the book she carried slipped from her hand and fell to the ground with a soft thud.

The sound made Darcy turn. She said nothing as she walked towards him, boldly wrapping her arms around his neck, and pulling his face to hers for a deep and passionate kiss. After kissing him soundly for some time, she whispered, "You are so handsome."

She felt his face breaking into a broad grin as she kissed him, her hands travelling down his bare back and caressing the backside of his breeches, before coming back around and feeling the muscles of his abdomen and chest. As she did, she felt him begin to unbutton the back of her dress. "What are you doing?"

"I want you to swim with me." So saying, he eased her dress over her shoulders.

She laughed, delighted with the notion. "We are not so far from the house. What if we are seen?"

He fumbled behind her until she turned in his arms, presenting her back to him for easier removal of her stays. "It is our duty, of course, to produce an heir for the estate. If we are seen, we shall send them off immediately and tell them we are tending to our duties, as should they."

"That sounds like you have something a good deal more scandalous in mind than merely swimming."

His only reply to that was a quick waggle of his brow that made Elizabeth laugh.

Elizabeth began to walk gingerly into the water, the chill welcomed yet requiring a cautious approach. However, her plan of easing into the water gradually was not to be borne, and she soon shrieked with delight and alarm as Darcy quickly swept her off of her feet, nearly tossing her into the deeper water.

Once she was fully soaked, she found she became chilled through, and she immediately placed herself within Darcy's warm arms. Unfortunately, the water she found herself in was too deep for her to stand comfortably.

"Put your arms around my neck," Darcy told her, and she did, clutching him tightly and trying to take advantage of the modicum of warmth he offered, but she soon found herself warmed by other means.

THEY EVENTUALLY RELOCATED to the sunnier, warmer bank, and as the afternoon drew on, they found themselves underneath a large, shady tree, pleasantly cooled by the water and a light summer breeze as they awaited their clothing to dry. For some time, they reclined, and Elizabeth read to Darcy from the book she had brought with her.

Finally Darcy stretched, asking her lazily, "I never did ask, why did you not go with Bingley and your sister to view Huddleston Hall? I had understood that to be your intention, though I could not be more pleased with how the alteration in the scheme has redounded to my own benefit."

Should I tell him? She did not wish to raise false hopes, but on the other hand she knew what joy he would have to know her suspicions. "I was sick to my stomach," she told him.

"You are?" Alarmed, he sat up. "I had no idea, I should never have—"

She put her hand against his chest to stop him. "I am not ill. Or, rather, I am not ill now, though I suspect I could be again tomorrow, and perhaps the days after that too."

Darcy considered that a moment, hope gradually lightening his countenance. "Do you think you might be…?"

"I think it very possible."

Darcy was so pleased, he laughed aloud. "This is a happy day, indeed one of the happiest ever I have known. I only wish we might know it for truth. When shall we, do you think?"

Elizabeth shrugged. "Likely another month, so for now, we must keep it only to us, though I do think Mrs Reynolds has her own suspicions."

He groaned, but mixed with it another laugh. "A month! It seems too long to bear."

"Perhaps so," she agreed. "But alas, it is not up to me."

DARCY'S happy anticipation was nearly too much to be contained. As the group gathered around the dinner table later, he found himself wondering whether he ought to just tell his sister. Of course, if Georgiana was told, then rightly, Jane ought to be told as well. But Fitzwilliam was like a brother to him, and Saye would be positively incensed if he was not among the first to know...and he would naturally tell Miss Goddard. Darcy rubbed his head, which began to ache with the pressure of withholding so much felicity.

Bingley provided some welcome diversion. As the footmen were entering with the soup, he cleared his throat and announced, "I have some happy news for everyone on behalf of myself...and Miss Bennet."

Jane? Darcy immediately turned his head to her. Had she at last accepted him? It appeared she had, for she had scarlet-hued cheeks and tears in her eyes—and Elizabeth did too.

"Several days ago, Miss Bennet did me the very great honour of agreeing to be my wife." This news was greeted with clapping hands and faces wreathed in smiles all around the table. "But she gave me one condition."

Jane laughed lightly and demurred, "No, no, not a condition, not precisely."

"She said I must vow to buy her a house near her dearest sister and friend. Well, I am happy to report that today I did just that. Huddleston shall be mine"—he stopped himself to give Jane a look, and amended his words—"*ours*, by the end of September."

This was greeted with still more delighted claps and smiles as the soup was ignored in favour of hugging and well-wishing and congratulating.

"I cannot bear to be long outdone by the likes of Bingley," Saye began as the group settled back into their seats. "As I *already* have a house in Derbyshire, I cannot delight anyone with news of estates or land. But I can tell everyone that..."

He paused, and Fitzwilliam groaned and said, "Come now! No time for theatricals."

"...Miss Goddard has agreed to be my wife," Saye concluded. "I must ask for your discretion as I do not as yet have her father's blessing."

"He would not dare withhold it," said Miss Goddard with a sweet smile.

"And I made certain to kiss her thoroughly enough as to render his objections immaterial."

Her eyes flew wide at his admission—though she did not disagree with him, Darcy noticed—and much laughter and still more congratulations ensued.

His own good news was threatening to burst forth, and he silently willed Elizabeth to look his way. When she did, he could see that her wishes were aligned with his own, and he silently mouthed, "May I...?"

Elizabeth gave the tiniest of nods, and he found himself almost immediately on his feet. "As we are overflowing with glad tidings today, I wished to add ours as well, though I must qualify it by saying nothing is certain as yet. But I wished to share it here, now, while we are all together..."

All eyes were on him, and from the soft smiles of the ladies and knowing nods of his cousins, he thought they likely already guessed it. They were as happy for him as he was for them, and he felt there was truly nothing better in this life than the moment he was experiencing.

"Do not tease us, sir," Jane begged and then looked at her sister. "Lizzy?"

It seemed wrong to say such a thing with an entire length of a table between them, so Darcy went to her, standing behind her and placing one hand on her shoulder. She reached up and covered his hand with hers as she echoed what he had said. "Nothing is certain yet, but...all the signs are there. We have every reason to hope."

All were quick to rise again to lend their well wishes, and dinner became a noisy, joyous affair filled with plans and questions and suppositions. The festivity continued into the wee hours of the morning, the young people finally taking themselves off to their beds just before the dawn.

But inasmuch as he believed he felt the fullness of his blessings that day, there was more to come. After what was surely the most terrible night of his existence came another dawn, a dawn heralded with the lusty cry of a new-born son with a full head of dark curls and his mother's eyes. Darcy settled himself onto the bed beside them, gingerly placing one arm around his wife, while his hand—which suddenly seemed impossibly enormous and clumsy—brushed against his son's head.

"What did we decide upon?" Elizabeth asked, her voice weary but happy. "Alexander? Or was it James?"

And he could not answer, for in that moment he felt in his heart the shift within him. He was no longer merely a man or a husband, but a father, and together, he and Elizabeth had made a family, and that was the greatest felicity of all.

HISTORICAL NOTES

The author has taken some liberty with the creation of the cocktail known as the Tom Collins. Although its origin is subject to debate, it was likely not created until the latter half of the 19th century and more than likely by an American.

The author and Quills & Quartos Publishing thank you for your purchase of this book. We hope you will consider leaving a review.

Subscribers to the Quills & Quartos newsletter receive advance notice of sales as well as bonus excerpts, deleted scenes, and other exclusive content. You can sign up on our web site at www.QuillsandQuartos.com. Thank you!

ACKNOWLEDGMENTS

I sincerely wish to thank anyone and everyone who had a hand in bringing this book to the published world, from all of those who read and commented back in its days on the online forums, to those who helped me wrangle it into actual publication length. Special thanks to Lucy Marin, Julie Cooper, Vickie Lewis and Jan Ashton for many hours spent helping me in development and my editors Gail Warner and Katie Jackson for their expert assistance. You ladies are the absolute best!

ABOUT THE AUTHOR

Amy D'Orazio is a longtime devotee of Jane Austen and fiction related to her characters. She began writing her own little stories to amuse herself during hours spent at sports practices and the like and soon discovered a passion for it. By far, however, the thing she loves most is the connections she has made with readers and other writers of Austenesque fiction.

Amy currently lives in Pittsburgh with her husband and daughters, as well as three Jack Russell terriers who often make appearances (in a human form) in her books.

So Material a Change is Amy's eighth book.

ALSO BY AMY D'ORAZIO

NOVELS

A Lady's Reputation

A Short Period of Exquisite Felicity

A Wilful Misunderstanding

The Best Part of Love

The Mysteries of Pemberley

NOVELLAS

A Fine Joke

Of a Sunday Evening

SHORT STORY ANTHOLOGIES

Dangerous to Know: Jane Austen's Rakes & Gentlemen Rogues (The Quill Collective)

Elizabeth: Obstinate Headstrong Girl (The Quill Collective)

Rational Creatures: Stirrings of Feminism in the Hearts of Jane Austen's Fine Ladies (The Quill Collective)

Yuletide: A Jane Austen-Inspired Collection of Stories (The Quill Collective)

Made in the USA
Monee, IL
12 June 2023